Lady Vengeance

By the same author

Maid of Honour
The Bargain

Lady Vengeance

Melinda Hammond

ROBERT HALE · LONDON

© Melinda Hammond 2003
First published in Great Britain 2003

ISBN 0 7090 7398 4

Robert Hale Limited
Clerkenwell House
Clerkenwell Green
London EC1R 0HT

2 4 6 8 10 9 7 5 3 1

Typeset in 11/13pt New Century Schoolbook
by Derek Doyle & Associates, Liverpool.
Printed in Great Britain by
St Edmundsbury Press, Bury St Edmunds, Suffolk.
Bound by Woolnough Bookbinding Ltd.

CHAPTER ONE

*In which a nobleman gives vent to his anger,
and five men of good birth show a lack of good
breeding.*

December 1745

The thunder of hoofs was like a drum-roll for the devil,
thought the young postilion: God save us, the master might
have been flying from Old Nick himself, the speed he chose to
travel! Within the coach Guy Morellon, Marquis of Thurleigh,
seemed impervious to the lurching and swaying of the vehicle,
but leaned back against the tabaret-silk squabs and gazed
idly out upon the wintry landscape. He scarcely noticed the
bare fields, nor the iron-grey sky; his thoughts were occupied
with the fortunes of the young Charles Stuart who, if reports
were correct, was even now sweeping south with his supporters to regain the crown for his father. The marquis wondered
if the messengers sent to the young prince had yet returned;
if all had gone well, they should now be awaiting him with the
others at the Black Goose, from where they would travel
together to join the Jacobite army.

My Lord Thurleigh considered his fellow conspirators: only
five men, including himself, but not without influence. The
youngest of these were Rowsell and Poyntz, whom he had sent
to advise the prince of the support that awaited him. They
were also the most idealistic, with little thought for their own
gain. Useful tools, as the Marquis acknowledged, but very

minor characters when compared to the third member of the party, James Boreland. Powerful both physically and politically, Boreland's wealth and influence would be a great asset to the Jacobite cause. Moreover, he had been a military man, distinguishing himself in recent campaigns., and thus would be invaluable not only for his experience, but also in winning over the British troops. The last member of the group had no military background, but as a pillar of the English Church Bishop Furminger could be relied upon to add respectability to their cause. My lord allowed himself an inward smile of satisfaction; when such an august group announced their allegiance to Prince Charles Edward Stuart, many would hasten to follow suit, and the Hanoverian dynasty would be rocked to its very foundations.

The chariot swept through a small village, the postilion making no attempt to check his horses' rapid pace. Knowing he was almost arrived at his destination, Lord Thurleigh shook out the fine Flanders lace at the cuffs of his grey satin coat, then put up one hand to his cravat, from whose snowy folds a large ruby glared out sullenly upon the world. At that moment the sudden slowing of the carriage nearly threw him from his seat, but he steadied himself as the vehicle came to a stand and with an oath he leaned out of the window, his thin face thunderous.

'What the devil is going on?'

The postilion fought to control the plunging horses.

'A woman, my lord – in the road!' cried the white-faced servant, struggling to maintain his seat on the frightened animal.

My Lord Thurleigh moved to the other side of the carriage and looked out; at the edge of the road stood an ashen-faced woman, her clothes liberally stained with mud. She was leaning heavily upon the arm of a young girl wrapped in a sage-green cloak, the hood of which had slipped back to reveal an abundance of rich chestnut hair that now tumbled about her shoulders. One of the servants had run to open the carriage door and let down the steps but, observing the muddy state of the highway, his lordship remained inside, merely calling across to the woman to ascertain that she had taken no hurt.

'No, my lord. I have no injury,' replied the woman in a faint and trembling voice.

'You relieve my mind,' came the cool reply and the marquis signalled for the steps to be put up again.

'What, does my mother warrant no apology?' cried the younger lady, stepping forward. 'Your carriage appeared at a reckless speed, sir. We are fortunate that we crossed when we did. A moment later and we would have been trampled to death.'

'Then mayhap you will take a little more care in future.' My lord's tone was dispassionate, but he was sensible of some surprise when he perceived the youth of the speaker: little more than a child, but now her green eyes flashed angrily at him.

'Nell, please,' murmured her mother, distressed, 'you should not speak so to his lordship.'

'I would speak no differently to the king himself!' declared the girl hotly.

A small crowd was beginning to gather about the scene and the marquis was eager to end this unseemly interchange.

'Be thankful no one was hurt, young woman!' he retorted curtly. 'And that I am too busy to deal with your insolence. Drive on!'

As the carriage pulled away, there was much bobbing of curtsies and tugging of forelocks as the villagers recognized the nobleman, but the red-haired girl remained motionless as the coach swept by, merely fixing Lord Thurleigh with a long, accusing stare.

'Impudent wench!' he muttered as he settled himself back into his seat. 'If I had the time I'd teach her to mind her manners, by God if I wouldn't.'

Inwardly, he cursed at the necessity of travelling in a closed carriage when he could have ridden to this engagement and enjoyed the exercise – but that would have left the carriage at Margaret's disposal, and there was always the possibility, faint but persistent, that she might disobey him and drive back to London.

Lord Thurleigh's face darkened at the thought of his wife,

the once-beautiful marchioness. What was she now – well past her thirtieth year, her face pitted with the powder and paint she relentlessly applied to it and her body raddled by the number of men she had taken to her bed. Perhaps he could have forgiven her the lovers, had she presented him with an heir, but after seventeen years of marriage they were still childless, a still-born son in the first year being the only bitter fruit of their union. He had also sought his pleasures elsewhere – and had suffered the penalty by contracting the pox and this latest dose was proving damnably difficult to cure, a fact that did nothing for his temper.

He shifted irritably. How my lady had sulked when he told her they were to come to Thurleigh Hall. Lady Thurleigh hated the country – in Town she had her freedom and as many lovers as she wished; at Thurleigh she was lady of the manor and expected to behave herself – his lips twisted into a bitter smile. No easy task for a woman with the soul of a harlot! She numbered more than a brace of government ministers amongst her bedfellows, and if he was to march into London with the rightful heir to the throne, 'twould be mighty embarrassing to find his wife abed with a Hanover man! The marquis was cold and ruthless, and those who knew him wondered that he did not cast off his lady and find himself a wife who could give him the children needed to continue the line, but they little guessed his weakness, when Margaret stood before him with her bewitching green eyes and soft lips so inviting. Her body might not be so firm as when he had married her, but she knew to a nicety how to please a man, and when he felt her move against him, he was powerless to resist his own desires – and he hated her for it.

By the time the chariot swept into the yard of the Black Goose, Lord Thurleigh had recovered his composure and he stepped down from the carriage to accept the innkeeper's obsequious greeting with his habitual indifference.

The landlord ushered Lord Thurleigh into a long, low-ceilinged room on the first floor. The apartment boasted an imposing canopied bed at one end of the room and at the other, long windows overlooking the yard. In front of these windows there was a round table, at which were seated three gentlemen in travelling dress and a fourth in a full-bottomed wig and the black raiment of a man in religious orders. They all rose from their seats as the marquis came in, but no one spoke until the landlord had retired, closing the door silently behind him.

'Well,' drawled my lord, drawing off his gloves, 'what news?'

The gentleman in black stepped forward, mopping his plump, glistening face with a fine lace handkerchief.

'My lord, it is all up with us! 'he cried. 'Our cause is lost!'

Thurleigh turned a contemptuous eye upon the speaker.

'My dear Furminger, I am aware your bishopric cost you a great deal,' he sneered, 'but did it cost you all your nerve as well?'

The clergyman's flushed face grew darker, but my lord's attention had already moved to a sandy-haired young gentleman in a brown frock-coat.

'Rowsell, did you see the prince?'

'Alas, my lord! Poyntz and I reached Derby by dusk on Saturday, only to find His Highness had already departed – northward.'

Lord Thurleigh regarded him steadily for a full minute, his cold face expressionless. At length, his hard grey eyes fell to a half-empty decanter upon the table and he stepped up to fill himself a glass, then in a leisurely fashion he lowered himself on to a convenient chair, signalling the others to do the same.

'You must forgive me if I seem a little dull, Rowsell, but why did you not go after him?' he asked softly.

The gentleman hesitated, and cast an anxious glance at Mr Poyntz, a corpulent young man who then took up the story.

'The army left Derby a full day ahead of us, my lord, and they were in retreat. To travel after them, and on a Sunday too, would have made us very conspicuous, and 'twould have shown our hand. We thought it best to report back to you – we have travelled with only the briefest of stops.'

'Word was in Derby that the Highlanders knew they were outnumbered,' put in Rowsell defensively. 'They had no wish to meet the Duke of Cumberland, or to engage the forces being assembled against them at Finchley.'

'Then they let themselves be frightened off by exaggerated

stories from the ill informed!' snarled a big bearded man in a coat of russet broadcloth, his fierce eyes burning.

'Very likely,' concurred the marquis, before turning his cold, pitiless stare upon the two young men once more. 'Did it not occur to you, sirs, that the prince might have been persuaded to turn south again, once he knew he could count upon our not inconsiderable support?'

There was an uncomfortable silence. Poyntz shifted uneasily under his lordship's hard gaze.

'There's little sympathy for the Stuarts at Derby, my lord; it seems that their army was told that they were turning north to meet Wade's forces, but it was generally held that the prince was in retreat. Cumberland is not far behind him—'

The bearded gentleman jumped up, banging his great fist upon the table as he did so, making the glasses rattle.

'Bah! You should have let *me* go to Derby, sir! I'd not have let you down. God knows, between us we could raise enough support to take London, if the prince would but make the attempt!'

'I feel sure you have the right of it, Boreland,' murmured Lord Thurleigh.

Bishop Furminger shook his head.

'No, no, Boreland,' he said, 'I think we are well out of it. There's been little enough support for the cause this side of the Border.'

'Only because the majority are waiting to see how the prince fares!' growled Boreland. 'They want to support the winning side. If His Highness would but press on, there's not a doubt that the people would come over. Do not underestimate Lord Thurleigh's influence, and my own men – why there's more than a score of fellows who dare not stand against me. Powerful men, too, who have needed my help in the past. I've not allowed one of 'em to slip away!'

'That is all very well,' put in Rowsell impatiently, 'but Charles Stuart is now half-way to Scotland. What are *we* to do?'

'Charge your glasses, gentlemen, and pray that His Highness comes safely out of this fiasco,' returned the marquis coolly. He refilled his own glass, saying, 'One golden opportunity has been missed, but while James and his line continue, there will doubtless be others.'

'We are well out of it,' repeated the bishop when they had drunk their silent toast. 'We have none of us shown our hand, so there's no danger for any one of us.' His bright, beadlike eyes flicked from one to another, but he met with only hostile glances. 'That is to say,' he hurried on nervously, 'we have aroused no suspicion and will therefore be able to assure His Highness of our full support in any future attempt.'

'And I'd wager you are praying there will not *be* a future attempt, eh, Furminger?' jeered Boreland. 'God knows why you elected to join us, for you've no stomach for this business. . . .'

The bishop's round face flushed a deeper crimson.

'At least 'twas not for greed, sir, nor to please an ambitious wife!' he retorted shrilly.

Boreland's eyes narrowed.

'Why you little—'

'Enough!' Thurleigh's voice was not loud, but it had its effect, for the two men resumed their seats and contented themselves with glaring at each other across the table. His lordship set his empty glass down with a snap. 'Poyntz, tell Bradgate to send up more of his best cognac.'

'Yes, my lord.' Poyntz hurried away, leaving the others in an uneasy silence.

The marquis unbuttoned his coat and crossed one elegantly shod foot over the other, while his keen glance ranged over the three men. Furminger, for all his cleric's robes, appeared the most agitated; his round, fat face was permanently flushed, partly with wine, partly with fear as he fidgeted nervously in his chair. In comparison, George Rowsell was outwardly composed, yet beneath their sandy brows his amber eyes were constantly shifting about the room and he drummed his fingers nervously upon the table top. My lord turned his attention to the large bearded man in the russet coat and brown bob-wig who was now sitting by the window, unconcernedly paring his nails.

'And you, Boreland,' the marquis addressed him, 'do you still wish to go after the prince?'

'Well – 'tis out of our hands,' replied the other without looking up. 'If Rowsell and Poyntz had carried on and overtaken His Highness, they could have given him proof of the support waiting for him—'

With an oath George Rowsell jumped up.

'Damn you, Boreland, are you saying we are to blame? I tell you the cause was already lost before we reached Derby! We had to choose whether to follow the trail of his Scottish rabble – and they were none too particular about other people's property, from what we heard in Derby, which did nothing for their popularity! It was follow them or keep our appointment here!'

'Very well, man, I'm not doubting your word,' replied Boreland testily. 'That red-hot temper of yours will be your downfall, Rowsell, unless I'm much mistaken!'

'I trust it won't prove to be ours, too!' muttered the bishop.

The marquis laughed softly.

'You may rest easy, Furminger, for I have hit upon a way of ensuring continued loyalty from every one of you!'

He reached up to his neckcloth and removed the ruby pin from its folds. His fingers moved around the intricate gold setting until they found the cunningly concealed catch. With a little pressure, the back of the jewel sprang open upon a tiny hinge.

'Gad sir, that's ingenious!' declared Boreland.

'It has its uses,' murmured the marquis, handing the jewel to him.

Boreland looked closely at the brooch. Upon the outer face of the gold backing, the Thurleigh coat of arms had been engraved, and as he opened it wide, turning the jewel to catch the light, he drew a sharp breath of astonishment.

'What is it, man?' Rowsell peered over his shoulder.

'The names of each one of us, neatly etched – it's a death sentence, my lord!'

Thurleigh sat in his chair, smiling as they crowded round to look at the jewel. At length he held out his hand for the ruby. He closed it up and replaced it in his neckcloth.

'Have no fear, gentlemen. That engraving shall not see the light again, so long as I have your unquestioning loyalty.'

He broke off as Poyntz re-entered, followed shortly by the landlord carrying a fresh supply of brandy and glasses, which he set down gently upon the table before quickly withdrawing.

'Well, we may as well drink a final toast to the Stuarts. It will be a long time before we see their standard raised again in England.' Boreland filled five glasses as he spoke, handing them to his companions.

The five gentlemen rose to their feet and tossed off the brandy, then Lord Thurleigh stepped forward to pick up the bottle.

'Drink well, gentlemen, for who knows when we may be together again like this.'

Having recharged the glasses, Thurleigh weighed the empty bottle in his hand, then with a sudden ferocity he hurled it at the fireplace, where it shattered noisily, covering the hearth in a myriad of jagged pieces.

At that moment the landlord returned, closely followed by a couple of his stable lads, scrubbed clean and each carrying a tray piled high with dishes. Bradgate's usually smiling face was anxious as he surveyed the scene.

'I do trust you will like the dinner, my lords.' His voice was strained as he tried to sound genial. 'My wife is still lying in, and it is my sister's cooking I put before you, but I venture to think you won't find it too disagreeable.'

'And where is this sister of yours, Bradgate?' called James Boreland. 'Are we not to set eyes upon a woman in this infernal place?'

'Ah, sir, my sister has been suffering sorely from the gout these past weeks, and cannot manage the stairs,' explained their host solemnly. 'I fear 'tis a sad fact, but we are neither of us as young as we used to be.'

'What?' cried Poyntz in high good-humour. 'Do you have no pretty young women here for our delectation?'

'As to that, sir, I am sorry to disappoint you, but you will find no females in this house save those I have mentioned,' returned Bradgate, setting down his tray. 'If it's female company you are wanting, I'd recommend the Bear, where they are more used to dealing with gentlemen like yourselves. We are but a quiet country inn.'

'Oh, very well, fellow,' laughed Poyntz. 'Take yourself off now, but if you can't provide us with female company be sure to keep us well supplied with your wine, sir!'

The day was drawing to a close when the young girl arrived at the Black Goose. She walked across the courtyard, the low sun breaking through the clouds long enough to glint on the copper tints of her hair, which hung down over the shoulders of her green cloak. Her wooden pattens clattered loudly on the uneven cobbles of the yard as she made her way to a small black-painted door some distance from the main entrance of the inn. As she approached, the door swung open and the landlord stepped out from the dark interior.

'Good day to you, Bradgate!' she greeted him cheerfully and with a confidence far in advance of her years. 'How is Mistress Bradgate today?'

'She – she's very much better, Miss Nell,' stammered the man, looking surprised. 'I did not look to see you here today.'

'Mama promised to deliver a restorative to your wife, so I have come with it.'

'That is very kind of you, Miss Nell, I'm sure, and if you'll but give it to me, I shall see to it that Mrs Bradgate takes some this very day, and I shall tell her you called—'

'You will do nothing of the sort!' laughed the young lady, holding her basket closer. 'I shall tell her so myself, and see the new baby! You need not look so anxious, Bradgate, for I distinctly remember the midwife telling me there can be no harm in a woman having visitors when she is lying in.'

'Perhaps another time, then, Miss Nell, for I feel sure we shall have some rain soon—'

'Nonsense, the clouds are dispersing now, and we shall have a clear evening, I have no doubt, but if you are concerned that I shall overtire your wife, I promise you I shall not stay above ten minutes.' She walked past him and into the dark shadow of the house, leaving the landlord to cast another anxious glance at the inn before following her inside.

Upstairs in the main guest-chamber the five gentlemen were finishing their repast. The table was littered with empty dishes and an impressive array of bottles spilled over on to the windowsill and mantelshelf, while the diners themselves sprawled in their chairs, swords and coats discarded, waistcoats unbuttoned to display the finest lawn shirts. The exception was the bishop, who sat thoughtfully at the table, his cheeks faintly tinged with colour, but his air of nervousness still much in evidence.

He drained his glass and rose from his chair, saying with a forced brightness, 'Well gentlemen, if you will excuse me, I believe I shall be on my way. The clearing sky gives me hope that it will be possible to make good time tonight —I will just step out and order my coach . . .'

Lord Thurleigh stretched out one elegant leg and barred his path.

'No, no, Furminger. We could not hear of such a thing,' he purred. 'This is, after all, your room, I believe. You hired it for the night, did you not? 'Twould be such a pity to waste it.'

Julian Poyntz rolled a bleary eye at the bishop.

'If I could find myself a willing petticoat I'd not waste it!' he said with a coarse laugh. 'Better than sharing a bed with Rowsell, at all events!'

'By God, Poyntz, do you view everything through the hole in your prick?' demanded Boreland. 'Can you not forget women for one night?'

'He may have the room with my compliments,' Furminger assured them all earnestly. 'As all our planning has come to nought I believe I might as well be away, for one cannot say how long this fine weather will hold, and the roads could become impassable overnight if we should have a heavy storm—'

'You'll stay!' snarled Boreland, his large frame swaying unsteadily as he came across the room to tower over the bishop. 'You were as keen as any of us to be free of that usurper, especially when there was a chance of glory! Well, tonight we are going to put this little set-back behind us and make merry, are we not, sirs?'

George Rowsell grunted as he refilled the glasses with an unsteady hand.

'Aye. As merry as grigs,' he said sarcastically. 'Thank God the brandy's tolerable, for 'tis the only amusement this place has to offer.' He muttered an oath as the brandy slopped on to the table. 'Light's so bad I can scarce see,' he complained.

'Admit it, Rowsell, you've caught a fox,' laughed Poyntz. 'There's light enough for a while yet.'

'I may well be half-sprung, but I'm in no wise incapable of filling a glass!' retorted Rowsell, offended by the allegation that he was drunk. 'Since Bradgate is now come to light the candles, I think that proves my point!'

The landlord smiled in a perfunctory manner and after he had performed his task he set to gathering up the dishes that were scattered over the table.

'I thought you said there were no women at the inn, Bradgate,' remarked Poyntz, looking out of the window.

The landlord looked up, startled.

'Nor are there, sir, saving my wife and sister.'

'Then what is that I see in your courtyard? An apparition?'

Bradgate swallowed nervously and came slowly to the window.

'Oh, that – that is just one of the village children. On some errand, I dare say.'

The marquis had been sitting quietly beside the fire, lost in his own thoughts behind an impassive countenance, but the landlord's obvious agitation caught his attention and he stirred himself sufficiently to rise and look out into the court-yard. There below was a girlish figure wrapped in a sage-green cloak, bending to stroke the inn's black cat as it rubbed around her ankles. My lord's lips drew back into a thin, cruel smile.

'You wanted some distraction, Rowsell. It seems you are in luck. Fetch her up here, Bradgate.'

The innkeeper paled.

'My lord – she is the daughter of a respectable family – her father is a very learned gentleman . . .'

His lordship remained unmoved.

'I have a score to settle with that young lady. Send her up.'

'But sir, she is just a child—'

'Do as you are bid!' snarled the marquis, his hard grey eyes snapping. 'Unless, of course, you have forgotten who owns this land. Perhaps you would like to find yourself another hostelry tomorrow. . . .'

White with fear, the landlord hurried away, to return moments later with the young girl at his side. Her hood was thrown back to reveal her glorious head of thick, red-brown tresses, framing a face alight with innocent curiosity. She gazed about her with puzzled interest until her eyes reached the marquis, who had resumed his seat. A faint blush tinged her soft cheek.

'Leave the child with us.'

After the briefest hesitation, Bradgate withdrew silently, leaving the girl standing alone by the door, clutching her basket. A large, bearded man came unsteadily towards her, rubbing his chin with one powerful hand.

'Well, here's a treasure,' leered Boreland, his tone slurred. He stationed himself by the door. 'Who would have thought to discover such a piece of perfection in this out-of-the-way spot.'

'I – I expect you wish me to apologize for my incivility today, my lord.' She spoke directly to Lord Thurleigh, her soft, well-modulated tones holding no hint of fear.

'Oh, more than that, my dear.'

'I am sorry, sir, I do not understand you.'

'We want the pleasure of your company for a little while,' explained Boreland, taking the basket from her and dropping it into one corner. Ignoring her protests he untied her cloak and tossed it after the basket. 'Come, sit with us and have a glass of wine.'

The girl allowed herself to be guided to the table, where a brimming glass of burgundy was pressed into her hand.

'I – I cannot stay,' she began, a faint tremor in her voice. 'I am expected at home—'

'All in good time, my dear.' Rowsell drew his chair closer. 'Tell me your name.'

'Elinor Burchard, sir. Of Rock Cottage.'

'And how old are you, Elinor Burchard of Rock Cottage?'

'Just sixteen, sir.'

'Fair sixteen,' he murmured, eyeing her appreciatively. 'Drink your wine, my dear.' He pushed the glass a little closer to her lips while his other hand slipped around her back. 'You must be very warm with your kerchief wrapped so tightly about you,' he murmured, tugging at the knot.

17

It came free almost immediately and he pulled the muslin from her shoulders, revealing the low bodice of her gown, leaving the snowy frill of her shift just visible, with the soft white skin above.

'A comely lass, and already well-formed,' remarked Poyntz, running his eyes over the shapely figure that was now exposed.

'I want to go home!' cried Elinor, jumping up. The wine from her glass spilled over as she set it down upon the table. She turned her green eyes pleadingly towards the bishop, who was still sitting silently at one side. 'Sir,' she beseeched him, 'I see you are a man of God – pray tell them to let me go!'

Bishop Furminger's pale blue eyes shifted uneasily towards the marquis, but there was no compassion in that cruel, thin face.

'Alas, my child, the bishop is unable to help you. His influence here is – minimal. In fact, I am the one you should appeal to. You know who I am?'

'Yes, my lord. You are Lord Thurleigh, Lord Lieutenant of this county.'

'Then why do you not ask me for leave to go?'

Hesitantly Elinor stepped towards him. He watched her approach, his face impassive.

'Kneel!'

After a slight pause, she sank to her knees, her head bowed. My lord reached out a hand and, cupping her chin, he tilted her face up towards him. Thurleigh noted the flawless skin, the fresh, innocent face with its straight little nose and soft inviting lips. She reminded him of his Margaret, when she had first become his bride – indeed, even the eyes were very nearly the same colour. The thought did not please him and he pushed it away, but already he felt the first stirring of desire. He looked into the girl's sea-green eyes: they were full of apprehension and wet with unshed tears.

'Please, my lord, I want to go home.' Her voice caught on a sob.

The anger that had been growing within him throughout the day boiled over; first the prince's retreat had put an end to his hopes, and now the girl dared to try her woman's tricks upon him! Weeping was one of Margaret's favourite weapons; she used it frequently to get her own way. Realizing his own weakness enraged him still further. Something of his anger showed itself in his countenance and with a small cry Elinor scrambled up and ran to the door, only to find it was locked. Boreland held up the key.

'No escape that way, my pretty, at least not before you have earned it!'

She banged upon the heavy door with her small fists.

'Help!' she cried, 'Bradgate, help me! Let me out!'

The marquis laughed softly, his anger under control now, ice-cold and pitiless.

'There's little hope for you from that quarter, young lady. Our host knows better than to cross me.'

She turned again to face her captors, her back pressed against the unyielding door. Boreland stepped up and laid one large powerful hand upon her shoulder.

'Now then, gentlemen! Who shall be the first to take their pleasure?'

CHAPTER TWO

Wherein tragedy follows dishonour

Julian Poyntz stepped forward, his chubby face flushed with wine and excitement. 'Fore Gad, 'tis an age since I had a virgin,' he muttered, reaching out one hand to run his short, stubby fingers along the top edge of her bodice.

She recoiled from his touch and turned aside, only to find another man beside her.

'I cannot recall ever having one!' laughed George Rowsell. 'There's no need to be afraid, chuck, only behave yourself and you will soon be free to go. Oh, but you have spilled your wine over your petticoat! Let me help you remove it.'

Slowly he unlaced the strings at her breast while Boreland held her arms to her sides to prevent resistance. The stiffened bodice came away and Rowsell tossed it aside, followed by the heavy skirts and the quilted petticoat. She felt another pair of hands around her waist untying the strings that secured the pockets beneath her gown. Then, as she stood in only her lawn shift, the hands explored her body. Boreland released his grip on her arms and moved his large hands up to push the shift from her white shoulders, revealing the small, firm breasts. Watching from one side, Poyntz ran his tongue around his dry lips.

'Let me take her,' he muttered hoarsely, stepping forward.

Overcome by fear, Elinor whimpered as hasty fingers drew off her final covering, leaving her naked. With Boreland holding her arms again she could not even cover herself, but merely bowed her head, allowing her hair to fall over her face, the thick tresses covering her breasts. At this point Bishop

Furminger jumped to his feet.

'Gentlemen,' he cried shrilly, 'this has gone far enough—'

'Hold your tongue!' snapped Boreland contemptuously. 'You have done nothing but whine like a whipped cur since you arrived!' He grinned suddenly. 'Don't worry, Furminger, you can take your turn with the rest of us.'

'I want no part of this!'

'Growing squeamish, Bishop?' jeered Poyntz.

'Perhaps you would object less if we could find you a pretty young man for your amusement,' drawled the marquis, enjoying the bishop's discomfiture, but as the clergyman could not be drawn to say more, my lord refilled his glass, then rose and carried it over to the girl.

'Perhaps, ma'am, you would care for another drink.' He held the glass to her lips.

The blood-red wine ran down her white body as she struggled against her tormentors and, as the marquis stepped away, she spat at him in one final, desperate gesture of defiance. Thurleigh's face darkened at the insult and he spoke with a deadly calm.

'Take her to the bed.'

Boreland swept her up and bore her to the large canopied bed, tossing her down upon the coverlet. At a signal from Lord Thurleigh he reluctantly withdrew and the marquis drew the hangings across one side of the bed, screening himself and the girl from the others. Unhurriedly he started to undress.

'Now, Elinor. You are a sensible girl. You know you cannot quit this room until I give you leave to do so.'

'Oh sir, if you have a daughter, pray consider if you would wish her to suffer in this manner!' She raised herself up on one elbow, her face blotched with tears.

My lord knelt upon the bed, still clad in his shirt and breeches. There were no candles at that end of the room but even in the gloom she saw once again the cold hatred in his face, and instinctively drew away.

'I have no daughter, thus such arguments are wasted upon me.' His eyes ran over her body and he added softly, 'But I did have a young bride, a long time ago, who looked very much as you do now . . .'

'Then for her sake, don't hurt me, sir! Pray let me go!'

The marquis laughed bitterly. 'For *her* sake! No, by God. 'Tis for her sake you are here!'

His fingers traced the red wine that had spilled down over her body. There were no tears now: the girl lay rigid, waiting her fate – only the green eyes burned in the white face, their terror evident even in the near-darkness.

'No!' Elinor suddenly came to life, struggling to free herself. Reason had forsaken her, and she fought wildly, her fingers tearing at his lace cravat as she tried in vain to keep him away. At first he laughed at her, enjoying what he knew to be an unequal struggle, but at last, tired of the game, he struck her hard across the face. With a cry she fell back and he knelt above her, breathing hard, his desire fuelled by her spirited defence. But mixed with the desire was another, less pleasurable sensation. The ulcers and open sores in his groin were so painful he knew they would prevent his taking the girl; even as he looked down at her he felt his lust receding and disgust at the thought of his own pox-ridden member caused him to pull away. He gathered up his clothes and with a last look at the semi-conscious figure on the bed he walked away to the fire to finish dressing.

'Are you done already, my lord?' Boreland's ribald laughter did not improve his humour. 'I had expected to be broaching another bottle before we saw you again'

The marquis gave a thin smile.

'A virgin may give you brief comfort, Boreland, but one needs a woman for true pleasure.' He glanced at the men around the fire, deciding which one would be least likely to notice his failure. 'Rowsell, why don't you try your luck with our little prize?'

The young man looked at him blankly while his wine sodden brain tried to make sense of the words. He rose unsteadily to his feet.

'Aye, my lord, I will!'

He found the girl motionless upon the bed, her eyes closed and her lips moving silently as if in prayer. The sight of her pale body excited him and he fumbled with the buttons of his breeches. Not waiting to remove his clothes he straddled her,

anxious to relieve the urgency of his desire. She lay unprotest-
ing as he thrust into her, pushing and grunting as he spent
his passion, then he collapsed beside her, breathing heavily.
The effort had sobered him a little and he looked at the still
form beside him. He found her lack of response unnerving and
was not sorry to return to the cheerful fireside with his
comrades. Elinor did not move. She was oblivious to the chill
air, her numbed brain conscious only of a wish that she might
die, and soon.

Julian Poyntz followed Rowsell. He hesitated when he
looked at the pale face, the half-closed eyes red-rimmed from
crying. His glance strayed to the coverlet, where even in the
gloom a dark stain proclaimed her lost virginity. The marquis
approached, bearing a lighted candle. His cold eyes took in the
scene in an instant.

'What ails you, Julian? Losing your nerve?' he taunted the
young man. 'I have brought you a light, that you may see what
you are about.'

There was more coarse laughter from the others.

'Aye, I've long wondered about your manhood, Poyntz,'
Boreland called out loudly. 'Perhaps you should become better
acquainted with our dear bishop.'

'Now there's a thought.' murmured Thurleigh, laughing
softly as he returned to the fire.

Poyntz resolutely turned his eyes towards the almost lifeless form upon the bed.

'Damn you, Boreland, you've no call to talk like that!' he
declared, and began to unbutton his small-clothes with grim
determination.

After Poyntz came Boreland, a big bull of a man with thick
black hair that covered most of his body. Elinor had shown no
emotion towards the previous two men, remaining inert and
submissive beneath them, but Boreland's huge frame rekin-
dled her terror and she tried unavailingly to hold him off. He
laughed at her feeble attempts to fight him, his massive
strength easily overpowering her. Elinor thought she would
be crushed by his weight upon her own small frame while the
thick hair of his body and the brandy fumes from his hot
breath threatened to suffocate her. She felt her strength fail-

ing and cried out at the pain as he abused her already aching body. Then, mercifully, she felt herself slipping away into blackness.

How long Elinor lay in the darkness upon the bed she could not tell, although she was aware of the chinking of glasses and the murmur of conversation in the room. The big bearded man forced himself upon her once more, but her body so ached with dull pains that she was beyond caring. At last, Lord Thurleigh came over and tossed her clothes upon the bed. She stared at him blankly.

'Get dressed, Mistress Burchard. We are finished with you.'

'She doesn't understand,' mumbled Rowsell, who had come up and was now leaning heavily against the bedpost. 'Come along, m'dear. I'll help you to dress.'

'So too will I!' declared Poyntz, struggling out of his chair and staggering across the room.

Amid much laughter and joking, the two men hustled the girl into her stockings and petticoats, and Poyntz claimed the privilege of tying the pair of embroidered pockets around her dainty waist. He turned his head carefully to look for them – sudden moves made him feel sick. When he observed that the pockets had slipped down from the bed and were now lying upon the floor, he did not even attempt to bend down and retrieve them, for to lower his head to such an extent would, he knew from experience, result in his making a most undignified descent to the floor and being quite incapable of standing up for a considerable period. Instead he lowered himself gently on to his knees. As he did so, his attention was caught by a dull gleam from just under the edge of the bed.

Carefully turning his attention in that direction, he picked up the object and squinted at it with drink-misted eyes. It was a heavy gold brooch, intricately wrought and set with a single large ruby. In the recesses of his wine-sodden brain Poyntz remembered seeing the ornament in the lace cravat of one of the gentlemen present, although he could not recall just who was its owner.

At that moment, a small sob from Elinor penetrated his thoughts and the first, faint pangs of guilt stirred within him.

He picked up the pockets from the floor and into one of them he slipped the ruby brooch before rising carefully to his feet and assisting his companion to complete their task of dressing the girl. Finally, the green cloak was tied about her shoulders and Elinor was set upon her feet, her basket pressed into her hands. Blankly she looked about her. The bishop still sat nervously in his corner, never daring to speak, while the marquis dozed in his chair with his feet resting upon a stool before the fire. James Boreland stood by the door, holding up the key.

'Here, chuck, open the door and you can go home.'

Some faint look of comprehension came to her at his words and she stepped up stiffly to take the key from him. As she did so, he jerked it out of reach, and grabbing Elinor about the waist, he gave her one final kiss before letting her go and giving up his prize.

'In another year or so you'll be a fine looking woman,' he told her. 'Mayhap I'll come back for you then!'

But Elinor was too busy fumbling with the lock to pay attention to his taunts. At last she unfastened the door and staggered out into the passage. To get out of the inn she was obliged to go down the stairs and through the tap-room, which was crowded with local workmen, but she noticed neither the men nor the silence that fell as she stumbled between the chairs, stiff and bruised from her ordeal, with her hair dishevelled and her eyes red and swollen from her tears. When she reached the door she did not stop to collect her muddied pattens which she had left at the porch, but staggered out into the night, her one desire to remove herself from the place with all speed.

It was nearly an hour later when my Lord Thurleigh roused himself sufficiently to take his leave. The fire had burned low, although none of them had noticed. James Boreland was stretched out upon the bed, snoring noisily, while Poyntz was slumped over the table, his head upon his arms, sleeping off the effects of a surfeit of wine. My lord rose from his chair, buttoned his waistcoat and buckled on his sword.

' 'Tis time I returned to Thurleigh. It was not my intention to remain here so long. My dear lady will be missing me.' He ended upon a bitter note, unable to picture his wife watching and waiting anxiously for his return. His eyes came to rest upon the bishop, sitting uneasily in a corner, biting his lip. The marquis gave a contemptuous smile. 'My dear Furminger, I wish you would look a little less anxious. I had thought your worries were at rest now that you have no need to pin a white cockade to your bishop's mitre.'

'I have no more wish than you to see the Elector upon the throne,' returned the bishop peevishly. 'It is to be hoped that His Highness will come off safely from this set-back.'

'There is a faint possibility that he can hold Scotland, but if he is to keep his head, he would be best advised to return to France,' drawled the marquis, easing himself into his coat.

Furminger cast a resentful look at him.

'You seem mighty indifferent to his fate, my lord!'

'Do I? Then it is because I refuse to concern myself over a matter that is out of my hands. You would do well to follow my example. Go home tomorrow and forget all about Charles Stuart for the present.' He gathered up his gloves, then paused, walked to the bed and looked around it and underneath it, frowning. 'Now where in heaven's name is my ruby?'

George Rowsell, who was busy with the poker trying to coax some life into the dying fire, glanced up.

'What's that, sir? Your cravat pin? I believe Poyntz picked it up earlier.'

The marquis walked back to the table and gave Poyntz a shake, but apart from a faint groan, his efforts met with no response.

'He's probably put it in his pocket. Try if you can rouse him, Rowsell, while I step below to order my carriage. There's moon enough yet for me to travel to Thurleigh.' He found the landlord in the taproom, and had just ordered his carriage to be set to when Bishop Furminger came hurrying down the stairs.

'My lord, he does not have it!' he declared in a frightened whisper.

When Bradgate had gone to do his bidding, the marquis turned a weary eye upon the cleric.

'What are you talking about, sir?'

'The ruby!' hissed Bishop Furminger. 'Poyntz says he does not have it! He gave it to the girl!'

'What!'

'Oh, I said it was madness to touch her!' muttered the bishop, wringing his hands. 'Now everything is lost!'

'Quiet, you fool! What do you expect the girl to do with it? She can't sell such a distinctive ornament, at least not before I have had a chance to recover my property.'

The landlord appeared at the outer door.

'Your carriage is waiting, my lord.'

Before the marquis could reply, an elderly gentleman came in behind Bradgate. His head was bare save for a grey tie-wig and his open greatcoat flapped about him. Distress was writ large upon his lined countenance. At the sight of Lord Thurleigh he stopped, breathing heavily.

'My lord, I must speak with you.'

The marquis waved a languid hand.

'In the morning,' he drawled dismissively. 'I am going home.'

'No, my lord. It must be now!' The old gentleman barred his way. 'I have a just and very serious grievance to take up with you.'

A sudden hush had fallen over the room, although no man looked up from his tankard.

'Mr Burchard, 'twould be as well to wait until morning,' muttered Bradgate.

Lord Thurleigh's eyes widened fractionally.

'Burchard – I have heard that name somewhere before, I believe.'

The old gentleman's countenance displayed his anger.

'Aye, sir! This very morning your carriage nearly rode down my wife, and now my child has come home to tell me she has been dishonoured!'

Lord Thurleigh's thin face was haughty.

'Indeed, sir? And whom do you accuse of dishonouring your daughter?'

Mr Burchard's steady gaze never wavered.

'She tells me, sir, that it was yourself and your party who forced themselves upon her.'

In the tense silence that surrounded them, my lord laughed softly.

'A fairytale, sir, dished up by the girl to save her own face. She came here, flaunting her charms, hoping to make a little money, I don't doubt. As a matter of fact,' he continued, watching the old man carefully, 'she stole something of mine before she left. A ruby cravat pin. Damme, would I give such a thing to the girl? Tell her to bring it back to me, there's a good fellow, and I will say no more about it.'

Still the old gentleman stood his ground.

'Nay, my lord. I demand justice!'

Lord Thurleigh's eyes darkened. He waved towards the bishop.

'Do you have the audacity to imply that I, or a man of the cloth, would be party to such an outrage as you describe?'

A pair of faded grey eyes stared accusingly at the two men.

'I cannot doubt my daughter's word, sir,' he said deliberately.

'And I say she is a liar,' replied the marquis coldly. 'Try, if you can, to find any here who will support her story.'

Mr Burchard looked around the crowded taproom, but as his eyes swept over them, the men shifted uncomfortably in their seats and averted their faces.

'What!' he cried desperately. 'Will no one here speak up for my little Nell?'

Thurleigh stood behind him, a full head taller than the old man and his fierce, hawk-like glance defied any man to speak. No one moved.

'Come away sir,' murmured Bradgate. 'You can do yourself no good here.'

The old man shook off his arm.

'No. I will not come away until my daughter's name has been cleared!' His hand moved to the ancient sword strapped to his side.

The landlord was horrified.

'Sir, you will not fight his lordship!' he muttered, but was ignored.

The marquis was slowly drawing off his gloves.

'Very well, clear a space. We will decide the matter now, and make an end to it.'

There was much scraping of boards as tables and stools were pushed back and the candles arranged to give equal lighting to the combatants, while the two gentlemen removed their coats and rolled up their sleeves, preparing themselves for the contest.

'My lord!' Bradgate made a feeble protest, but a malevolent look from the marquis silenced him and he drew back unhappily.

'This is most irregular!' declared the bishop, unable to contain himself. 'It will be nothing short of a brawl in a common ale-house! You need seconds, and a surgeon – arrange a proper meeting, my lord, in heaven's name!'

He received a sneering look for his pains.

'If it offends your sensibilities, Furminger, then I suggest you go back upstairs with the others.'

At last, the two men were ready. The marquis, tall and lean, his agile body in stark contrast to that of his opponent, a man well past his fiftieth year and so short and slight that he looked no match for his powerful opponent. The two men drew their swords, gave the briefest of salutes and with the scrape of steel upon steel they began. It soon became apparent that the older man was no expert with a sword. He parried where he could, the blades ringing together in the hushed room, but all too soon Lord Thurleigh's lightning blade darted inside his feeble guard and buried itself deep in his chest. Without a sound the old man crumpled on to the floor and lay there, motionless. Bradgate jumped forward and turned the body, urgently looking for a sign of life. There was none. Lord Thurleigh wiped his bloodied sword upon the dead man's shirt before returning it to its sheath. Then he looked around him.

'Let that be a lesson to you all,' he said. 'It is not wise to cross the Marquis of Thurleigh.'

With that, he drew on his coat, and without another word he stepped over the lifeless body of his opponent and went out to his carriage.

'My lord!' Bishop Furminger ran out after him. 'What of the ruby?'

The marquis curled his lip contemptuously.

'Do you expect me to convey Burchard's body to his house and demand my cravat pin tonight? Calm yourself, man. My men shall call upon the widow and her daughter first thing in the morning, never fear.'

The following morning Lord Thurleigh's men arrived at Rock Cottage to find the house deserted, and their enquiries in the village were met with blank stares. The hapless widow Burchard and her daughter had vanished.

CHAPTER THREE

*In which one acquaintance is renewed and
another begun*

September 1753

It had been a fine, sunny day and although darkness had now
closed over Paris, there was no chill in the air, for the richly
carved stone buildings which had basked all day in the sun's
rays now surrendered their bounty to the night. The Duc du
Bellay made his way at a leisurely pace up the steps to the
ballroom of Madame de Briare's grand town house.

'You are sure Madame will have no objection?' said his
companion, a corpulent gentleman who wheezed slightly from
the exertion of mounting the stairs.

'My dear Julian, she will be enchanted to have you at her
soirée.'

'And shall we find Monsieur de Briare at home?' asked the
corpulent gentleman as they reached the top of the stairs.

The *duc* chuckled and shook his head.

'Our host dislikes such evenings as these and invariably
absents himself. Madame has no shortage of attendants willing to take his place at table – or in bed, when necessary.'

He bowed to a diminutive lady who now appeared through
the crowd. She was dressed in cream figured silk, powdered
curls piled high upon her head and at the corner of her mouth
she wore a scarlet patch that gave her countenance a charm-
ingly roguish look as she smiled her welcome.

'*Monsieur le Duc* – why are you *always* so late!' she chided him gently, as he bowed over her hands. 'I had quite given up hope! It is too bad of you.'

Monsieur le Duc spread his hands in a helpless gesture.

'Alas, Madame, I have no defence and must crave your pardon. However, I have hopes of regaining your favour by bringing my good friend Julian Poyntz along with me! I believe you are old friends.'

For the first time Madame's dark eyes moved to the *duc*'s companion and they widened slightly as she took in the heavily laced coat of salmon pink satin over an embroidered waistcoat that was cut generously to cover the gentleman's ample proportions. She gave a little trill of laughter.

'Truly, *m'sieur*, I would not have known you.' She smiled disarmingly, holding out her hands to him.

'I, on the other hand, could never forget you, Madame.' The Englishman gallantly kissed her fingers.

The lady made no reply but allowed her eyes to dwell expressively upon the rounded form before her.

'I have grown a little stouter since we last met, eh?' chuckled Poyntz.

Madame de Briare laughed up at him and tucked her tiny hand into his arm.

'That is a certainty, *m'sieur*! Henri, you may go away and amuse yourself for a while,' she commanded imperiously. 'It should not be difficult, for you are acquainted with everyone present, I think, and I wish to have *M'sieur* Poyntz to myself!'

The *duc* shrugged his shoulders.

'If that is your wish, Madame, of course I will go. But I am mortified that you should prefer such a *stout* English gentleman to myself!'

'Careful, Henri, or I shall be forced to call you out!' laughed Poyntz, wagging a fat finger at his friend.

'Observe, you have terrified me, *m'sieur* – I go at once.'

With another graceful bow, the *duc* sauntered away, leaving Madame de Briare to lead her guest across the crowded room.

'Come, Julian, we will sit and talk. There is a quiet corner where we can find a little privacy. Do you object if I call you Julian? It used to please you.'

'It does that still, Madame.'

She pouted. 'Ah, but you do not call me Thérèse! Have you been away from Paris for so long that you have forgotten we were once lovers?'

His faintly protuberant blue eyes grew misty.

'How could I forget anything so delightful?' he murmured. 'But after so many years I hesitate to remind you of the fact, lest I offend.'

They had reached a secluded alcove set between stone pillars and part-shielded from the main chamber by heavy drapes. Madame de Briare settled herself upon a sofa, carefully arranging the folds of her dress to make room for her escort. She patted the seat beside her.

'And what brings you to Paris, Julian? Are you perhaps on your way to Rome to visit your Stuart king?'

'I am on my way back from there,' replied the gentleman, sitting beside her, 'I have also been to Avignon to see the prince.'

'Ah, such a charming man!' Madame sighed. 'But so much changed! I saw him shortly before he was obliged to leave Paris. So many years of disappointment. They are taking their toll of him. But tell me, is there another plan to restore the Stuarts to the English throne?'

'There is always another plan,' came the weary reply.

'And it is still milord Thurleigh who makes these plans for you to obey?' Her sharp eyes observed his sudden wary look and she smiled. 'Oh Julian, you must not be alarmed, there is no one to overhear us.'

'What do you know of Thurleigh's plans?' he asked her cautiously, but the lady only laughed.

'Why, Julian, nothing more than the gossip that surrounds every Englishman who comes to France these days. But you need not be concerned – I do not think anyone here really cares about your little intrigues.' She paused, her smile slightly teasing. 'Except . . . there is perhaps one who would be interested, a young English milord who is exceedingly handsome . . .'

Poyntz gave a nervous laugh. 'Then pray do not tell him anything about me, Thérèse, for it is all nonsense, you know!'

'Have no fear, *mon cher*,' she told him, patting his hand. 'I chatter, but I do not give away my secrets. Now, I have had you to myself long enough, and if I do not let you go, we shall find ourselves the target for mischievous tongues' – she tapped her fan playfully against his bulging waistcoat, her eyes twinkling wickedly – 'I do have my reputation to consider! But you need not be too unhappy. I know of at least one lady here tonight who truly admires men of your stature. She really is very agreeable, *m'sieur.*'

Poyntz chuckled as he struggled to his feet. 'Thank you, ma'am, but I shall survive, I believe, without your kind offices! I see du Bellay over there and as he has been kind enough to house me during my sojourn here in Paris, I must not neglect him. In any event, should I require an introduction, I am sure he can serve me admirably.'

With a parting bow Mr Poyntz walked away, leaving his hostess smiling after him for a moment, tapping her fan thoughtfully against her fingers, until the demands of her guests once more occupied her attention. She moved between the little groups, a word here, a smile there, but she would not be detained. Madame had spotted her quarry, a tall gentleman, standing apart from the main company, and she made her way purposefully towards him.

'Ah, Viscount Davenham.' she gave him her enchanting smile. 'You do not mix, sir. Does the company not please you?'

The gentleman's blue eyes rested upon her, but Madame could not read the thoughts behind his steady gaze. She was aware of a faint tingle of excitement within her: this tall Englishman with his plain dark coat and no jewellery, she was reminded of a blackbird in a flowerbed, yet his very austerity attracted her.

'Your pardon, Madame. My mind was taken up with business. Indeed, I have no fault to find with the company, only with myself for being such a poor guest.'

'No, no my lord, you are not that,' she returned, keeping her dark eyes fixed upon his face. 'I am sorry we do not dance tonight, for you clearly need some – diversion.' She smiled invitingly up at him and stepped closer, until the scarlet petals of the roses in her corsage brushed his sleeve. 'Perhaps, my lord, our little poetry reading after supper will help you to forget your – business. We have the finest wits in Paris here tonight.'

His smile was perfunctory.

'I shall look forward to hearing them, Madame.'

His hostess sighed audibly, making great play with her fan.

'I am most disappointed in you, *m'sieur*. I do not believe you wish to be entertained!' Her pouting accusation drew a boyish grin from the viscount.

'I fear that on this occasion our ideas of entertainment do not coincide! A thousand apologies, Madame!'

'Oh, I cannot be angry with you! But can I do nothing to increase your enjoyment of this evening? Is there no one to whom I might introduce you?'

The viscount was about to make his denial when his attention was suddenly arrested by a movement by the door, a late arrival. His eyes widened fractionally.

'You may tell me, an you will, who is the lady just come in. The one dressed *en grisaille*.'

Madame looked across the room. 'Oh, that is Madame de Sange.'

'From her dress one would suppose her to be a widow.'

'That is correct, my lord. Philibert de Sange has been dead all of fourteen months, yet still she wears her widow's weeds. She never wears anything but grey.'

'Doubtless she was greatly attached to her husband.'

His hostess laughed. 'That is difficult to believe, my lord! He was very old, and word has it that he treated her abominably, although the lady herself never speaks of it. 'She observed his interested gaze. 'Pray do not allow yourself false hopes, my lord. No one has yet succeeded in breaching *that* citadel. In Paris she is known as the Lady of Stone.'

'Indeed?'

'You can well imagine that when de Sange produced such a young and beautiful wife there was no shortage of admirers, all ready to pay court, but it seems the lady is as virtuous as she is lovely. There has never been a breath of scandal attached to her name. Even now she holds herself aloof – but I can see it is no use. You are enchanted! Very well, I shall introduce you!' She led him across the room. 'Madame de Sange, I have with me one who is anxious to be known to you.'

'Your servant, Madame.' The viscount bowed over the gloved hand, his lips barely brushing the fingers before letting them go.

Madame de Briare watched with no little amusement as the two exchanged civilities, the viscount's attempts to open a conversation bringing little response from the lady. However, when their hostess had moved away he tried a different approach.

'Perhaps, Madame, my mastery of the French tongue is incomplete?'

'On the contrary, sir, it is perfect, as I am sure you are aware,' she replied coolly. 'If you prefer it, we can talk in English.'

'Your tone is not encouraging, Madame de Sange.'

'That is very observant, my lord.'

He regarded her with some amusement. 'It is easy to see why they call you the Lady of Stone. With your powdered hair, that widow's garb and such a cold, unfriendly manner, I am forcibly reminded of a block of granite.'

The lady's green eyes widened a fraction. 'And do you regularly talk to blocks of granite, my lord?' she asked him.

'Not *regularly*, ma'am, but I feel I am becoming more practised at it now.' He observed a small dimple appear at the corner of her mouth. 'Come, that is much better. Even widows are allowed to smile, you know.'

'Your conversation argues a most unstable mind sir,' she told him, her lips curving into a reluctant smile. 'Now, if you will excuse me—'

'No, please don't run away!' He put out his hand to detain her, and was rewarded with an icy stare.

'I run away from no one, sir!'

'Then prove it to me, Madame. Allow me the pleasure of your company for but a few moments longer. Who knows but that you might melt a little, given time.'

'One does not melt granite, my lord,' she countered, eyeing him warily.

'No, you are quite right. One chips away at it, little by little.'

'That would take a very long time.'

He smiled. 'I am in no hurry.'

At this point Elinor de Sange sensed danger. She had thought herself immune to any man's charms, but as the viscount smiled down at her she was shaken to discover that she wanted to respond, to know more of this tall Englishman who could make her laugh so readily. To cover her agitation, she turned to the mirror behind her and gave her attention to straightening the long strands of pearls that were roped about her throat.

'They are going down to supper,' remarked Lord Davenham, glancing about him. 'Perhaps, Madame, you would do me the honour. . . .' His speech trailed away as he caught sight of her reflection, for the Lady of Stone now bore every appearance of petrifaction. She was still standing before the mirror, but her face beneath its light powdering was quite as grey as her gown. She was staring fixedly into the glass and following her gaze, the viscount realized that she was watching the Duc du Bellay and his pink-coated companion as they approached. Slowly, like one in a dream, the widow turned to meet them.

The Duc du Bellay beamed at the lady as he came up to her.

'Your servant, Madame, and Lord Davenham, my dear sir, how goes it with you?' He waved a hand toward his companion. 'Madame, Monsieur Poyntz was very desirous to be presented. I hope you do not object to our interrupting you?'

'Not at all.' she replied mechanically, her fingers gripped tight about her ivory fan.

'It was my hope that I might have the pleasure of taking you to supper,' began Mr Poyntz, 'but I think Lord Davenham has the advantage of me.'

The viscount glanced again at the lady, but she appeared to be having difficulty with her speech, so he gently drew her hand on to his arm, saying, 'You have the right of it, sir. Your luck is quite out tonight. Now, gentlemen, if you will excuse us?'

He led Madame de Sange away, although she seemed unaware of his presence, and it was not until they entered the supper-room that she came out of her trance-like state, for my lord then felt her tremble.

'Are you ill, Madame? Shall I send for our hostess to attend you?'

'No, no. I am quite well, sir. I assure you.'

The viscount led the way to a vacant table.

'You seemed distressed at the sight of the *duc* and his friend,' he observed casually.

The green eyes flew to his face. 'What? Oh – no. I – I was feeling a little faint when the two gentlemen came up. . . .' She gave a flutter of laughter. 'A silly thing, but I am quite recovered now. The salon has so little air.'

Lord Davenham looked unconvinced, but he did not pursue the matter. He noted silently the lady's lack of appetite, and although she responded to his remarks, she seemed preoccupied, and it did not surprise him that she excused herself as soon as they had finished supper. She would go home, she told him. A little rest was all that was needed to set everything to rights. When my lord suggested that he should call upon her the following day, to assure himself of her well-being, the lady would have none of it.

'There is no need for you to trouble yourself, my lord. I shall be quite recovered by the morning and I have no doubt there are any number of things for you to attend to before your return to England.'

'Nothing that cannot be postponed, ma'am.'

'No, sir. I will not hear of it.' She met his gaze squarely as she added meaningfully, 'I thank you for your concern, Lord Davenham, but truly there is nothing to be gained by such attention. You would be wasting what little time you have left in France.'

With a faint shrug Davenham bowed.

'As you wish, Madame.'

The viscount returned alone to the salon. Spotting the salmon-pink coat across the room, he made his way directly to the wearer.

'Ah, Davenham!' Julian Poyntz greeted him cordially. 'What have you done with the lovely widow?'

'She has left by now, I daresay. She was feeling unwell.'

'Pity, I was hoping to try my luck there – not that I'd much chance against a handsome young dog like yourself, eh?' He gave a fat chuckle. 'Quite a fetching lady, though, don't you agree? A piece of perfection.'

The viscount assented, and took out his snuffbox.

'What brings you to Paris?' He offered the box to Mr Poyntz, who shook his head at it.

'Oh, a mere whim, sir,' came the casual reply. 'I wanted to look up old friends. Very much like yourself, I've no doubt.'

Lord Davenham helped himself to a pinch of snuff and returned the box to his pocket.

'Not quite a whim on my part, Poyntz. It fact it was more a suggestion of my father's. He wants some information.'

'Indeed?'

'Yes,' nodded my lord. 'You see, there is a certain English nobleman who is being – shall we say – less than honest with his fellow countrymen. He holds a great deal of power and influence already, but it is not enough for him, sir.'

'It is not?' Poyntz looked wary.

'No. He wishes to restore a Stuart to the English throne, hoping thereby to become even more powerful.'

'Surely not, my lord!'

'But it is true,' returned the viscount. 'In fact, sir, I can tell you that this nobleman is suspected of treachery by many in the government, but he is cunning. There is no proof against him, and such is his influence at court that more than rumours are required to denounce him.'

'Then it seems the gentleman is secure,' replied Poyntz, nervously biting his lip.

Observing signs of unease in his auditor, Lord Davenham smiled faintly.

'Oh, but that is far from the case! You see, my father has no love for this man – due, I suspect, to some age-old quarrel – and he is determined to gather enough information to bring down the marquis. Oh, did I forget to mention that the nobleman in question is a marquis?'

'I'm sure it doesn't matter to me, my lord, since I know nothing about it,' said Poyntz, in a voice that was not quite steady.

'No, no, of course not. However, my father tells me that he already has information concerning several of the fellow's accomplices. There is a deal of information to be gained from these – ah – fellow-conspirators, which would doubtless help us in our task, and gain clemency for the informants at the same time.'

Mr Poyntz eyed the viscount warily for a few seconds, then he laughed, saying with a fair assumption of confidence, 'Seems to me you've been sent to shoe a goose, Davenham! If there is treachery afoot, would your time not be better spent in London, watching this nameless gentleman?'

'Perhaps you are right,' murmured the viscount, moving away. 'I intend to return to London very shortly in any event, although my hosts, Madame and Monsieur Charrière, are holding a masquerade ball in a sennight, and I have given my word I shall stay until then. Mayhap I shall see you there, Poyntz. It seems to me that all of Paris has been invited – and will doubtless attend,' he added thoughtfully, 'for the Charrières are renowned for their hospitality, are they not?' And with a final bow, Viscount Davenham sauntered away, leaving a pensive Mr Poyntz to stare after him.

CHAPTER FOUR

Madame de Sange is transformed

After the noise and activity of the de Briare's soirée, Elinor found the Hôtel de Sange sepulchral. A solitary light burned in the hall, where she surprised a sleeping servant, who had not expected to see his mistress for another two hours at least. The jewelled heels of her shoes tapped loudly across the marble floor and up the wide staircase, but the thick rugs on the upper floors deadened all sound save the soothing rustle of Madame's skirts as she made her way to her bedchamber. Just as she reached her room, an elderly lady in a black gown appeared.

'You are returned early tonight, Madame.' She spoke in perfect English and with some surprise.

'Yes, Hannah. It was a tedious affair. I am very tired.' Elinor avoided the woman's searching look as she entered her bedchamber.

After the briefest hesitation, Hannah followed her. She watched as Madame threw off her cloak and sat down at her dressing-table to remove her jewels, paying no heed to her companion, or the constant chatter of her voluble French maid. After a few moments, Hannah addressed the servant in English.

'Thank you, Bella. I will attend to Madame tonight. It is no good babbling away at me in French, young woman, for you know I don't understand the half of it, nor ever shall, no matter how many years I live here! Off you go to bed!'

'Poor Bella. I fear you have offended her.' Elinor smiled

41

slightly as the maid was hustled out of the room, still muttering. 'You should not wait up for me, Hannah. You know I asked you to live here to give me respectability, not to be my servant.'

'Heavens, ma'am, have you forgotten that I was your nurse? Did you think that when your sweet mama died I would go back to England and leave you here alone with all these foreigners?'

Madame's lips twitched, but she replied gravely, '*We* are the foreigners here, Hannah.'

'You know what I mean, Miss Nell. Now, let us get you into your wrap and I will let down your hair.'

Obediently Elinor allowed her old retainer to help her out of the heavy grey satin with its numerous petticoats and cumbersome hoop, replacing it with a cream wrap of fine wool. She then resumed her seat at the dressing-table while Hannah brushed the grey powder from her chestnut hair with soothing, regular strokes.

'It is seldom that you leave a party early, Madame.'

Elinor avoided the sharp old eyes that watched her reflection in the glass.

'As I told you, 'twas a tedious affair. I could scarce conceal my boredom.'

The regular brushing stopped.

'Now Miss Nell, I've known you too long to be fobbed off with such a tale!' came the blunt reply. 'When I saw you come in, you looked for all the world as if you had seen a ghost.'

'Mayhap I *did* see one, Hannah.'

'Nay, child, what sort of talk is that?'

'I saw a man, Hannah. A fat Englishman named Poyntz. He did not recognize me, but I knew *him* at once—' Her voice trembled and she took a long breath before continuing, 'He was one of the men at – on that night—'

The older lady's face grew pale.

'Oh no, child! Surely you are mistaken!'

Elinor turned in her chair and caught at the frail hand that held the brush.

'There was no mistake! But I want to know, Hannah, could he be – was he the one who killed my father?'

The servant stared down into the troubled green eyes and shook her head sadly.

'Miss Nell, I do not know. So long ago, I hoped you had forgotten.'

Elinor dropped the hand as if she had been stung.

'Forgotten!' she cried, jumping up. 'How could I forget that I was used for the pleasure of five so-called gentlemen, or that one of them murdered my father? I tell you, Hannah, those five faces are burned into my memory, and will never be erased! But to see this man Poyntz, so – so jovial and prosperous. Did *all* of them go unpunished?'

Hannah Grisson shrugged. 'That I do not know, for since our flight to France I have had no word from England. But why revisit your pain, my lady?'

'I do not revisit it, Hannah. It has never left me. But now. . . .' She paused, then glanced up at her servant, a little smile playing about her lips. 'Whatever my late husband's faults, he has left me in complete control of my fortune, so perhaps it is time I began to make use of the money.' She rose. 'I shall go to bed now, Hannah. I am sure it will please you to know that I have decided to leave off my grey gowns. Tomorrow, I shall set about replenishing my wardrobe with more cheerful colours.'

'Your sainted mother would be pleased to see you wearing colours again, Miss Nell,' said Hannah, her face brightening as she helped her mistress into bed. 'Perhaps some good has come of this night after all is said and done. Talking can do a deal of good, and perhaps your ghost is laid to rest.'

Elinor lay back against the soft pillows, her green eyes glinting.

'Not quite,' she said softly, 'but I hope he soon may be.'

Madame de Sange rose from her bed very early the following morning and issued her orders: she would see no one but her *coiffeuse*, and the dressmakers, milliners and the most fashionable mantua-makers in Paris who passed through the Hôtel de Sange in a constant stream. When at last she emerged once more into the Paris street a few days later, gone were the grey cloak and gown, replaced with a morning robe in emerald-green lustring and a cream woollen shawl thrown over her arm as a precaution lest any chill breeze should suddenly spring up. Her hair, previously dressed in thick powdered curls, was now pinned up neatly under a wide-brimmed straw hat, with little tawny ringlets framing her face. Today, however, this transformation was not for the benefit of any society acquaintance. Madame de Sange stepped up into her waiting coach and was borne away to the outskirts of Paris, where she could indulge in her favourite pastime. It was her habit, on fine days, to take her carriage to a small wooded glade where she could alight and walk undisturbed beside a stream that meandered through the trees. There she felt at peace. On this particular morning Elinor revelled in the solitude, for the past days had been so busy that she was glad of a respite to collect her thoughts. It was with some annoyance therefore that she observed a figure before her on the path. As she drew closer, she recognized the tall figure of Viscount Davenham. He sketched a bow as she came up to him.

'Good day to you, Madame de Sange.'

'Sir, I come here to be alone. Pray be so good as to go on your way.'

He raised his brows at her direct speech.

'I am sorry if I interrupt you.'

'You do interrupt me. Good day, sir!'

'Pray, hear me, Madame!' he cried, walking beside her. 'I have called at your house a dozen times since the de Briare's soirée and on each occasion you have refused to see me.'

'With good reason. I have been engaged.'

'Then allow me now but a few moments of your time.'

'No.'

She walked on briskly, hoping he would turn back and leave her in peace. However, she soon realized that he had fallen into step behind her. He followed her in silence for some time, then:

'Faith, spirit,' she heard him say, 'whither wander you? Do you go, perhaps, like Shakespeare's fairy, *over hill, over dale, thorough bush, thorough brier* to serve some fairy queen?' Receiving no answer, he continued in a conversational tone: 'It

44

is exceeding pleasant here, is it not? The trees provide us with their leafy shade, birds delight us with their song, and a stream, too, a veritable paradise! I vow I could walk on for ever. Indeed, I am beginning to think I shall be obliged to do so!'

Elinor stopped and turned to face him, trying to hide a smile.

'My lord, upon first meeting you, I discovered that you liked to converse with blocks of stone – granite, was it not? Now I find you talking to yourself!'

'The latter case is easily remedied, ma'am.'

'Is there nothing I can say that will persuade you to go away?'

'No, Madame, nothing.'

'Then faith, sir, I must capitulate. You may walk back with me to my carriage.'

'Would you not care to stroll on a little further?' he asked her hopefully.

Quelling any desire to prolong their meeting, Elinor turned her steps resolutely back the way she had come.

'How did you know I would be here, Lord Davenham?'

'After trying unsuccessfully to call on you, I made a few enquiries and discovered that you walked here most mornings.'

'Have you then been here, lying in wait for me?'

'Oh no. As I told you, I have tried each day to gain entry to your *hôtel* and having failed to do so, I watched for your carriage.'

'And did your sources fail to inform you that I detest company on my walks?'

'They told me of it, but I thought I should succeed.'

'Oh?' When he did not speak, curiosity forced her to ask, 'Why should you think you would succeed when others had failed?'

'Because we are both English. I learned from my informants that you came to France as a child. Thus, we have something in common.'

There was a pause and, glancing down at the lady, my lord was somewhat surprised to see the look of annoyance upon her countenance. When at last she spoke her voice was low and taut.

'You are mistaken, sir. I no longer consider myself English, nor do I have any affection for that country.'

'Do you never come to England now?'

'No, never.'

'Then how can you be so sure you would not like it there?'

'My lord, I pray you will not question me too deeply. Let it suffice that England holds for me . . . unpleasant memories.'

He stopped, obliging her to halt beside him. 'Then I would wish, Madame, that you would but take the trouble to come to London, and mayhap we could replace those memories with something a little happier.'

She shook her head, keeping her eyes lowered. 'I doubt you could do that.'

'I would willingly take up the challenge.'

With a tiny shake of her head Elinor resumed her walk.

'No. I am sorry. It will not do.' She spoke firmly. 'I have given you enough of my time, sir. You may escort me back to my carriage, if you so choose, but then I must ask that you do not trouble me again.'

'I must in any event return to England at the end of the month; surely there could be no harm—'

'No!' she cried, stopping once more. 'It cannot be! I have other plans.' She drew a deep, steadying breath and looked up at him, forcing herself to meet his puzzled eyes squarely. 'I am sorry for it, my lord. If it were not for . . .' she broke off, then tried again. 'There are things that I must do. A course of action that I *must* follow, and it allows no room for . . . other interests, my lord.'

'What?' He smiled at her. 'Are you about to take orders and enter a nunnery?'

'It would be all the same for you, sir, if I were,' she told him earnestly. 'Pray believe me, there is no place for you here.'

Steadily she faced him, returning look for look. At length Davenham shrugged.

'Very well, Madame. I can see you are resolved, and I will trouble you no further.' He smiled again, this time a little wryly. 'A pity, mistress, for I believe we should deal extremely well together!'

Elinor held out her hand but would not meet his eyes. She said softly, 'I am sorry.'

The viscount took the outstretched fingers and lifted them briefly to his lips.

'So too am I,' he replied, then, without another word, he turned and strode off, leaving the lady to make her way back to her carriage alone.

CHAPTER FIVE

A gentleman is in peril of his life, and a lady of her soul

Madame de Sange dressed with care for the masquerade at the noble residence of M. Charrière, choosing a gown of gold-coloured silk embellished with quantities of blond lace and clasping about her neck the magnificent de Sange diamonds which had remained in their case since her husband's demise. She completed her costume with a voluminous cloak of dark green and an elaborate gilded headdress. Surveying her reflection in the mirror, Elinor allowed herself a smile: no one would recognize her – faith, with nothing more than her mouth and chin visible beneath the headdress she hardly knew herself! Elinor shivered, but it was not the anticipation of an enjoyable evening that caused her to tremble. Her sole purpose was to confront Julian Poyntz, and she foresaw little pleasure in the encounter.

The Charrière family was one of the very few in Paris that Philbert de Sange had deigned to recognize and his widow knew the house well. She moved confidently up the wide sweeping staircase to the ballroom, her nervousness gone now that she was so close to her goal. The room was already crowded, and very hot, and Elinor was glad to take a glass of champagne from a hovering servant. There was no sign of Poyntz, but she was not unduly worried: it was early yet. The dancing commenced and at once the ballroom seemed full of swirling, laughing couples. She watched them somewhat envi-ously, and took a second glass of champagne. An undignified

48

collision between several of the dancers caused her to laugh out loud and a tall figure in a black domino immediately turned to stare at her. Unaware of this scrutiny, Elinor sipped at her glass, her foot tapping in time to the music.

'Your pardon, Madame, but it is against the rules of the house for any guest merely to observe the dancing,' remarked the gentleman in the black domino, removing her half-empty glass and setting it aside. Then, without waiting for a reply he led her on to the dance-floor. They were already dancing before Elinor had realized where she had heard his voice before.

'English manners, my Lord Davenham?'

He smiled, squeezing her hand, while through the slits of his mask his blue eyes glittered, causing her heart to pound in a most alarming way.

'I fear a hesitant approach would have met with a refusal.'

Since she could not make a denial, Elinor remained silent, allowing herself to enjoy the music and the dance. The viscount was a good dancer, expertly guiding his partner through the steps of the courante, avoiding collisions which were always a danger in such a crowded room. The atmosphere was exhilarating, and Elinor found herself in such harmony with her partner that she readily agreed to remain with him for the galliard, subduing her conscience with the thought that even if Julian Poyntz had arrived, it was still too early in the evening to approach him. The orchestra was playing a very lively tune, and many of the dancers whooped and shrieked as they whirled about the room, taking advantage of their disguises to abandon formality. Elinor and the viscount danced amongst them, twirling and skipping so fast that Elinor felt her senses reeling and when at last the music came to an end, she was obliged to lean against her partner for fear of losing her balance.

'Sweet heaven, my lord! I have not danced like that for many a year!' She laughed, allowing him to lead her from the floor.

'But you danced perfectly. I would have said you were used to dancing every night!'

'Flatterer!' She tapped his arm with her fan before unfurling it and vigorously fanning her glowing cheeks. Observing this, Lord Davenham led the lady towards an embrasure where the glass doors had been opened to allow a little air into the ballroom. Breaking away from her partner, Elinor stepped out on to the terrace, thankful to feel the cool night air upon her heated skin.

'I cannot think when I have enjoyed myself so much,' she remarked as the viscount came up beside her. 'When I set out tonight I had no anticipation that the evening would be so pleasant.' She turned to face him, smiling. 'Thank you, my lord.'

She saw the gleam of his teeth as he smiled back at her.

'I told you we should deal well together, did I not, Madame de Sange?'

Before Elinor could reply, he had removed his mask and bent his head to kiss her, locking her into a crushing embrace. Elinor's blood raced. For a few seconds she returned his kiss with equal fervour, pushing her body hard against him. Then reality swept back upon her and she struggled to thrust him away.

'No!' She freed herself and stepped back, her hands out before her to keep him away. 'That should not have happened!'

'Would you tell me you did not want me to kiss you?'

'Yes, no – oh, I wish you would go away!' Elinor pressed a kerchief to her lips with a trembling hand. 'It was the champagne and the dancing – you took advantage of me!' His laughter made her angry and she stamped her foot at him. 'You are no gentleman, sir, to treat me thus!' Her voice trembled as she fought to hold her tears.

The laughter died from his face and Davenham stared at her in amazement.

'By God, you are serious!'

Elinor drew a deep breath. With scarcely a tremor in her voice she replied, 'I have already told you, sir, you waste your time with me. I enjoyed our dance, but I have no further use for you!' Looking up as she finished this speech, she trembled at the angry look in the viscount's eyes. For an instant she wondered if he might strike her, and in her heart she would not have blamed him, for her words had been insulting, calculated to repulse, but he made no move towards her. His lips had set into a thin line, and without another word he made her a stiff little bow, turned on his heel and strode back into the ballroom.

As soon as he had gone Elinor felt the tears welling up, but she blinked them away, resolving not to give in to such weakness. Besides, she told herself sternly, she had not yet accomplished what she had set out to do – she must put this silly incident out of her mind, for all her courage would be required for the task ahead.

When Julian Poyntz and the Duc du Bellay arrived at the Charrière residence, the promised masquerade was in full swing. Du Bellay had provided his guest with a grey domino and mask, and both gentlemen donned their disguises before entering the ballroom. Mr Poyntz, already mellowed by the *duc*'s generous dinner, found the noise and excitement intoxicating and was soon swept up in the dancing from which he emerged some time later feeling very hot and not a little thirsty. There was no sign of du Bellay, so Poyntz set off alone in search of some refreshment, making his way to an adjoining salon where a magnificent supper had been laid out. The main passion of Mr Poyntz's life was food and he gazed rapturously upon the feast.

It was some time later that he reappeared in the ballroom, having sampled almost every dish and refilled his glass with more of his host's excellent wine. He stood gazing with a detached interest at the dancers until he became aware of a tall figure in a black domino standing but a short distance away. Poyntz recognized the gentleman, despite his disguise and, tossing off his wine, he bestirred himself to speak.

'Lord Davenham – your servant sir.' He sketched a small bow. 'Thought I'd see you here. Dashed glad to be able to converse in English, too!'

'It was always my expressed intention to attend tonight.'

Hearing the cold tone, Mr Poyntz wondered who could be responsible for putting the viscount into such a black mood. He tried to dismiss Lord Davenham's obvious ill-humour with a nervous little laugh.

'Yes well, I've been thinking over the little matter we were talking of—'

'Have you, perhaps, some information for me?'

'Perhaps, perhaps,' murmured Poyntz warily, 'but it has occurred to me that it might be safer to take up residence here in Paris and to say nothing.'

The viscount bowed, apparently unmoved.

'As you wish, sir, although I am informed that His Majesty's government would not be – ah – *ungenerous* to one who helped them in this matter. Also, one must remember' – he paused to brush a speck of dust from one velvet sleeve – 'when a traitor falls, his accomplices are liable to fall with him.'

'Wait! I own I would be pleased to be out of it, after all these years,' muttered Poyntz, almost to himself. 'Oh very well!' he added decidedly. 'I will call upon you here tomorrow, my lord, with your permission?'

'Certainly, sir. I shall look forward to it.'

The viscount moved off and Mr Poyntz returned his attention to the dancing, where the excitement was now much more intense. A figure suddenly appeared beside him, a lady swathed in a large cloak of green and gold, with a gilded headdress that concealed all of her hair and half her face, save for a dainty chin and a pair of cherry-red lips that now smiled invitingly. She pulled him into the whirl of dancers and Poyntz entered into the spirit of the occasion, gallantly leading his partner around the floor and performing the rigaudon as energetically as was possible for a man of his stature, but after a few minutes he drew her to one side, wheezing and panting from the exertion.

'A – a thousand – apologies, madam, but – I must rest – not as young as I was!'

'It matters not, *monsieur*. Let us take a glass of wine together.'

He stared as the masked face, frowning. The lady's English was perfect, with scarcely a trace of accent.

'Have we not met before? I would swear I know your voice.'

'Oh, 'tis quite possible, *m'sieur*.' The lady's eyes glittered through the slits of her mask, a warm smile curving her red lips.

'Come then! Let us sit here while I try to discover your identity!' cried the gentleman gaily. He led his partner to a vacant sofa, provided two glasses of champagne and spent a very pleasant half-hour in dalliance with his mysterious partner.

Nothing could have exceeded the lady's amiability. She gently flattered him, laughing at his attempts to name her and ensuring that he was kept supplied with drink. The gentleman pushed his round, flushed face close to hers.

'Well, this I will say, madam! You're dam' – dashed good company, whoever you may be!' He stumbled over his words, but the hand gripping her knee was very sure.

She did not move away, and through the slits of her mask the green eyes were inviting.

'It will soon be time for the unmasking,' she said softly. 'A pity that it is so noisy here. Shall we find a quieter spot in which to declare ourselves?'

There was no mistaking the eagerness in the gentleman's voice as he agreed. The lady led the way out of the crowded ballroom and along a corridor to the wide staircase. By the time they reached the next floor the noise from the ballroom was but a distant murmur.

'You appear to know the house well, ma'am,' remarked Mr Poyntz as he followed her along another corridor.

'I have often stayed here with my husband.'

'I trust that gentleman will not disturb us tonight.' He gave an uneasy laugh.

'He need not concern you, sir. He is dead.'

She stopped at a door. Poyntz followed her into a large guest-bedchamber, handsomely appointed with gold hangings at the windows and around the large bed. A cheerful fire blazed merrily in the hearth and the lady stepped forward to light a taper from the flames, then she proceeded to light candles until the whole room was illuminated. Poyntz looked about him curiously.

'Your room, perhaps, madam?'

'I do not stay here tonight,' she said, untying her cloak. 'Doubtless it has been given over to some guest, but it will do for our purposes.'

He laughed, moving towards her.

'By Gad, lady, you are a cool one!' He reached out to pull her into his arms, his lips eagerly covering her mouth with hot kisses while one hand tried to remove the concealing head-dress.

'Not yet, *m'sieur!*' She struggled to hold him off. 'Someone may discover us. Let me lock the door.'

She went to the door and turned the key, afterwards slipping it into her pocket. Turning back she saw that the gentleman had removed his domino and mask.

'Will you now let me see your face, fair charmer?' he asked her.

She put up her hands to take off the headdress, revealing her face and an abundance of thick auburn curls, gleaming in the candlelight. It was a few moments before Poyntz recognized her and his look of surprise when he did so was almost comical. 'Madame de Sange! This is indeed a pleasure I did not expect! At our last meeting you gave me no reason to think—'

'That night, Mr Poyntz, I was still in mourning.'

The gentleman laughed, and began hurriedly to unbutton his coat.

'Then, tonight, Madame, it is time to celebrate!'

She stepped close to him, assisting his fumbling efforts to remove his tight-fitting coat; then, as he struggled with the buttons of his florid waistcoat, she unbuckled the ornate dress-sword with her long, steady fingers. He glanced at her, his round face glowing with eager anticipation.

'In grey you were enchanting,' he told her rapturously, 'but now, with that glorious hair and such exquisite eyes, I vow I have never before seen such a combination!'

'Oh I think you have, Mr Poyntz.'

She stepped back and he found himself staring at the blade of his own dress-sword, its point pressed lightly against the fleshy folds of skin beneath his chin. He tried to retreat, but found the way blocked by a heavy wooden writing-table behind him.

'I – this is dangerous funning, ma'am!' He tried to laugh.

'But I am deadly serious, Mr Poyntz. Please do not attempt to move, or I shall be forced to pierce your throat. Put your hands behind you.'

The very calmness of her speech unnerved him and he did as she ordered.

'What – what is this?'

'Do you not remember me?'

He began to shake his head, then remembered the steel at his throat.

'No, I cannot recall having seen you before, save at the de Briare's soirée. Pray put down the sword and let us talk sensibly.'

The blade pressed deeper into his flesh and he feared that at any moment the point would puncture the skin. The lady's eyes were hard as stone as she watched him.

'Think back, Mr Poyntz. Think back to a winter's day in December, eight years ago.'

'Eight years!' he repeated in astonishment. 'How the devil can I recall—?'

The look on the lady's face made him break off and he said in a quieter tone, 'Well, let me think – that would be 'forty-five. I seem to remember I spent most of that winter chasing over England – Good God!'

She watched as astonishment and recognition crossed the gentleman's features and she smiled grimly.

'The – the girl at the inn?' he asked her incredulously. 'But you cannot be – Thurleigh said you were dead! He told me that when he had recovered the ruby he dispatched you—'

'I know nothing of that!' She cut him short impatiently.

A wary look came into Poyntz's eyes. He tried to move, but the steel at his throat never wavered from its target and he changed his mind.

'You – you appear to have done very well for yourself, Madame de Sange. What is it you want from me? Money for some by-slip of that night? Damme, but I don't see how you can tell which of us fathered your love-child . . .'

A look of loathing came over her face.

'How dare you talk of love!' she cried in disgust. 'There was nothing but hate and violence on that night and I thank God he spared me a bastard from such a time!'

He looked perplexed.

'But if it is not a child – what is it you want from me?'

'Did you think, sir, that if we should meet again I would let any of you go unpunished for what you did?'

' 'Twas nothing more than a little dalliance – ahh!' He screamed and fell to his knees as the sword bit into his skin and he felt a trickle of warm blood running down his neck.

'Next time it will go deeper!' she promised, her voice low and quivering with anger. 'You must now realize how much I should like to drive this point through your throat right now – it is only the fact that I need information from you that prevents me from killing you.'

He did not doubt her sincerity, and beads of perspiration stood out on his forehead, the colour ebbing and flowing from his cheeks.

'P-please, Madame, consider what you are about! You cannot wish to damn your soul by committing murder!' he cried shrilly, but she regarded him with cold, contemptuous eyes.

'But you could save me from sin, and save yourself, Mr Poyntz, if you will but tell me who killed my father.'

'I don't know – please!' He screamed again as the sword once more pierced his neck, 'I swear I know nothing of this!'

'My father was an old man, a peaceful man, but he went to the inn in search of justice. They brought him back to us on a litter – one of you had killed him!'

He read the accusation in her eyes and trembled.

'Not I, believe me! Pray Madame, consider – it was I who showed you some little mercy and gave you the ruby as some recompense for your suffering. True, I did not then realize—' He broke off, sweat glistening upon his brow. 'I – I remember nothing after you had gone, I swear it! Most likely I passed out. I recall nothing more of that evening.' He held his breath as she stared down at him, then she drew back slightly and he closed his eyes in relief as the sharp point came away from his neck. His heart was still pounding heavily, making it hard for him to breathe, but he struggled back to his feet, nervously eyeing the blade that still hovered menacingly before him.

'But, Madame, did not Lord Thurleigh come to you to reclaim his ruby?'

'I know nothing of such a jewel,' she told him dismissively.

'I have not seen the marquis or any of you since that night.'

'Then he did not get it back. He has no hold upon any of us,' Poyntz muttered to himself, before the lady's sharp voice brought him back to his present predicament.

'You will find paper, pens and ink upon the table behind you,' she told him. 'I want you to write the names of the men who were with you that night. Move slowly, sir, for I would still very much like to kill you.'

Poyntz sat down at the table and drew the small writing-case towards him, thinking quickly. If he could only get the sword away from her, he could overpower her, but the deadly steel remained between them and he read murder in the lady's eyes.

'Write the name of the inn and the date you were there at the head of the paper,' she commanded him.

'But I cannot recall the inn—'

'The Black Goose. Write it!'

He gave a shrug and picked up the pen. What did it matter now, if he did give her the names? He had, after all, decided to turn king's evidence, and bring an end to Thurleigh's continual plotting. God knows he was tired of it! He wrote steadily, and without a break, hesitating only over the marquis's name. Thurleigh could be a deadly enemy, as many had found to their cost, but a moment's reflection convinced Poyntz that he was in no danger. The letter to Charles Stuart that they had all signed was burned and if the ruby was lost, then there was nothing to connect Julian Poyntz with any serious Jacobite plot. He finished the list, put down his pen and sat back, rubbing his left arm, which had begun to ache.

'Sign it!' ordered the lady.

When he had finished she motioned him to move away, then she glanced quickly at the paper.

'There are some very dangerous men on that list,' he warned her, mopping his brow with a handkerchief. He was feeling very uncomfortable, and was beginning to wish he had not eaten quite so freely at the supper table. 'You would be well advised to stay away from them.'

Elinor cast him a contemptuous glance.

'I do not fear them,' she said coldly. 'I fear nothing now, not even death.'

A sudden, strangled cry from Poyntz made her raise the sword again, suspicious of his actions: he was leaning heavily upon the table, one hand pressed to his chest. 'My heart!' he gasped. 'Help me!'

She frowned, suspecting a trick, but the gentleman's pallor was real enough. He was on his knees now, gasping for breath.

'Pray, Madame – quickly, summon help for me!'

She did not move.

'What help did you give *me*, sir, eight years ago?' she asked slowly.

His faded blue eyes grew wide with terror as she spoke, then all expression left them and he keeled over, hitting the floor with a dull thud.

Elinor stared down at Poyntz's lifeless body: blood from the small wounds upon his neck had made crimson stains upon the snowy white lace under his chin and his eyes stared out unseeingly from the livid face. Shuddering, she turned away and it was some moments before she could collect her scattered thoughts. Then, placing the dress-sword carefully upon the table, Elinor worked quickly, dusting the list of names before folding the paper and slipping it into her pocket. She fumbled for the key and, with trembling fingers, fitted it into the lock and opened the door. With a final glance back at the inert form upon the floor, she snatched up her cloak and left the room, shutting the door quietly behind her. Elinor hurried along the deserted passageway, tying her cloak as she went. She reached the stairs before she remembered that her head-dress was still in the bedchamber. It was too late to go back, already a clock somewhere in the house was chiming the hour and she had given instructions for her carriage to be waiting. In any event, she told herself, the unmasking would have taken place by now and she would look conspicuous if she continued to hide her face. She drew her cloak around her, the hood pulled up over her hair, and hurried down the stairs, hoping to slip out of the house unnoticed. Her heart thudded painfully as she descended and the noise from the ballroom grew steadily louder. Elinor turned a corner and gave a frightened gasp as she collided with a large figure coming up the stairs. Panic threatened to overwhelm her as the black figure seemed to tower above her, blocking her way. Without looking up she muttered an apology and hurried away, scarcely pausing until she was out of the house and being carried homeward in her carriage.

Elinor did not allow herself to relax until she had reached the safety of her own bedchamber. Dismissing her maid, she drew the paper from her pocket and unfolded it with fingers that were not quite steady, then she sat at her dressing-table to study the list. With the exception of Lord Thurleigh, the names meant nothing to her, but she did not doubt that she would be able to trace them and perhaps, just perhaps, she could exact revenge. The following morning found her still considering her plan of action as she sipped her hot chocolate. There was a light scratching upon the door.

'Miss Nell?' Hannah entered the room. 'Bella told me you were not quite yourself last night, and I have come to see how you go on this morning. Would you like me to summon a doctor?'

'Of course not, Hannah! As you can see, I am very well.' She put aside her cup. 'Hannah, when my mother died, I gave you her jewel-box, do you recall?'

'Why yes, Madame,' replied Hannah, surprised, 'the box and all its jewels! You would have none of them, and said I might do with them as I wished.'

'Yes I know, and I meant it, Hannah, but I should like to know what became of them.'

The older woman regarded her fondly.

'Why, they are still in their box, safe and sound in my room. Bless you, Miss Nell, what would I want with fancy jewels? And since you have been kind enough to house me *and* to give me a pension, I want for nothing, and have had no need to sell any of the gems.'

'Could I perhaps look at them, Hannah?' asked Elinor, getting out of bed and reaching for her wrap.

'But of course, Miss Nell! And you may keep them all, with my blessing: I have no need of them.'

Hannah hurried away, returning a few minutes later carrying a small wooden box, its dark surface highly polished and inlaid with an intricate pattern of ivory. She placed it down upon the dressing-table in front of Elinor, who turned the key and slowly opened the lid. Inside, her mother's jewels lay just as she had left them, the strings of pearls and gold chains tangling together, with the occasional glint of a precious stone shining through from beneath. Elinor's long fingers sifted through the ornaments until she found what she was looking for, buried deep at the back of the box. Her fingers closed around a large brooch and she brought it out into the light.

'Do you know when Mama was given this, Hannah?'

'Why no, Miss Nell. I never saw your dear mama wearing such a thing. Indeed, I did not know of its existence until now, for I confess I have never liked to sort through the sainted lady's things.'

Elinor stared down at the ornament; from the centre of its ornate gold setting the large ruby glared sullenly back at her.

'Will you let me keep this, Hannah?'

'But of course, Madame! You may keep the whole box with my goodwill.'

'No, thank you, you shall have the rest. Take the box back to your room, Hannah, and you may as well begin to pack your things. We are going to England.'

'England!' Hannah gasped. 'Dear lady! When do we depart?'

'As soon as may be,' came the brisk reply, 'so you can give orders immediately to begin packing up.' Elinor dismissed her companion and turned her eyes back to the jewel. 'Lord Thurleigh's ruby,' she murmured. 'With blood did we pay for this, and in blood shall I return it.'

CHAPTER SIX

The viscount learns of an old mystery

The house in St James's did not stand out from its neighbours: there were no outward signs that it was not a private residence, and if the burly individual who opened the door to Lord Davenham was in danger of bursting the seams of his tight-fitting livery coat, the viscount showed no concern. He ran lightly up the stairs to a large, well-appointed salon on the first floor where candles burned brightly in their sconces and little groups of gentlemen were gathered around the tables, indulging in various games of chance. The viscount's entrance caused little stir, most of the gentlemen being too concerned with their fortunes to observe his entrance, but a richly clad gentleman at one of the green-baize tables called out to him in a bluff, good-natured voice.

'Davenham, my dear boy! Come and join us – I'm about rolled up, but we can include you in the next rubber.'

'Thank you, Derry, but no.' Lord Davenham smiled faintly as he approached the table. 'I came in search of Lord Hartworth – is he not here?'

Lord Derry inclined his head towards a door at the far end of the room.

'Your father's been in there playing euchre for the past couple of hours.' He paused, surveying the viscount's frock-coat and riding-boots with some disfavour. 'How came Jacob to let you in, dressed like that?' he demanded.

'Jacob knows a rich patron well enough!' laughed another gentleman at the table.

Lord Derry shook his head sadly.

'There was a time when they wouldn't let you into this club unless you was properly dressed. No – well, look at you, lad! Never saw such a plain coat in all my life! A touch of gold lace would not go amiss.'

'I'll wager Davenham picked up these bad habits from those damned Frenchies!' added a freckle-faced gentleman. 'When did you get back, my friend? I did not look to see you in London again this side of Christmas.'

'I am but this day arrived, Sir Robin.'

'Have you come from Paris?' asked Derry. 'Heard about poor old Poyntz, I don't doubt.'

'Yes – in fact I would have come back sooner, but I took over the poor fellow's affairs. There was no one else to do it, so I remained in Paris to act on behalf of his family.'

'Bad business,' remarked Sir Robin, shaking his head. 'I heard of it from George Rowsell a couple of weeks back. Poor fellow was most upset.'

'They were always close friends,' put in Lord Davenham.

'Aye, but from what I hear he's found consolation in the arms of yet another beautiful woman,' grinned Derry. 'Damme if I know how he does it, but Rowsell is rarely seen without some fair charmer upon his arm.'

'He falls in and out of love at the drop of a hat!' declared Sir Robin. 'Although I must say, having seen the lady I can well understand the fascination. The woman is captivating!' His attention was caught by a movement at one end of the room and he added, 'Here's Lord Hartworth now, Davenham. 'Tis mighty unusual for him to leave the table so early. I pray for your sake, lad, that the luck's not been against him.' Davenham pulled a wry face.

'I shall soon discover the truth of it, sir.' He bowed to the gentleman and moved away to greet his father.

There could be no mistaking the tall, grey-haired gentleman in the silver-laced coat who now crossed the room to approach the viscount. The resemblance between father and son was striking. The older man favoured a more elaborate style of dress, with the skirts of his coat stiffened to swing out from the waist and a quantity of fine Mechlin lace at his cuffs and neck contrasting sharply with the viscount's plain coat of dark-blue velvet and snowy-white neckband. However, both men shared the same high cheekbones and square jaw-line, and if the earl's blue eyes had lost a little of their colour, they were no less keen as they fell upon the viscount.

'Well, this is an – unexpected – honour,' murmured the earl. 'To what do I owe the pleasure of seeing you, Davenham?'

The viscount took the long slim fingers that were held out to him and bowed over them.

'I called at the house, sir, to pay my respects to you 'pon my return from Paris – your man told me I should find you here.'

'Your sense of filial duty is most touching, Davenham, but I believe I would have survived another few hours without knowledge of your safe return. You could as well have waited until morning.'

The viscount's eyes held his parent's gaze unwaveringly.

'I have yet to hear of you quitting your room before midday, sir, and as your temper is never at its best until dinner-time, I cannot but feel that this is a more propitious moment for our meeting.'

Lord Hartworth raised his brows at this cool speech, but there was the merest hint of a smile upon his thin lips.

'Perhaps you are right, dear boy,' he admitted in his quiet way. 'Give me your arm and we will abandon this hell.' His eyes lighted upon the viscount's dress and he added, 'Much as I applaud your eagerness to inform me of your safe return to these shores, it was not at all necessary for you to come to see me directly you arrived in Town. A few moments spent at your rooms to change your travelling clothes would have been quite understandable – may I say, *desirable*.'

Davenham grinned.

'I *have* taken the time to change, sir, before presenting myself to you. As for my coat – I have already been informed that it is too plain.'

Taking his son's arm, the earl sighed audibly as they sauntered out of the salon.

'It is my misfortune to have fathered a child with no sense of fashion.'

'Much you care for that!'

Lord Hartworth looked pained.

'But I *do* care for it, my dear boy! I am relieved, I admit, that you do not favour the *excesses* of the mode, I even take pride in the fact that your coats require no additional padding at the shoulders, and your excellent leg is much admired—'

'Two gifts of heredity sir?' queried the viscount drily.

'Undoubtedly.' It was a warm night, the chill of autumn had not yet descended upon the town and the earl waved away the offer of a cab and set off with his son to walk the short distance to Hartworth House. 'Have you spoken with your mother?'

Lord Davenham shook his head.

'She, too, was out when I called, dining with friends I believe, but I was informed that you were both expected to be at home for supper, so I left word that I would join you.'

'The countess will be delighted.'

The younger man glanced sharply at his father.

'And you will not, sir?'

'Of course, my dear boy. I am always happy to see you. In fact, I would like to hear a little more of your sojourn in Paris, although not at the supper-table. You do not appear to have had any marked success there.'

Davenham's countenance was grave.

'I had great hopes that Julian Poyntz would help us. Indeed, I believe he was ready to do so!'

'Then it was unfortunate that he died before he could be of use. The word in Town is that he expired in the arms of his lover.' He paused, observing his son with interest as the young man kicked a stone from the flag-way with an unwarranted amount of force. 'Of course, one cannot always believe such tales—'

'There is no reason to doubt this one!' retorted Davenham. 'The only incredible point is that any woman could bear to have such a barrel of a man near her!'

A smile touched the earl's lips as he glanced at his son's tall, slim frame. He asked, 'Were you in the vicinity when Poyntz died?'

'It occurred on my doorstep, you might say. Charles Charrière held a masked ball, and one of my fellow houseguests went up to his room to find Poyntz stretched out upon the floor. It was assumed he was involved in some amorous intrigue, and upon his collapse the lady was thrown into a panic and fled the scene.'

'And do you share that view of the situation, Jonathan?'

'It seems the most probable explanation. There was one odd thing – Poyntz had blood upon his neckcloth and when I looked closer, I found two small cuts upon his throat. Nothing but scratches, in truth.'

'But there is the possibility that someone killed Poyntz to prevent him talking to you.'

'It cannot be discounted, yet . . . '

'Who knows what kind of amusements our friend was enjoying with his lady before the excitement became too much for him?' murmured Lord Hartworth, finishing the line of thought for him.

'Aye, damn him!'

The earl once more turned his head to study his son's grim countenance, but he chose not to pursue the matter. They walked on in silence until the viscount was ready to speak.

'I suppose Thurleigh is still in favour at court?'

'Even more than that. He is now a regular visitor at Leicester House. He has the princess's favour and the trust of her son, and at the same time the King will hear nothing against him. He sees him as some sort of mediator – believes he is trying to bring about a closer understanding between the monarch and his heir. Pelham is furious, for he sees his own position as first minister in jeopardy if Thurleigh continues to gain influence in both courts.'

'Do you believe he is trying to reconcile the Princess of Wales with the King?' asked the viscount.

The earl did not answer immediately.

'I have studied Guy Morellon for a long time,' he said at last, 'and I have no doubt that he is up to some mischief. It's my belief that he still hopes to bring down the House of Hanover. Doubtless, rather than reconciling the King and his daughter-in-law, he is nurturing her feelings of ill-usage, in order to assist his own plans. You will recall that at the beginning of this year the Privy Council met to investigate allegations that the young prince's sub-governor, Andrew Stone, was a Jacobite. It was nothing more than a malicious scandal spread about to discredit the man – perhaps there would have been some truth in it if the finger had pointed at my Lord Thurleigh. In any event, the Princess of Wales does not trust Stone, or for that matter the boy's governor, Waldegrave, and I understand that she has more than once requested that Thurleigh be given the post.'

'He is treading a very delicate line,' mused Davenham, frowning. 'Can it be that he has abandoned hopes of a Stuart revival, and is securing his position with the young prince?'

Lord Hartworth shrugged.

'It is undoubtedly true that he gains favour with the boy through his mother: the prince is very young and impressionable, certainly. However, that does not tell us why Thurleigh sent Poyntz to see the Stuart in Rome.'

Davenham shook his head.

'There's some deep game afoot, I've no doubt of it, sir, but I would be happier had I spoken at length to Poyntz.'

'Since that is no longer possible, what will be your next move?'

The viscount laughed harshly.

'At the present time to forget all about this damned affair!' Realizing the earl was regarding him with raised brows, he continued, 'Your pardon, sir, but gathering evidence to accuse a man of treason is not a task I enjoy! I agreed to talk to Poyntz for you, since I chanced to be going to Paris at a time when you knew him to be there, but I was not aware that you required me to carry on with the investigations!'

'My dear boy, you can hardly leave the matter as it stands. There is sufficient evidence against Thurleigh to make one suspicious, you will agree, but nothing yet that would convict him of treason – and I want him brought to justice!'

Davenham glanced curiously at his father.

'I wish you would tell me why it is that you have such an aversion to the marquis.'

'My own devotion to the King, naturally.'

'Pray do not try to fob me off, sir!' retorted Davenham. 'At some point in the dark and distant past Thurleigh has crossed you. What was it, a woman?'

The earl looked pained. He said quietly, 'I wish you would get it out of your head that every quarrel arises from an *affaire de coeur*! No, this is a much simpler matter. Murder.'

'Pray continue, sir.'

'There is little to tell. Some years ago it came to my notice that a gentleman of my acquaintance had been killed in a duel with Lord Thurleigh.'

'That is not murder, sir.'

'I am aware of that, my son. Under normal circumstances, I would have mourned my friend's passing, and left the matter there, but circumstances were very far from normal. My friend was a peaceful man, a scholar, in fact, with little interest and even less skill in the art of *duello*. The fact that he could be persuaded to fight at all argues great provocation, and when I learned the identity of his opponent and that the duel was conducted in the taproom of a country inn, my suspicions were aroused. I made enquiries, but had little success. Thurleigh's associates could not be brought to speak of the matter, and when I travelled to the inn where the event took place I found that the landlord had already quit the area, and since the marquis is Lord-Lieutenant of that particular county, I could find no one willing to talk to me.'

'I agree, sir, it sounds most suspicious. Have you no idea why Thurleigh should wish to murder the fellow?'

'No, none. As I have told you, the man was a scholar. He had no interest in affairs of state, or struggles for power. Indeed, the last I heard of him before he was killed, he was living quite retired.'

'Had he no family?'

'Yes. A wife and one child, a daughter. My enquiries concerning their welfare met with no success. The cottage that was their home is now a ruin; apparently it was burned down soon after the death of my friend, and his family have vanished.'

'Done to death by the villain of this tale, I shouldn't wonder.'

'Or fled for their lives.'

'I never did like Thurleigh,' remarked the viscount, 'but I

always considered him eccentric rather than dangerous.'

'You should not underestimate the man,' the earl told him. 'He is very clever: there is nothing to connect him with any plot against the monarchy, yet I *know* he was responsible for at least two – for example, were you aware that Charles Stuart was smuggled into England a few years ago, to be received into the Anglican Church? And doubtless, Thurleigh has had a hand in other plots, too.'

'But if you have had so little success in catching him, why do you suppose that I will do better?'

'Because, my son, time is running out for the Stuart cause. James is growing old, his son Henry is now a cardinal in the Church of Rome and Charles is drinking himself into his grave. Thurleigh must know that if his plans are to succeed, an attempt will need to be made soon. Thus he sent Poyntz to Rome. What he will not have foreseen, I trust, is that his followers are not so eager for the game. You said yourself that Poyntz was ready to give it all up. If Thurleigh cannot rely on his minions, he will be forced to show his hand.' Lord Hartworth gave a slight cough. 'Much as I would like to deal with Thurleigh, my advanced years make me too slow for such work.'

'And you would like me to complete the task?'

'I would like him brought to trial.'

'Then I think I had best seek out George Rowsell,' said the viscount, pensively. 'He was always a good friend to Poyntz. If there was another plot afoot, you may be sure Rowsell will know of it. I must persuade him to tell me.'

Lord Hartworth smiled faintly. 'You make it sound a very simple task, Jonathan.'

'You may be sure it will not be that, sir!'

'But you will succeed, my son, I have no doubt of it,' purred the earl as they reached the steps of Hartworth House. 'You have all the tenacity of a terrier.'

Davenham grinned. 'Another hereditary trait, sir?'

My lord cast a reproachful look at his son. 'Useful as a terrier may be, my dear boy, it is scarcely a *noble* beast.'

'Then I am indeed a sad disappointment to my family,' remarked the viscount as he followed his parent into the house.

'Pray do not let it concern you,' replied the earl kindly. 'You have barely reached your thirtieth year. There is time yet for change.'

CHAPTER SEVEN

A lady weaves her plans

The huge rotunda at Ranelagh was crowded when George Rowsell arrived. A heavy shower of rain had forced the revellers to abandon the pleasure gardens with the Venetian canal and the pagoda, and take shelter indoors. Mr Rowsell advanced into the throng, his sandy brows drawn together, for he was unable at first to spot any acquaintance; then a group of gentlemen descended upon him, hailing him with good-natured raillery.

'Never expected to see you here, Rowsell,' called a young gentleman in a peacock-blue coat, 'I didn't think this sort of thing was your line. Bad night tonight, too,' he continued, shaking his head. 'No masquerade, and with Vauxhall now closed for the winter, there's a deal too many people here.'

'We're for going back to town,' put in another gentleman. 'Come with us, Rowsell?'

'No, I thank you. I am come to meet someone.'

'Not another beauty, sir! 'Fore gad, you change your women as I change my coat, I swear it!'

'Have you not heard?' laughed another. 'This one is different. Rowsell thinks himself in love with this lady. Ain't that so, sir?'

'Careful, man,' someone warned him. 'Rowsell has been known to call a fellow out for such remarks.'

But Rowsell was not attending to their banter. He had spotted a familiar face a short distance away and with the briefest of farewells he left the gentlemen to their own devices and fought his way through the crowd until he came up with his quarry.

'Madame de Sange – your servant!' He pressed her hand to his lips.

'Mr Rowsell.' She smiled warmly at him. 'You are acquainted with Lord and Lady Hare? They were kind enough to befriend me when they learned I was a stranger to London.'

'What? Oh – yes, of course.' He sketched a bow to the lady and gentleman but his eyes returned immediately to Madame de Sange. 'Your servant, my lady – Lord Hare. Madame, may I offer you my arm?'

Elinor hesitated, glancing uncertainly at Lady Hare, who nodded at her.

'Go along, child, there is no reason why you should not give Mr Rowsell the pleasure of your company.'

With a smile, Elinor put her fingers lightly upon Mr Rowsell's sleeve and allowed him to lead her away through the crowd. The gentleman immediately began to speak.

'When we last met in Town – was it only three days ago? It seems like a lifetime! You were putting up at an hotel, but they told me today you have moved out. Are you now staying with Lady Hare?'

'No, Mr Rowsell, I have hired a villa at Knight's Bridge.'

'Surely you will not live there alone!'

'No, sir, I have a companion with me.' She gave a soft laugh. 'You look disapproving sir. I am used to running my own establishment, you know.'

'Of course. Forgive me, Madame. I did not mean to censure you. I am merely concerned for you – but there, I have no right—' He broke off, then confided, 'I was anxious that you might not come here tonight, and when I saw the crowds, I felt sure I should never find you.'

'When we last met, I gave you my assurance that I would look out for you, sir.'

'After we had danced but twice together!' he cried, 'Why, 'tis the sort of polite reply anyone might make. How could I be sure you were in earnest?'

'So you doubt my word,' she murmured.

Rowsell stopped and pulled her round to face him.

71

'How could I believe you would favour me, when every man in the room was vying for your attention?'

'Not every man, sir,' Elinor teased him, but her smile was not unkind and he relaxed visibly.

'I believe the rain has ceased,' he observed. 'Would you care to stroll through the gardens, ma'am? If we keep to the gravel paths, I think we may find it is not too wet underfoot.'

'Yes, I should like that, sir, I thank you.'

The gentleman smiled happily and proceeded to spend a very agreeable hour escorting Elinor about the gardens. At eleven o'clock he escorted her back to the rotunda, to join Lord and Lady Hare who were waiting patiently for them. He took his leave and strode off, flushing slightly under the knowing smile of Lady Hare, who lost no time in congratulating Elinor upon her conquest.

'If ever I saw a young man head over heels in love it is Mr Rowsell!' she exclaimed. 'You have bewitched him, child.'

Elinor smiled, but brushed aside my lady's teasing, preferring to sit quietly in her corner of the coach as they sped back to town. She too was well pleased with the evening.

Two days later, George Rowsell found himself riding out of London to the small village of Knight's Bridge. Madame de Sange's villa was set well away from the main highway, and lay at the end of a long, leafy lane. Upon his arrival, Mr Rowsell was informed that Madame was busy out of doors. A servant directed him to the secluded rose-garden. The plants were sheltered upon three sides by a high stone wall and the ground sloped away to the south, giving a view of the open pasture and parkland beyond the villa's grounds. He spotted the lady immediately. She was turned slightly away from him, engaged in collecting the few late roses that remained unblemished upon the bushes. Rowsell stopped, admiring the picture and after a few moments the lady looked up, as if aware of his gaze.

'Mr Rowsell!' She smiled at him. 'Do you like roses, sir? There are some particularly fine specimens in this garden, although it has been allowed to run wild for some time, I believe. I have set the gardener to work clearing the weeds but perhaps I should take on another man; the grounds are far too much work for one. In any event, I fear we shall not see this garden at its best until next summer.'

'It can only be at its best when you are in it, Madame.'

'How gallant of you to say so. Who knows where I shall be this time next year? Shall I pick a rose for your coat?' She snipped off a beautiful yellow bloom, but after a glance at the gentleman's face she placed it gently in her basket with the others, saying, 'No, that will not do. I suspect from those sandy brows of yours that your hair is a very fiery colour. Do you always powder it so white, sir?'

'Aye. 'Tis the fashion. But you are right about its true colour, it accounts for much of my hot temper.'

She moved to the next bush and snipped another rose, then she put down her basket and scissors while she placed the flower carefully in his buttonhole.

'Then a white rose might cool you, Mr Rowsell.'

'Not when you stand before me, my dear,' he murmured huskily, 'for you rekindle the flame!'

Leaning forward, he planted a gentle kiss upon the lady's lips. Elinor froze, and taking her inactivity for compliance, Rowsell folded her in his arms, covering her face and neck with kisses. At last she came to life, fighting to hold him off.

'No, sir, I beg of you. You go too fast for me!'

'How can you say that, when you know you do not want me to stop?' He tried once again to take her in his arms, but she broke away.

'No, Mr Rowsell, this will not do! Besides, you will crush your poor rose – does it mean so little to you?'

'Of course not, ma'am, it means the earth to me!' He fell to his knees before her, his arms imprisoning her as he buried his face in the folds of her yellow skirts. 'Only tell me when I may claim the greatest gift from you, dear lady – when will you give yourself to me?'

A look of revulsion crossed Elinor's face as she looked down upon the powdered head that pressed against her, but she forced herself to keep still.

'Soon, sir, soon, I promise you,' she murmured, schooling her voice into gentle tones. Her eyes strayed to a straggling pink rose that she had so far overlooked: growing up amongst its glossy foliage was a dark-leaved intruder, whose purple bell-shaped flowers had mostly disappeared, giving way to plump, shiny black berries. An arrested look came into her eyes and she scarcely heard Rowsell's words as he rose to his feet.

'I shall hold you to your promise, ma'am, for I fear I cannot survive many more days without you!'

The lady gave him a faint smile.

'You may be assured, sir,' she told him as she stooped to pick up her basket, that I shall soon release you from your misery.'

Templesham House was overflowing with guests when Lord Davenham arrived. He knew then that he would not enjoy the evening, but he had not come for pleasure. Having decided that George Rowsell could be of use to him, the viscount was seeking out the gentleman. Rowsell was known to be a man of fashionable habits: he loved women, gambling and fighting. At Lady Templesham's rout, a gentleman could almost certainly indulge in at least two of these passions. The viscount greeted his hostess, who was more than a little surprised to find the notoriously unsociable Lord Davenham at her party. He then moved on, avoiding the main chamber and making a leisurely tour of the smaller chambers where Lady Templesham had ordered card-tables to be set up. He was disappointed and a little surprised to find Rowsell in none of these salons and he returned to one which held a number of gentlemen whom he knew to be friends of his quarry. A noisy game of silver loo was in progress, with both the gentlemen and ladies in high spirits. Davenham did not enquire after Rowsell, but entered into conversation with one of his acquaintance, hoping that one of the crowd would mention the gentleman. His patience was soon rewarded when a chance remark from one of the ladies brought a raucous laugh from her escort.

'You may wave goodbye to your hopes in that direction, my dear, for Rowsell is almost a married man now!'

'What's this, Blythe?' cried another gentleman. 'Rowsell about to tie the knot? I cannot credit it! I know he's constantly

hankering for a wife, but until now she's always been someone else's!'

'Aye, well, he's serious this time,' laughed Mr Blythe. 'The
fellow's infatuated. He can scarce think of anything but his
lady. I tell you he will wed her ere the year is out! Never seen
such a change in a fellow.'

'And shall we see the happy couple here tonight?' drawled
a large, bearded gentleman seated at one end of the table.

'He's dancing with her now, I believe,' remarked another
player, 'and if George Rowsell forsakes the table for the dance-
floor, it *must* be serious!'

'Then fetch them in at the end of the dance. I have a fancy
to see Rowsell's little love-bird.'

'Oh she's a diamond of the first water, Boreland, I assure
you!' cried Blythe. 'French, I think. The only wonder is that
she sees anything at all in George Rowsell!'

There was general laughter around the table, and an air of
excitement as a lady standing by the door announced that Mr
Rowsell and his partner were approaching. The couple
entered the room to a confusing medley of greetings. The lady
appeared a little shy in the face of such blatant curiosity, and
she hung back slightly behind her escort, but with a smile of
encouragement Rowsell led her forward into the room, where
the candlelight gleamed upon the green and gold of her robe
à la française. There was a murmur of appreciation from the
gentlemen present as they gazed upon the lady. She was as
tall as her escort, her glowing chestnut hair unpowdered and
arranged in thick curls about her head, with one glossy
ringlet falling across a white shoulder. Emeralds gleamed at
her throat and wrist, matching the green sparkle of her eyes.
Rowsell laughed in delight at their admiration.

'No, no gentlemen! Carry on with your game. This is not the
time for formal introductions, Madame would never remember you all, would you, my dear?'

Elinor lowered her eyes and murmured a reply: she had
recognized James Boreland at the table and was only too
pleased to avoid closer acquaintance, at least for the moment.

Lord Davenham stepped forward with the smallest of bows.
'Madame de Sange and I have met before, in Paris.'

'Paris?' remarked Mr Rowsell, helping himself to a glass of wine from a convenient tray. 'You've been there recently, Davenham?'

The viscount inclined his head. 'I have not been back in London above a sennight.'

'Then 'tis most likely you saw poor Julian there.'

'Yes, I did. I talked to him shortly before his death.' Lord Davenham turned to Elinor. 'I believe you were acquainted with Julian Poyntz, Madame de Sange?'

'I? No – that is – I believe we were introduced at some time . . .'

'Did I not hear you were there when he died, Davenham?' enquired Boreland, overhearing their conversation.

'I was one of the first upon the scene, yes.'

'There was a woman involved, was there not?'

'I believe there was,' said Davenham, 'but I cannot applaud the lady's choice.'

For a brief moment Elinor thought she might faint. The viscount's eyes seemed to accuse her, although common sense told her he could not possibly know of her involvement with Poyntz. She steadied her nerves and forced herself to parry his uncomfortable gaze with a haughty stare. The conversation continued to flow around them, but she heard none of it until Mr Rowsell asked her if she would care to join in the next game of loo. Elinor shook her head.

'I have little sense for card games,' she smiled. 'I am afraid I should disappoint you. However, I have no objection to watching, sir, while you are at play.'

Lord Davenham stepped forward. 'Perhaps, Madame, you would permit me to lead you back to the ballroom.' He observed Rowsell's sudden frown and added smoothly, 'There is little likelihood that Rowsell will be finished here for a least an hour. It would be very dull work for you to stay and watch for such a time.'

Rowsell nodded. 'It's a good notion, Davenham. Yes, you go on and enjoy yourself, my dear. I know how you love to dance.'

'Really, I would as lief stay and watch you—' put in Elinor, but Rowsell grasped her fingers and held them to his lips.

'Bless you, you are an angel! But Davenham is right, you

will find me tedious company when I am at play. Off you go now, but one dance and no more – I shall expect you at my side after that!'

The viscount offered his arm and, realizing that argument would only draw unwanted attention, Elinor placed her fingers upon the velvet sleeve and walked with him out of the small salon.

'I seem to recall, ma'am, that when we last spoke you told me you never came to London.'

'At that time, my lord, I had no desire to do so.'

'May I enquire what has changed your mind?'

The blunt question caught Elinor off her guard.

'I cannot think that my motives concern you, sir,' she retorted at last, and was surprised to observe the tightening of his jaw, as if he was curbing his temper.

'No, thank God, they do not!' he replied harshly. He led her into the ballroom where they took their places in the set and executed the steps of the minuet without a word. If the viscount derived any pleasure from the dance, Elinor saw no sign of it, for his face remained stern and forbidding throughout. She was at first puzzled by his behaviour, but by the time the dance had ended, her perplexity had turned to anger and she felt herself compelled to speak as he led her off the floor.

'I wish you will tell me, sir, why you asked me to dance, when it is very clear to me that you did not enjoy one moment of it!'

'Alas, Madame, I scarcely know that myself.'

She gave a scornful laugh. 'Pray, sir, do not be afraid of wounding my sensibilities! After a half-hour spent dancing in silence I feel sufficiently insulted that I daresay I shall scarce notice any further abuse you may care to level at me!'

The viscount's countenance grew darker still and his mouth tightened to a thin line.

'Very well, Madame!'

He took her elbow in a vice-like grip and guided her out of the ballroom to one of the empty smaller salons. He almost thrust her inside, closing the door after them with a snap. Elinor turned to face him: she was considered a tall woman, but even with the added height of the Pompadour heels on her green silk shoes she was forced to look up at his face, and she was aware of a tiny tremor of unease as she regarded his thunderous countenance. He turned away from her, and when at last he spoke his tone was harsh.

'You accuse me of insulting you, Madame de Sange – if you want to know the truth, I am disappointed! It is perhaps my own fault. In Paris you were pointed out to me as the saintly Lady of Stone. I was intrigued, I admit it, and when we talked—' He threw out his hands in a hopeless gesture. 'I was attracted to you, by your manner and your readiness to laugh at the ridiculous.' He turned to face her, and Elinor saw that the anger had died from his face. 'Doubtless you will laugh at *me*, Madame, when I tell you that even after that one brief meeting I felt that in you I had met a friend, that I had found a kindred spirit. Hah! Is that not absurd?' Elinor felt not the smallest desire to laugh, but neither could she trust herself to answer him steadily and he continued bitterly, 'I know now that my impression upon such a short acquaintance was totally misguided. How Paris was fooled into believing you to be virtuous beyond reproach is a mystery to me, Madame, for I am forced to the conclusion that you have less honesty than a common harlot!'

She stared at him.

'How dare you say that!' she whispered, pale and trembling with rage. She raised her hand to hit him, but immediately she found her wrist caught in a grip of steel.

'I shall not give you that satisfaction, Madame de Sange.'

His sneering tone brought the colour flooding back to her cheeks. Her eyes blazed, but she fought to control her anger.

'You can have nothing more to say to me,' she told him in an icy tone. 'I would thank you now to let me go!'

He released her and Elinor turned towards the door, but as she placed her fingers on the handle he stopped her with another question.

'Does Rowsell know that you and Poyntz were lovers?'

She threw him a contemptuous glance. 'Why don't you ask him? Knowing his quick temper, I should think he is likely to kill you for your impudence – in fact I very much hope he does!'

She swept out of the salon and on to the card-room where she found Rowsell counting up his winnings during a break in the play.

'My dear, did you enjoy your dance—' He broke off as he caught sigh of her stormy countenance. 'What is it, Elinor, What has occurred to upset you?'

'It is nothing sir, I assure you. Pray continue with your game.' She did her best to sound calm, but even to her own ears her voice was strained. Rowsell pushed back his chair and stood up.

'You are distressed!' he challenged her, concern writ large upon his face. 'Where is Davenham? If he has done aught to—'

'No, no, 'tis nothing serious, I promise you,' she hastened to reassure him. 'It – it has nothing to do with Lord Davenham. I have a slight headache this evening, and it has spoiled my enjoyment. This thundery weather, I fear,' she ended lamely.

'Then let me call your carriage – I will escort you home at once!' He scooped up his guineas from the table and guided Elinor downstairs. As they waited in the grand hall for her carriage, a flurry of activity announced a late arrival. A young gentleman entered with a lady whom Elinor guessed to be at least twice his age. His lover-like demeanour dispelled any thoughts that he might be escorting his parent to the Templeshams' rout, and Elinor turned her attention back to the lady. She had an uneasy feeling that she had seen her before, and her suspicion was strengthened when the woman glanced across, hesitated, then turned from the stairs to approach Elinor. Despite the powdered hair and heavily rouged cheeks, the woman still held some remnants of beauty, with her finely boned features and sea-green eyes that sparkled beneath heavily darkened brows. A sumptuous silk gown in the latest fashion and a jewel-encrusted aigrette set amongst the powdered curls suggested a woman of some consequence. Elinor looked a question at Rowsell, who muttered an oath under his breath before bowing to the lady as she came up to them.

'Lady Thurleigh, your servant, ma'am! May I present to you Madame de Sange?'

Elinor felt a shock of surprise, but she concealed this behind a smile and gave a small curtsy. The marchioness acknowledged Rowsell with a slight nod, but her green eyes remained fixed upon Elinor's face.

'Madame de Sange . . . you are a Frenchwoman, perhaps?'

'My husband was French, Lady Thurleigh.'

'I do not think I have seen you in London before.'

'This is my first visit, ma'am.'

Lady Thurleigh stared at her. 'But you are English?'

'My family moved to France when I was but a child.'

Lady Thurleigh looked as if she would say more, but at that moment a servant announced that Madame de Sange's carriage was at the door and the marchioness turned away and carried on up the stairs with her escort.

'Pray, Madame, do not concern yourself over Lady Thurleigh,' remarked Rowsell, leading her out to the carriage. Her manners are a little odd, to be sure, but in the wife of so powerful a man as the marquis such things are overlooked.'

'Oh. And – and is Lord Thurleigh in Town?'

'I don't think he can be, or his wife wouldn't have that young pup as her escort. It's common knowledge that my lady is very free with her favours, but she don't usually flaunt her paramours under her husband's nose!'

He handed Elinor into the coach. 'Will you not let me come with you? I do not like you to be alone!'

'I have Hannah – Mrs Grisson. She will attend to my needs.'

The door closed upon her but she leaned out of the window, holding out her hand for him to kiss.

'But 'tis a man's attentions you need, Madame,' he told her, retaining her fingers. 'You are no innocent young maiden, who has never known a man's caresses – your eyes tell me you want me – how much longer with you make me wait for you?'

She shook her head at him, casting a warning glance towards the coachman.

'Not now, sir. I cannot talk of such things here I . . .' She broke off, searching for words.

'You have promised to join my party for Drury Lane on Friday,' he said urgently. 'I will be denied no longer. My own carriage shall call for you. If you decline to come with me I shall have my answer and trouble you no further.' He kissed her fingers once more before releasing them, and gave the word to the coachman to move off.

'Until Friday, Madame!'

CHAPTER EIGHT

In which a gentleman's temper proves his undoing

Alone in the dark seclusion of her carriage, Elinor's thoughts raced through her head, but even at a decorous pace the journey to Knight's Bridge was not long enough for her to unravel the tangle of her emotions. When the carriage drew up at the villa, she alighted in silence, and spoke not a word until she had discarded her heavy ballgown in favour of a light wrap, and had allowed her new English maid to brush her hair, leaving it hanging in thick, shining waves down her back. Then, in a quiet voice, she dismissed her servant. When the girl had withdrawn, Elinor went to her dressing-table and drew out from one of its drawers a folded sheet of paper which she spread upon the table.

She stared at the untidy lettering: the list of names seemed to dance upon the paper in the wavering candlelight. There were but five names written there, and that of Julian Poyntz had a neat black line drawn through it. She glanced down the page, her eyes coming to rest upon the name of James Boreland. She had recognized the big, bearded figure immediately; it had been difficult to conceal her loathing of the man, and she found herself longing to be able to cross his name from the list, but her plans for George Rowsell were so near completion she dare not change course now. Lord Davenham's lean and angry face intruded into her thoughts, but she quickly pushed the image away. What did it matter if he thought ill of her? She drew herself up, squaring her shoulders as she carefully refolded the paper and replaced it in the drawer. She had set herself a task and nothing, no one, would divert her from her goal.

Elinor awoke late on Wednesday morning to the sound of heavy rain lashing against the windows. She was forced to abandon her plans for a solitary walk, and instead spent the day pleasantly enough with Hannah, attending to her household duties. However, when the weather showed no signs of improvement the following morning, Hannah noticed a change in her mistress's demeanour. Elinor was restless, unable to concentrate upon one task for any length of time and frequently going to the window to stare out at the sodden landscape.

'Oh will this rain never stop!'

'When the Lord wills it, Miss Nell,' replied her companion, not looking up from her mending. 'A little occupation would help you to bear with it. Why do you not take up your embroidery?'

Elinor gestured impatiently.

'I have not the humour for it today. I would prefer a more lively diversion.'

At that moment a servant entered to announce that a visitor had arrived and wished to speak with Madame.

'A visitor!' cried Elinor. 'Who would wish to drive here in this weather?'

'The lady would not give her name, ma'am,' replied the servant, 'but begged to be allowed a few words with you in private. I have shown her into the small parlour.'

'You were seeking some diversion from this dreary weather,' remarked Mistress Grisson, smiling faintly, 'so you had best see the lady. Do you wish me to come with you?'

'No, thank you, Hannah. I shall go alone.'

Elinor crossed the hall and quietly entered the small parlour. Upon recognizing her visitor, her brows rose slightly.

'Lady Thurleigh! Forgive me, I did not expect—'

'No, it is you who must forgive me.' My lady smiled, holding out her hand. 'It is very bad of me to descend upon you so suddenly.'

'No, no, not at all, ma'am. Won't you sit down?'

Lady Thurleigh chose a straight-backed chair by the window, giving Elinor the opportunity to study her visitor more closely. In the daylight Lady Thurleigh looked older than when Elinor had last seen her. Without its heavy coating of powder, her skin looked sallow and lined, but the green eyes still sparkled luminously, and the copper curls piled artlessly around her cap of finest Brussels lace may have faded over the years, but they were only faintly streaked with grey.

'You will be wondering why I am calling upon you,' she began, her fingers nervously playing with the sticks of her fan. 'You see, Madame, when I saw you the other night, I was struck by your resemblance to – to an old acquaintance of mine.' She smiled at Elinor. 'You will think me very impertinent, but I would be honoured if you would tell me just a little of your history.'

Elinor stared at her in surprise.

'My parents lived very quietly, ma'am, and I cannot think that you could have known them.' Her response was stiff and uneasy, and my lady threw up her hands.

'Oh I have offended you! I beg your pardon. Pray, Madame de Sange, I realize it may seem very odd to you, yet if you would but tell me your father's name, and in which part of England you were living before you moved to France. . . .'

Elinor eyed her guest warily.

'Forgive me, Lady Thurleigh, but does the marquis know of your visit here?'

Lady Thurleigh looked startled.

'My husband? He is not in Town, and does not even know I have seen you. Why do you ask?'

'Oh, it does not signify. You asked my father's name, did you not? It was Burchard.'

'Was?'

'Both my parents are dead.'

'I am sorry. Burchard.' She murmured the name slowly, as if committing it to memory. 'And where were you living?'

Elinor told her of the small village in Bedfordshire. Lady Thurleigh said quickly, 'But you were not born there?'

'No, ma'am. I was born in Oxford.'

An expression that was hard to read flitted across the older woman's face and she stared hard at her hostess.

'And did you have a happy childhood. Madame?' she whispered.

'Until the death of my father I was extremely happy,' replied Elinor coldly, 'but I do not see—'

'No, no, you must think me impolite to question you so!' The marchioness sat very still, tapping her foot, and just as Elinor was wondering what to say next she rose quickly, holding out to Elinor a hand that was not quite steady. 'I am sorry, Madame de Sange, to have troubled you. I must go! Pray do not think too hardly of me!'

After the briefest touch of fingers Lady Thurleigh hurried from the house, leaving Elinor in speechless amazement.

Came Friday evening, and Mr Garrick's theatre in Drury Lane was overflowing with people from all levels of society. George Rowsell's party arrived only minutes before the performance was due to commence. There could be no doubting that gentleman's happiness as he escorted Elinor to the box he had secured for the evening. The lady had done justice to the occasion with a new gown of green watered silk, laced with silver and falling open to reveal a white quilted petticoat delicately embroidered with silver thread. Her powdered curls cascaded about her bare shoulders, and she wore no jewels save for one brooch, a single large ruby that was pinned to the lace of her bodice. There was little time for Elinor to become acquainted with the couple that Rowsell had invited to share the box: the brief introduction made it plain that the young matron, one Mrs Shaw, was not escorted by her husband, although the gentleman's attentions soon gave Elinor a firm indication of their relationship. This was confirmed when Rowsell leaned closer to whisper in her ear that their companions had a dinner engagement, and would be leaving them after the play.

'So it will be just a quiet little dinner for you and me, my sweet,' he murmured, 'and afterwards—' He broke off, taking advantage of some lively entertainment on-stage to place a kiss upon the white skin of her shoulder, while one arm slid around her waist, his fingers moving up until they reached the softness of her breast beneath its covering of lace. Elinor felt a sudden panic, but she forced herself to remain still, not to repulse him. Keeping her eyes fixed upon the actors, she reached up one hand to touch Rowsell's cheek: for her purposes, dinner alone with George Rowsell would be an ideal situation.

At the interval, Mrs Shaw slipped away with her paramour to take a stroll in the lobby. As soon as they were alone, Rowsell turned to Elinor, taking her hands in his own strong grasp.

'Madame – Elinor! I thought this day would never arrive, and when it dawned, I was even then afraid you would not come!'

She said nothing, but allowed him to press kisses on to each of her gloved fingers, while a faint blush touched her cheeks, for she was very conscious of their situation. She was relieved when the door of their box opened and she looked around, expecting to find that Mrs Shaw and her escort had returned, instead of which she found herself staring up at the towering figure of James Boreland. The gentleman bowed, explaining that Rowsell had promised an introduction to Madame de Sange, and he wished to present his lady. Gripping her fan to conceal her trembling fingers, Elinor forced a smile to her lips. She repressed a shudder as Boreland took her fingers and bowed over them. With no little relief she turned to greet Mrs Boreland. She found herself facing a woman of medium height, strikingly dressed in a robe of turquoise silk with such a wide hoop beneath her skirts that she had difficulty in moving about the box. She wore a fixed smile and her cold blue eyes held a calculating look that made Elinor think her affability as doubtful as the jet-black curls that covered her head. After the introductions, Mrs Boreland took a seat beside Elinor and asked her a number of questions concerning her history.

'Is your son in Town with you, ma'am?' enquired Rowsell.

Temporarily silenced, Mrs Boreland glanced anxiously towards her husband.

'No, not this time,' Boreland said smoothly. 'Andrew's health

86

has been a little troublesome during the summer and we thought it best to leave him at the Hall.'

'And how are you enjoying the entertainment, Madame?' Mrs Boreland hardly waited for her husband to finish. 'I do think this theatre is so much better since dear Mr Garrick has had the running of it. We shall not stay to see the farce, however, for we are going on to Derry House.'

Boreland turned to his friend. 'Do you intend to go, Rowsell? Derry told me you were invited.'

Rowsell hesitated. 'No, I think not—'

'Oh, Madame de Sange, pray *do* say you will come!' Mrs Boreland laid one gloved hand upon Elinor's arm. 'It promises to be *quite* delightful and the Derrys are renowned for their delectable suppers!'

Elinor shook her head. 'No, I am sorry, we cannot—'

'Oh come now, Madame.' James Boreland stepped forward and it took all Elinor's strength of will not to shrink away from the man. 'Surely you will not deny my wife the pleasure of your company for a little longer this evening? It is obvious that Mrs Boreland has taken a liking to you and as she is returning to Weald Hall in a very few days, there will be so little time for you ladies to become acquainted!'

Elinor hesitated, glancing at Mr Rowsell, who gave the smallest of shrugs, saying, 'Perhaps, ma'am, we could look in for an hour.'

Mrs Boreland clapped her hands together. 'That would be *most* enjoyable!' she cried, with what Elinor considered to be an unwarranted show of delight. 'If you would but have supper with us there, Madame, I should be most grateful, for I have so few real friends in Town these days that I confess I quite *dread* attending these parties! But look, Mr Boreland, we must get back to our seats, for the players are coming on to the stage even now.'

They rose to take their leave and Boreland stepped closer to bow over Elinor's hand. His eyes rested briefly upon the ruby brooch. Elinor held her breath.

'I look forward to seeing you at Derry House, Madame. Until then, *au revoir!*'

There was a general confusion as the Borelands left the box

and Mrs Shaw and her partner resumed their places. Rowsell, observing his lady's troubled countenance, took advantage of the noise to speak to her.

'I am sorry, my love. Boreland was quite insistent that we go and he is not a man one can easily refuse! We need not remain above the hour, my sweet.'

She nodded, unable to trust herself to speak. She was resolved upon her course of action, and determined to carry it through, but this sudden change of plan had unnerved her. However, by the time they left the theatre she had regained her composure and had reconciled herself to having supper with the Borelands.

Rowsell's carriage took them on to Derry House, where they found Mr and Mrs Boreland already arrived and looking out for them.

'Why do you think they are so anxious for us to join them?' Elinor asked her escort as they alighted from the coach.

'It is most likely that they want company. They are not universally popular, you see, although *he* is so powerful no one dares to cut them direct. Nothing will persuade the ladies to show more than common politeness to his wife, though.'

'I can understand that,' murmured Elinor, fixing on a smile as they came up to the couple.

'My dear, *such* a shocking squeeze!' laughed Mrs Boreland as they moved through the crowded rooms. 'I vow there is scarce room to breathe in here and so noisy, too!'

'I had heard all of London was invited,' remarked her husband, glancing about him. 'It seems Derry has allowed the scaff and raff of the town to join us. Let us repair to the supper-room.'

Elinor took Rowsell's arm and together they made their way to a large room which had been set out for the occasion with a number of small tables. The gentlemen led their partners to an empty table, Rowsell taking a chair beside Elinor and calling for a bottle of claret and one of champagne to be brought for the ladies. A servant scurried away, to return moments later with the refreshments.

'You are in good spirits, Rowsell,' remarked Boreland, smiling faintly through his beard.

Rowsell held up his brimming glass to salute Elinor.

'Oh, I am, James. I am the happiest man in London tonight!'

Elinor could not meet his eyes and looked away, a faint blush stealing over her cheek.

'I am glad to hear it,' murmured Boreland. He looked at Elinor, then said slowly, 'Your pardon, Madame, if I appear to stare, but – have we not met before? Your countenance seems so familiar.'

She shook her head, setting her powdered curls dancing. 'No, sir. I have never before been to London. Could it be that you were ever in Paris? No? Then doubtless you are thinking of someone else.'

She held her breath for a few seconds as he continued to stare at her, then he shrugged and drained his glass.

'Perhaps. I do not doubt it will come to me presently. Rowsell, the Rausan is excellent – let us have another bottle!'

'I do so enjoy these evenings, Madame,' said Mrs Boreland with her cold, glittering smile. 'It is quite delightful to me to see so many people enjoying themselves, and to study how the ladies dress in Town these days. I vow I find it monstrous entertaining!'

There was no shortage of entertainment for Mrs Boreland during their meal, the room was already quite full and a constant stream of guests flowed through the apartment, some looking for an empty table, others merely promenading through the lesser rooms whenever the ballroom grew uncomfortably warm. Among those fortunate enough to find a table was a lady in a blue silk gown trimmed with blond lace, who took one look at the crowded supper-room and immediately bullied two mild-mannered young gentlemen into giving up their places. Her escort remonstrated with her as they sat down at the vacated table.

'Really, Mama, it is a great deal too bad of you to browbeat people in that way,' he told her, smiling.

'Nonsense, Davenham!' retorted Lady Hartworth, her blue eyes twinkling. 'You are a great deal too sensitive! Those young men were only too pleased to move for us.'

'Aye,' laughed the viscount, 'after you had informed them that, being well acquainted with their families, you had most likely bounced them both upon your knee when they were still in the nursery!'

'Well, and why should you complain of it? We have our seats do we not? And as soon as I have had a glass or two of good wine to restore my energies, we shall quit this place with all possible speed! Whatever possessed Lady Derry to send me an invitation I shall never know! Such an odd woman, to be sure. I swear there are any number of *low persons* here! And why your father should think it a good thing that we come is beyond my comprehension. I have never enjoyed myself less, I can tell you that, for if there is one thing I dislike it is being jostled and herded like so many milch cows!'

'I share your dislike of these affairs, ma'am,' agreed her son feelingly, 'and this one is worse than most, I'll admit. I shall be happy to escort you home as soon as you are ready.'

'I can see that!' snapped the countess. 'You have been as restless as a colt in a halter since we arrived here! But what of this man Hartworth wanted you to see, is he here? Oh don't look so surprised, Jonathan,' she continued, observing her son's raised brows, 'there's very little of your father's business I don't know, and I am well aware you accompanied me to this, this *May Fair* for more than just the pleasure of my company!'

'George Rowsell might be here tonight. Father thinks he could tell us something of Thurleigh's plans. I intended to speak with him at the Templeshams' the other night, but it did not prove possible. Now I am to try again.' He gave a sudden laugh. 'A fruitless task in this crowd, Mama! There's little chance of learning anything of note tonight. The sooner we leave the better!'

Across the room, Mrs Boreland was commenting to Elinor upon the excellence of the suppers, but although she nodded in agreement, Elinor tasted nothing of what was before her. She forced herself to eat a little to prevent her escort becoming concerned. The gentlemen were both in good spirits and it seemed to Elinor that she had scarce finished her second glass of champagne before they had started upon their third bottle of claret. Conversation was now flowing as freely as the wine, but Elinor took very little part in the pleasantries; while the others were laughing at some little joke, she slipped her hand through the folds of her gown and into the embroidered pocket beneath, where her fingers curled around a small glass phial. She drew it out, her heart pounding hard within her as she held the little container tightly in her hand below the table, waiting for a suitable moment to make her move.

Within seconds there came a diversion. A gentleman who was patently the worse for wine cannoned into a footman and they crashed to the ground, taking with them any number of dinner plates. The resulting confusion drew all eyes, including those of her companions, and Elinor took the opportunity to uncork the phial, then she leaned forward to reach across the table towards a dish of sugared fruits. As her hand passed over Rowsell's half-filled glass, she allowed the inky black liquid from the phial to fall into the wine, where it remained for one heart-stopping moment in a small cloud before dispersing into the claret. Scarcely daring to breathe, she carefully returned the phial to her pocket as Rowsell turned back to her, a fiery glow in his eyes.

'I vow, Elinor,' he muttered huskily, 'we must be going soon, if I am not to disappoint you tonight!'

'Oh, but I have not yet finished my champagne.' Elinor forced her dry lips into what she hoped was a persuasive smile. 'Also, my dear, your own glass is not yet empty.'

Rowsell laughed gaily. 'You have the right of it, my sweet!' he declared. 'We shall not leave until I have drunk one more toast!' He picked up his glass and held it aloft. 'Boreland, we must honour our delightful ladies! Fill your glass sir, and join me in drinking to the source of all our happiness!'

James Boreland looked amused. 'But of course, my dear fellow.'

Elinor sat very still, outwardly calm, while inside her raged a tumult of emotion. Rowsell had turned in his chair to face her, his eyes glowing with happiness, his glass held up in readiness while he waited for Boreland. The seconds ticked by, Elinor summoning every ounce of willpower to remain still. The noise of the supper-room seemed very distant, unreal: she watched in fascination as Boreland poured his wine, taking what seemed to Elinor an inordinate amount of care in pouring the claret and setting the decanter down gently upon the table while his wife chattered ceaselessly. At last he was ready and the two gentlemen faced their ladies. Rowsell smiled lovingly at Elinor.

'To you, my dear. To us!'

Elinor held her breath. She was surprisingly calm now. She watched while he raised the glass closer to his mouth, then suddenly she wanted to scream at him to stop, but it was too late, the words would not come and the glass was at his lips. Yet before he could taste one drop of the sweet, deadly wine, a group of revellers passed the table, one of them losing his balance and falling heavily against Rowsell. The glass flew from his hand and Elinor gave a small cry as the poisoned claret spilled over her petticoat. She watched in horror as the blood-red stain spread slowly across the white silk. With an oath Rowsell jumped to his feet, sending his chair crashing to the ground.

'You drunken oaf! I'll have an apology for the lady!'

The man swayed on his feet, supported by a companion in much the same condition. He shook his head at Rowsell's furious ranting.

'T'morrow, sir – I'll talk to you 'morrow—'

'No, by God, we shall settle this now!' cried Rowsell in a towering rage.

'My dear boy – give him your card,' advised Boreland. 'Can't start a brawl in Derry's supper-room!'

But Rowsell did not hear him; he flew at the offender, knocking him down with the first blow. For a few moments confusion reigned, ladies screamed and Lord Derry's servants looked helplessly at one another, not at all sure what was to be done. As the reveller picked himself up from the ground it seemed that some of his intoxication had left him. A crafty gleam came into his eyes as he looked at Rowsell standing over him, fists clenched. The man came slowly to his feet, keeping his head bowed, then with a lightning move he snatched up a carving-knife from a tray of ham on a nearby table. With a cry of warning, Boreland leapt to his feet and ran forward, but he was too late. Rowsell had closed with his opponent and even as Boreland and several of the footmen pulled the protagonists apart, Rowsell sank to his knees, the carving-knife having been driven to the hilt up under his ribs and into the very heart of him.

For a full minute there was silence, then several cries of Shame! Coward! As the killer was led away Rowsell was laid upon the floor, but there was no flicker of life from his inert form and Boreland called for a cloth with which to cover the bloodied body. Some of the ladies in the room were crying, but, looking up, Boreland observed that Madame de Sange was still sitting rigidly in her seat, her face immobile and those green eyes staring blankly at Rowsell's lifeless form. He switched his gaze to his wife.

'Take Madame de Sange away, Isobel. I will arrange matters here, and follow you when I can.'

Mrs Boreland rose and went to Elinor, keeping her eyes averted from the still form lying not six feet from their table. Silently she helped the widow to her feet and guided her gently out of the room. As they neared the door, a gentleman stood before them. Viscount Davenham bowed slightly, but Elinor's stunned gaze went through him, unseeing, and he stepped aside to let the ladies pass.

'Poor child,' murmured Lady Hartworth to her son. 'How very distressing for her to lose an admirer in such a way.'

'Really, ma'am?' he replied coldly. 'I begin to think she is making a habit of it.'

CHAPTER NINE

Madame de Sange receives comfort – and an invitation

The journey to Knight's Bridge seemed an endless one for Elinor. She sat in the carriage, staring fixedly before her, while Mrs Boreland remained at her side, patting her hands and making soothing noises. Not by nature a compassionate woman, she found it difficult to give succour to the young woman, who was obviously distraught by the death of George Rowsell. Had she but known it, the grieving widow was quite oblivious of her attentions, and was conscious only of a desire to reach the seclusion of her own room. At last they arrived at their destination. Madame's footman was on hand to hold open the door, and Mrs Boreland led her charge gently but firmly into the lighted hallway. Almost immediately Hannah Grisson appeared, looking drawn and anxious.

'God in heaven – what has happened!'

'Your mistress has sustained a shock.' Mrs Boreland led Elinor into the drawing-room and guided her towards a chair. 'There was a most distressing incident at Lord Derry's supper party. Poor Mr Rowsell is dead.'

'Lord have mercy on us!' gasped Hannah, sinking on to a sofa, her face as white as her kerchief.

'Yes,' affirmed Mrs Boreland. 'A group of monstrous low, rough fellows were in the supper-room – I cannot think what Lord Derry was about, to let such people into his house! There was a most unseemly fracas, and poor Mr Rowsell was fatally wounded, struck down by a carving-knife.'

'He – he was *stabbed*?'

Mrs Boreland looked impatient.

'Have I not said so? Come, woman, your mistress needs attention. Will you not fetch her a cordial, or a little brandy—'

For the first time since entering the house, Elinor spoke. 'No, please, that is not necessary.'

'But Madame, you are in distress. I would urge you to take something – perhaps a sleeping draught—'

'No, I thank you for your concern, ma'am, but I swear I am much better now. Hannah shall fetch me a cup of hot chocolate, but I need nothing stronger.'

Muttering anxiously under her breath, Mrs Grisson rose and went out of the room, leaving Mrs Boreland to hover solicitously around Elinor, who was still deathly pale, although the blank look had now left her eyes. After a short while she spoke again.

'I must thank you for accompanying me, ma'am. I am most grateful for your support. Shall I order my carriage to take you back to town, or would you like me to have a room prepared for you here?'

'No, no, my dear, there is no need for you to put yourself out at all.' Mrs Boreland's words were warm enough, but, as ever, her smile was fixed, never reaching her eyes. 'Mr Boreland said he would follow me here and take me up. But there is no need for you to sit up waiting for my husband to make an appearance. Here is your servant returned with the chocolate. Pray, Madame de Sange, will you not drink it and go to bed? A good night's rest will help to ease your distress.'

Elinor took the cup from Hannah with a word of thanks, but shook her head at her visitor.

'You are monstrous kind, ma'am, but I could not sleep. For a while, at least.'

'But of course, dear ma'am. I can understand that, after such a scene as we have just witnessed, you would wish to have company, lest your thoughts become too morbid and disturbing.' Mrs Boreland nodded sympathetically. 'It is unfortunate that you live so secluded. There is nothing like a little company to relieve the spirits.' She paused, considering

her words. 'Forgive me, Madame. I hesitate to speak, and yet
– pray do not be offended! Our acquaintance has been brief, I
know, but even so I should be pleased to be of assistance to
you, if you will allow it. Perhaps, ma'am, you would care to
return with me to Weald Hall? I must go back there shortly,
but I do not care to leave you in this house – you should not
be alone at this time! And do not think I wish to throw you
into a round of social engagements. Mr Boreland and I entertain very rarely, but even so I venture to think you will not
find us *too* dull.'

'I do not think Madame de Sange could consider such an
idea at present—' began Hannah, but Elinor silenced her with
a wave of her hand.

'Thank you, ma'am. Perhaps when I have had a little time
to reflect. . . .'

'Of course,' returned Mrs Boreland. 'I do not mean to press
you. Mayhap you would prefer to travel to Weald in a week or
so – but you need not answer now; I shall come to see how you
go on in a day or two, and we will discuss the matter more
fully.' She raised her head as there came from outside the
sound of a vehicle approaching. 'That will be my husband. He
will be happy to see you have recovered a little, Madame.'

They heard a knocking upon the door, and moments later
James Boreland strode in. His big frame dominated the room
and, as Mrs Boreland stepped forward to greet her husband,
Hannah moved across to stand beside Elinor's chair, protec-
tively close to her mistress. Boreland bowed to the ladies, and
spoke first to Elinor, who was still sipping at her chocolate.

'Madame, my condolences to you. I know how close you
were to poor Rowsell.'

'Thank you sir.' Elinor's voice was scarcely above a whisper.

'How do matters stand, sir?' asked his wife. 'Did you see
Lord Derry before you left?'

'Aye. He's most upset about the whole business, naturally.
The young fellow who quarrelled with Rowsell has been
apprehended. He was drunk, of course, but that does not
excuse his actions.' He shook his head. 'Dashed pity about
Rowsell, though. I always said he should make efforts to curb
that temper of his—'

'Yes, well, never mind that now, sir. We must go back to Town, and leave Madame de Sange to rest. Unless, that is, Madame, you wish me to remain to keep you company?'

'You are very kind,' returned Elinor, summoning up a smile, 'but I have Hannah, and I shall be well now that I am home. My thanks to you both for your trouble.'

'No, no, do not get up,' said Mrs Boreland, pushing Elinor gently back into her seat. 'We will leave you now, but I shall call again in a few days. Now, come along, Mr Boreland, we must be on our way!'

So saying, the couple went out, leaving Elinor and her companion alone in the drawing-room. They sat in silence, listening to the sounds of departure, but neither woman moved until they heard the Borelands' coach moving away from the house, then Hannah threw herself at Elinor's feet in great distress.

'Oh Miss Nell, Miss Nell, what mischief are you about?'

Elinor put down her empty cup, her hands trembling a little.

'I am sure I don't know what you mean.'

Hannah took hold of those hands, giving them a little shake.

'Oh my dear child, will you deny that you wanted revenge upon the gentleman? After you had gone out, I went to your room to return the petticoat 'pon which I had mended a torn flounce, and what should I discover hidden in a corner of your cupboard but a pair of old kid gloves, darkened with juice, a stained muslin handkerchief and a small bag that had recently held berries. One or two even remained. Devil's cherries, Miss Nell: deadly nightshade. . . .' She broke off, wiping her eyes. 'You were so eager for the rain to cease, to go out into the garden alone – I made sure you had planned to poison Mr Rowsell, and I have been in dread here since, expecting any moment to hear that you had been clapped up for murder!'

Elinor gazed down at her companion, a strange look in her green eyes.

'But I poisoned no one, Hannah. I confess, that it was my intention to kill George Rowsell, for what he had done to me.'

'Oh, my poor, poor child!' wailed Hannah, burying her face in her apron.

'I discovered the nightshade growing amongst my roses. What could be easier than to collect the berries and put their juice into a little bottle that would fit into my pocket? I even managed to drop the poison into his drink.' Elinor paused, looking at the dark stain upon her petticoat. 'I did everything, Hannah, everything I had planned, to avenge myself upon George Rowsell, and it was all . . . unnecessary.' She began to giggle, then to laugh hysterically.

Hannah stared at her, aghast.

'Stop it, Miss Nell.' She took Elinor by the shoulders and shook her. 'You will do no one any good by this. Stop it, I say!'

To Hannah's relief, the wild laughter abated, to be replaced by a flood of tears. Hannah embraced her, crooning to her and gently stroking her hair, much as she had done when Elinor had been a child. At last Elinor grew calmer, and Hannah drew her gently to her feet, keeping one arm tight about the widow as she helped her up the stairs to her room.

A few days later Mrs Boreland paid a short visit to Knight's Bridge and came away feeling very well pleased with the results of her labours. She returned to the elegant apartment she and her husband had hired for their stay and entered it, wearing a satisfied look upon her rather hard features. She received a grim smile from her husband, who was writing at a small desk by the window.

'Well, madam,' he greeted her, 'what business have you been about, that you should resemble a cat that's taken the cream?'

'I have been to visit Madame de Sange,' she replied, stripping off her kid gloves. 'And I have secured from her the promise that she will come and stay with us over Christmas.'

'The devil you have!'

Mrs Boreland's hard eyes snapped.

'You knew it was my intention to invite the widow to Weald Hall – do you now object to the arrangement?'

'Not to your arrangement, my dear, but to your timing. I have to go to the Continent very soon, though I expect to be back before Christmas. However, I have plans afoot that require discretion and I'd as lief have no prying eyes at Weald during the winter.'

The lady shrugged. 'I would have taken her down with me when I leave Town, had she been agreeable, but the lady was not to be persuaded. Perhaps it is for the best, however, for I shall now have time to prepare Andrew. As to your own affairs, you need not trouble yourself about our guest. I will ensure that Madame is well entertained, with Andrew's assistance. After all, I want her to know just how pleasant it is to be mistress of Weald Hall.'

Boreland looked amused.

'You think you can make a match between our son and the lady?'

'That is my intention.'

'You were born an optimist, Isobel.'

'What is so outrageous in my plan? The poor child has suffered a severe loss with Rowsell's death. She has no family or friends here to support her, nor, as far as I can ascertain, has she anyone to advise her. The alternatives are for her to return to France, or to make a life for herself here. And what could be more natural than that she should be drawn towards those of us who knew George Rowsell and loved him as a brother?'

'A brother!' he repeated, laughing. 'I didn't think you ever cared much for the hot-headed fool!'

'We will not speak ill of the departed,' replied his wife, unperturbed. 'The widow needs a refuge and I intend that she shall find one at the Hall. If, at the same time, she can be persuaded to bestow her hand—'

'And her fortune!' he put in drily.

'To bestow her hand upon a member of the family that has taken her to its bosom, I shall of course be delighted.'

'I applaud your ambitions, Isobel. I daresay if you had been born a man you would have been a powerful force to reckon with.'

She gave him a thin smile.

'As it is, sir, I leave that rôle to you. I believe you have not been entirely unsuccessful in it.'

'Thank you. And if this latest trick can be brought off—' He paused, gazing thoughtfully into space, then he recollected himself and smiled across the room at his wife. 'I hope you succeed with your matchmaking. Andrew needs a wife and the girl would be a monstrous good catch. Her fortune is not tied up in any trust, I believe.'

'I have already ascertained that her money is under her own control. She is her own mistress.'

'And a devilish handsome one, too,' remarked Boreland. 'A widow with no ties or constraints upon her fortune – 'tis an ideal opportunity for Andrew. She looks somewhat familiar,' he added thoughtfully. 'I cannot quite place her. . . .'

'Possibly you knew her mother.'

Boreland's keen eyes rested upon his wife, challenging her to say more, but she remained silent. At length he shrugged, saying carelessly, 'I daresay I did.'

She watched him tidying the papers on his desk, then he moved towards the door, collecting his hat upon the way.

'You are going out?'

'Yes. I have business to attend to at the coffee-house. Pray do not enquire the nature of it.' He spoke quickly, forestalling her question. 'It is safer for you to know very little of what I do. Apply yourself to finding a wife for our son, and leave other matters to me.'

The golden shades of autumn were fading into winter and Elinor decided that until her visit to Weald Hall she would withdraw from society; in the fashionable salons and drawing rooms that she had visited so briefly, it was whispered that Madame de Sange was so overset with grief at the death of her lover that she had taken to her bed and was in decline. Hearing this, Viscount Davenham assured himself that it did not concern him. After all, he reasoned bitterly, if one could tell a man by the company he kept, the same must surely apply to a lady and her lovers. Yet as November wore on he found himself unable to banish the lady from his mind, and on a bright but chilly morning, he rode out to Knight's Bridge.

News of the visitor was brought to Madame as she sat at her dressing-table, where Hannah Grisson was putting the finishing touches to her hair. The servant's shrewd old eyes did not miss the delicate flush which mounted to Elinor's cheeks before that lady said coolly, 'I will not see him. Tell him I am not at home!'

Hannah met her mistress's eyes in the mirror.

'You have spoken with no one but your servants for over a week, ma'am. Will you not give him a few minutes of your time?'

With a little cry Madame flew from her dressing-stool.

'Oh, am I to be hounded here, in my own house? You go to him, Hannah. Tell him I *will not* see him!'

'If it is the same Lord Davenham who came calling in Paris, Miss Nell, he is not so easily discharged.'

Elinor turned away, anxious to avoid Hannah's searching gaze and pulled a warm cloak from the cupboard. 'I am going for a walk in the garden, so you may safely tell my Lord Davenham that I am not in the house!'

Mrs Grisson went downstairs to the marbled hall, where the viscount had been left to kick his heels. As she approached the young gentleman, she remembered his visits to the Paris house. Then too, she had been charged with the task of refusing him admittance.

'My lord, Madame de Sange is not receiving visitors. She sends her apologies.'

'The devil she does!' He smiled ruefully. 'Come, tell me! What exactly did she say?'

Hannah was not proof against his coaxing tone.

'Sir, she will not see you.' She read the disappointment in his eyes. 'I am sorry, my lord.'

'Aye. So too am I.' He sighed, and with a slight bow he turned and strode out of the house.

'Sir!' Hannah ran to the door.

The viscount halted on the path and looked back, his blue eyes enquiring. She stepped outside.

'She – my mistress – is even now in the garden, sir.'

'But she will not see me.'

Hannah bit her lip. 'There is a narrow track, my lord, at the side of the house. It runs beside the garden wall.'

'A track, you say?'

101

'Yes, sir. And – there is a tree at the side of the track, a tree whose branches reach right over the wall. It has been used by the village boys to come in and steal apples from the orchard.' Hannah flushed and looked down at her apron, which she was twisting between her hands. 'It is not so high that it could not be climbed by someone wishing to enter the garden. . . .'

'But you said that she will not see me. What would she think of . . . an intruder?'

Hannah looked up, fixing her eyes at some point past the viscount's shoulder.

'Certainly there are some gentlemen whom I should not wish to see in my lady's garden, sir.'

The viscount lifted an eyebrow. 'Indeed?'

'Yes sir.'

'But you think . . . I should look for this tree?'

Hannah retreated back up the steps.

'Oh, do not ask me, my lord. I could not advise you against my lady's wishes!' She went inside quickly and shut the door. As she listened to his footsteps on the gravel drive, she smiled to herself.

Elinor moved swiftly from the rose garden to the shrubbery, making a mental note of the instructions she would give to her gardener later in the week. The air was warm within the sheltered garden and she pushed her cloak back over her shoulders as she walked, lifting her face to the sun. She turned on to a side path and stopped abruptly, her mouth opening for a cry which never came. Before her stood Viscount Davenham, showing no sign of discomfiture as he bowed to her. Madame's eyes flashed angrily.

'I gave orders that you were not to be admitted!'

'Nor was I. I came over the wall.'

'Over the – how dare you, sir! You behave like a common thief!'

'I did it to steal time with you, Madame. Pray allow me to explain myself.'

She turned and began to walk quickly back towards the house.

'You did that very effectively at our last meeting! There can be nothing left to say!'

In a couple of long strides he was beside her.

'Lady, I mean you no harm! I want to apologize.'

'Too late, my lord!'

'No, I will not allow that!' He jumped in front of her, grabbing her arms and forcing her to stop. 'Pray, at the very least, hear me! When we last met I was angry. I gave you no chance to defend yourself. That was wrong of me; will you not explain to me *how* I have misjudged you?'

Elinor glared at him, her breast heaving. She bit her lip, stormy green eyes meeting cool blue.

He said gently, 'I am willing to listen, and more than ready to believe I was in error.' He watched the fire die from her eyes, but she remained cautious. He continued, 'Will you not walk with me, Madame de Sange?'

She made no remonstrance as he drew her hand through his arm and led her back along the sheltered paths of the shrubbery. She remained tense, and there was an edge to her voice when she spoke to him.

'Well, sir?'

'Well, Madame! I saw you with Poyntz, in Paris, the night he died. I met you on the stairs as you ran away from his room. Even wrapped in your cloak I knew you.'

'Oh.'

'I cannot believe your affections were engaged?'

'They were not.'

'Then there was George Rowsell.'

'Yes.'

'Would you tell me you were not his mistress?'

'I am no man's mistress.'

'Yet they are both dead.'

She said in a tight voice, 'I did not kill either of them.'

'I know that, but to see you with Rowsell, a womanizer, a man so coarse, and you—'

'You know nothing of me.'

He heard the wistful note in her voice and stopped, pulling her round to face him.

'I *do* know you! I know you did not love Rowsell – you *could* not love such a man! Will you not tell me why you gave him to believe you would marry him?'

Elinor looked up and realized her mistake as she found her eyes held by his intense gaze. She wanted to trust him, to tell him everything, but he was a man, and she could not bring herself to believe he was so very different from the rest!

'If – if I tell you that I have – I had my reasons for befriending Rowsell, would that be sufficient?'

'No.'

The word stood between them, stark and uncompromising. Elinor realized it was important to explain, and she fought against herself in her attempt to do so.

'I did not – love him.'

'And Poyntz?'

Her lip curled. 'He died of over-indulgence.'

'But you were there.'

'Yes.'

'Why?'

'I was his Nemesis.'

'Will you not explain?'

'I cannot!' She closed her eyes against the bewilderment she saw in his face. 'Pray, my lord, do not question me further. I have told you more than any other living soul, save my faithful Hannah. At this time I can give you no more.'

'At this time – does that mean that one day you will tell me?'

Aye, if I live! Aloud, she said, 'If you will keep faith with me, sir, and trust me.'

His wry smile appeared.

'I have no choice, since you will not let me help you.' He lifted her fingers to his lips and felt them tremble as he kissed them. 'I am your servant, ma'am, now and always.'

'Thank you.' The viscount had retained her hand and Elinor felt her resolve weakening. She said, 'You must go now, if you please.'

'And must I climb back over the wall?'

A reluctant smile curled her lips. She shook her head.

'I have a key to the wicket gate. I will let you out.'

She led him to a shady corner of the garden and unlocked the small door set into the wall.

'When will I see you again, Madame?'

'I – I am going out of town for Christmas. I do not yet know when I shall return. I—' She looked up to find him staring down at her. Instinctively she stepped away, only to find the garden wall at her back. He put his hands on the wall on either side of her, trapping her. She knew he was going to kiss her, and as panic immobilized her body, a whimper escaped her constricted throat.

The viscount stepped back, frowning at the terror he saw in her face.

'Elinor? Do I frighten you so much?'

She was trembling violently.

'N-no. It – it is not you, sir, it is – all men!'

'My dear child, what is it? Will you not tell me?'

No, I cannot!' She leaned against the wall, afraid that her limbs would not support her. 'Please, please go now.'

'But will you not—'

'Please – you must leave me now!'

Davenham hesitated, but Elinor waved him away, and once he had stepped through the door she locked it as quickly as her trembling hands would allow, before giving way to her tears.

As the year drew to a close, Elinor made her plans for her forthcoming visit to Weald Hall. Since no time limit had been agreed for her stay, the house at Knight's Bridge must be kept open, she decided, with Hannah remaining in charge of a skeleton staff. This arrangement did not suit Mrs Grisson at all, as she was quick to inform Madame as they were packing her gowns into a large trunk, but Elinor was adamant. Seeing the older woman's distress, Elinor put her arms around Hannah and hugged her.

'My mind is quite made up, Hannah, I must go alone. Pray do not look so frightened, my dear. Boreland is merely flesh and blood, like you or me, and just as vulnerable.'

Mrs Grisson broke out of the embrace and paced the room, her emotions plain upon her face, although she did her best to conceal them. At length she turned to her mistress, her faded eyes pleading.

'Miss Nell, pray do not go! If you kill that man you will be found out and hanged for sure, and if he should remember who you are, he will most certainly do away with you!'

Elinor gave a small, twisted smile.

'In that case,' she said,' you may inform upon our friend Boreland, and have him executed for murder.' She held up a yellow gown, ignoring Hannah's anguished looks. 'Now, what do you think of this canary-coloured sack? Too many knots and ruffles for a lady in mourning for her lover, do you not agree?'

Realizing my lady would not be moved, Hannah sighed audibly, but refrained from any further argument.

CHAPTER TEN

*Wherein we learn of a lady's trust
for a most untrustworthy person*

In one of the small apartments of Leicester House, a lady stood by the window, looking out at the wintry sky. The December day was short and the room was already growing dark, but when a servant had disturbed her, bringing in a taper to light the candles, she had waved him away. There was still light enough, she reasoned, and the rosy glow of the blazing fire gave the room an air of intimacy. Nervously she pulled at the lace handkerchief between her fingers as she waited for her visitor to come upstairs; she had seen him arrive, but it seemed an age before she heard the discreet scratching upon the door, and the gentleman was shown in. She gave a faint smile of relief as she watched him enter, his elegant coat of grey silver-laced satin glowing richly in the firelight and, as he made his bow to her, the diamond stud in his hat flashed its own greeting.

'Your Highness.'

'My Lord Thurleigh.' She greeted him warmly as she came away from the window. 'I have anxiously awaited your return to Town. You have seen my sons?'

He shook his head. 'I called at Savile House, but was informed that the prince was engaged and could not see me.'

'And my Edward?'

'Similarly engaged, ma'am.'

The Princess of Wales made a little sound of annoyance.

'It is always the same,' she complained, her Teutonic accent

107

still strong after seventeen years in England. 'Since that man Waldegrave has been their governor, my children are kept very close. I fear they are not being taught as they should be, yet the King will not listen to me! He has surrounded his grandsons with Jacobites but cannot be made to see it!'

'There was an inquiry into the matter, ma'am,' he reminded her gently. 'The allegations proved groundless.'

The princess looked sceptical. 'What do I care for inquiries? I would that *you* were governor at Savile House, my lord. Then I would know my children were in safe hands.'

Lord Thurleigh's hard grey eyes gleamed for a moment before the lids concealed his triumphant look.

'I should be honoured by such a trust,' he murmured, bowing modestly, 'but although I dare to think that His Majesty regards me in a favourable light, I do not think that he is about to bestow that post upon me. He is too well disposed to Waldegrave at the present time.'

'He cannot see what is under his nose!' The Princess was scathing. 'It is the same with the current rumours concerning the Stuart. His Majesty will not take them seriously. He says they are put about by mischief-makers here in England, but how can he be sure?'

The marquis spread his hands. 'As you know, Your Highness, I have ordered my own people to look into the matter. . . .'

'And have you any proof, my lord?' she asked him eagerly. 'Anything that will make the King take this threat seriously?'

'Alas, as yet I cannot bring His Majesty proof that Charles Stuart is planning another attempt upon the crown. If only I could, then mayhap plans could be made to safeguard the young prince.' He paused, watching the Princess closely as he continued: 'Unfortunately, His Majesty will not listen to those of us who believe there is a real threat. It is almost as if some-one did not wish him to see the danger. . . .'

The lady's petulant expression turned to one of anger.

'He is being misled by his brother!' she said savagely. 'Cumberland would like nothing better than to have Charles Stuart dispose of my children. Then he would be free to wrest the crown back for himself.'

Since this was exactly what Guy Morellon wished to imply, he could not but be pleased with this speech, but the lady's vehemence caused him to go cautiously.

'Indeed, ma'am, I have never heard aught against the duke . . .'

'I live in constant dread of him!' came the bitter reply. Suddenly, she stepped forward and caught one of his hands between her own nervous fingers, glancing around her to make sure they were alone.

'Pray, my lord,' she spoke now in a quiet, urgent tone, 'you once told me you would do anything to serve your future king. I am a widow, sir. My son is defenceless! If Charles Stuart – or any other – should attempt to steal away his birthright . . .'

'I would indeed do my utmost to protect His Highness, and all of your family, ma'am, But, would you trust so much to me, rather than His Majesty's advisers?'

'In truth I would, sir!' she told him earnestly. 'I would put myself and my children totally in your charge. Did not my dear husband tell me you were his very good friend? My son attains his majority in a little over two years and then, my dear sir, you may be sure that your loyalty to us shall not be forgotten. George has a very warm regard for you, Lord Thurleigh, and will welcome your attendance upon him when he sets up his own household.'

Guy Morellon smiled to himself as he uttered a few more comforting words to the princess while triumph sang within him. It was too easy: the lady was so set against the Duke of Cumberland that she was willing to believe him capable of any infamy. He decided he had done enough for the present.

'I must go out of Town again for a short while,' he told her as he took his leave. 'My man is due back from France very soon, and I go to meet him.'

'I pray he will bring you good news, my lord.'

'As you say, ma'am. In the meantime, it would be best if you spoke of this matter with no one,' he warned her.

She held out her hand to him, smiling trustingly up into his face.

'Of course, sir. I would do nothing to endanger my family.'

'Then I will say *au revoir*, Your Highness, and I hope that upon my next visit, I shall be able to give you better tidings.'

As he was driven away from Leicester House, Lord Thurleigh laughed softly to himself. Everything he had planned was falling into place. Those skilfully spread rumours of a Stuart revival could never be traced back to him, and what did it matter if the King and his advisers dismissed them? The Princess of Wales believed them, and doubtless many of her supporters, too. He laughed aloud as he recalled his last conversation with the princess: there was not a thought in her head that had not been put there by someone else, and now that he had her trust, it was simple to put in the occasional word or suspicion to keep her at odds with the King. Had she not told him she trusted him above all others? It did not matter after all whether Boreland's visit to Charles Stuart had been fruitful: Thurleigh was sure now that he did not need a full-blown invasion to stir up a rebellion. With his influence over the princess, it would be an easy task to set the Hanoverians against one another. Thurleigh settled himself into one corner of the coach and closed his eyes, still smiling. With the country in turmoil, who could say what an ambitious man might not achieve?

CHAPTER ELEVEN

Mistress Boreland proves unusually hospitable

Two weeks before Christmas, the Boreland coach carried Madame de Sange away from Knight's Bridge. Elinor's scant knowledge of the country prevented her from recognizing the route, although she knew from the occasional milestone that they were heading north. Except for a brief stop to change horses at Hadley Green, they travelled throughout the short winter day. Elinor had no way of telling how far they travelled and she dozed fitfully as the carriage rumbled on, only waking when she felt a change in pace, and found they were turning off the main highway to follow a much narrower track that took them between two thick walls of trees. Elinor suppressed a shudder, and took comfort from the knowledge that an armed guard was sitting upon the box beside the coachman, to protect them from highwaymen. A thick bed of rusty leaves covered the ground between the trees and scrunched under the wheels of the coach, and the bare branches overhead formed a dense lattice above the road, reducing the wintry afternoon light to a dusk. Occasionally a break in the trees allowed a shaft of sunlight to finger the road, but to Elinor even this seemed strange and unreal. She pulled her fur-lined mantle closer about her and hoped that they were nearing their journey's end.

At last the coach broke free of the forest, emerging from the semi-darkness into the late afternoon sunshine and Elinor had her first view of Weald Hall. At the edge of the trees the ground fell away in a gentle valley, with the house set high upon the opposite ridge, bathed now in the golden rays of the setting sun. The road did not traverse the valley, but followed its length, gradually descending to curve over a stone bridge across a small stream, then beginning an equally gradual ascent back along the eastern slope, eventually coming to a halt upon the gravelled courtyard of the house. Elinor descended from the carriage and stood for a moment, regarding her surroundings. The house was a fine Jacobean mansion, built of red brick, which was partially hidden by a thick covering of ivy, and the small leaded windows were aflame now in the sunlight. She was still looking up at the gabled roofline and the tall, twisted chimneys stretching skywards when her hostess came out to greet her. Elinor noted Isobel Boreland's plain gown of dark blue wool, its severity only relieved by bands of white lace at the neck and wrists, and the wintry smile that curved the lips but never reached her dark eyes.

'My dear Madame de Sange! You are very welcome! I trust your journey was not too tiring?'

'Not at all, ma'am, thanks to your consideration for my comfort. And to terminate my travels at such a beautiful spot has made the excursion most worthwhile!'

'You are seeing the Hall at its very best,' replied Mrs Boreland. 'I cannot think there is a house in England better situated than this one. But although the sun is most welcome, there is little warmth in it at this season. Let us go indoors, Madame, where you may take off your wrap and warm yourself by a good fire.'

Mrs Boreland led her guest inside, explaining as she went that her husband and son were out shooting.

'It was such a fine day there was no stopping them,' she continued as they entered the drawing-room. 'I made sure you would not object if they were not here to meet you. I thought you would perhaps prefer to have a little time to yourself.'

Madame de Sange could only nod in mute agreement. Her hostess was in full command, and after they had partaken of wine and biscuits before the cheerful drawing-room fire, the new guest was borne away upstairs to the room that had been set aside for her. Dinner would be in an hour, she was informed, and the maid who had been hired to wait upon her would be up directly. With a final suggestion that Elinor should take a short rest, Mrs Boreland went out, leaving her guest to stare after her in some amusement.

Recovering a little from Mrs Boreland's overbearing style of hospitality, Elinor made a brief inspection of her apartment. It was a dark room, the walls covered with faded blue flock-paper and wainscoting that was dull from lack of polish. There was a door leading to a small dressing-room, and although the bedroom itself was not large, she felt that this could only be an advantage, for the blazing logs in the corner fireplace were able to keep it comfortably warm. A pair of rather dark paintings adorned the walls, but apart from these, and an unremarkable marble bust upon the mantelshelf, the room was bare of ornament.

With a small sigh she turned away from the cheerless surroundings and went to the window. Her room faced east, looking out over the terrace and formal gardens to the parkland beyond. Small tendrils of ivy encroached upon the glass and Elinor wondered idly how often the servants had to cut back the vines to prevent the windows from being completely overgrown. A scratching at the door brought her out of her reverie, and she turned to find a young maid hovering in the doorway, anxiously awaiting her commands.

At the appointed hour, Madame de Sange made her way downstairs. The velvet skirts of her russet-coloured gown brushed the floor as she crossed the hall and was shown into the drawing-room. She paused in the doorway, aware that her burnished curls would be glowing in the candlelight. Across the room, beside his wife, stood James Boreland. For a brief moment Elinor wondered what madness has prompted her to put herself into his power, but it was too late to go back. Summoning up her courage, she moved forward, head held high, her eyes and her smile fixed upon her hostess. Mrs Boreland smiled in reply and rose to meet her.

'My dear, you look enchanting, does she not, Mr Boreland?' She turned to her husband, but he had already stepped forward to greet their guest.

'Indeed, indeed,' he murmured. 'Your servant, Madame!'

Steeling herself, Elinor held out her fingers, but as he reached out to clasp them, her eyes noted the mass of thick black hair upon the back of his hand. The sight brought a vivid memory of the night at the inn, when his large, hairy frame had borne down upon her so mercilessly. . . . With an immense effort she pushed aside the thought and with it the fear and revulsion that threatened to engulf her. She forced herself to reply calmly and to exchange a few civilities, but could not deny the relief when she could at last turn away from him as Mrs Boreland presented her only child.

Andrew McCallum Boreland proved to be something of a surprise to Elinor: all her energies had been taken up appearing calm before the father so that she had not noticed the son and, when at last he was introduced to her, she turned to face him, expecting to see a younger version of her host. She was instead confronted with a slight young man, little taller than herself and wearing a distinctly nervous look upon his countenance. He wore his own dark hair unpowdered, and tied back loosely with a ribbon, from which one or two lank strands had already escaped. He made her an awkward bow, asked about her journey to Weald Hall and then stepped back, looking anxiously to his mama for guidance.

'Go and fetch Madame a glass of ratafia from the tray, Andrew,' suggested Mrs Boreland. As he moved away she smiled at Elinor. 'My son does not go much into society, Madame, and he was very anxious about this moment. However, he will recover presently when he is more used to you and then you will find him a charming companion. His health has never been good, you see, and we were unable to send him away to school.'

'I – I learned a lot from Mr Avery, Mama,' put in Andrew, coming up to give Elinor a glass. 'You said I could not have learned more if I had gone to the best school in the country.'

Mrs Boreland looked a little put out at this speech, but she gave him one of her thin smiles.

'I am sure you did, sir, for Mr Avery was an excellent tutor. And, what is more, you have an excellent understanding of how the Hall and the estates are run, which is far more to the point than too much book-learning, do you not agree, Madame de Sange?'

Elinor was saved from the necessity of answering by Mr Boreland's remarking, 'Your own estates in France must need considerable attention, Madame. Doubtless they are handled by your late husband's executors?'

'I have complete control over the de Sange inheritance, sir. However, I have now sold off most of my land, and I have an excellent steward who attends to the rest.'

'I seem to recall Rowsell telling me that your family came originally from England,' put in Boreland, regarding her closely.

Elinor's pulse quickened.

'That is so, sir, but it was such a long time ago I cannot help but think of myself as a Frenchwoman.'

'Father has recently been to the Continent.' Andrew looked pleased to be contributing to the conversation. 'Is that not so sir? First to Rome, was it not? And then on to Paris—'

'Madame has no interest in my business journey.' His father cut him short, frowning so fiercely that the young man visibly blanched and sank back into his chair, not daring to speak again. James Boreland turned his searching look back to Elinor. 'Madame, are you sure our paths have not crossed? Your face haunts me, yet I cannot think where I have seen you before.'

Elinor met his gaze squarely: there could be no half-hearted evasion of this gentleman.

'Well, sir, let me see. My father was a scholar, a man of peaceful habits and a retiring nature. After his death my mother took me to her relatives in Dijon, where we continued to live quietly until I married Philbert de Sange. If you were in Paris within the past five years or so then it is *possible* you saw me there. Yet, if we had met, sir, I am sure I would remember it.'

'You make too much of it, Mr Boreland,' put in his wife without looking up. 'Pray do not tease our guest any longer with your musings or she will be sorry she came!'

At that moment the door opened to admit a servant and with relief Elinor heard the announcement that dinner awaited them.

Later, with the last glowing embers still burning in the hearth, Elinor lay in her bed reviewing her first day at Weald Hall. Not for one moment did she consider Mrs Boreland had invited her purely out of sympathy. Even in her own home, where she should have been most relaxed, the lady had shown no spark of warmth: despite her smiles she seemed cold and hard as stone. Elinor smiled to herself, remembering that the epithet had once been applied to her; had *she* ever appeared so cold and unapproachable? Certainly Lord Davenham had not thought so, he had even considered himself capable of – what was his expression – *melting* the Lady of Stone!

With something of a sigh she put away these agreeable memories and tried to concentrate upon her immediate task of revenging herself upon James Boreland. However, she found her thoughts wandering and she realized that she was indeed very tired. With a yawn she pulled the bed covers a little closer, resolving sleepily to let events show her the way. Fortune had brought her thus far, surely it would not desert her now.

Madame de Sange slept long and deeply, waking only when her maid came in the following morning to pull back the heavy curtains and allow the sun to stream into the room. Discovering the lateness of the hour, Elinor rose and dressed swiftly, going downstairs to find only her hostess still at breakfast. Mrs Boreland greeted her with such a profusion of smiles and honeyed words that Elinor wondered if the lady's coldness the previous evening had been due to fatigue, or perhaps some disagreement between husband and wife. Mr Boreland had already left the house upon business, she was informed, but Andrew was at that very moment in the stables choosing a suitable mount for Madame in order that he might show her over the Boreland acres.

'We mentioned it last night,' Mrs Boreland reminded her, smiling fixedly at her guest, 'but perhaps you might not wish for so much exertion today, although it would be a pity to delay the excursion, for one can never be sure how long this fine weather will last.'

'No, no, I would very much like to ride out today, but I must beg your son's indulgence while I break my fast and then change my dress.'

Mrs Boreland beamed even more broadly.

'But of course. I will have a message sent to the stables immediately. Will an hour suffice you, Madame?'

Slightly less than an hour later, Madame de Sange emerged from Weald Hall wearing a close-fitting riding habit of brown camlet, silver laced and with a matching cocked hat pinned firmly over her burnished curls. Three horses were saddled, a groom mounted upon one of the animals, holding the reins for Mr Boreland's horse, while a stable lad stood at the head of the lady's mount. Andrew was waiting to throw her up into the saddle, a task which he accomplished with some nervousness, due mainly, Elinor guessed, to the fact that his mother was at hand issuing a multitude of instructions to the young man upon how to treat a lady.

'Off you go now, and enjoy yourselves,' she concluded, when both riders were settled upon their mounts. 'And be sure, Andrew, that you do not bore Madame de Sange by talking constantly of hunting!'

The result of all these strictures left Andrew so tongue-tied that it was Elinor who had to initiate all attempts at conversation for the first part of their journey, her companion answering each time with a self-conscious monosyllable. She thought with an inward smile that he was very much like a child upon a duty call to some fearful aunt. Indeed, she was rapidly coming to the conclusion that Andrew Boreland had no more understanding than a boy half his age.

'Do you know,' she remarked, after this state of affairs had continued for some time, 'I do not think I should be too bored if you were to tell me about your hunting. It is a sport I have never experienced, although I used to watch the hunt go by from our cottage in Bedfordshire when I was a child, but neither my father nor my husband enjoyed the hunt and thus I was never introduced to it.'

'Then you must come out with us here,' returned Andrew, losing some of his shyness. 'My father keeps a pack of hounds – they are kennelled by the stables, quite a distance from the house, yet often at night you can hear them baying. Sometimes we can be out hunting the hare all day, but if you do not wish to be in the saddle for so long you may always turn back and wait for us at home.'

'What happens to the hare?'

'Often it gets away,' said Andrew, unconcerned. 'The hounds are prone to riot, you see, and part of the skill is to keep them 'pon the right scent. Occasionally we have a good, fast run, but usually it's steady riding – no reason at all why you should not enjoy it.' He saw the doubt in her face and blurted out, 'Mama is very anxious that you enjoy your stay here. She says if I am very good and – and entertain you properly, you will want to stay here, and one day be mistress of Weald Hall.'

'Oh.'

'Perhaps I should not have told you that.' He paused, frowning. 'Mama tells me sometimes that I must not repeat things – she will be angry with me—'

'You need have no fear upon this occasion, Andrew, for I shall not tell anyone what has passed between us.'

His face brightened and he turned to smile at her. 'You are very kind. I like you very much, you know. I think I shall enjoy being married to you.'

'I think it is a little soon for you to be considering marriage! You hardly know me.'

'But I heard Mama telling my father that you would make me a perfect match.'

'Perhaps that is so,' replied Elinor, torn between surprise and amusement, 'but I cannot think it right to decide such matters upon so short an acquaintance.'

'You do not like me!'

'Oh Andrew, that is not true!'

Bringing his horse a little closer, he leaned across and gripped her wrist.

'Yes it is! If you liked me you would marry me – why do you dislike me?'

The thin fingers were surprisingly strong, and Elinor could feel his nails digging into her flesh. She said as calmly as she could, 'Please, Andrew, you are hurting me.'

'I would never do so if you liked me!' The words were child-like, but that fact did nothing to lessen the unease that Elinor was beginning to feel. With relief she heard the groom's voice close behind them.

'Come along now, Master Andrew. You are alarming the lady. Let us get on with our ride, sir, or we won't cover the half of it before we have to turn back.'

For a fleeting moment Elinor thought the boy would ignore the advice, but although he looked mutinous, Andrew released her.

'Let us race to those trees over there.' He pointed to a small copse on the skyline. 'There's a good view from the ridge!'

Upon the words he set his horse to the gallop, leaving Elinor and the groom to follow as best they might. By the time they reached the copse, Andrew's ill humour had disappeared and he grinned an apology at Elinor.

'Are you still angry with me, Madame?'

'Of course not.' She paused. 'I would very much like to be your friend, Andrew.'

The young man looked at her doubtfully. 'Really?'

'Yes, *really*! But I wish to hear no more talk of marriage.'

'Oh, very well. But may I call you Elinor?'

'If you so wish.'

'Good!' He smiled sunnily. 'Now I truly feel we are friends!'

CHAPTER TWELVE

Of plot and proposal

In the gleaming candlelight of the latest hell to become the fashionable haunt of London's gamblers, Viscount Davenham surveyed the company with a critical eye. Such was the obsession with games of chance that almost every noble house of the country was represented within these large rooms and indeed the surroundings were sumptuous enough for any company. The ornate plaster ceilings were freshly painted in sky-blue and gold, with rich velvet hangings in a matching blue covering each window, defying guests to tell if dawn had yet come. The noble lords and gentlemen were grouped around the green baize tables, eagerly watching the tumbling dice or awaiting the turn of a card. An occasional shout of triumph or groan of despair broke above the general low rumble of conversation, while soft-footed waiters replenished glasses and trimmed candles, lest a guttering flame should cause offence to any player, and over-dressed females draped themselves over sofas, their carmined lips smiling as they waited to share in the celebrations of the lucky few, or to provide succour to the losers.

Lord Davenham felt a light touch upon his arm.

'Well met, sir!' Lord Derry's cheerful tones carried across the room, earning him one or two disapproving glances. 'So you have discovered this little place – what d'you think of it? Company's a little thin, but everywhere's the same this time of year.'

The viscount shrugged. 'The wine's tolerable.'

'Gad! Is that all you can say?' Derry laughed. 'You're devil-ish hard to please, my boy! Don't know why you come to these places, damned if I do!'

'Oh, merely to be sociable, Derry.' The reply was accompa-nied by the ghost of a smile. 'Who's that sitting over there at Exeter's table – thin fellow in the brown coat?'

Derry glanced across the room.

'Oh, Lord Thomas. He's but recently come to Town, I believe.'

'He seems to be on very good terms with Thurleigh.'

'I should think so – the marquis brought him here. I'm going down for some supper, Davenham – care to join me?'

Lord Davenham turned to accompany his friend.

'How is your mama?' enquired Derry as they made their way downstairs. 'In good health, is she? Haven't seen her since we had that supper party.' He shook his head, 'Bad busi-ness that! Poor Rowsell, and in front of the ladies, too! Very bad form. I tell you, my mother was particularly cut up about it, vowed she'd not have another rout! All humbug, of course. When everyone's back in Town in the spring you wait and see, she'll be sending out the invitations once again. I only hope this business with Rowsell doesn't keep people away.'

'Oh I doubt that. In fact, 'tis most likely to lend a morbid attraction to her parties in the future!'

My lord Derry was much struck by this thought and he said, brightening, 'Yes, by Jove! It might just do that! I pray you, Davenham, don't think I am condoning people going around killing each other at fashionable parties,' he added hastily, 'but since it has happened, we've to make the best of it, ain't that so? Besides, I didn't know Rowsell very well – not my crowd. Too hot-tempered for my liking. I don't suppose there will be many to mourn his passing. Except perhaps the lady he was escorting that night. I heard that they were about to be married. Strange, I didn't think Rowsell was in the market for a wife.'

'But then the lady *is* very beautiful' put in the viscount, at his most casual.

'Aye, of course, so maybe there was some truth there,' agreed Lord Derry. 'Locked herself away after Rowsell's death, you know, only came to Town a few times after that. Rumour has it that she was distraught with grief.'

The viscount nodded. 'I believe so.'

'Well, if she was she's over it now,' remarked Derry as they entered the supper-room. 'I heard she's gone off to spend Christmas with James Boreland and his family.'

The news did nothing to improve Lord Davenham's temper and he ate his meal in silence, allowing his companion to rattle on uninterrupted throughout the meal. If Lord Derry noticed his friend's unusually taciturn manner he did not show it, but happily returned to the gaming-tables alone after supper, when the viscount announced his intention of going home. Davenham made his way to the door, where he encountered the Marquis of Thurleigh preparing to depart.

'Ah, my dear viscount.' The marquis bestowed a brilliant smile upon him. 'How fortunate that we should meet like this! Do you have your carriage waiting? No? Then you must allow me to take you up in my own.'

With an inward shrug, Lord Davenham climbed into the luxurious equipage that was awaiting the marquis, and once settled inside, he observed his host, who was quietly humming a tune as the coach set off in the direction of Warwick Street.

'You seem in very good spirits tonight, Lord Thurleigh.'

The other smiled, his white teeth flashing in the darkness.

'Oh I am, my dear sir, I am! I would like to share my thoughts with you, but I am not at all sure you would find them a cause for celebration.'

'I am quite certain I should not!'

Again the gleam of white teeth.

'Then I regret to say that my happiness must be your sorrow, Davenham.'

'I wish I knew what mischief you are planning!' snapped the viscount.

'Come, sir, do you doubt my loyalty?' demanded the marquis in a pained tone.

'The only loyalty you have is to yourself.'

Lord Thurleigh laughed softy. 'You are very like your father, Jonathan Davenham.'

'And, like my father, I distrust *you*,' came the blunt reply. 'We will catch you out, sir, you may be sure of it.'

The marquis leaned forward in the darkness.

'Then you must be quick, sir,' he hissed, 'for I am growing ever more powerful. Soon no one will be able to stop me!' The coach slowed and he glanced out of the window. 'Ah, Warwick Street – your lodgings, I believe, Lord Davenham?'

The viscount jumped down and turned, his eyes searching the older man's face.

'Tell me, Thurleigh, whose cause do you espouse – the House of Hanover, or that of Stuart?'

'Really, my dear young sir, do you expect me to answer you? Nay – I will give you an answer, although you know it already. I espouse my own cause! By the bye, I am taking my wife out of Town tomorrow, so you may relax your vigilant watch upon my activities. I shall be hatching no new plots while I am away!'

At Weald Hall, Isobel Boreland was well satisfied with the progress of her schemes, but her guest was feeling much less sanguine about her own position. After almost a week at the Hall, Elinor felt she was no nearer to knowing how to deal with James Boreland, and she had come downstairs that morning to hear that her host had risen early and departed, leaving his family with little notion of when he would return. Elinor's suggestion that she should curtail her visit brought a swift response from her hostess. There could be no question of Madame leaving them so soon. Mrs Boreland was only too happy to have her company, especially now that her husband was obliged to go away. She added that Andrew, too, would be sorry to see her depart and would wish to hear no more about leaving unless, and here Mrs Boreland paused eloquently, Madame de Sange was not enjoying her stay at Weald Hall? Elinor hastily disclaimed, but behind her smiles her heart sank, and she returned to her room after breakfast feeling tense and frustrated.

She had missed her chance, Elinor told herself angrily. Her host had offered to teach her to shoot: why had she not accepted his offer and taken the first opportunity to put a bullet through his black heart? She knew there was little chance of persuading such a powerful figure to confess that he had murdered her father, or to tell her who had done so, but she had held back from attempting her revenge. What had stopped her? she asked herself bitterly. Did she expect the man to drink a trifle too much at dinner one night and confess his sins of his own volition? Now he was beyond her reach, and she was left to continue in a most uncomfortable rôle.

A feeling of oppression settled upon Elinor. She felt trapped and, she had to confess, it was in a web partly of her own making. A casual enquiry brought the information that Weald Hall could be cut off for weeks at a time in winter, when the rain and snow made the twisting road leading to the house impassable. Riding out with Andrew one damp and chilly morning, Elinor asked him if this was true.

'Lord, yes!' came the cheerful reply. 'It becomes a quagmire when the rain starts. The stream usually floods too, down in the valley, and covers the road.'

'Perhaps I should cut short my visit,' she murmured, 'for I would not wish to be stranded here.'

'No, no, you cannot leave!' cried Andrew, his face flushing with disappointment.

'But I have a house near London that I must return to some day, Andrew.'

'But you must stay for Christmas – it is but two days away, and Mama is expecting Father home any time now. We always have guests here on Christmas Day, you see, it is a tradition. The vicar and his wife and daughters, and one or two of our other neighbours come to dine – you would like that, Elinor, would you not?'

'I am sure I should, Andrew, but—'

'Don't leave me! I don't want you to go! Mama said you would stay here with me for ever, that you would never go away!'

There was a note of panic in Andrew's voice, and Elinor forced herself to speak calmly.

'Then that is something I shall discuss with your mama.' She shivered. 'It is growing dark. We had best be turning back.'

They cantered back through the park, but as they approached the house, shadowed now in the fading light, Elinor knew a moment of panic. She wanted to turn her horse and set it galloping away from the Hall, never stopping until she had left the Boreland estate far behind. She tried to shake off her unease, telling herself not to be foolish, but as they clattered into the stable yard she could not help glancing over her shoulder at the sturdy, wooden-faced groom who accompanied them on every ride. Surely his mount was not the usual type of servant's horse, it looked too well-bred, too fast. The thought came unbidden to her mind: he could easily catch up with me if I tried to run away! Thrusting such unpleasant thoughts aside, Elinor allowed Andrew to help her dismount and lead her indoors. She must have faith in her own destiny.

CHAPTER THIRTEEN

Discovery

The short December day was fast drawing to a close as James Boreland reached his destination. A caped servant ran out of the house to take his horse and a stony-faced footman ushered him inside, relieved him of his rain-sodden outer garments and overnight bag and showed him into the library, where his host awaited him beside a blazing fire.

'Ah, that's a welcome sight!' Boreland stepped up to warm himself before the flames.

'Not the most pleasant weather for your journey,' remarked Lord Thurleigh, rising from his chair and going over to the sideboard.

'Damnable! It has not stopped raining all day!' He glanced at his host. 'Is something amiss, Thurleigh?'

'You notice some stiffness in my movements? I have been in some pain lately.' Lord Thurleigh's thin lips stretched into a mirthless smile. 'The wages of my sinful youth, I suspect. Too many pox-ridden whores.' He proceeded to fill two glasses from one of several decanters standing upon a silver tray, then, coming back to the fire, he handed one of the glasses to his guest. 'I shall summon my physician when I return to Town.'

'Aye, you have little chance of getting him to come here,' declared Boreland, remembering his earlier grievance. 'The roads around here are an abomination! I have spent the past two days travelling through some of the most inhospitable country I have ever experienced! For God's sake, sir, why could we not have met at Thurleigh, or even your Leicestershire lodge? At least the roads are passable there.'

'Did you meet any acquaintance upon your journey here?'

Boreland gave a snort of laughter.

'That I did not! I have always considered Norfolk a god-forsaken place, now it seems that all men of any sense have forsaken it, too!'

'Then you see why I chose to come here.' Guy Morellon allowed himself a faint smile. 'Here there is no need for furtive disguises or suspicious actions. The chances of meeting someone who knows you are very remote.'

'I only hope we may not be stranded here!'

'You are tired after your journey,' replied the marquis soothingly. 'Let me ring for my man to show you to your room. Then, after we have dined, we will get down to business.'

The dinner was a good one, a saddle of mutton and a couple of dressed capons meeting with Mr Boreland's approval, although he decided against the spiced beef, and later chose only the almond pie from the array of sweet dishes that were brought to the table. At length, the covers were removed and the servants withdrew, leaving the two gentlemen to refill their own glasses from the bottle of brandy set on the table between them.

'Now,' began the marquis, sitting back in his chair, the stem of the wineglass turning gently between his long, thin fingers. 'What news from France?'

'Precious little. In fact,' said Boreland, thinking of his two-day journey, 'nothing that could not have been put in a letter.'

'Forgive me, Boreland. You know it is not my way to commit anything to paper. Men may be persuaded to forget one's words, but material evidence. . . ! Only once have I ever made *that* mistake. . . but we digress. You spoke with the King?'

Boreland nodded. 'Yes. I travelled to Rome, but found no joy there, so I went to Avignon and succeeded in gaining an audience with the prince.'

'And how did you find Charles Stuart? Well?'

'As well as ever a fellow can be in his situation. By the bye, it came out in conversation that he was smuggled into England a few years back – were you aware of it?'

127

'But of course. He came to be received into the Anglican Church.'

His companion shot a suspicious glance across the table.

'You arranged it?'

'I had some hand in the affair.'

'You told me nothing of this!'

'My dear sir, no one knows all my cards. There was no reason for you to know of the matter. Furminger handled the whole.'

'That old woman!' He gave a snort of derision. 'The fellow's a fool.'

'Nevertheless, he is a bishop, and managed things quite satisfactorily. But that is enough of the past, my dear Boreland. Tell me of the prince.'

'He's a father now, did you know?'

'I heard rumours – a boy?'

'If only it had been! A son might perhaps have given Charles Stuart the will he needs to try his luck here once more.'

'He will not come?'

'No. I told him of your plans, but it proved of little use. Poyntz had apparently tried such persuasion but without success. He will not make any attempt upon England unless he is assured of the crown, and for that we need the backing of the French.'

'Which is not forthcoming?'

'No.'

'And the gentlemen I told you to contact – they could not help you?'

'I had meetings with them all, in Paris and Versailles, but to no avail. The most I could get them to agree upon was the troop ship movements in the Channel ports, although even these will not be as extensive as you had requested. It seems they do not consider the moment *propitious* for opening hostilities with England.'

Thurleigh shrugged.

'How disappointing.' He refilled his glass. 'But not entirely unexpected, after all.'

'Hell and damnation, my lord! You had me chasing all over France—'

'Calm yourself, Boreland. I set you no unnecessary task. If Julian Poyntz had not been fool enough to kill himself with his unaccustomed debauchery he would have reported back to me and saved us both a deal of trouble. As it is, I needed to know how much Poyntz had achieved before his untimely end. Very little, it would appear. However, all is not lost. While you were hard at work pleading our cause across the water, I have been equally busy here at home. I now enjoy the full confidence of the Princess of Wales, and, to some extent, that of her eldest son, although he is set about by a bunch of the most admirable men, who make sure no one wins too much influence with the heir to the throne. However, I am certain I have gained favour.'

'It is never a bad thing to have friends in the highest places,' came the somewhat sneering reply. 'I fear 'tis a great pity that there will be no invasion, for you are obviously well placed to put an end to the line of Hanover.'

'But there will be *news* of an invasion, I can promise you that,' smiled Thurleigh. 'Rumours are already rife in Town and the movement of men and arms to the western shores, however small the actual numbers, can only fuel the speculation.'

'And what good will that do us?'

'I have told you, my friend, I never pass on more than it is necessary for you to know. But . . .' he paused, thoughtfully regarding his guest, 'in this case, I am so pleased with my little scheme that I will tell you. The Princess thinks me her only friend: she hates the King and distrusts Cumberland, fearing that he wishes to be rid of his nephews and take the throne for himself. You may smile, Boreland, for you know as well as I that the duke has no such notions. His current unpopularity is mainly undeserved, but it suits my purpose admirably! To continue: the lady is already disturbed by the rumours that are flying about Town concerning the French and Charles Stuart, and is in no way comforted by the King's dismissal of such reports. Thus, as speculation grows, she will become ever more concerned for the safety of her children. I shall then come to her aid, and at a suitable moment I intend to spirit the whole family away to a place of safety.' He smiled.

'Think of it, Boreland: the disappearance of the heir to the throne! There will be chaos. I shall make sure some suspicion falls upon Cumberland. That should cause a few riots! Then perhaps the Jacobite cause may again raise its standard, and once it is seen abroad what turmoil the country has been cast into, I have no doubt that France will wish to turn it to her own advantage. England will be at her mercy; Charles Stuart will reclaim his throne, with the help of his French cousins, to whom he will of course show due gratitude. . . .'

'And also to yourself, my lord?' grinned Boreland.

'There you have it, sir. If, however, no such success is forthcoming for the Stuarts, I shall, of course, protect my royal charges until such time as the young king may return safely to his court.'

'Young king?' Boreland frowned.

The marquis met his eyes with a bland smile.

'Oh, did I forget to mention it? At the same time that I spirit away the royal children, the King is to be assassinated.'

Boreland awoke the next morning in no very good humour. He had a splitting headache, and since no one could doubt the quality of the wines Lord Thurleigh allowed to grace his table, Boreland realized his present state must be due to the quantity consumed the previous evening. Indeed, he thought grimly, his host's mellowness was some proof of that, for rarely was Guy Morellon so forthcoming about his plans. As he rose unsteadily from his bed, Boreland found himself wondering if his brain was playing tricks on him: had Thurleigh really said that he planned to kill the King? He walked over to the washstand, filled the bowl from the heavy jug and plunged his head into the icy water. The shock of cold revived his memory, and last night's conversation came floating back to him.

'If *you* are busy with the heirs to the throne,' he had said to his host, 'who is to dispose of the King?'

He remembered Thurleigh's cold grey eyes watching him over the rim of his glass.

'Why, it must be you, of course, Boreland. A man of your standing should have no difficulty in obtaining a private audience with our revered monarch.'

'And how do you propose that I get away after completing my task?'

'That is for you to arrange. I have no doubt you will hit upon a solution.' Thurleigh had leaned forward, his voice suddenly urgent. 'There is no one else I would entrust with the task! Oh, I have no doubt I could find a dozen willing to attempt it, men with grievances to avenge, or a liking for murder, but they cannot be relied upon should things go wrong. Poyntz is dead: so too is Rowsell, that leaves only you or Furminger, and the bishop really does not have the stomach for the task.'

No, thought Boreland, and in the cold light of morning neither did he relish the thought. Thurleigh's plan was a bold one, the stakes were high, but if they succeeded! The sudden excitement died within him as he looked out of the window at the sodden landscape. The rain fell straight and heavy, relentlessly beating into the ground; there would be no travel today.

For two days the rain continued, filling ditches and rivers to bursting point and when at last it eased and the servants ventured out for fresh supplies, they returned with ominous reports of flooding in the surrounding farms and villages. Lord Thurleigh's lodge was built upon a slight rise, and they had no fear that the house itself was in any danger, although the lawns were waterlogged, and my lord's dour butler announced gloomily that the cellars were growing damp. Boreland cursed his bad luck and could scarcely conceal his impatience at the continuing bad weather. Coming into the breakfast-room one morning, Lord Thurleigh found his guest standing by the window, his countenance every bit as forbidding as the louring sky. The marquis smiled faintly.

'Is my hospitality so poor that you cannot wait to get away?'

Boreland joined his host at the table, his ill-humour unabated.

'Damme, sir, 'tis Christmas Eve! I had hoped to be back at Weald Hall by now. It's the custom for the parson and his brood to dine with us tomorrow, plus various other respectable neighbours – a parcel of dowds, but I'm expected to play the great lord now and again! With the roads near impassable we could be imprisoned here for weeks! Hell and damnation, Thurleigh, how do you stand this place?'

'Easily, my friend. Unlike you, I have no loving family awaiting me. My Lady Margaret scarcely notices whether I am at home or not. I believe she has taken to amusing herself with the stable lads at Thurleigh. . . . Very bad form; I really wonder if I should put an end to it. . . .' He broke off from his musing, his hard eyes coming to rest upon his guest. 'You are mighty keen to get back to your – what did you call them? Your *parcel of dowds*! Or is it perhaps the attractions of this female you have chosen for your son?'

'As I have already told you, that was Isobel's idea, not mine!'

'Is she fair?'

'A veritable beauty! 'Tis strange, the girl looks familiar. Can't quite put my finger on it, but sometimes there's a look or a word, and I feel certain I know her. Impossible, however!'

The marquis showed a mild interest: after all, the weather was so bad, there was little point in hurrying breakfast.

'My dear Boreland, nothing is impossible. Tell me about this beauty.'

'She's somewhat older than Andrew, widow of some Frenchman, and very rich, apparently. Came over from Paris not long ago. If you'd been in town recently you would have met her – Rowsell was hot for her, even wanted to marry her, would you credit it? When he died, Isobel decided to bring the girl to Weald Hall and see what could be done to promote a match with Andrew. I was surprised she agreed to't. I had the impression she didn't like us above half when we first met her. But there, women are strange creatures.'

'As you say. She came from Paris? How long ago?'

'Only been in England a few months, I believe. It seems Rowsell had no sooner clapped eyes on Elinor de Sange than he was captivated. Never stopped singing her praises.'

The marquis had stopped eating, and now regarded his guest very intently.

'Elinor – and what does she look like, this paragon?'

Boreland shrugged.

'She's tall, good figure, a pretty face, but too solemn for my taste.'

'And her hair? What colour?'

'A reddish-brown. In Town she mostly kept it powdered, so I doubt that poor Rowsell often saw its glory, unless he managed to get her into bed, which I doubt. I suspect her virtue was part of the attraction.'

My lord was sitting very still.

'Would I be correct if I were to hazard a guess that her eyes are green?'

'Aye, you would.' Boreland nodded. 'Very striking. In fact, she's very like your own lady, when she was younger, of course—'

'And you say you've never met the woman?' Thurleigh sneered at him, his eyes glittering dangerously. 'You are a fool, man. She was more of a child at the time, but of course you've seen her before, following our disappointment in 'forty-five. You raped her!'

James Boreland stared uncomprehendingly across the table, then as the realization broke upon him, he brought his fist crashing down upon it, cursing violently.

'Tell me,' continued Thurleigh, 'do you know if she met Poyntz in Paris?'

'No. That is, it was mentioned once – I think she did say something. . . .'

My lord sat back in his chair, gazing up at the ornate plasterwork of the ceiling.

'Does it not seem odd to you,' he remarked, 'that this woman should have met Poyntz, who subsequently died in a most mysterious fashion, that she should then turn up in London with Rowsell at her heels, and that, upon his untimely demise, she should accept an invitation from you to stay at the Hall?'

Boreland's countenance darkened as his brain worked back over events. Suddenly he looked up, fixing his fierce stare upon the marquis.

'The ruby! I thought I had seen its like before!'

Thurleigh brought his own grey eyes down from their

contemplation of the ceiling to meet his guest's harsh stare. He sat very still.

'Go on.'

'She wore a large ruby brooch – 'twas the night Rowsell was murdered, which circumstance put it out of my mind until now, but I recall that at the time I thought it an unusual piece, more suited to a man – in fact, my lord, it bore a striking resemblance to a certain large cravat pin you yourself possess – *if* you still have it!'

The two men stared at each other for a full minute, then the marquis spoke coolly.

'As you have already surmised, my dear Boreland, it is the very same. It was not to be found after the girl had left the inn that night. I sent my men to recover the stone the following morning, but the wench and her family had vanished. No word could be got from the villagers, despite all my – er – persuasions, and you may be sure that I scoured the countryside for news of them.'

'By God, sir, you're a cool one! You know that stone contains evidence to send us all to the gallows!'

'That is why I let you all believe I had recovered the ruby. It ensured your continued loyalty to me.'

'And have I ever given you cause to doubt me?'

'No, sir, *you* have not, and for all his tempestuous nature, I believe George Rowsell could be trusted, but Furminger would undoubtedly like to cut all ties with me, if he thought he could safely do so, and Poyntz – well, I think he too was growing tired of the game. Pray do not look so disapproving, my dear sir! I have been ever vigilant, waiting for the stone to come to light, but there has not been the slightest sign – until now.'

'Do you think the woman knows what is in the brooch?'

'It is possible. The compartment is well concealed, and would not easily be discovered, but if it has been in her possession for the past – how long would it be now, eight years?' The marquis shrugged. 'She could have found its secret. Yet if that is so, why has she not passed it to the proper authorities and had us all arrested?'

'That may have been her reason for coming to England.'

'Perhaps, Boreland, but is it not also possible that she came here purely for revenge, and that she wears the ruby to remind herself of the task? The idea has a certain romance, I think.'

With sudden decision Boreland rose from the table.

'There's only one way to find out,' he said, making for the door. 'I'll beat the truth out of her!'

A faint, malicious smile spread over Thurleigh's face.

'My dear fellow, you can't go yet – the roads are still awash!'

Boreland paused at the door, fury burning in his eyes.

'Then mayhap I will have to *swim* home!'

Christmas Day dawned cold but dry; the rain that had persisted during the past few days had eased, but the easterly winds that drove off the clouds brought a sharp drop in temperature, and as the Weald Hall party set out to attend the service at the village church, Elinor was thankful for the hot bricks her hostess had ordered to be placed in their carriage. Apart from the servants, there was only Mrs Boreland, her son and Elinor in the corner of the church set aside for the family, James Boreland not having returned. His wife's disapproval of his absence showed plainly in her face, but to anyone who mentioned the subject she merely remarked that the bad weather had no doubt prevented him from coming home. After the service, during which time Elinor had felt her feet turn into blocks of ice on the chill stone floor of the church, they returned to Weald Hall, where a welcoming fire awaited them in the morning-room.

'Perhaps, Elinor, you would like a game of billiards with me?' suggested Andrew, warming himself before the flames.

'That is out of the question,' Mrs Boreland interrupted before Elinor could reply. 'Have you forgotten that we have visitors coming today? Madame will want to rest and change before they arrive, will you not, my dear? And you too, Andrew, would be the better for lying down upon your bed for an hour. I was most put out when you fell asleep during the sermon!'

Her son flushed slightly, but cast a mischievous glance across ar Elinor as he replied, 'Well, 'twas a mighty tedious tale, Mama!'

'That has nothing to do with the matter. If Mr Tidwell questions you about the text tonight, you will look nohow if you cannot answer him! Now off you go to your room, sir, and let me have no more of your nonsense!'

Realizing that her hostess wished to be free to check over the arrangements for the forthcoming dinner, Elinor excused herself and went up to her room. She did not feel in the least tired, and after changing her sober-hued morning-gown for a loose wrap she sat down at the small dressing-table and unpinned her hair, brushing out the tangled curls as she gazed absently at her reflection in the mirror before her. When she had finished she put down her brush and upon impulse opened her jewel box and took out the ruby brooch, which she had not worn since the evening of George Rowsell's death.

The stone held so many memories for her that Elinor felt a slight tremor run through her as she held it in her hand. To her, its red depths seemed to reflect the blood that had been shed – the stain of her own lost virginity, her father's tragic end and the death of two of the five men she held responsible. It was symbolic of her quest for revenge and yet it was nothing more than an ornament, just what was needed to complete her toilet for that evening. It would secure the muslin kerchief to the bodice of her gown. Why should she not wear it? The jewel seemed to mock her misgivings, and with sudden decision she rose to put the brooch upon the mantelshelf, tucking it slightly behind the marble bust so that it could not slip off into the hearth: it would be ready at hand when she came to dress.

As she closed the jewel box she thought she heard the faint sounds of voices in the hall below. Could the visitors be arriving already? She thought she must be mistaken, for it was still early. Elinor looked around for some occupation. The light was fading, and she decided against trying to read. The servants would be busy preparing for the evening, so she did not ring for a taper, knowing that when her maid came to help her to dress, she would bring a light with her. Kicking off her shoes, she lay down upon the bed to await the girl's arrival.

Elinor had scarcely made herself comfortable when she

heard the door open. Thinking it was her maid, she sat up in leisurely style, but her languid air deserted her when she saw not a servant but James Boreland standing in the doorway. As he shut the door firmly behind him, she slipped off the bed, her eyes wary. He had exchanged his top-boots for a pair of soft-soled slippers, but apart from that he was still dressed in his muddied travelling clothes. Elinor felt a pang of fear, but when she spoke she tried for a light note.

'What, sir, is the house afire that you must enter in all your dirt?'

'You may well wish that it were!' he growled, advancing towards her. 'What were you planning to do, murder me as you did Julian Poyntz?'

'Faith, sir, I do not understand you!' She spoke calmly, yet her heart was thudding so hard she feared she would faint.

'Oh I think you do! Were you not the mysterious woman who lured Poyntz to his death in a Paris bedroom?'

'Julian Poyntz died of a weak heart.'

'You must have been mighty rough on him, Madame! But how did you plan to dispose of me? A knife between the ribs, perhaps, as poor Rowsell died?'

She turned away from him, hunching a shoulder.

'All this is nonsense. You are talking like a madman.'

'Oh? And what of the ruby?'

'What ruby?'

Boreland strode across to the dressing-table and snatched up the jewel case. He tipped it up, spilling the contents across the tabletop. After a brief glance at the scattered gems he threw down the box with an oath and turned back to Elinor.

'Where is it?'

'Do you think I would be fool enough to bring it here?' Her tone was scathing and she kept her eyes on his face, although she longed to glance towards the mantelshelf. Even in the dim light she could see his anger growing, then he smiled suddenly, which frightened her more than any rage.

'Well, there's no hurry. You will tell me what I want to know, eventually. You've grown into a very beautiful woman, Elinor. I said you would, that night at the inn. Do you remember?'

'No!' She tried to evade his grasp, but his hands caught her wrap and tore it away, leaving her covered only in her shift. Grabbing her wrist, he savagely twisted her arm, sending her crashing back on to the bed, where he threw himself upon her, pinning her beneath him, his hands firmly anchoring her arms above her head. Unable to move, Elinor looked up into his face, just inches from her own, and alight with savage triumph.

'I made the devil's own journey to get back here after Thurleigh told me about you and by God, madam, I intend to be paid in full for my trouble!'

She turned her head away as he tried to kiss her, and instead he buried his face in the thick red-gold tresses of her hair. As she felt his hot breath upon her neck, Elinor shuddered, panic rising within her. *Dear God*, she cried silently, *am I to suffer again at this creature's hands?* Suddenly, as if in answer to her prayer, a voice as cold as steel cut through the room.

'Could not your whoring wait until our guests have departed?'

Boreland raised his head. He was still pinning Elinor to the bed but she could see Isobel Boreland standing in the doorway, stiff with outrage.

'I have never objected to you taking your pleasures in London,' she continued in an icy tone, 'but has it come to this, that you must bring your doxy to the Hall?'

He released Elinor and slowly climbed off the bed.

'A whore she is, ma'am, but not mine! You forget, madam wife, that it was your idea to bring her here! A fine mate you have chosen for our son. The girl came here for mischief. She intended to kill me.'

His lady looked contemptuous.

'Do you expect me to believe that?'

'Believe what you will, madam, 'tis the truth.'

'As to that, we must talk later. There are a dozen people below waiting for dinner. What am I to tell them?'

'Tell them I have but this moment come in, and must needs change.' He looked back at Elinor, who was still upon the bed, raised up on one elbow. 'There is more I need to know from you, Madame de Sange, but it can wait. For now . . .' He bent to scoop up her wrap and shoes which he took over to the dressing-room. He tossed them inside, then shut and locked the door, pocketing the key. 'Just in case she tries to escape,' he told his wife. 'There was a frost on the air even as I rode in and she'll not get very far without shoes or clothes. Now, off you go downstairs and look after our guests, my dear. I will join you as soon as I can.' He shepherded his wife out of the room, and taking the key from the lock he held it up with a last, mocking glance at Elinor.

'We will give your apologies to Mr Tidwell and the others, Madame. Perhaps a period of quiet reflection will help you to realize that it would be better for you to co-operate with me. If you do not . . .' – he shrugged – 'either way I shall get what I want from you.'

He closed the door and she heard the scrape of the key as he turned it. There was the soft pad of retreating footsteps, then silence.

Elinor slid off the bed. She did not try the door, for she knew it would be locked, as was the dressing-room. She took the coverlet off the bed and wrapped it around her. The fire was dying down and without its blaze the room was now very dark. She went to the window and, after a few moments spent fumbling with the catch, she managed to open it. The icy air took her breath away and she pulled the coverlet tighter about her shoulders. It was completely dark now, save for the light of the stars that sparkled in the velvet black sky. It was very still, with no breath of wind to stir the ivy that clung about the window, and it was bitterly cold. Boreland was right, she thought, only a fool would venture out unclothed on such a frosty night.

Elinor closed the window and returned to the fire, what was left of it, and sat down before its glowing embers to consider her situation. From below the sounds of merriment drifted up to her. They would all be at dinner now, she guessed. If her room had overlooked the drive there was a chance that she might have called to the guests as they left and made them aware of her plight, although most likely their host would have told them she was deranged, and not to be taken seriously.

139

She jumped up angrily and paced the room, berating herself for being fool enough to come to Weald Hall. She had never made any plans; what had she expected to achieve? The anger, fear and frustration within her welled up and she threw herself upon the bed, relieving her emotions with a bout of tears and finally falling into an exhausted slumber.

How long she slept Elinor could not be sure, but when she awoke the house was silent and her room was dark save for the starlight that gleamed palely at the window and showed her the barest outlines of her prison. Suddenly she heard a noise outside her door. The key was fitted into the lock and quietly turned. She sat up, ears and eyes straining to know who was there. The door opened quietly and someone entered carrying a single lighted candle in its holder. For a moment she could not see the figure behind the light, but as she recognized her visitor she gave a sigh of relief. 'Andrew!' she whispered. 'What are you doing here?'

'Papa said you were going to run away. He said he had to lock you up to keep you here.'

'And how did you get the key?'

'I took it from Papa,' he said simply, locking the door behind him and dropping the key into his pocket. 'He's asleep downstairs in his chair.'

Although he was dressed for dinner in a black velvet coat and knee-breeches, she observed in the candlelight that his neckband was loosened and his flowered waistcoat unbuttoned, while a few strands of lank brown hair fell across his pallid brow. From his appearance and the strange glitter in his eyes, Elinor guessed that he had been drinking. It seemed most likely that Mr Tidwell and the other guests had already left Weald Hall, for Elinor could not imagine Andrew escaping from his mother's vigilant eye while visitors were present. She thought it must be quite late, and in all probability most of the staff – and their mistress – had now retired, leaving Andrew in his father's care. Elinor saw a glimmer of hope. She spoke softly.

'Will you give me the key, Andrew?'

'Can't do that,' he said, putting the candle down carefully upon the mantelshelf, 'Papa would be angry with me.'

'But he will be angry when he knows you came to see me.'

'He won't know. Shan't tell him.'

'Give me the key,' she coaxed. 'I won't tell on you, you have my word,' she added. 'I thought we were friends.'

'We are. That's why I want you to stay.'

'But surely not if it makes me unhappy!'

'Mama says you are a wicked woman.'

'That's not true, Andrew.'

'She says you never wanted to marry me.'

'I have never told you differently.'

He continued as if she had not spoken. 'Papa says you'll marry me anyway. He'll see to it, and when we are married you will stay here with me for ever. You need not be afraid of me, Elinor. I know how to treat a wife. Papa took me to London once, to a house where there were lots of ladies. He said he wanted me to learn about women and how to please them. . . .'

Elinor suppressed a shudder. At last a plan was forming in her head, and she needed to stay calm.

'What are your parents doing now?'

He shrugged. 'Mama is in her room, I think. Papa is asleep in the library. We had guests for dinner, you know, and Papa drank a lot of wine. He never allows me more than a couple of glasses – and then he told me to go to bed, almost before our guests had gone home.' He giggled. 'That's why I took the key. I'm old enough to decide my own bedtime *and* I shall decide which bed I sleep in!' He moved forward, and as he did so Elinor stepped back, glancing up at the marble bust behind her.

'Yes, of course you are,' she said soothingly. She reached up and took the ruby brooch between her fingers. 'Look, Andrew. I want to show you this.' She held out the brooch. He reached out to take it, but the jewel slipped from her hand. 'Oh how clumsy of me. It's fallen in the ashes. Quickly, Andrew, can you find it?'

The boy stooped, peering into the cooling embers, and as he did so she picked up the marble bust and brought it down upon his skull. He crumpled to the floor without a sound. Fearing she had killed him, Elinor knelt beside the boy and put her hand inside his shirt. With relief she felt the gentle thud, thud of his heart. Satisfied that he was still breathing, she set to work.

CHAPTER FOURTEEN

A flight and a chase

Moving as quickly as her trembling fingers would allow, Elinor stripped Andrew of his clothes. The coat and waistcoat were soon removed, but the shirt proved more difficult, since it had to be pulled up over his head and she was obliged to lift the boy's unexpectedly heavy form in order to complete this operation. At last it was done and she paused for a moment, panting with exertion, before dressing herself in Andrew's clothes. The soft linen shirt covered her easily, the sleeves coming well past the ends of her fingers, but she scarcely gave this a thought, merely pushing them back out of her way as she pulled on the black knee-breeches. As she had hoped, they fitted her quite well, and when she had tucked in the shirt and put on the waistcoat she was not displeased with the result. Her heart sank when she tried on the shoes: they were far too big and would be useless for her needs.

Upon a sudden impulse, she knelt down and stretched out one arm under the bed. With a faint sigh of relief her fingers found a pair of satin slippers that had been pushed out of sight and overlooked by her maid when she had cleared the room. They were not intended to be worn outside the house but, thought Elinor as she put them on, they were better than nothing. Quickly she fastened the buckles of the knee-breeches over her own silk stockings and shrugged on the boy's velvet coat.

Elinor carried the candle to the dressing-table and scooped up her jewellery, dropping it into the capacious pockets of the frock-coat. Looking up, she caught her reflection in the mirror. Forgetting for a moment her predicament, she smiled at the boyish image she presented: she thought the thick curls tumbling about her shoulders rather spoiled the effect, and snatching up a length of ribbon that had been thrown carelessly over one corner of the mirror's frame she tied back her hair.

A door banged somewhere in the house and immediately she forgot her appearance. She must hurry; she had no idea of the time but Andrew could soon be missed, and she wanted to be well clear of the house before anyone realized what had happened. She opened the window and listened intently. There was no sound. Despite her coat, the night air made her shiver and she glanced back at the still form lying by the hearth. With only a second's hesitation she crossed the room, picked up the coverlet that she herself had so recently discarded and dropped it over the boy's near-naked form. The movement disturbed the ash in the fireplace, which rose in a little cloud, settling again around the ruby brooch. Elinor reached out and picked it up, blew away the worst of the ash and pushed it deep into one pocket, then she went back to the window and climbed out into the night.

Elinor felt strangely calm as she eased herself off the window ledge and pushed her feet into the tangled mass of ivy. To fall and break her neck would, she felt, be preferable to remaining in the house and at the mercy of James Boreland. In the silence of the night the rustle of the leaves was very loud and the old thick stems creaked ominously as she made her descent. Slowly she inched her way downwards, trying to spread her weight evenly between her hands and feet.

A brief glance down showed her that she was now no more than ten feet above the terrace. To descend further she would need to move to her right, where the ivy grew up between two of the large ground-floor windows that looked out over the gardens. She put out her right hand, her fingers searching for a strong vine, and when she had found a suitable handhold she carefully eased herself across, moving one careful foot at a time, her toes in the thin slippers probing the ivy for a new support.

Unfortunately for Elinor, where the ivy had been trained upwards there were no lateral boughs and in desperation she tried to wedge her foot between the gnarled and twisted stems that covered the lower walls. Without a proper foothold, her grasp upon the ivy tightened as she struggled to support her weight. Then, with heart-stopping certainty Elinor knew she was going to fall. There was a rustle of leaves and a loud cracking as the ivy came away from the bricks and she dropped the last few feet to the ground.

For a few seconds she lay still, dazed. She felt bruised, but not seriously hurt and, although her own heart was hammering, she could hear no sound from within the house. All the windows on this, the east front, were in darkness but still Elinor quickly moved off the exposed terrace to hide herself amongst the bushes of the formal gardens. There was just enough moonlight to see her way and once she was out of sight of the house she paused. From her riding expeditions, she knew that the house was surrounded on three sides by relatively open parkland that eventually gave way to the fields in use by Boreland's tenant farmers. On the fourth side, the house looked out to the west over the valley along whose winding road she had travelled when she had first come to Weald Hall. The valley itself was exposed, but if she could just get across to the forest on the other side, she would be but a few miles from the main highway.

Having decided that this route offered her the best chance of escape, Elinor lost no time in making her way around the house to the west front. She crept along quietly, keeping as much as possible to the shadows of the bushes and outhouses. At last she could see the sweep of the drive and the parapet, beyond which the ground fell sharply away. To reach it Elinor knew she would have to cross the open lawns.

Praying that no one would be standing at their window at such an hour, she started to run. Without the restriction of her petticoats she felt she was flying across the ground and she was soon at the parapet. Scrambling over the low stone wall she ran on, almost revelling in the freedom of her male attire. The newly risen moon was still too low to light the valley, thus affording her the protection of the shadows, but she had to strain her eyes to see as she slipped and slithered down the grassy slope. The cold air played upon her bare hands and face, chilling her skin, but she scarcely noticed.

Nearing the bottom of the valley her ears could detect the sound of running water. and she was soon standing beside a small stream. She turned and walked along the bank, her eyes searching for a crossing. She was in luck, coming soon to a place where a few large rocks had been tumbled into the water to make a series of rough stepping-stones. It took her but a few seconds to cross and then she began the steady climb up to the wall of trees that stood tall and silent above her.

The exertion warmed her and by the time she reached the cover of the woods she could feel the warm glow in her cheeks. In contrast, the cold air rasped in her throat and she threw herself down upon the ground, leaning back against a tree-trunk while she regained her breath. It was dark under the trees, the moonlight barely penetrating the thick canopy. Keeping within the shadow of the trees, she looked back across the valley. She could clearly see Weald Hall standing black against the sky, but even though the moon was higher now the valley was still deep in shadow. She froze. There was movement, surely, amongst the shadows surrounding the house. She could not quite see the menace but her ears confirmed her worst fears. The baying of hounds came clearly to her; they were in the valley, and there could be only one quarry that James Boreland would pursue at such a time – herself.

Elinor turned back into the forest and set off between the trees. She made slow progress, for she was hampered by the undergrowth that covered the forest floor. She felt she was in a nightmare, slowly pushing her way through a dense tangle of leaves, constantly tripping over roots and branches she could not see. Ahead of her she thought the blackness was less intense and with a sob of relief she came upon a rough track. She guessed it was the same lane she had travelled to reach the Hall and if so, then it would lead her to the Great North Road and, she hoped, to some village where she could find shelter. With renewed energy she set off at a steady pace, while at her back the baying of the hounds drew ever nearer. The sharp stones cut through the thin soles of her slippers and her toes ached with cold, but she kept moving, the sound of the hunt providing a spur to her aching limbs. She must cover as much ground as possible, for she knew that once her pursuers reached this track they would soon overtake her.

She ran on for what seemed like hours, each breath of raw cold air burning her throat, but she dared not stop. The sounds of pursuit were rapidly increasing, and she guessed that they had now reached the lane. She thought she could hear shouting amidst the hounds' cries and tried desperately to quicken her pace. She stumbled and fell, a faint cry of frustration escaping her as she scrambled to her feet. A quick glance showed her that the hounds were in sight: she made out their white coats showing as grey smudges in the darkness behind her. She ran on, blind panic threatening to overwhelm her senses. On each side the trees stood in black unbroken ranks, ahead lay only darkness. There were no lights to be seen, no signs of a house or building to offer her protection. In another few moments the dogs would be upon her – she had no illusions, they would tear her apart as they would any other hunted animal.

Out upon the Great North Road, there was but one solitary traveller. A horseman, dressed all in black, from the plain tricorn pulled low over his eyes to the tips of his muddied riding-boots. His mount was also as dark as the night and since they kept to the side of the road where the stones gave way to mud and grass, the horse's hoofs made very little sound, so that anyone chancing to see them could be forgiven for thinking he had stumbled upon some ghostly shadow of the night, and could certainly not be blamed for turning about and making haste to depart from such an unnatural sight. In fact the traveller's reason for keeping his horse to the soft grass verge was quite simple: despite his relaxed style in the saddle, the gentleman's senses were ever alert to the sounds around him. If his ears detected the rattle of a coach, or the clatter of hoofs on the road, he would turn his horse and they would melt into the darkness of the trees that skirted the highway. However, apart from the sudden rustle of the bushes as they disturbed some animal at the roadside and the scream of a fox somewhere in the woods, there was little to interest the gentleman. He sighed and reached out with one gloved hand to smooth the glossy neck before him.

'Well, Devon, we may as well head for home.' The animal's ears twitched at the sound of the deep, familiar voice. 'Business is very quiet. Just one coach tonight, and that yielded little more than a slim purse and a battered watch!' The horse snorted, drawing a soft laugh from his rider. 'So you didn't like my giving the old fellow back his timepiece, eh, Devon? Well, 'tis Christmas, when all's said and done, and never let it be said that Ralph Belham has lost all Christian feeling! Besides, it would have fetched very little at the fencing-crib. And what a story he will have to tell his cronies! Well, come up, lad! We'll leave it at that and get you back to that warm stable!'

He set his horse to the trot, untroubled by the darkness, for both horse and rider were very familiar with this stretch of the highway. After a few minutes they slowed again, this time the rider bringing his mount to a complete stop. The horse stood with ears pricked, snorting nervously.

'So you hear it too, do you? Hounds at this time o' night? Let's take a look.' He turned Devon off the main road, picking a path through the trees with scant regard for the darkness that would hamper a man less familiar with the territory. The baying of the hounds grew louder, confirming his direction, and he rode on, intrigued.

Elinor's lungs were at bursting point. Terror kept her moving, but she knew it was only a matter of minutes now before they caught her. Suddenly, a large shape broke away from the shadows just ahead and blocked her path. Unable to stop in time, she cannoned into the shape and found herself pressed against the warm flank of a horse. Her senses reeled, her first thought was that James Boreland had in some way overtaken her, and it was with relief that she heard the cheerful voice of a stranger.

'Here, lad, take my hand.' The rider reached down to her. 'We'll make the odds a little fairer!'

Without hesitating, Elinor took the gloved hand, then placing her foot upon the toe of the rider's boot she allowed him to pull her up so that she could scramble up behind him. There were shouts from her pursuers, and calls for them to stand, but the rider only laughed as he turned his horse and set it cantering away. There was a shot, then another, and Elinor clung even more tightly to her rescuer.

'Don't worry, boy, they'll never hit us at this range, and in the dark, too. Just hold on and we'll soon have you safe and sound.'

He settled the horse into a steady canter and they rode on, the stranger whistling nonchalantly into the darkness, while Elinor clung on behind him, her head resting wearily against the rough cloth of his greatcoat. She had no idea how long they travelled, nor in which direction. They crossed roads and fields and splashed through numerous icy streams, the sure-footed steed never once stumbling over the frosty ground. Now that she was no longer active, the cold air pierced the velvet coat and thin knee-breeches that were Elinor's only protection against the elements and she tensed her tired limbs to prevent herself from shivering. She kept her head down, sheltering her face behind the broad shoulders of the rider, but she could do nothing to prevent the cold wind biting into her bare hands, which were clasped around his body.

At last the pace changed and they slowed to a walk, then to a complete stand.

'It's time we gave old Devon a rest. You can be sure we've lost those hounds now. Jump down, lad, and we'll walk a little.'

Elinor slid to the ground, but as her feet touched the ground she feared that her numbed limbs would not support her and she clung to the saddle cloth to prevent herself from falling. The rider dismounted and came to stand beside her.

'Now, what's this, are you hurt?'

'No, it – it's only the cold.'

Her companion paused, then taking her by the shoulders he pulled her into the moonlight, staring hard into her face. He whistled softly.

'Why, 'fore Gad, 'tis a wench!' His eyes appraised her, and

from the depths of his thick beard she caught the gleam of his white teeth as he smiled. 'A fair dainty one at that, too, I'd wager! Why in heaven's name – but we can talk later,' he said briskly, as he felt her body shivering beneath his hands. 'The first thing to be done is to set you before a warm fire! Come on, Devon's rest will have to wait!'

Without ceremony he threw her back into the saddle. She sat astride the great horse, her rescuer smiling up at her.

'There now, are you comfortable? Good. I'll lead you for a while. Just try not to fall off.'

Elinor gave a tired smile.

'I'm not in the habit of falling off horses, sir.'

He laughed. 'That's the spirit!'

'What is your name, sir?'

He stopped, took off his hat and made her a flourishing bow.

'I am Ralph Belham, at your service, ma'am!'

'I am *very* pleased to meet you, Mr Belham.'

'And you, ma'am, do you have a name?'

Elinor shook her head.

'No, I beg you will let me keep my name a secret a little longer. I promise to explain everything later.'

'Very well, and I look forward to the explanation!'

They set off again, the gentleman leading his horse along the easiest course while Elinor concentrated on staying in the saddle. She had never used a man's saddle before, and it took her a little while to get comfortable, but once she was accustomed to her mount she found it difficult to stay awake. They had travelled about a mile when Belham, glancing up, saw Elinor swaying dangerously.

'Sit forward,' he commanded, climbing into the saddle. 'Poor child, your hands are so icy you can hold nothing! Swing your leg across – that's it,' He settled Elinor before him, sitting her across the saddle and cradling her in the crook of one arm. 'I cannot trust you to sit up behind me, you are so chilled that before we knew it we should have you sliding off and cracking your head upon the ground! Much better that I should have you here, where I can look after you.'

Elinor was too tired to protest.

'You are very kind,' she murmured.

'Kind!' he laughed. 'Aye, call it that if you will, my dear, but when I rescue a comely lass I expect my reward! Let's get you back to my quarters, where we can warm you with a hearty meal and a good fire, then we'll see how grateful you can be. What do you say to that?'

Receiving no response, he glanced down at his charge. Her head was resting against his chest, the face turned in towards him, yet even so he could make out the dark lashes lying upon her pale cheek. She was asleep.

When Elinor awoke she lay very still, unwilling to shake off her sleepy comfort. She opened her eyes and looked up at the pattern of blackened roof beams; although she recognized nothing of her surroundings, Elinor felt strangely calm and untroubled. Without moving her head from the soft pillows she looked about her.

The steep pitch of the roof and roughly plastered walls made her think the building was a cottage, or perhaps a farmhouse. She guessed it must be night, for the room was lit only by the fire that blazed high in the large open hearth at one end of the room, causing the shadows to dance upon the ceiling and walls. Wooden shutters were tightly closed across the windows, which were set low under eaves that came nearly to the floor. The room was sparsely furnished: a small chest beside the bed, a cupboard in one corner and a small round table.

Shifting her gaze to the fire, Elinor could see beside the hearth two wooden chairs, in one of which sat a large, bearded man, smoking a pipe. There was something familiar about him, but she felt too tired to search her mind and was content to lie still and watch him. He wore no coat, and the sleeveless waistcoat over his loose shirt was unbuttoned. His legs were encased in buckskins, and his feet in their shining black riding-boots were stretched out before him. He had thick, dark hair held back by a thin ribbon, but for all his casual dress he looked to be no farmer. As if aware of her scrutiny, he turned his head towards her and seeing she was awake, he laid his pipe upon the hearth and rose from his chair.

'So you have come to life at last!' He spoke in a deep, mellow voice and smiled as he came up to her. He leaned over and rested a hand gently upon her brow. 'No fever now. That's good. Are you thirsty?' He picked up a cup from beside the bed and held it before her, deftly slipping his free hand behind her shoulders to help her to rise. His smile grew as he saw her eye the glass suspiciously.

'It's only barley water. Megs made it up for you.'

'Megs?'

'Mistress Carew, the landlady.'

He helped her to drink and when she had done he laid her gently back against the pillows.

'There now, would you like some food?'

'Thank you, no. I would like to talk.'

'Very well.' He sat down on the bed. 'What would you like to talk about?'

'Where am I? And who are you?'

'You are at the Green Dragon, a small inn a few miles from Hoddesdon. It's well off the main roads and our host, Jem Carew, helps his brother with the neighbouring farm. Out of necessity, I daresay, for the inn itself would scarce support him and his wife.'

'And you?'

'Ralph Belham. I introduced myself to you upon the road, but doubtless it has slipped your mind.'

Elinor continued to stare blankly at him.

'Why am I here?'

'Can you not remember?'

She stirred uncomfortably in the bed.

'I'm not sure. There are dreams – nightmares. . . .'

'Aye, 'tis often so with these cases,' he murmured, almost to himself. He smiled at her again. 'I came upon you in a lane close to the London road. I was hidden in the trees, having come to see who could be making such a devil of a commotion!'

'Yes, I remember – the dogs.' Elinor closed her eyes, shuddering. 'They were almost upon me. . . .'

'Aye, you should be thankful they were leashed, or you would not be here now!' he told her grimly.

Elinor stared up at the blackened rafters, a faint crease between her brows. She felt very tired, her powers of reasoning frustratingly slow.

'Don't try to think too much now.' His voice seemed to be drawing away from her. 'You need to sleep.'

'Yes.' She closed her eyes. 'I think I do.'

When Elinor woke again the room was much brighter. The shutters had been removed from the windows to allow the daylight into the room. A good fire still crackled in the hearth, but the chairs beside it were now empty. She was alone. She lay still, trying to piece together the hazy memories that seemed to float around in her head, defying her to put them into order. She recalled waking to find the bearded man smiling down at her, what had he said was his name? Belham. Ralph Belham. She was pleased to find her thoughts were more coherent. She could also remember a woman being in the room at times, a round, rosy-cheeked woman in a snow-white cap, who had wiped her brow and given her a soothing draught to help her sleep, but she could not be sure – perhaps it was a dream. The noise at the door made her turn her head and she saw the bearded gentleman entering the room.

'Well, ma'am! You are looking a deal better this morning,' he told her, coming over to the bed. 'There's more colour in your cheeks today.'

'How long have I been here?'

'Four days – don't look so shocked, lady! When I brought you in you were so cold that our good landlady despaired of saving you. However, thanks to her ministrations you seem to have survived.'

'Who – who put me to bed?'

'Mistress Carew, of course! She stripped you, washed off the dirt and provided one of her own night-gowns for you to wear.' He grinned and added teasingly, 'Not that you'd have known, had it been the King himself tending you! Rest easy, child. I am here as nursemaid, nothing more. Megs has much to attend to and once it was clear you were out of danger I agreed to stay with you and allow her to return to her housework. You have been delirious, you know, and it was not safe to leave you unattended.'

'Did – did I say a great deal?'

He shook his head.

153

'Little of any worth, although I am curious to know your history. But you need not worry yourself with that just yet. Your health is the first consideration.'

'It seems I owe you a great deal, Mr Belham.'

'Call me Ralph – it would seem in order, since you are in my bed.' The quizzical gleam in his eyes changed to a look of surprise. 'Faith, madam, I was speaking in jest!' He frowned as he saw the terror in her eyes, and he stepped back a little, murmuring, 'Poor child, I'd wager you have suffered at some man's hands, am I right?' When she did not answer him he continued. 'Think, child! If I had wanted to take you I could have done so any time during these past four days! You must learn to trust me, my dear.'

He knelt beside the bed, holding out a hand to her. Silently she gave him her own, and he squeezed it gently. 'You need have no fears for your safety, ma'am. It is not my way to take advantage of a lady in your circumstances. I have no designs upon your virtue. At least, not yet!' he added with a grin.

Elinor was surprised to find his improper speech did not shock her, rather it allayed her fears and she found herself smiling back at him.

'I should hope not, sir!'

Ralph Belham seated himself upon the edge of the bed, saying gently, 'Will you tell me your name? I cannot call you "madam" for ever!'

She hesitated, her fingers nervously plucking at the coverlet.

'Elinor.'

'Just Elinor?' He picked up her left hand, glanced at her wedding ring and looked an enquiry.

'I am a widow,' she said quietly, withdrawing her hand.

'Well, that is some relief. At least we shall not have an irate husband to deal with. Would you like to tell me why you were abroad in the middle of the night, dressed as a boy and pursued by a hunt in full cry?'

For a full minute Elinor lay staring up at him, a speculative look in her green eyes.

'I – I was escaping from a man who thought I would destroy him.'

'You were on Boreland's land.'

She nodded.

He – he had imprisoned me in his house and – I think he would have killed me, had I not run away.'

'From what I know of the man I can well believe it. But if that is so, why did he not order his men to loose the dogs? They would have made short work of you.'

'He – I think he wants information from me . . . in fact – where are my clothes?'

'They are safely stored away in the cupboard. And while we are on the subject, why the boy's clothes?'

The question brought a faint flush to Elinor's pale cheek, and the hint of a smile to her eyes.

'I had nothing else to wear. It was far too cold to venture out without some protection, so I took what I could find.'

He grinned down at her. 'And mighty fetching you looked too, my dear. But I don't doubt you would like something a little more feminine once you are on your feet again. I've asked Megs to see to it – you can trust her to provide you with all you need.'

'Th-thank you,' she stammered. 'You are very kind – but I cannot stay here. . . .'

'Well, I think for the moment you have little choice. If James Boreland is looking for you it is most probable that his men are still scouring the countryside and watching the roads, too, I don't doubt. He's not a man to give up easily. It would be best for you to lie low for a while and get your strength back, then we can decide what's to be done with you.' He rose. 'Now, I'll go and find Megs and tell her to bring you some food. Oh – one thing more. Since you are loath to disclose your identity, I think it would be a good idea to adopt a new name. Megs will want to call you something: will Mistress Brown do? Not very inventive, but it will suffice, I think.'

'Yes. As you wish.'

She watched him go out. She felt too weary even to think properly. It was only a few minutes before the door opened again, this time to admit the landlady, carrying a tray. Elinor remembered seeing her face, the ruddy cheeks and kind eyes, during the more lucid moments of the past few days, and she smiled shyly at her hostess.

'Well, my dear, it's good to see you looking so much better!' Mistress Carew set down her tray and helped Elinor to sit up, arranging her pillows behind her and saying as she did so, 'Master Ralph said you was awake, so I've brought you a little broth, and some chicken too. Do you think that you can manage to eat just a little of it? You need to build up your strength, you know, for you have not eaten for quite a time!'

'I'll try to do justice to it,' murmured Elinor as the tray was placed down before her.

'Well, I'll just sit here while you do.' The landlady drew up a chair. 'There's little pleasure in eating alone.' She smiled as she watched Elinor spooning up the broth. 'I admit I didn't think to see this. When I first saw you I thought we'd never save you, and that's a fact! Chilled to the bone, you were, and so pale I thought you was past hope, but Master Ralph carried you in and we got you to bed, popped a couple of hot bricks between the sheets to help warm you and I do think that between the two of us we didn't do such a bad job of bringing you round.

'Not that I liked the idea when Master Ralph said you was to have his room, for anyone could see that you was a lady, and we don't cater for the Quality, but he said you had to be hidden away, in case they came looking for you, and he was right, too, for only yesterday my Jem found a rascally fellow snooping around the bedrooms. Said he'd lost his way, but Jem soon sent him packing!'

'S-someone has been looking for me?'

'Now don't you fret yourself over it, Mistress Brown. Haven't I just told you that you are as safe as anything here? You just finish your food like a good girl.'

'You are very kind – you know nothing about me.'

'It's enough that Master Ralph has befriended you, ma'am.'

'But you could be in trouble if I am discovered here.'

She was surprised to hear the landlady chuckle.

'We should be in a great deal more trouble if 'twas found that Ralph Belham lives here!' she said, rising. 'Now, you've done very well but I can see that you're not going to eat any more, so I'll take these dishes away and leave you to get some rest.'

'Why *does* Mr Belham live here, in hiding?' asked Elinor.

Mrs Carew stopped in the doorway.

'Lord love you, do you not know? Well, then, it's not for me to say. You'd best ask him – he'll tell you, an he wishes it!'

CHAPTER FIFTEEN

Madame de Sange finds a friend

For a long while after the landlady had departed Elinor lay back upon her pillows, considering her situation. Her recollection of events since her flight from Weald Hall was incomplete and touched with a dreamlike quality that refused to be dispelled. Elinor summoned her strength to get out of bed. The effort of standing made her pause, her legs feeling weak, and she stumbled shakily across to the large oak cupboard. She pulled open the doors. It was filled with clothing, a couple of black, three-cornered hats on the top shelf, and an assortment of shirts, waistcoats and coats neatly arranged below. It took her some time to find what she was looking for but at last with a sigh of relief she spotted the black velvet jacket and knee-breeches that she had taken from Andrew Boreland. They had been brushed and folded and put away in one corner of the cupboard. Elinor pulled out the jacket and reached her hand into one of the pockets. It was empty. Quickly her trembling fingers searched the other pocket, that too held nothing.

'Is this what you are looking for?'

The voice behind her made her turn sharply, a startled look in her green eyes. Ralph Belham was standing in the doorway, holding a small leather pouch from which he pulled one of her necklaces.

'Megs found them when she was cleaning your coat. Is this the reason you were being hounded?'

'I did not steal them.'

'That does not answer my question.' He walked to the table and tipped the contents out of the bag; it was all the jewellery she had swept into the coat pocket when she left Weald Hall, and in the centre was the ruby brooch. She reached out her hand but Ralph was quicker, snatching up the ruby. 'Well?'

'Very well – yes. The rest is my own jewellery, but I believe this one, the ruby, is what Boreland wanted of me.'

Belham studied the brooch with renewed interest.

'Is it so valuable then? 'Tis a handsome gem, undoubtedly, but the setting. . . .' He shook his head. 'Too elaborate for my taste, and too large for the stone.'

'Please give it to me.'

He eyed her speculatively.

'Why not let me sell it for you? I can get you a good price, and we can split the money . . .' He stopped and laughed at her. 'Don't look like that, child. I'm only teasing you! Here, have your trinket. Will you tell me what makes it so important to you?'

Elinor looked into his face, and was surprised to see the gentleness and sympathy in those brown eyes. She looked away, confused. It was so long since she had trusted anyone.

'No – that is, not yet! I – I cannot!'

'Pray, then, do not upset yourself. It can wait, but there is a matter that I must discuss with you.' He picked up a shawl from the bed. 'Here, put this around you and come and sit by the fire. There. Are you comfortable?'

'Yes, thank you. What is it you wish to say?'

'We must come to some arrangement about this room.'

'The matter is easily solved.' She smiled faintly. 'Now that I am recovered, I shall be on my way.'

'It is not going to be quite that simple, Elinor. James Boreland is a dangerous enemy. I have already said that I do not doubt he is still looking for you, so you would be advised to remain out of sight for a little longer.'

'But there is my house to consider! I must advise Hannah, my companion. She needs to know that I am well, and – and I must warn her, for he may search for me there!'

'Undoubtedly he will do so. I think it could be arranged that a note is sent to your home, but it need not disclose your present location. You are not yet recovered sufficiently to fend for yourself, so I suggest you remain here, where you need not worry about being discovered, until we can decide what's to be done with you.'

'But this is your room. I could not possibly—'

'My dear child, I do not live here permanently, and when it is necessary for me to be here, I can quite easily make do with a truckle bed somewhere.' He grinned, his eyes twinkling. 'You will have noticed that there is but one bed in this room and I don't suppose you would like to. . . ? No, I can see the idea does not find favour with you! To be serious, for the present we need to keep you hidden away, but my activities make it necessary for me to use this room occasionally – with your permission, of course, ma'am! I shall do my utmost not to inconvenience you.'

'And just what are your – er – *activities*, Mr Belham?'

He grinned at her. 'Have you not guessed? I work the high toby. I'm a prigger. A *highwayman!*'

If Ralph Belham expected to shock her he was disappointed. Elinor's brows rose fractionally in surprise, then she chuckled.

'And I was afraid you might think I had stolen the blood stone! No wonder you want to sell if for me.'

'Blood stone? Why do you call it that?'

She did not answer immediately, but stared at the brooch, turning it between her fingers so that the ruby glowed in the firelight.

'It came into my possession following a series of – of tragic events,' she said at last, her eyes still fixed upon the ruby. 'It reminds me of the blood that was shed – that must be repaid.'

'If Boreland is involved you had best leave well alone, Elinor,' he advised her, and earned for his trouble a scornful glance.

'I have no intention of giving up now, I will have vengeance.'

Belham shrugged. 'Well, 'tis no business of mine.'

She gave him a rueful smile.

'Very true, but let us return to your business. Why is it so important that you use this room?'

'Because it has a secret stairway set into one side of the

chimney, that leads directly to the stables. It means I can come and go from here without anyone knowing. Very useful for one in my line of business. Would it disturb you if I continue to use those stairs? If you do not trust me, I will let you have one of my pistols to protect yourself.'

Elinor laughed; odd, she thought, that she felt so at ease with this man!

'That will not be necessary. I am so much in your debt that I cannot refuse to help you in this little way.'

'Good.' He rose. 'You look tired. I won't detain you any longer, my dear. You should rest.' He put a hand on her shoulder as he passed her chair. 'Don't worry, Elinor. Megs will look after you while you are here. You will be perfectly safe.'

'Thank you. But – you said you could get a message to my servant?'

'Certainly, although to do that you must tell me your name, do you not agree?'

Elinor sighed.

'I must do so. After all, it would be a simple matter for you to discover it, would it not, once I give you my direction.'

'Good. I will have paper and pens sent up. Write a brief note, tell me the direction and I will see to it all.'

'Thank you, Mr Belham.'

'Ralph.'

'Thank you. Ralph.'

When he had gone, she remained by the fire, a faint smile still playing about her mouth. She felt strangely at peace, and was surprised to find she was not at all concerned to be sharing her room with a highwayman. Her amusement deepened as she thought about her rescuer. What an odd man he was! A gentleman, to be sure, even if he now lived on the wrong side of the law! Mistress Carew obviously idolized *Master Ralph* as she called him and Elinor wondered if the landlady knew anything of his earlier life. She made up her mind to question her hostess at some suitable moment, but for the present she must turn her mind to what she could put in her note to Hannah. Poor Hannah! How shocked she would be when she learned of her mistress's adventures, although for the present it must suffice her to know that she was safe: explanations could come later.

The following day was market day and Mistress Carew returned to the inn laden with packages which she took up to Elinor. There were two gowns, one in green calamanco, the other a grey silk with a quilted petticoat, which she laid out upon the bed for Elinor's inspection.

'I'm sorry they are so countrified,' she apologized as she shook out the dresses, 'They aren't what you are used to, I'm sure, but I didn't want to draw attention to myself by buying anything too fancy. I had to guess your size, ma'am, too, and looking at you now I think we're going to have to take a little bit out of the waist of the calamanco, but if you'll just try it on, I'll have it altered in a trice.'

'They are just what I need,' Elinor assured her, 'I shall be pleased to be able to wear something other than your night-gowns! And as for style, I should look very out of place here wearing London fashions, besides being most uncomfortable. These will suit me perfectly. Thank you, Mistress Carew. I would not have chosen differently myself!'

That dame flushed deeply at this praise.

'Well, I don't think you'll look too badly in them, ma'am. There's some flannel petticoats and everything else I could think of that you might need in the last parcel.'

'You must let me know how much all this has cost you.'

'Oh, but I haven't paid for a thing!' replied the landlady, puzzled. 'Master Ralph gave me your purse and told me to take what I needed – did he not tell you he had done so?'

'What? Oh – oh yes,' returned Elinor, making a mental note to speak to Master Ralph later. 'I had forgotten all about that.'

She had no chance to speak to him during the day, but the idea that Ralph Belham had bought her clothes disturbed her thoughts so much that she lay awake that night long after the fire had burned down, and consequently her ears caught the muffled sound of footsteps coming softly up the stairs, followed by a faint click and the whisper of the wall panel opening upon its near-silent hinges.

Daring to peep out, she saw a greatcoated figure with a lantern crossing the room. It must be Ralph, she thought, but even so she lay very still, the blankets pulled well up over her face. As he came to the foot of the bed he stopped and she shut her eyes, pretending to be asleep, but her body was rigid with fear. After a few seconds, the figure moved on, out of the door and down the stairs to the main part of the inn.

Elinor's opportunity to speak to her benefactor came the following day when she received a message that Master Ralph considered it would be safe for her to take a little walk, since the road was clear of strangers and the sun was making a brief appearance. Glad to quit her room, even for a short period, Elinor emerged from the inn, a warm scarlet cloak about her shoulders and her feet enclosed in serviceable but clumsy wooden clogs. She found Mr Belham waiting for her and smiled at the look of surprise upon his countenance when he beheld her.

'Did you expect to see me in a hoop and silver lace, sir? I fear you are disappointed.'

'Not at all, ma'am. The country style becomes you admirably.' Taking her hand upon his arm Ralph led her along the lane away from the inn. 'Tell me if I go too fast. I do not wish to overtax your strength.'

'No, I shall go on very well. In fact, I am glad of this opportunity to speak to you – about these clothes. Mistress Carew thinks – that is, the money . . .'

'Megs told you I had found your purse, and we both know you had no money with you,' he said helpfully.

'But it is not right that you should buy my clothes,' she murmured, her cheeks hot.

'No, of course not, and knowing that that is just how Mistress Carew would look at the matter, I decided it would be best to tell her it was your own money and save any embarrassment.'

'Yes, of course. I would not for the world upset our hostess, but that does not mean I can allow you to keep me. You can sell some of my jewellery!'

The gentleman looked amused.

'Of course I could, an I needed to! Calm yourself, Elinor. Why will you not let me help you?'

'I – I do not wish to be in your debt.'

'Then you may look upon my assistance in this matter as a loan. When it is safe for you to return to your proper station, I shall of course expect to be repaid.'

'And you shall be, sir. Every penny!'

He stopped. 'My dear, there is no need to be so vehement. Lovely as you look with that angry flush upon your cheek, and the sparkle in your eye, I would prefer to have you smile upon me!'

For a full minute she struggled with herself. Anger and indignation warred with her sense of humour, but at last the humour won and she laughed, not the affected trill of a light-heart, he noticed, but a low, melodious sound, full of warmth.

'You do well to mock me, Mr Belham. In recent days so much has happened to me that to fall out with you over a few shillings would be absurd and very ungrateful too, but from an early age I have tried always to pay my debts, not to be beholden to anyone. I fear it has become something of an obsession with me.'

He glanced down at her, intrigued again by the repressed passion in her voice. He said gently, 'I would like to hear your history, Elinor, an you would allow it.'

Her gaze flew to his face: he saw again the fear in her sea-green eyes before the thick lashes concealed her thoughts from him.

'Perhaps sir, I will tell you, in time, but it is no tale with which to sully such a beautiful winter's day! Tell me instead if your messenger has yet returned from Knight's Bridge.'

Belham shook his head. 'I do not expect him before tomorrow. When he has delivered your note he is to go into Town for me, to learn what news there is. I have heard rumours that the French are poised to invade in a fresh attempt to set the Stuart back on the throne and I shall be interested to know what is being said in the coffee-houses. These matters are rarely without some substance.'

Elinor shrugged. 'It is always in someone's interest to keep the pot boiling. But what shall you do today?' she asked, suddenly changing the subject. 'Will you try your luck upon the – the high toby?'

'Madam, I beg you!' cried he, feigning horror. 'Such cant

terms upon your lips! But no, I do not go out tonight. I fear Devon may have strained a fetlock – nothing serious, but I'm going to let him rest for a day or two. Normally I would have returned home, but I thought perhaps you might care for a little company this evening.' He sketched a bow. 'Mistress Elinor, would you do me the honour of dining with me tonight?'

The lady responded immediately with a curtsy. 'I should be delighted, sir. A little company is never unwelcome.'

'Good. However – pardon the indelicacy, ma'am – I must beg permission to use your room for the occasion, since I fear 'twould be tempting Providence for us to use the private parlour downstairs.'

'But of course!' She stepped back to make him a most regal curtsy. 'Pray consider my room as your own, sir, and make such arrangements as are necessary.'

He caught her fingers and raised them to his lips.

'I vow 'tis an honour to have your acquaintance! I shall instruct Mistress Carew to prepare dinner, and shall wait upon you at four o'clock!'

'You are looking very well, ma'am, if I may say so!' Mistress Carew arranged a white kerchief about Elinor's shoulders and stood back to admire the effect. 'That walk today has done you the power of good, for it has put the roses back in your cheeks, that it has! Now, I must be off downstairs to see how Becky's doing in the kitchen – my daughter's a good girl, ma'am, but she needs watching if we're not to have burnt offerings for dinner! I'll send her up later, ma'am, if you're agreeable, and she can build up the fire and set the table for you, so that you and Master Ralph can enjoy your dinner in comfort.'

'Megs?' Elinor did not look up from adjusting the sleeves of her grey-silk gown. 'You do not think it – wrong – that I should be having dinner here, alone, with Mr Belham?'

Mistress Carew looked at her blankly for a few moments, before bursting forth in merry laughter. 'Bless me, no my dear!' she said, when she could at last command her voice. 'Master Ralph has told me how important it is that we keep you out of sight here, and I can quite see that it would be impossible for you to use the private parlour, for you never know who might just happen to glance in at the window, or come into the inn and discover you! I'm a good, Christian woman, madam, never doubt it, but I don't see as having dinner with Master Ralph will do you much harm. In fact it's more likely to help you, for mayhap you'll eat a little more if there's someone to keep you company, for it's precious little you've been taking up to now. Hardly enough to keep a bird alive! And another thing,' continued the good woman, in a much more serious tone, 'if it keeps the master indoors for a night it will be a blessing, for I don't mind telling you, Mistress Brown, that I worry about him when he's out o' nights, for he's no need to do it, as I've told him often and often, and it'll be Tyburn Tree for him if he's caught, and no mistake!'

With this dark warning, the landlady retired, shaking her head.

CHAPTER SIXTEEN

A chapter of histories

At precisely four of the clock, Ralph Belham arrived at Elinor's room. He had done justice to the occasion by donning his best suit of plum-coloured velvet, the coat and waistcoat embellished with silver buttons and silver lacing. A froth of white lace adorned what was visible of his shirt above the waistcoat, and there were matching ruffles at his wrists. His hair was held back by a silver buckle and, for the first time, she noticed the streaks of silver in his dark hair. A dress sword hung by his side and a cocked hat was tucked under one arm, completing the picture. Elinor was impressed.

'If I had known it was to be such a grand occasion, I should have had my dressmaker send me a new gown, sir!' She smiled, giving him her hand.

'You look charming,' he assured her, kissing her fingers. He grinned ruefully. 'It is unfortunate that however fine my own dress, my beard ruins the effect by giving me such a piratical appearance!'

Elinor laughed, pleased to find that his words had effectively dispelled the nervousness she was experiencing. The wine was already opened and awaiting them at the table. Ralph escorted Elinor to her seat and filled her glass, and a few moments later Mistress Carew and her daughter entered carrying trays laden with dishes. Some were set out upon the table, others were arranged upon a side table brought in for the purpose, and after checking that everything was to their satisfaction, the landlady followed Becky to the door, pausing only to instruct the diners to enjoy themselves.

They took their time selecting from the array of dishes. There was roasted fowl, a glazed ham and spiced brisket with a rabbit fricassee keeping warm in a large covered pot beside the fire. Turnips and carrots tossed in butter glistened in the candlelight and on the side table a plum-pudding, apple-pie and a large jug of cream awaited their attention. There was no servant to wait upon them, the landlord requiring all his staff in the taproom and kitchen during the evening, but the diners did not consider this a disadvantage; in fact, as the meal progressed, Elinor was surprised to find herself relaxing and conversing with Ralph with the easy intimacy of an old friend.

'Will you tell me about your life?' she asked, as he refilled her glass.

'There is little to tell. I am the younger son of a very respectable family in Warwickshire. My father owned a small estate there, and he wanted me as a younger son to become a parson. Can you imagine a worse profession for me? Having no taste for the religious life, I went to London where a brief spell of high living soon disposed of my allowance. In an effort to recoup some of my losses, I turned to highway robbery. I worked on the notorious Hounslow Heath for a while, quite successfully! I found the excitement suited me so well that I decided to settle into a regular way of life as a highwayman.'

'Why did you come here?' she asked, intrigued by the unconcerned manner in which he spoke of his illegal activities. They had finished their meal, and Elinor sat with her elbows upon the table, resting her chin upon her clasped hands.

'Hounslow is by far too dangerous to work for long.' Ralph leaned back in his chair, studying the wine in his glass. 'Almost every coach upon that road has outriders, or an extra guard. The risks are too great. Besides, one cannot spend every night upon the road. I assist the vicar of Hoddesdon in the running of his charity school there. The pay is meagre, but sufficient for a gentleman down on his luck, and I have lodgings adjoining the school, so I am free to come and go very much as I please, except for a few hours' teaching.'

'But surely your frequent absences are remarked?'

'I put it about that I have a widowed mother living nearby, so no one questions my movements.' He laughed suddenly, a hearty, lively laugh, full of energy. 'Doubtless they think me a most devoted son! I have a broken old nag that suits my schoolmaster image perfectly, and Jem takes care of Devon for me here. With a little cross-country riding I can work any of the northern roads out of the capital, and with much less chance of getting caught. Do I shock you?'

'No, but I am curious to know why you do it.'

'Oh, for the adventure, mostly. Don't worry, I haven't harmed anyone yet – frightened a few, I don't doubt! No, I take a few gewgaws, or a purse, just sufficient to keep me in comfort. Jem and Megs don't really approve, but they say very little about it and if I suggest that it would be safer for me to move out, Megs won't hear of it. I think she's quite attached to me, in her own way.'

'I am sure of it,' smiled Elinor, 'for she is always talking of Master Ralph! But what of your family – have you no wish to see them? Surely your father would make you an allowance.'

'Doubtless he would, an I would be a dutiful son, but there's the rub! I prefer to go my own way, and after so many years I'm too old to change now! Don't look so troubled, sweetheart, there is very little love lost in my family. I daresay they are all the better for my absence.'

'But your mother – or – surely there must be someone you care for, some lady you once loved?'

'My mother died when I was a child, and as for the ladies. . . .' He threw back his head and gave a loud, merry laugh. 'Aye, I've loved a few in my time, but never seriously! That's the secret, Elinor, care for nobody, 'tis the only way to survive. Once you allow yourself to become a victim of the tender passion you are lost, you become vulnerable. But perhaps you would care to argue the point with me?'

She shook her head. 'No, I think you are right, for that is how I too have survived.' Before she could continue, there was a scratching upon the door and Mistress Carew came in.

'If you have done, ma'am, Becky and I will clear away these dishes, for you will be more comfortable to have a tidy room, I daresay, and Jem's sent up a bottle of brandy for you, Master

Ralph, if you are agreeable, for he knows it's what you like! And there's a bottle of ratafia for you, ma'am, which is about all we have in the house suitable for ladies, excepting my elderberry wine, which I thought would not be quite what you would want at the end of a meal. Put down that tray, Becky, there's a good girl, and then you can help me pack up these things.'

She bustled about, chattering inconsequentially as she loaded the dishes on to the trays ready to be taken away. While this was being done, Ralph escorted Elinor to one of the chairs beside the fire, where he pulled up the small table and set upon it the brandy and ratafia, pouring out a glass of each and handing the ratafia to Elinor. By this time Mistress Carew and her daughter were ready to depart and Ralph held open the door for them to go out. Megs thanked him, adding that it was not for a gentleman to be holding open doors for such as she, and adjuring him to remember that Mistress Elinor was not yet in full health and not to keep her sitting up till all hours.

When he had closed the door, he stood there for a few moments, with such a comical look of relief upon his face that Elinor laughed.

'Megs is so kind,' she said, her voice quivering with amusement, 'but she does like to talk, does she not?'

'Her tongue runs on wheels, sometimes, but as you say, she has a very kind heart. However, I will take heed of her last words, for you are not yet fully recovered and we must take care that you do not become overtired.'

'Oh, but I am not in the least fatigued,' she said quickly. 'Please, sit down and enjoy your brandy.'

He lowered his long frame into the chair, stretching out his legs until his shoes with their large silver buckles were almost in the hearth. For a while they sat in companionable silence, gazing at the flames. Ralph reached forward to pick up another log and throw it on to the fire, and as he sat back in his chair he glanced at Elinor's thoughtful countenance.

He said gently, 'I have told you my history, Elinor. Will you not honour me with yours?'

She gazed at him, her green eyes seeming to look through

him, never seeing the man at all. She smiled faintly.

'Mine is not an edifying tale, sir. Are you sure you wish to hear it?'

'I would like you to tell me.'

'Very well.' She paused, returning her gaze to the fire, as though the words could be found there. Belham watched her, listening in silence as she spoke of her happy childhood, the only daughter of devoted parents. He observed the play of emotions, clearly visible in her features, as she spoke haltingly of her ordeal at the hands of Lord Thurleigh and his cronies, of her father's subsequent death and the flight to France. Her tale was plainly told, and he could only guess at the anger and sorrow that was held in check within the slim young woman sitting opposite. When she paused in her story, he went over to the small table and refilled their glasses.

'You lived peacefully in France?' He handed her the ratafia. 'Were you happy in your new life?'

Elinor shrugged, a faint smile touching her lips.

'I learned to live with my memories. Poor Mama was not so fortunate – or mayhap I am wrong,' she murmured, almost to herself, 'mayhap she was more blessed than I, for at the end she lost all memory of those last days in England. She never really recovered from her grief, you see, and she died just two years later, having convinced herself that Papa was alive and soon to join us in France. How I prayed then that God might take me too!'

'I am glad he did not.' Ralph smiled faintly. 'What happened to you after your mother's death?'

'I was married by that time. My relatives had arranged it all for me – a very good match, considering my circumstances! Philibert de Sange was very old, very rich, something of a recluse – and an eccentric. He offered a good settlement, and in truth I did not care what became of me.'

Ralph had resumed his seat by the fire and from his chair he had a clear view of Elinor's profile. Now as he watched he saw the sudden tightening of her jaw, the lips compressed to withhold some secret she was not yet ready to share with him.

171

'He owned a house near Paris, although he entertained very little, and rarely went about – there were but two or three houses he deigned to visit. He was an old man, but his – his appetites were not weakened by age. I learned to please him, to degrade myself for his enjoyment, and to suffer his petty tyrannies.'

Her fingers clenched around the stem of her glass. 'At night I would flatter him, praising his wasted body, pressing my kisses upon the shrivelled flesh, and suppressing any revulsion I might feel for the living, lusting skeleton that was my husband! I complied with his every wish, submitted to every caress – I sank to the level of the lowest trull from the gutters of Paris. And every night I prayed that I might die, each night for four long years I begged God to release me from my living hell.' She gave a trembling laugh. 'And it seems He heard me at last, for de Sange died very suddenly one night and I was a widow – a very, very rich widow! No, pray don't come near me!' she cried out in alarm, as Ralph leaned forward in his chair. 'If you comfort me now I shall dissolve into tears, and I am resolved to finish my story! Let me but pause a moment to savour again the thankfulness I felt at that moment!

'I was then but one-and-twenty, but I felt I had already lived through two lifetimes. I did not know what to do. I had gone from a child of fifteen to a widow of twenty-one, I had severed all connection with my mother's relatives – I could not forget it was they who had arranged my marriage, and they had been amply repaid for their trouble! My one friend was Hannah, the English servant who had been with me since I was a child. It was she who arranged the burial, ordered my mourning clothes and persuaded me to accept the few invitations that came my way.' She looked at him. 'Paris would have opened its arms to me, had I so wished, for you see, the de Sange family is a very old and noble line, as well as being exceedingly rich! But I preferred to live quietly, until September last, when I met an Englishman named Poyntz, who . . . awakened old memories.'

She paused, but Ralph Belham remained silent, watching her and at last she began to speak again, her words almost tumbling over themselves as she told her story, her eyes never wavering from the crackling fire, as if she was reading her tale in the flames.

For some minutes after Elinor had finished, there was a heavy silence. Ralph Belham sat in his chair, a deep frown creasing his brow and his normally smiling eyes very sombre. The sound of a log settling into the ash of the fire roused him from his reverie, and he leaned forward to throw more wood on to the flames.

'It is a fantastic tale, Elinor.'

'I know. But it is a true one.'

'The list of names – where is it now?'

'At Knight's Bridge. I hid it before leaving for Weald Hall. Should Boreland's men search my house, I doubt they will find it. And even if they do' – she shrugged – 'the names are so engraved upon my mind I am not likely to forget them.'

'And what is your plan? To murder all the men upon that list?'

'If that is the only way to bring them to justice, yes.'

'You are a determined woman, Elinor de Sange.'

'I have years of hatred to repay.'

'Revenge is a canker, my dear, it will eat away at your soul.'

The green eyes regarded him steadily. 'It is all that keeps me living.'

He reached out for his pipe. 'Do you know, a very wise tutor of mine once told me that a man who studies revenge keeps his own wounds green.' He glanced across at her. 'You would do well to put your anger behind you, Elinor.'

'Sir, I cannot.'

'Aye, you have told me what you endured and in your place I too would want to be avenged, but the risk you run!' He saw the stubborn set to her chin and shrugged, knowing she would not heed his arguments. He rubbed his beard, staring thoughtfully into the fire.

'Let me see: Poyntz, Rowsell, Boreland and Thurleigh – you have yet to tell me the fifth man upon your list.'

'A clerical gentleman, Bishop Furminger – now what have I said to give you such amusement?'

Ralph Belham shook his head at her, still chuckling.

'Not content with wishing to tangle with one of the most powerful lords in England, you must needs add a bishop to your list! Well, madam, let no one say you lack courage!'

CHAPTER SEVENTEEN

Revelation

Bishop Furminger was dozing before the fire at the modest little house in Islington which he had hired. A mild recurrence of the gout that had plagued him of recent years had coincided with an unfortunate misunderstanding between himself and one of his footmen (a very pretty young man who had quite misinterpreted his master's friendliness) and the reverend gentleman had thought it prudent to follow his physician's advice and take a break from his not very arduous duties. He had thus removed himself from his diocese for a period of recuperation, hoping that by the time he returned to his flock the rumours concerning himself and the young man – who had been paid handsomely to disappear discreetly – would have died down.

Raised voices penetrated his reverie and the sounds of a violent entry caused him to sit up with a jolt, turning a startled countenance towards the door. As the sight of his visitor, his round face grew pale, but he waved away his servant, who was vociferously protesting that he had been unable to prevent the unseemly intrusion.

'Yes, yes, go away now! I will deal with this! Well, my dear Boreland, this is – ah – an unexpected pleasure. Will you not sit down? You must excuse me for not getting up to greet you, but as you can see, I am indisposed.' He waved one fat hand towards his left leg, which was heavily bandaged and resting upon a footstool.

'Your man told me as much.'

This reply was unencouraging, but the man of the cloth summoned up his most charitable smile.

'And what can I do for you, my dear sir?'

'I need your help to find a woman.' Boreland observed his host's look of surprise and gave a bark of laughter. 'Not just any woman, Furminger: the one I seek could be very dangerous.'

'And do I know the lady, sir?'

Boreland's dark eyes were fixed upon the bishop, watching him closely.

'Aye, my friend, you do. Perhaps you will recall a certain winter's night back in 'forty-five when we were gathered together with certain – friends.'

The bishop shuddered, his small mouth pursed in an expression of distaste.

'That is a time I have tried hard to forget! So close to disaster—'

'You were ever the coward!' cut in Boreland contemptuously. 'Mayhap you remember we had a girl there that night?'

'*You* had a girl there!' Furminger was quick to correct him. 'I had nothing to do with that disgraceful episode!'

'Nevertheless, you were present, and as I recall you did precious little to prevent it! But we'll let that pass, for the moment. The fact is that the girl is now a woman. A remarkably beautiful woman, I might add! And she is bent on revenge.'

The bishop shifted uncomfortably on his chair, and when he spoke his voice was little more than a petulant squeak.

'But what has this to do with me?'

'I think she means to kill us all. Doubtless you are aware of the untimely demise of Julian Poyntz, and of Rowsell's sudden death?'

'Of course, but—'

'I believe the woman was involved in both. I was to be her next victim, but I foiled her plot.'

'Well, I am sure you can deal with this matter without my help. After all, she is merely a woman; how can she hope to hold out against the mighty James Boreland?'

'How indeed, but I have yet to find her! The witch has

disappeared. I had her safe, as I thought, at Weald Hall, but she escaped. I have scoured the countryside, and my men are watching her own house lest she return, but there is no trace of her. That is why I have come to you. It is possible that she has taken refuge with some parish priest, and while the fellow might not disclose the lady's presence to me, he would undoubtedly do so to a bishop! I want you to make enquiries, discreetly, of course, and should you be successful, you will inform me immediately, do you understand? The woman calls herself Elinor de Sange. She is the widow of some rich Frenchman.'

'Then is it not more likely that she has returned to France, or taken her husband's religion?' put in Furminger hopefully. 'I have no influence with papists.'

'My wife ascertained that although the woman lived for some time in France, she did not adopt the Catholic faith,' replied Boreland. He added drily, 'Trust Isobel to discover that! No. Elinor de Sange is still in England. I know it, and I intend to find her.'

'But surely the woman is mad to seek revenge upon such a powerful man as yourself! Why put yourself to such trouble over a lunatic?'

For some moments Boreland did not answer, merely stood looking down upon the bishop. Should he tell him that the ruby brooch was missing, and that in all probability it was in the hands of Elinor de Sange? Observing the corpulent figure of the bishop, the protuberant blue eyes glancing up fearfully, then away, unwilling to meet his own stern gaze, he decided against it.

'Lunatics are always dangerous enemies. I would that this one was put safely away. Now, will you help me?'

'Oh, very well, sir! Pray summon my servant and I will send out letters today, seeking news of the woman.'

'Good. Then I shall leave you to your labours. And remember, Furminger, be discreet. I must not be connected with this matter.'

'Pray go, sir, and leave me to my task!' retorted the bishop peevishly. 'I am well aware that your opinion of me is not high, but you may rest assured that if there is one thing I have learned these past years it is discretion!'

James Boreland laughed, but as the servant entered at that moment he refrained from comment and took his leave, confident that his efforts to find Elinor de Sange would soon be rewarded.

Ralph Belham did not attempt to dissuade Elinor from her quest, merely extracting from her the promise that she would remain at the Green Dragon at least for a few more weeks until she was fully recovered. The return of his messenger from London the following day added a further reason to remain hidden. The young man had delivered Elinor's note to Hannah, as requested, and reported that the servant had been much relieved by the news that her mistress was safe. However, she sent a warning to Elinor: twice in recent days a stranger had been seen loitering upon the road outside the house, and Hannah was convinced they were being watched. Ralph's messenger had managed to steal away unnoticed under cover of darkness, but his tidings dashed Elinor's hope that Boreland would quickly give up his search, and she resigned herself with a good grace to a prolonged stay at the inn.

Despite her desire for revenge, she was grateful for the peaceful interlude. It could not last for ever, she knew, but for the moment she was content to ignore the future. In Ralph Belham she felt that she had found a friend and they were soon upon the easiest of terms. He visited the inn as often as his teaching duties would allow, and although he could not disguise the warm look in his eyes when they rested upon her, he gave no sign of wanting more than her friendship.

His conduct set Elinor at her ease, so much so that she no longer shrank away from the friendly kiss he bestowed upon her cheek whenever he took his leave of her, nor did she object to the brotherly hugs he would sometimes give her. That he wanted her she had no doubt, and on the evenings when he rode out, coming back up the hidden staircase to her room in the early hours of the morning, she would invariably wake at the faint scraping as the wall panel opened and lie in her bed, holding her breath as he crossed the room. She kept her eyes tightly closed, but was aware that his footsteps halted beside her bed and she could imagine him, standing there, looking down upon her before moving on. And gradually, as the days passed, her nervousness subsided. She came to trust him.

Elinor had been at the Green Dragon for nearly three weeks when the weather worsened. The ground had grown ice-hard over the past few days, with clear skies producing sparkling morning frosts and clear, sunny days, but now the wind had changed, and the heavy clouds brought the threat of snow. Despite Megs's misgivings, Ralph continued to patrol the night roads. The landlady shook her head over his fool-hardiness, and was still voicing her concern one windy evening when she brought Elinor's supper to her room.

Elinor did her best to ally Megs's fears, but as she prepared to retire she could not but feel a little anxious for her friend. The wind was whistling about the house, and a glance through the shutters showed Elinor that it had begun to snow, tiny white flakes that swirled around on the frozen earth. Elinor built up the fire and retired to her bed, snuffing out her candle and burying her head under the covers, but she was unable to sleep. Twice she slipped from beneath the blankets to throw more logs upon the fire, but the night was well advanced when her straining ears caught the sound she had been waiting for: a muffled footstep upon the stairs, then the faint click as the wall panel swung open and Ralph Belham entered the room, wrapped from head to foot in black, with a scattering of white powdery snow upon his hat and shoulders. A cold blast of air accompanied him and Elinor pulled the blankets a little tighter about her. She lay still, watching him in the firelight and, as if aware of her scrutiny, Ralph looked around. He smiled at her, taking off his hat and shaking the snow from it on to the fire, where it hissed faintly before disappearing.

'I am sorry, did I wake you?'

'No. I could not sleep. I put more wood upon the fire – in case you need to warm yourself.'

'That was kind of you.' He threw his hat on the table, then discarded his greatcoat and sat down before the fire.

Elinor slipped out of bed and put on her wrap, drawing it

closely about her as she came across to the hearth, where she helped him to pull off his boots. Ralph laughed softly.

'Why, thank you, ma'am! Ah, that's much better! 'Tis a damned cold night and for all the luck I had I might as well have stayed indoors instead of getting chilled to the bone!'

Having placed the boots on one side of the hearth, she returned to his chair and stood before him.

'There's snow on your collar, Ralph. Let me brush it away before it melts into your neckcloth . . .'

Her fingers flicked over his collar and, aware of his eyes upon her, she looked into his face, a faint smile in her eyes. She did not protest as he pulled her down on to his lap and kissed her; instead her own arms crept around his neck.

'Your skin is very cold,' she murmured, 'my bed is warm. You had best share it with me.'

He held her away from him, a mixture of disbelief and amusement in his eyes.

Elinor touched his cheek. 'Come to bed, Ralph. It is quite ridiculous that you should have to sleep on that narrow truckle-bed downstairs when this one is wide enough for us both.'

She rose and he followed her across the room.

'My dear, are you sure this is what you want?'

'Yes.' She reached out for him. 'Yes, I am sure.'

Taking her hand, he sat down upon the bed and leaned over to kiss her. Elinor felt the rough tickling of his beard, still chilled from the night air. Then, when he had shrugged off the rest of his clothes he slipped between the sheets and Elinor warmed his cold limbs with her own soft body. She found herself considering the moment: it was the first time she had willingly embraced any man. She knew a fleeting moment of panic as she first touched his naked body, but it was replaced almost immediately with a feeling of comfort, a security that she had not known for many years.

He kissed her, gently at first, then with a growing intensity as Elinor responded to his touch. For the first time she felt pleasure in a man's caresses; his hands gently explored her body, his fingers moving lightly over her thighs, arousing in her a passion such as she had never known before. His body, firm and unyielding, was pressed against her and Elinor abandoned herself to the new and delightful sensations, forgetting everything in the pleasure of the moment.

Daylight was peeping through the cracks in the shutters when Elinor awoke, her body still wrapped around her sleeping companion. She lay very still, wondering at the feeling of peace that enveloped her. Until now the men who had used her body had done so purely for their own pleasures, but Ralph's gentle caresses had drawn responses from Elinor that had both surprised and delighted her. No man had ever given her such pleasure.

Sensing her wakefulness, Ralph stirred. Even in the gloom she thought his eyes smiled at her.

'Elinor.' He raised himself on one elbow, watching her face in the gloom, 'I know your story, I am aware that you have no cause to like men. Why did you take me to your bed? Was it for my sake, because you think you should repay my kindness, or did you truly desire it?'

He felt her stretch beside him, like a cat.

'Oh, for any number of reasons. I hope you do not regret it, Ralph. I do not.'

'Not at all,' he murmured, kissing her hair. 'I have been wanting to do that since the first day I brought you here.'

She smiled and moved willingly back into his arms.

'Well, I have been here for more than three weeks, sir, we have a little time to make up, have we not?'

She kissed him.

'You're a damned fine woman, Elinor,' he murmured, his lips close to her ear. 'You should be consorting with nobility, not a common highwayman.'

'My experience of noblemen leads me to believe that they are a great deal more villainous than you will ever be!'

He pulled away from her, taken aback by the bitterness in her retort.

'What, did you never meet one honest gentleman?'

For an instant the disturbing image of Lord Davenham flashed into her mind. She pushed the thought away.

'They consider only their own pleasures,' she answered

shortly and, taking his face in her hands, she pulled him close, kissing him with an intensity that aroused their passion once again.

They breakfasted late, giggling like children in their new-found happiness, and neither of them sharing the landlord's gloom at the prediction that the heavy snowfall during the night would keep them indoors for at least a week.

'Poor Jem, he'll be very short of customers for a while,' said Ralph, returning to Elinor's room after a brief descent to the taproom. 'He says there are high drifts in the lanes, so there's no likelihood of visitors today. It should be quite safe if you would care to come downstairs for a while. I've asked Jem to have a fire made up in the private parlour. I must return to Hoddesdon.'

'Oh, surely not – the snow is too deep!'

Touched by her disappointment, Ralph took her hands in his own.

'I can walk across the fields. I will be needed at the school, Elinor; I must try and get back. I will return to you just as soon as I can – trust me!'

With Ralph gone, Elinor found the days at the inn dragging by. She was pleased to be able to leave the seclusion of her room, for as her health and strength returned she was increasingly frustrated at being forced to remain hidden away.

Jem Carew's gloomy prediction proved correct. The snow remained with them for a week, during which time no traveller came within sight of the Green Dragon. At last there was a break in the weather and a steady thaw set in. Within a couple of days the snow was diminishing rapidly, leaving only patches of white upon the landscape where the drifts had been thickest. Waking one morning to this changed world, Elinor felt her spirits lift. She went downstairs, alert for any sign of strangers. Upon meeting her hostess at the foot of the stairs and being assured that the inn was empty, Elinor made her way to the private room set aside for the use of such travellers as did not wish to mingle with the rough working men who frequented the taproom. Ralph found her there some time later. She was sitting in one of the high-backed armchairs beside the fire, deep in thought, turning the large ruby brooch idly between her fingers.

'How's this, Mistress Brown?' he rallied her. 'Have you no occupation for those idle hands of yours? I will ask Megs to find you some small task – what shall it be? There's a chicken to be plucked and drawn for dinner, or shall I set you to some sewing?'

'Ralph!' She jumped up and ran into his waiting arms. Only after he had kissed her did she answer his question, saying with mock severity, 'I have not prepared a dinner, but I would inform you, sir, that I have already mended a dozen torn sheets! Oh, I have missed you! Can you stay?'

'Only for a couple of days. But you were lost in your own thoughts when I arrived – will you not share them with me?'

She held up the ruby.

'I have been pondering why this jewel should be so important. Julian Poyntz told me he thought I was no longer alive, and that Lord Thurleigh had recovered the stone, and James Boreland, too, was most anxious to find it. There is a mystery here, Ralph, and this, this blood stone holds the key.'

'Let me look at it.'

She handed him the brooch. He went over to the window and began to examine it closely.

'I thought when I first saw it that the setting was too large for such a stone,' he said, turning the ornament over and over between his fingers. 'I wonder. . . .'

Elinor followed him.

'Do you think there might be some secret catch?' she asked, watching as his fingers moved delicately over the finely worked casing, examining every detail of its pattern of leaves and flowers.

'I don't know. If there is a catch it's well hidden amongst the ornate detail of the setting. Yes! Yes. . . I have it!' He pressed a tiny flower bud, and the plain gold backing of the brooch opened upon its hidden hinge. Peering over his shoulder, Elinor could see the back of the ruby, and was surprised to note that it was cut exactly as the front of the stone, as if the ruby had originally been intended to be seen from both sides. Ralph turned the brooch slightly to allow the light to play upon the inside of the gold casing. He gave a low whistle.

'I think we have discovered the secret.'

The inside of the cover had been engraved with letters so small they were difficult to read without the aid of a glass, but by turning it to catch the very best of the light, Ralph could just decipher the words.

'Well?' demanded Elinor. 'What does it say?'

'Enough to cost men their lives,' he replied quietly. 'Look here: "Loyal subjects to the true King James." And there is a list of names: "Guy Morellon, Marquis of Thurleigh – Bishop Furminger – James Boreland – George Rowsell – Julian Poyntz." And there's a date, "1745".'

Elinor stared at him.

'But – those are the very men – I don't understand. . . .'

'When exactly did you see these men, Elinor? Think hard, love.'

'It – it was some eight years ago . . . it would be December, 'forty-five.'

'Then there we have it! Charles Stuart was in England then. These men must have had the intention of joining forces with the Stuart as he marched south. Fortunately for Thurleigh and the others the Jacobites started north again before they had openly declared themselves. No doubt the night you saw them they were gathered together to await news from the prince.'

Elinor took the brooch and stared at it, turning it slowly between her fingers.

'Lord Thurleigh must have been very sure of the outcome to commit himself so openly to the Stuart cause.' She looked up, 'Ralph, do you think this is sufficient evidence of treason?'

He shrugged, saying slowly, 'Used properly, I don't doubt it could ruin Thurleigh, at least.'

'Then it is just what I need! Did I not tell you Fate is using me in this matter?'

Ralph looked as if he was about to reply, but he checked himself, merely saying, 'Well, the weather is still too uncertain to travel far, so there's nothing to be done about it today. Put the brooch away, Elinor, and forget about it for the present, if you can.' He clapped his hands, saying brightly, 'Now, what would you care to do this morning, ma'am? I am entirely at your disposal. I had the forethought to bring a backgammon board with me; would you care for that, or shall we play at cards?'

The thaw continued and the roads that had been impassable because of the snow now became rivers of mud, causing just as many problems for travellers, but it ensured Elinor's seclusion. Ralph Belham was the only visitor, and his patience and gentleness continued to work their magic, Elinor responding to his caresses as she had never done to those of her husband. Philibert de Sange had been interested only in his own sensual pleasures and his wife's humiliation. For her own survival, Elinor had learned to repress her revulsion and indeed all other emotion, protecting herself from further pain with a cold, impenetrable barrier of reserve. Ralph had broken through that barrier and she gave herself to him willingly, pleased at his enjoyment of her body and astonished that she, too, should find pleasure in their union.

By the time the snow had disappeared from even the highest ground, Elinor felt that something inside her had melted too. She tried to explain this to Ralph one morning as she lay in bed, still wrapped in blankets, watching him dress.

'I did not know there could be such pleasure between two people,' she told him, smiling. 'Until I met you, dear Ralph, I had only known men who considered their own pleasure. I cannot think that I have ever been so – so comfortable as I am with you. I would like to stay here for ever and ever!'

Ralph laughed and when he had finished buttoning his waistcoat he sat down on the side of the bed, his eyes smiling tenderly at her.

'There is nothing I would like more, my dear, but we both know it cannot be.'

Her green eyes smiled up at him. 'Oh? And why is that?'

He took her hand, his voice gentle. 'You do not love me, Elinor. I am not the man for you.'

'How can you say that, after these past few days?'

'They were very special, but I am not the only man who will give you such pleasure, believe me. Besides, child, I have twice your years. You are far too young and beautiful to waste your life with me.'

She sat up, frowning. 'You are serious! Ralph, do you – do you not love me?'

'Aye, child. Too well to keep you here with me.'

'But it is where I want to be!'

'For the moment, perhaps, but that will change. Already I have seen the restlessness in your eyes.'

'Oh but—'

'Pray now, child, do not argue with me.' He smiled tenderly at her anxious face. 'Our time is not yet over, and we can enjoy each other's company for a little while longer, but some day you must leave here.'

'No!' She sat up, flinging her arms about him and burying her face in his shoulder. 'You have made me happy, Ralph! You are the only man who has ever made me so!'

'Aye, child, but you have told me that your experience of men is limited. Soon you must go back to your world, take up your old life. I doubt not that you will find a good man – a young man – who will make you happy.'

'But why should I do that when I have found happiness here, with you? Why should I give that up now?'

'And what of this solemn quest for revenge that you have pursued so diligently?' he teased her, but gently. 'Is that over?'

'Yes, yes! I will hand the ruby brooch to someone else – a government minister, or even the King! They can make of it what they will!'

He laughed softly. 'Oh Elinor, I wish I could believe that! But I have come to know you too well. Come now, dry your eyes. This is not a moment for tears, my love. Let us enjoy the time we have left.'

'I'm sorry.' Elinor sniffed, gratefully making use of the handkerchief he held out to her. 'You are right, Ralph. There is no reason for us to be downcast. Wait for me to dress and we will breakfast together.' *And mayhap, given time, I can persuade you to let me stay*, was her unspoken thought.

It was a full week before the weather had improved suffi-ciently for Ralph to resume his nocturnal activities. There was little traffic on the highway, for he found the roads to be thick with mud, some of them flooded, making travel almost impossible. There was just the occasional farm wagon, or a post-chaise taking advantage of the moonlight to continue its perilous journey to London. For the first time since embarking upon his nefarious career, Belham was aware of a desire to get back to the inn, put Devon in his warm stable and enjoy a cosy supper with Elinor beside a blazing fire. He laughed to himself as he turned his horse off the highway.

'I must be growing old! You'd be glad of the rest though, eh, Devon? Let's go home.' He patted the horse's neck, staring thoughtfully ahead of him. 'I think another time we should go west and try the Barnet-Hatfield road, where there's more likelihood of taking a decent purse.'

Adhering to his decision, the next night Ralph rode west from the inn, joining the London road just south of Hatfield. The weather continued dry, although it was a little blustery, with heavy clouds moving across the sky and occasionally obscuring the moon. Keeping to the shelter of the woodland bordering the highway, he turned his horse south, moving slowly through the trees, his senses fixed upon the road a few yards away. He was wrapped warmly against the chill wind that moaned through the trees, and Devon moved steadily beneath him, as silent as his master.

Little passed along the road: a gentleman with his lady riding pillion behind him had come along, but the moonlight had shown the fellow to be a clergyman, and not a very prosperous one, Ralph guessed, if his living did not run to a carriage; he had let them pass unhindered. Now there was silence, save for the wind's sighing. Ralph judged it to be about ten o'clock; he guessed that anyone who had gone visiting that evening would soon be travelling home if they were to take advantage of the moonlight.

Sure enough, the rumble of a carriage sounded in the distance. Devon pricked up his ears and snorted expectantly: he knew the game. Ralph gathered up the reins in one hand and with the other he took out his pistol. Then, in the shadow of the trees, they waited. Ralph could hear the coach quite clearly now; it seemed to be moving at speed through the darkness. A few moments later the dark shape could be seen, the carriage lamps bobbing and twinkling as the coach swayed over the broken roads. As it thundered nearer, Ralph pulled his silk kerchief over his face and, at a touch from his heels, Devon sprang forward, appearing before the coach so suddenly that the leaders shied and reared, and the coachman instinctively reined in his team. Observing that this worthy fellow was wholly engaged in regaining control of his horses, Belham turned his attention to the footman clinging to the straps at the rear of the coach. He waved his pistol at the man.

'Come along now, me lad!' he cried in a hearty voice. 'Just you climb down and stand out on the road, where I can see you. That's better. Now, stand there nice and peaceful and it's no harm will come to you.'

'What the devil is going on!' demanded an angry voice from within the carriage.

'Just step down, sir, before I spoil your elegant carriage by putting a bullet through one of your new glass windows!' called Belham jovially.

The carriage door opened and a large gentleman jumped down to the road. The brim of his lace-edged hat kept his face in shadow, until he looked up at Belham, when the full light of the moon illuminated his countenance. Ralph's brows rose fractionally in surprise, then he threw back his head and laughed as he recognized the bearded face of James Boreland.

CHAPTER EIGHTEEN

Ill-met by moonlight . . .

The two men regarded each other, Boreland scowling as he looked up at the highwayman.

'So this amuses you, does it?' he growled. 'Only get down from that horse and I wager you would not find it so congenial!'

'Damme, Boreland, do you take me for a fool? Just hand over your purse and your watch and you can be on your way.'

'So, you know me, eh? How is that – were you in my employ, mayhap, and turned off for dishonesty?'

'Devil a bit!' retorted Belham cheerfully. 'You were ever too much the villain for my taste! And tell your men to keep very still,' he added sharply, as the footman tried to edge back towards the coach. 'This pistol is aimed at your heart, Boreland.'

At a barked word of command from his master, the footman froze, and having assured himself that the coachman, with his team now under control, showed no signs of reaching for a shotgun, Ralph returned his attention to the carriage.

'Who else is in there?'

'My wife.'

'Then she had best come out and join us. Quickly now!'

Boreland helped his wife to alight from the coach and she stood, pale and still beside the steps. Belham inclined his head towards her.

'Good evening, ma'am! No need to look so anxious. I'll not trouble you.' He chuckled. 'By God, being married to this

189

fellow must be trial enough for you, ma'am! But now you, sir, empty your pockets!'

With a sly glance at the masked horseman, Boreland reached into his pocket. Keeping his eyes upon the pistol that remained steadily pointed at his body, he slowly drew forth his purse. As he brought his hand clear of his pocket, the purse slipped from his fingers, and with a muttered oath he bent to retrieve it. Too late Belham saw the small silver pistol in his hand; there was a loud retort, Devon snorted and drew back, feeling his master jerk in the saddle.

'That's for you, my pretty villain!' snarled Boreland triumphantly. 'I'll take great pleasure in watching you rot from a gibbet!'

Belham backed his horse, and despite the pain he managed to laugh.

'Not yet, Boreland!' he said, taking careful aim. 'I'm not that easy to kill!'

Even as he spoke he squeezed the trigger. Isobel Boreland screamed as her husband staggered, then collapsed. As if released from a dream, his footman ran forward.

' 'Fore Gad, he's dead!' he cried shrilly. 'You've killed 'im!'

'That was my intention,' muttered Belham, putting away his gun. The servants were too busy attending to their mistress, who had fallen into hysterics over her husband's lifeless form, to hear him. He turned his horse and dug in his heels, sending Devon off across country at a gallop.

Elinor was dozing before the fire when her ears caught the first faint sounds of a footstep on the stair. As the wall panel opened she turned, but the words of welcome died unspoken on her lips when Ralph staggered into the room. She jumped up and ran forward, reaching him just as he was about to collapse. It took all her strength to support the wounded man and she was obliged almost to carry him to the bed. As he sank down on the covers she caught sight of the blood upon her hands, and with a smothered exclamation rushed to the door to summon help.

Returning to the bed Elinor felt a cold chill run through her. Ralph's greatcoat was undone and in the dim lamplight she could see the dark stain spreading over his velvet riding jacket. Feverishly she unbuttoned the coat and the waistcoat beneath, finally tearing away the blood-soaked shirt to reveal the small wound in his flesh, just below the ribs, from which the blood still oozed. Elinor looked around for something to stanch the blood and in desperation she snatched the kerchief from around the neck of her gown, almost sobbing as she bundled it up and pressed it over the wound. Ralph's eyes flickered open and he smiled faintly when he saw her.

'Damned fellow caught me unawares,' he breathed. 'I should have known better.'

'Hush now, don't talk,' Elinor told him, trying to keep her voice level. 'Save your strength. I have told Becky to send for a doctor.'

'Too late for that.'

'No!' muttered Elinor, blinking back the tears. 'I won't let you die!'

The kerchief was now red with blood, and it was with relief that Elinor saw Mistress Carew enter the room, carrying a jug of water and a pile of fresh cloths over one arm. The landlady took one look at the figure on the bed and hurried across the room, firmly but gently easing Elinor aside and applying herself to the task of cleaning up the wound, all the time keeping up a constant flow of small talk.

'So it's come to this! I knew how it would be if you didn't give up this way of life. I hope you're satisfied, Master Ralph, and it's the Lord's help we shall need now to get you out of this pass!'

Elinor was engaged in wiping his face with a damp cloth, and she was heartened by the faint chuckle with which he greeted the landlady's words.

'No sermons, Megs, I beg of you. Just get me into bed – I'm damned tired!'

'Aye, all in good time, sir. First we must bind you up so that you don't bleed to death before the doctor can get to you. I've sent Jem to see if old Doctor Brookes will come out to you, but I don't expect to see him much before morning.'

Together the women set to work: it was clear that Ralph was in great pain, and Elinor could not be sorry when he fainted. When they had finished, she pulled up a chair, expressing her intention of sitting beside him until the doctor arrived.

'One of us must do so, surely,' muttered Megs as she gathered up the bloodstained rags ready to take them away. 'I confess I don't like the look of him. The bullet's lodged somewhere inside, and heaven knows what damage it may have done.'

She went away, shaking her head, and leaving Elinor to watch over the injured man. He lay still, even in the dim lamplight his face looking unnaturally pale. Elinor sat beside the bed, her senses alert for the smallest change in his condition. She had no idea how long she remained thus, although it must have been some hours, for the fire was almost out before she noticed it and got up to pile on more wood and bring it back to life. When she returned to the bed, Ralph was stirring: his eyelids flickered, and he looked at her blankly for a few moments before recognition dawned.

'Elinor . . .' He began to cough, and Elinor dropped to her knees beside the bed.

'I'm here, my dear.' She wiped his lips, observing with dismay that there was blood in the spittle.

'Fetch me some brandy.'

Elinor shook her head, reaching for the glass that stood nearby.

'There's only water here, or if you are in pain, Megs has left you a sleeping draught . . .'

'Give me the water, then.' His words were scarce above a whisper. 'Elinor, I must tell you . . .'

'Later, love. Here, let me help you up a little.' She supported him while he took a few sips from the glass that she held to his lips, gently lowering him back on to the pillows when he had finished.

'No, it can't wait.' He reached for her hand, his grasp so weak it made Elinor's heart ache with sadness for him. 'It was Boreland, Elinor! James Boreland was on the road tonight.'

'Dear God, no!'

He smiled at her shocked countenance.

'Aye, a merry jest, ain't it m'dear? I thought how we'd laugh over it when I told you.'

'Oh, Ralph!' Elinor felt the tears prick her eyelids and she blinked rapidly, unwilling to let him see her distress. His grip upon her hand tightened.

'He'll not bother you any more, Elinor. With his bullet in me I knew I had to finish him. He's dead, child, another name off your list. . . .'

Ralph closed his eyes, exhausted by his efforts, and Elinor felt the long fingers that enclosed her hand losing their grip. She heard a faint sigh, as if he was at last relieved of the pain, and then he was still. She called his name, but there was no response, no flicker of movement in his face. With trembling hands she felt for a heartbeat, but there was none. Then, clutching at his lifeless hand, Elinor buried her face in the covers and cried.

Viscount Davenham's enquiries into Lord Thurleigh's affairs were proving fruitless, until chance took him one evening to an exclusive gaming hell in St James's. It was not one of Davenham's usual haunts, but having previously agreed to meet a party of friends there, the viscount attended somewhat reluctantly. His pleasure in the evening diminished still further when Lord Thurleigh joined the table, but as the cards were dealt for a fresh hand, a name was mentioned that claimed his attention and, he noted, Lord Thurleigh's.

The marquis looked up from his cards to enquire casually, 'What was that you were saying about Boreland?'

The gentleman concerned was too busy studying his own hand to look up, but he replied readily enough.

'I was saying, 'twas a pity about the poor fellow. Roads aren't safe for anyone these days.'

'Why, what happened to him?' asked Davenham.

' 'Od rat it, sir! Do ye not know?' cried a red-faced gentleman in a brown bag-wig. 'The fellow's dead. Shot, you know, by some rascally highwayman!'

The viscount was surprised by the news, but a glance at Lord Thurleigh showed the marquis looking stunned. His naturally pale face looked ashen, and a muscle worked at the side of his mouth.

'When was this?' he asked quietly.

'Oh, about a week since,' replied the red-faced man. 'I heard that Boreland was returning to Weald Hall with his wife one night when he was set upon. His servants carried him to the nearest inn, but he was dead before they could fetch a surgeon to him.' He noted the sceptical look upon Lord Thurleigh's countenance and added, by way of explanation, 'I had it from old Browning. He was staying at the inn that night on his way back to Town. The arrival of Boreland's wife and servants with their master's body caused no small commotion, and when Browning discovered the cause of all the fuss I believe he almost went off himself, with fright!'

'I can well believe it!' laughed a fellow-player.

'And he was certain it was a highwayman?' Thurleigh spoke coolly enough, but Davenham's close scrutiny detected a faint tremor in my lord's fingers as he sorted his cards.

'Aye, no reason to doubt it! There have been several accounts of villains working that road in recent months. There was one thing, though: Boreland's men said their master put a bullet in the fellow before he got away.'

'Well, let's hope it proves fatal,' muttered a gentleman in a flowered waistcoat. 'Never liked James Boreland above half, but I don't say I wished the fellow any harm. His wife's had a run of dashed bad luck recently.'

'Oh?' Davenham could not resist the question.

'Come now, Jonathan!' laughed the red-faced gentleman, 'Surely you knew that Isobel Boreland has been trying to find a bride for that half-wit son of hers? Carried off that French widow – what was her name, now. . . ?'

'de Sange.'

'Aye, that's the one! She took her off to Weald Hall before Christmas, hoping to make a match there, if rumours are to be believed, but it came to nought. By all accounts the woman quit in something of a hurry, leaving Boreland and his wife as mad as fire. He even sent to Town, looking for her, but she's gone to earth, disappeared!'

The marquis had regained his composure and he asked in a faintly bored voice, 'Did not the lady have a house in Town?'

The gentleman in the flowered waistcoat shook his head.

'Lived out at Knight's Bridge, Northaw's place, I understand. But there's only her servants living there now. 'Fore Gad sir, what a hand you've dealt me! Call for another bottle of burgundy while I decide upon my discard.'

The game once more became the main interest but the viscount played mechanically, his attention taken up by the effect of what had been said upon the marquis. Lord Thurleigh seemed completely taken aback, and it was not long before he excused himself from the game and left. Davenham remained a little longer, but as he made his way back to Warwick Street that night he had much to think about. Thurleigh had clearly been upset by the news of Boreland's death, so perhaps the two men had been hatching some plot together. Davenham had not considered it necessary to have Thurleigh watched when he returned to Town, but now the viscount changed his mind. He wanted very much to know what the fellow would do next. Thoughts of Madame de Sange disturbed him. Was she in some way involved in Boreland's murder, too?

He pushed the thought away, telling himself it was absurd. She had asked him to trust her and he very much wanted to do so, yet the doubts continued to haunt him and after two restless nights he decided to act. From his lodgings in Warwick Street, Viscount Davenham knew it was but a short drive westwards along Piccadilly and out of town to the small hamlet of Knight's Bridge. On summer days, the village could be filled with carriages whose occupants were intent upon enjoying themselves in the tea-gardens, but on a cold January day, with a biting easterly wind that cut through the thickest coat, there were very few travellers abroad and no one to impede the viscount's progress.

Despite the noise of his arrival as the coach swept around the drive, no servant appeared to usher the viscount into the house. He jumped down from his carriage and signalled to his coachman to take the vehicle around to the stables and wait for him there. Then he trod up the shallow steps to the front door and rapped loudly upon it with the hilt of his sword. He waited for a few moments, and was about to knock again when he heard the rasp of a bolt being drawn back. Shortly after this the door opened a fraction and he found himself being regarded by a young serving-maid.

Sensing the child's apprehension, he said in a kinder tone than he was wont to use, 'Is your mistress at home?'

The girl shook her head.

'Is there anyone I can speak to?'

'There's nobody here, 'cept me and Mrs Grisson,' came the reply, scarcely above a whisper. 'She's my lady's companion – came with my lady from France,' the girl volunteered, overcoming her fear.

'Ah, then we have met. Will you tell her that Viscount Davenham would like a few words with her?' He read the doubt in her face and added helpfully, 'You may lock the door again while you go and find her. I shall not come in until she gives me leave to do so.'

The door was closed against him, and he waited in the cold, the suspicion that something was amiss helping him to bear the delay. At last the door re-opened and he was shown into a small parlour at the back of the house by the same young maid, her nervousness only slightly abated. The viscount regarded the occupant of the room, a spare female dressed entirely in black standing before the fireplace. The woman's features were harsh, but even so it was possible to detect a look of strain around the eyes, and her hands were never still, the fingers continually pulling at each other.

'Mistress Grisson – you remember me?' She eyed him warily, yet he was sure she recognized him. 'Where is Madame de Sange?'

'I do not know, my lord.'

Something in her tone made Davenham glance at her, frowning, but after a slight pause he said gently, 'I wish your mistress no harm, if you will but tell me the truth.'

'It *is* the truth, sir! I have already told them all I know!'

'Who? Has someone been here before me? Come, woman, you can speak freely, there is no need to be afraid.'

'Can you protect my mistress from Lord Thurleigh?' she demanded, her tone sceptical.

'Thurleigh has been here?'

She nodded. 'He came yesterday, with several of his men.

When I could not tell him where to find my lady he became abusive,' She broke off, pressing a handkerchief to her lips with one shaking hand.

The viscount quickly crossed the room, putting out a hand to support the woman as she swayed.

'Come and sit down, mistress. Is that Madeira upon the tray? I shall pour you a glass and you will oblige me by drinking it, if you please, before you resume your story.'

He poured two glasses, handing one to the woman, then he took a chair opposite her own, watching her closely as she sipped her wine. When he judged her to be more composed he spoke again. 'Did he threaten you?'

'Not me, but his men frightened the footmen so much that they would not stay on here – there is only Cook, and Clara and myself here now. Lord Thurleigh demanded to know what had happened to Madame de Sange. I told him I did not know, that I had no news of her.'

'And is that true?'

She smiled grimly. 'Not entirely. I *did* receive a message from her, a week or so after Christmas, saying that she had left Weald Hall and was quite safe, but I was not to try to discover where she was, and that she would contact me presently. I burned the letter as soon as I had read it.' The tired eyes met his steadily, a measure of trust in their depths. 'You are the first to know of it since that moment.'

'Was Thurleigh satisfied that you knew not where your mistress might be?'

'He – he was very angry, and threatened dire consequences if he found I was lying, but he did not fright me – my little one has suffered too much at his hands for me to feel anything but hatred for such a man! Then he asked for the ruby. I told him it was not here, but he set his men to search the house.' She took another sip of the Madeira and a few deep breaths to calm herself before continuing.

They turned out every jewel-case, broke open every cupboard, even in the servants' quarters! But of course, they did not find it.'

As the wine took effect, Hannah Grisson began to relax and the viscount refilled her glass.

'What is this jewel that my lord Thurleigh was so anxious to find?'

'It is a large brooch. A ruby set in gold. He claims my mistress stole it from him years before, but that is not true, sir, for never would Miss Nell do such a thing! If it was Lord Thurleigh's, he must have given it to her, and later changed his mind! When I think of what my poor lady has already endured at his hands, that he must add this insult. . . .' She broke off, her voice suspended in tears.

The viscount waited patiently while she checked her sobs and grew calm again.

'Madam, you say your mistress was previously known to the marquis? Forgive me, but I thought Madame de Sange had lived in France since her childhood.'

Hannah hesitated, gazing uncertainly at the viscount.

'Come,' he said, 'I think your mistress is very dear to you, and you must see that she might be in need of a friend now. I wish you would tell me everything.' He smiled encouragingly. 'You can trust me.'

The smile won. She began, haltingly at first, to give Lord Davenham an account of Elinor's history. The viscount listened attentively, interpolating a question upon occasion when some point was not clear to him, and when she had finished her tale he remained perfectly still for some minutes, a faint crease upon his brow as he pondered all he had heard.

'I pray you, sir, do not think too harshly of my mistress!' begged Hannah, worried by his serious mien. 'I confess that when we came to England and she told me of her intention to be avenged upon the men who had ruined her life, I did not believe her to be serious.'

'Surely the death of Julian Poyntz should have convinced you.'

'But my lady did not kill him, it was his heart.'

'How fortunate for Madame de Sange.'

The old woman bit her lip. 'You do not believe it.'

'Nay, mistress, I know it to be true, but I believe Poyntz had been frightened out of his wits beforehand, which doubtless caused his heart to fail. But let us turn our attention to the death of George Rowsell. That was also convenient for your mistress, was it not? And yet you tell me she had no hand in it.'

'I swear to you she did not!'

'How can you be so sure of that? You have told me she showed you the list of names she obtained from Poyntz – at sword-point, if your mistress is to be believed! Why then should she scruple to arrange for Rowsell's death? A bag of gold and a word in the right quarter . . .'

'My mistress had no need to hire anyone!' cried Hannah, much incensed.

'Oh? How do you know that?'

'Because she planned to kill him herself!'

'What!'

She looked sullenly across at the viscount, resenting his persistence that made it necessary to tell him so much.

'She planned to poison him that night, but by chance he became involved in the brawl. 'Tis the truth!' she added, seeing his look of disbelief. 'I wish it were not so, for it has led my lady to believe that some divine spirit is aiding her, and thus she accepted Mrs Boreland's invitation to go to Weald Hall. She did not think she could fail – and now Heaven only knows what has become of her. . . .'

'And Boreland is dead.'

Hannah looked up from wiping her eyes.

'And you blame my lady for that also?'

He stood up and walked to the window.

'I don't know,' he said quietly. 'The coincidence is too marked to ignore.'

The housekeeper stared at him for a moment, then gave way to her grief. She threw her apron over her face and cried unrestrainedly. Lord Davenham remained at the window, almost oblivious to the weeping figure behind him. After a while the tears subsided, and Hannah emerged from her apron, her face blotched and red, but composed.

'Your pardon, sir. It – it is not my custom to – to . . .'

'Would you like me to summon the maid?'

'No, thank you. It will not be necessary.'

'Then let us now work to find a way to help your mistress.' He took a turn about the room, rubbing his chin thoughtfully. 'You say your mistress had a list of names – where it is now?'

'I know not, sir. She may have hidden it here, or taken it with her to Weald Hall.'

'You are sure Thurleigh's men did not find it?'

'I am certain of that, my lord.'

'Can you remember any of the names upon that list?'

She shook her head. 'I never read it, sir. The only name I know to be on the list, apart from those we have already mentioned, is Lord Thurleigh himself.'

'And he is the most dangerous man of all.' He laughed suddenly. 'I thought Madame de Sange to be in league with him, when in fact – the cunning little vixen!'

'It seems to me, sir, that you do not approve of my mistress!' observed Hannah, listening in growing indignation.

'Approve! How should I approve of her becoming involved in something that is likely to get her killed?' He saw the fear in her face and continued in a milder tone, 'We must hope that your mistress is still safe, but if she should contact you again, you must come to me, immediately! If you will permit me, I will arrange for some of my own people to stay here until such time as Madame returns. You may trust them to protect you from any future unwelcome visitors. Also, you must persuade your mistress to let me help her, for I, too, have an interest in bringing about the downfall of Lord Thurleigh.'

'But if she does not contact me, how then shall we find her?'

'I will set about the business this very day,' replied Davenham, preparing to take his leave. 'There's little doubt that his lordship is already looking for your mistress, but we must hope that I find her first!'

CHAPTER NINETEEN

Of threats and surprises

During the next few days the viscount made discreet enquiries concerning Madame de Sange, but without success. He began to wonder if she had returned to France, until an unexpected visitor convinced him that she was still in hiding in England. Lord Davenham entered his rooms one morning to find Lord Thurleigh idly perusing a news-sheet. Upon the viscount's entrance, the marquis tossed aside the paper and stood up.

'Ah, Davenham! You will forgive the intrusion, I am sure. Your man let me in.' He paused, a faint, unpleasant smile touching his lips as he observed the viscount's look of displeasure. 'A good fellow in many ways, I am sure, but perhaps you should turn him off. My own servants know that I will permit no one to enter beyond the hall if I am away from home. It is a rule they dare not disobey.'

'Perhaps you have more need of such precaution,' retorted Davenham, tossing aside his hat and beginning to strip off his gloves. 'What can I do for you?'

The marquis took out an elegant silver snuffbox.

'I believe you have been making enquiries concerning a certain lady.' He helped himself to a pinch of snuff. 'Do you know where she is?'

'What is that to you?'

'My dear fellow, why so brusque?' murmured my lord, looking pained. 'My interest in the lady is not of an amorous nature. No. I am interested only in retrieving some property that has been – shall we say, lost? That is all. I have no other interest in the woman.'

'I am sorry, I cannot help you.'

'But you did visit the lady's house recently, did you not?'

'Only to find you had been there before me.' The viscount watched his visitor carefully. 'You seem to have made quite an impression upon the staff. Very few now remain.'

The marquis inclined his head. 'Thank you. That was my intention. It did not, however, help me to find what I am looking for.'

'I realize that. You would not otherwise be here.' Davenham looked across the room, holding Thurleigh's cold grey eyes with his own straight gaze. 'Do you know what happened to Madame de Sange when she left Weald Hall? Where did she go?'

The marquis shrugged. 'She disappeared. Have you spoken to Boreland's widow?'

'She refuses all callers.'

'How wise,' Thurleigh murmured. 'And should I be similarly reticent? It is my way, I know, and yet . . .' He hesitated briefly before continuing, 'I can tell you that Madame de Sange left Weald Hall on Christmas night – through a window, I believe.' Again the sneering smile was in evidence. 'It proves my point about servants – most of them will be indiscreet, at a price.'

'And just what did you learn – at a price?'

'That the lady escaped from a locked room by way of an open window. A little careless of Boreland, would you not agree, to overlook such a possibility? The servants were sent out to bring her back. Hounds were used, I understand.' He observed the tightening of the viscount's jaw and shook his head slightly. 'The orders were that she should be taken alive. However, she had an accomplice waiting in the woods, and they rode off, never to be seen again. It had crossed my mind that you, my Lord Davenham, might have been that accomplice.'

'I?' cried the viscount, surprised. 'Why should you think that?'

'I had thought – but no, I can see that you knew nothing of this.'

'Perhaps the lady has returned to France.'

'I doubt that. I have had the ports watched since I learned

of her escape. There has been no word from there. And would she leave the country without her devoted servant, who waits still at Knight's Bridge? No. She is still in England somewhere. I shall find her, never doubt it, and I should very much prefer to do so without interference.'

'Is that a threat?'

The marquis picked up his hat and gloves, and turned to smile coldly upon the viscount.

'Merely a warning. I do not look kindly upon those who stand in my way. If you should have news of Madame de Sange, it would be wise for you to inform me of it.'

'What is it that you want from the lady, Thurleigh? It must be a thing of great importance to make you come to me for help.'

A shadow of annoyance passed over the marquis's usually impassive countenance, but it was gone in an instant and he replied coolly.

'You mistake, Davenham. I did not come here to ask for your help, merely to offer you a little advice. The jade is not worth your attention. 'Twould be a great pity if you were to risk your very existence for a common thief.'

The marquis left the apartment without another word. Despite his outward calm, Lord Thurleigh was greatly vexed by Elinor's disappearance. He knew that Boreland had failed to recover the ruby brooch, but had relied upon his assurances that it was only a matter of time before he found Elinor de Sange, and with her, the jewel. The news of Boreland's death had come as a most unpleasant surprise. While the ruby was out of his hands there was always the possibility that its secret might be discovered, even though he knew how cleverly it had been concealed. And if news of it should ever reach Leicester House! His plans depended upon the continued trust of the Princess of Wales; with her help he hoped to spirit the young princes out of Town, but all his planning would come to nought if it was discovered that he had supported the Stuart in 'forty-five. His painstaking arrangements were very near completion; to make his move too early would greatly increase the chances of failure, yet if he delayed he knew there was a risk that the ruby could betray him. However, my lord was ever a gambler and he had always trusted to his luck. He would bide his time.

He entered Thurleigh House just as his wife was descending the wide staircase to the hall. At the sight of her husband she hesitated, eyes widening in surprise, then with a little cry of delight she hurried down the stairs towards him, her hands held out in greeting and a tantalizing smile upon her painted lips.

'Fie on you, my lord! I was told you would not be back before the dinner hour, and now I have made arrangements to amuse myself until then!' She gave him her hands to kiss, which service he performed dutifully as she continued to talk. 'Shall I cancel my coach, sir? 'Tis only a courtesy call to Lady Upton, and can easily be put off.'

'No need for that,' drawled the marquis, letting go of her fingers.

My lady's green eyes narrowed at his indifference, but her smile remained fixed and she followed him into the library, saying in a caressing tone, 'Then I promise you I will be as quick as possible! You will be home for dinner tonight? I am glad, for we have seen so little of each other of late, my lord.' She carefully closed the door and stood against it, eyeing the marquis speculatively. 'Did your business go well this morning sir? I – I understand you are trying to trace a certain – lady?'

Thurleigh's piercing gaze came to rest upon his wife. 'How the devil did you know that?'

'One hears these things,' she said vaguely. 'Have you had any success in finding her?'

'No, damnation. The chit's vanished.' Again that searching look. 'Why are you so interested, my dear Margaret? Jealous?'

My lady laughed and disclaimed, but her husband did not fail to note the tell-tale flush that crept into her cheek.

'I wish you would tell me why you want this woman, Thurleigh,' she said softly. 'It is possible that I might be able to help you.'

Her green eyes taunted him as they had always done, and he felt the stirring of desire as she moved closer, a provocative smile curling the corners of her mouth. With an oath

Thurleigh pulled her to him and kissed her savagely, but not before he had seen the flash of triumph in her eyes. As he let her go he gave a cruel laugh.

'Do you think I don't know your tricks by now, beloved wife? What's your interest in Elinor de Sange?'

'None, I swear it, save to help you, my lord.'

'Is it to help me that you bed every man who comes your way?' The marquis noted her angry flush, and the way her lips were pressed together to hold back the retort he knew she wanted to make, the taunt that his pox-ridden body could no longer give her pleasure. His lip curled. 'Such restraint, my dear. I admire you for it, but it will not persuade me to tell you anything more than you already know.' He forced his painful joints to walk across the room without limping and he opened the door. 'Your carriage will be waiting, my love. You had best be going, for you know how I dislike my horses to be kept standing.'

My lady glared at him, but without deigning to reply she swept out of the room, venting her wrath upon the hapless footman waiting to hand her into the coach.

The year advanced. Spring sunshine tempted travellers back on to the roads. Lord and Lady Hartworth, who had been in London all winter, left town to spend a few months at Hart Chase, their principal seat near Huntingdon, while many of those who remained in the capital welcomed back their friends and acquaintances. Still Madame de Sange's house at Knight's Bridge remained shut up.

The viscount remained in Town, dividing his time between trying to discover where Elinor de Sange might be, and observing the movements of Lord Thurleigh. In neither quarter could he have boasted of any great success, although his lordship's activities provided him with some diversion for his thoughts. Davenham noted that the marquis had renewed his acquaintance with Lord Thomas. Under normal circumstances, the viscount would have given the matter scarcely a thought, but his close scrutiny of the marquis made him more acutely aware of his actions and it seemed that Thurleigh was deliberately cultivating the fellow's friendship.

A casual word of enquiry elicited the information that Lord

Thomas was a relative newcomer to the court, a man of moderate means, with a small estate in Derbyshire, and that he had recently been appointed Lord of the Bedchamber. Interesting, thought Davenham, but hardly suspicious.

Much more intriguing were the frequent visits of my lord's groom to the squalid drinking-houses of Holborn and St Giles. Davenham learned of these forays from one of his own servants whom he had at one time set to watch the Thurleigh household. The young footman was devoted to his master, quick-witted and eager to please, so that when, having executed an errand in the City, he spotted Lord Thurleigh's man making his way towards one of the more iniquitous quarters of the capital, he had promptly followed him and reported his findings to his master. The viscount was at first inclined to dismiss the incident, but when subsequent observation proved that the fellow made regular excursions to such haunts he began to feel uneasy. The marquis prided himself upon the relative sobriety of his servants, and he was well known as a harsh master. Surely his head groom would not risk offending such an employer, or did he perhaps have his master's approval? An interesting point, but although Davenham watched the marquis closely during the following weeks, he was no nearer to answering the question when he received a summons from his father to join him at Hart Chase.

The viscount was greeted warmly by Fletton, the butler, who informed him in a fatherly way that Lord Hartworth had gone out but that my lady was at home, and in her room, should he wish her to be informed of his arrival.

'Don't bother,' said the viscount, giving up his greatcoat to a hovering footman, 'I'll announce myself. See to my bags, will you, Fletton?'

Lord Davenham took the stairs two at a time and made his way to his mother's apartments on the second floor. He knocked softly upon the door, but did not wait for an answer before entering. The countess was reclining upon a sofa by the window, her head resting upon a cushion and her eyes closed. One slender hand rested across her fashionable apron, an exquisite creation embroidered with dainty silver flowers, while the other arm hung down at her side, the book that had slipped from her fingers lying open upon the floor. The viscount trod quietly across the room and stooped to pick up the tome, dropping a kiss upon the lady's forehead as he did so. Lady Hartworth opened her eyes and, observing her visitor, gave a stifled shriek and sat up, throwing out her arms to wrap her son in a fond embrace.

'Jonathan! You wicked boy – how dare you come in upon me unannounced!'

Grinning, he returned her embrace. 'How dare you to look so charming when you are asleep, Mama! You are more beautiful each time I see you!'

'Flatterer!' she admonished him, trying to sound stern. 'Is that my book you are holding? Give it to me.'

'Here you are. What is it, another romance?'

'Yes, and quite tedious it must be, or I assure you I should not have fallen asleep! Now, my boy, come sit by me and tell me, when did you arrive?'

'I have but this moment come in, Mama. Yes, I know what you will say, I should have changed before coming to see you, but how could I wait to see my favourite lady, and I assure you I wiped my boots most carefully before coming indoors!'

'Fie on you, sir! When have I ever scolded you over a little mud when we are in the country? Pray be sensible, Jonathan. Your father is not yet returned?'

'No. Fletton told me he had gone out, so I came directly to you. Did I disturb you?'

'Not at all, my love. I had no intention of sleeping. There was an hour or so to spare before I needed to change my dress for dinner, and I thought I might be usefully employed improving my mind.' This prim speech was belied by the mischievous twinkle that gleamed in her eyes.

The viscount smiled back at her. 'What is this talk of changing your dress? Is that in my honour, ma'am? If so I am most flattered.'

My lady gave her attention to smoothing the creases from her snowy apron.

'I did not see your father's letter, Jonathan. What did he say to you?'

'Oh, it was the briefest of notes. He merely requested the pleasure of my company here for a few days.'

'Then you know nothing of . . .' she broke off and looked up as the door opened, saying in a voice tinged with relief, 'My lord! You are just in time. Jonathan is here.'

'So I was informed,' murmured Lord Hartworth, strolling across the room and bending to salute his wife's upturned cheek. Straightening, he smiled at his son. 'How are you, my boy?'

'Well, sir, I thank you. No need to ask how you go on. Chase has always agreed with you.'

The earl smiled faintly. 'Indeed it has.' He turned to his wife. 'My dear, if you do not object, I will take Jonathan away with me. There are one or two things I should like to discuss with him.'

'Of course you must go. Besides, it is time I was thinking of what I am to wear this evening.'

The two gentlemen took their leave of her, Lord Hartworth leading his son downstairs to the library, where a decanter and glasses were set out in readiness for them.

'You'll take a glass of Malmsey with me, Jonathan?' Lord Hartworth poured two glasses without waiting for a reply. He handed a glass to the viscount and bade him to be seated before continuing, 'When I left Town, you were attempting to find a certain lady. Madame de Sange, do I have that correct?'

'Yes, sir. As I told you at the time, Guy Morellon is also anxious to trace her, but so far my luck has been quite out. She seems to have vanished without trace. The only consolation is that Thurleigh's luck appears to be no better than my own. I have been keeping an eye on Thurleigh and I'll swear he has no more notion than I do where to find the lady.'

'Much less notion, in fact,' purred the earl, sipping his wine.

'Sir?'

The older man smiled faintly, his eyes gleaming with amusement.

'Did I forget to mention it in my letter to you, Jonathan? Madame de Sange is staying here, as my guest.'

CHAPTER TWENTY

In which a lady loses her temper

For a full minute the viscount could only stare at his father, whose amusement deepened at the young man's obvious confusion. At last he took pity upon his son and volunteered an explanation.

'I came upon Madame de Sange in a small village in Bedfordshire, where I had stopped to pay my respects at the grave of my late friend Ambrose Burchard. It did not take me long to discover her identity and to persuade her to put herself under my protection.'

'To put herself. . . ! Sir, I think I should tell you—'

'She is a most unusual young lady,' the earl interrupted him smoothly. 'She has told me her history.'

'What, sir, all of it?'

'I believe so, and I must say I find her resolution and fortitude most remarkable.'

'I wonder that she should be so forthcoming upon such short acquaintance,' observed the viscount drily. 'You appear to be on the best of terms!'

The earl's eyes gleamed. 'You forget, Jonathan, that I have the advantage of my years. I am old enough to be her father.'

'I wonder if that is how she views the matter.'

'You do not appear to like the lady, my son,' observed my lord, smiling.

Davenham threw up his hands. 'Like her! In faith, sir, I know not what to make of her! When she disappeared I went to Knight's Bridge to discover what information I could get there, only to find Thurleigh had gone before me, searched the house and had terrorized most of the servants into running away.'

'And it seems our dear friend Thurleigh is very anxious to find Madame de Sange.'

'From what I have heard, I believe it is not so much the woman as a jewel he wishes to find. A ruby brooch that she stole from him years ago.'

'Did Thurleigh tell you the lady stole the jewel?'

The viscount shrugged, his face harsh. 'Does it matter? The woman is involved in more than one murder. A little robbery would not be out of place.'

'Perhaps you will revise your opinion when you have heard Madame's story.'

'Oh, I had that from Hannah Grisson, the companion, who has known her all her life. A very touching tale!'

'You did not believe it?'

'I believe Madame de Sange to be a scheming jade, whatever her history!'

Over the rim of his empty glass the earl regarded his son steadily, an enigmatic gleam in his blue eyes. A clock somewhere in the house chimed and he rose from his chair.

'I must not keep you any longer. You will be wishing to change out of those travelling clothes before we join the ladies for dinner. And I hope, my son,' he added, with the ghost of a smile, 'that when you discard your muddied raiment, you will also rid yourself of that forbidding scowl!'

Despite his father's advice, when Lord Davenham presented himself in the drawing-room at the appointed hour, it could not have been said that he was in the sunniest of moods. He found his parents there and, as he joined them, they broke off their conversation to greet him.

'Jonathan, my boy, how gratifying that you are so punctual.' The earl raised his glass to observe his son's raiment. The frock-coat of dark-blue velvet was well cut, and hung open to display an embroidered silver waistcoat and an abundance of snow-white lace at his throat, but the absence of any ornament caused his parent's expressive brows to rise. 'Such plain dress, my son! Perhaps you should have taken orders!'

The viscount's solemn countenance was transformed when he laughed.

'Hardly, sir! You must forgive me if I eschew the more extravagant style of dress. An abundance of fobs and jewels is not for me!'

'Evidently!' Lord Hartworth shuddered elegantly and turned aside as his lady stepped forward, holding out her hands to her son and pulling him close so that he could kiss her cheek.

'My lord has told you that we have a visitor?' She smiled up at him. 'I want you to be very kind to her, Jonathan. From the little she has said of your previous meetings, I think she has formed a poor opinion of you!'

'Indeed, ma'am?'

'Yes *indeed*!' retorted his fond Mama, tapping his cheek with her fan. 'But if you mean to look so disagreeable and behave in that odiously haughty manner, you may go away and I will have Cook send dinner to your room!'

The cold look left his face.

'Doubtless you would send me a stomach powder, too, since I am so obviously colicky!'

'Of course!' She saw he was amused and pressed home her advantage. 'Now I pray you, Jonathan, be kind to the child, and do not look too critically at her gown. Your father wants as little attention as possible drawn to our guest so I dared not send out for more clothes, and we had to make over some' of my own dresses. I must say, though, it has answered very well, for apart from being obliged to let down the hems, and adding a flounce or two to accommodate the lady's height, they fitted her admirably. Hush now, here she comes, and remember, my dear, be *kind*!' With this final whispered admonition, the countess went forward to greet Madame de Sange, who was standing hesitantly in the doorway.

Lord Davenham's first thought was surprise that his mama had ever worn such a fetching gown as the one that now adorned Elinor de Sange. The peacock-green silk shimmered in the candlelight, and scallops of blond lace decorated the full skirts, with matching ruffles at the lady's elbows and about her neck. Her red-brown hair was unpowdered and pinned up in artless curls, framing a face that was as pensive as it was beautiful.

'My dear Elinor, pray come in!' My lady drew her guest forward until she was standing before the viscount. 'I am sure you remember my son, Jonathan, for I know you have met any number of times in Town.'

Elinor glanced up, uncertain of her reception, but she found the viscount regarding her with nothing more menacing than a faint, polite smile. She relaxed slightly and gave him her hand.

'Yes, of course. How do you do, my lord?' Her tone was cool, but not unfriendly, and the viscount answered in kind, although he made no effort to engage the lady in conversation.

'You can have no idea how pleasant it is for me to have Elinor to bear me company,' remarked Lady Hartworth, sensing the restraint. 'Your father always has a great many things to attend to when we are here and one cannot be forever driving abroad paying morning calls. To have so charming a guest is a veritable blessing.'

'You are too kind, ma'am,' murmured Elinor, blushing faintly.

'I trust, Madame, you do not find Hart Chase a trifle dull,' remarked the viscount, unable to keep the acid note from his voice. 'I believe you have been used to a more *eventful* way of life.'

Even as the words left his lips Davenham regretted them. He observed the expression of pain and confusion that momentarily shadowed Elinor's countenance, but before he could offer an apology, Lady Hartworth intervened. Casting her son a look of burning reproach, she carried Elinor off to sit beside her until they went into dinner. Somewhat to his mother's surprise, the viscount begged to be allowed to escort their guest. Elinor acquiesced silently, but as they followed the earl and his lady across the hall, Davenham detained her, allowing his parents to move away so that he could speak to her privately.

'Madame, pray forgive me for my incivility. I have not yet recovered from the shock of finding you here.' He tried to

speak jokingly, but realized to his dismay that he had merely
succeeded in sounding even more cutting. He felt the lady's
fingers tremble upon his arm.

'It is of no consequence, sir. I pray you will not allow my
presence to destroy all your pleasure in coming here. For my
part I shall endeavour to inconvenience you as little as possible!' Removing her hand from his sleeve, she walked quickly
away, leaving the viscount to follow her into the dining-room.
During the meal it was left to Lady Hartworth to maintain a
flow of inconsequential chatter, with the earl obligingly
adding the occasional remark. The countess could only be
thankful when the time came for her to remove with her guest
at the end of the meal, leaving the gentlemen to their own
devices.

Upon entering the drawing-room some time later, the earl
and his son found only my lady, dozing in a chair beside the
fire. She sat up as they entered, stifling a yawn and smiling
upon the gentlemen.

'So here you are at last! I vow you have been so long about
your cognac that I had almost given you up! Poor Elinor was
so tired she could scarce keep her eyes open, so I have sent her
to bed. I think she has the headache, for she was unusually
quiet at dinner, was she not, my lord? However, she makes you
both her apologies. Although in my opinion,' she added, fixing
her son with a reproachful eye, 'it is you, sir, who should be
making the apology for your cavalier behaviour before dinner!
How came you to be so unkind to our guest, Jonathan?'

'It was not my intention, Mama, and I am indeed sorry for
it. However' – he looked at her, frowning – 'how much do you
know of the lady's history, ma'am?'

Lady Hartworth met her son's eyes steadily.

'Enough to know that she has suffered quite dreadfully at
the hands of evil men!'

'And do you also know, Mama, that she came to England
seeking revenge?'

'In her position I hope I would have the courage to do the
same!' she retorted with unwonted spirit.

'Madame de Sange has favoured us with a full and, I
believe, true account of events,' remarked the earl. 'I think it

might be best if you were to discuss this with the lady herself on the morrow.'

'Yes, I agree,' put in his wife, a note of weariness creeping into her voice. 'It is far too late to talk of such weighty matters now.'

'Poor Mama, you too should have retired,' said the viscount, looking closely at her. 'There was no need to wait up for us.'

'Nonsense, Jonathan, I am not in the least bit tired!' she retorted, sitting up in her chair. 'How could I go to bed without seeing you, and on your first evening with us, too! Now come and sit down with me, my son, and tell me all the latest gossip from London.'

The viscount obliged her with half an hour of the most interesting stories from Town, but after this time he excused himself, pleading fatigue. For a long moment after he had left the room the countess remained staring at the door.

'Well,' she said at last, shaking her head, 'I must say tonight has been one of the most uncomfortable evenings I have ever endured! Elinor hardly touching her food, and blushing every time one spoke to her, and as for Jonathan, he scarcely said a word at dinner! I really cannot make it out!'

'Can you not?' murmured her spouse, looking amused. 'And I have always considered you a romantic!'

She stared at him.

'Surely you cannot mean – but they scarcely know one another!'

'Does that matter? I knew I loved *you* the moment I first saw you.'

A rosy blush coloured my lady's cheek.

'And I you, my lord, but that was different!' She observed his smile and sighed. 'Mayhap you are right, my lord, you usually are. Well, all I can say is that I hope they will soon get over it, for there is nothing more uncomfortable than to be obliged to share one's house with a pair of quarrelsome lovers!'

The morning dawned dull and wet, with a damp mist shrouding the countryside. It suited Elinor's mood, for she had awoken with an almost tangible depression hanging over her. However, after taking breakfast in her room, she dressed and went down to the library, where she took some comfort in the cheerful fire she found blazing in the hearth. She sank down into a chair and closed her eyes, hoping that a little quiet reflection would drive off the threatening headache. She fell into a doze and when she awoke some time later it was to find the viscount standing over her.

'Oh! I – I am sorry! You were perhaps wishing to use the library? I will go!' she started to rise, but Lord Davenham waved to her to remain in her seat.

'Please, stay where you are.' He gave her a slight, perfunctory smile. 'My father suggested we should talk. I was unpardonably rude to you last night. I apologize.'

Elinor blinked in surprise, regarding his back as he walked away from her to stand looking out of the window, staring out at the pleasant prospect of shaved lawns and orderly flowerbeds that glistened in the rain.

'Will you – that is, I would be honoured if you would tell me how you come to be here.'

'Has not Lord Hartworth—?'

'I wish to hear the story from you!' he broke in, turning to face her. He saw her stiffen and added, 'If you please, Madame.'

After a moment, Elinor nodded.

'Very well. Won't you sit down, my lord? To have you standing over me puts me at a disadvantage.'

He drew up a chair and sat down facing her.

'There. Now will you begin?'

She could not explain why his presence should cause her hands to tremble so, and she clasped them in her lap to disguise the malaise.

'I was visiting my father's grave when Lord Hartworth first approached me. He told me he had known me as a child, when he had come upon occasion to visit Papa.'

'Wait.' The viscount stared at her, frowning. 'Who was your father?'

'Ambrose Burchard.'

'But of course! I should have realized – my father's dear friend!' He subjected her to another searching look. 'He died in a duel?'

The lady's face darkened.

'He was brutally slain by Lord Thurleigh or one of his cronies! My father was a peaceful man, no more adept at swordplay than – than I am! And as if his death was not enough, my mother and I were forced to flee the country, for fear of being arrested as thieves!'

'Ah. The ruby.'

'What do you know of that?'

'I called upon your companion, Mistress Grisson. She had just endured a visit from Lord Thurleigh, who made it clear to her that he was anxious for news of you and, it would seem, for the return of a certain ruby brooch.'

'When – when was this?' she asked him, growing pale.

'Soon after Boreland's death – you knew of that, of course?' His sarcasm was lost on her, and she merely nodded.

'Poor Hannah, was she hurt?'

'No, but very frightened – and more for your sake than her own.'

'I must write to her again, tell her I am safe—'

'That would not be wise at present!' he said quickly. 'Thurleigh has not given up his search for you. But we digress from your tale, Madame. Why did you come to Hart Chase?'

'Your father seemed to know something of me.' She shot a speculative glance across at the viscount. 'From you, perhaps?'

'I told him what I knew of you, but that was scant knowledge.'

'Then I am doubly grateful to his lordship for befriending me, since what you know of my life has led you to believe only the worst of me!'

'Since you would not trust me with the whole story! But let us not fall into an argument. I suspect my father told you that you could help him to bring down Lord Thurleigh. Am I right?'

Elinor nodded. 'The ruby brooch bears an inscription, naming Thurleigh and four others as loyal to the Stuart cause in the uprising of 'forty-five. Your father believes it will provide damning evidence against those named.'

'Where is the brooch? May I see it?'

'I have it with me,' she said, reaching into her pocket. 'I was going to give it to Lord Hartworth for safekeeping this morning.'

'Very wise.' The viscount leaned forward to take the brooch from her outstretched hand. 'A fine piece of craftsmanship,' he added, turning it between his fingers.

'You will see it has the Thurleigh crest on the back, and there is a small catch concealed on one side. Amongst the smaller leaves.'

His fingers roamed over the finely wrought gold until he felt a slight movement in the setting. A little gentle pressure and the back of the brooch fell open. The viscount carefully studied the inscription. At last he looked up.

'Three of the men named here are no longer alive.'

She met his gaze squarely. 'I am aware of that.'

For a moment an unasked question hung between them. Then, 'Did you arrange for their deaths?'

'No.' She continued to hold his gaze. 'I wanted them dead, I do not deny that I was quite prepared to – to kill them myself, but it was not – necessary.'

Davenham looked away. Thoughtfully he walked over to a large desk in the centre of the room, opened a drawer and dropped the ruby into it, closing and locking the drawer afterwards and pocketing the key. Elinor watched him; now that she had shared her burden and handed over the stone, she felt as if a weight had been lifted from her shoulders.

The viscount returned to stand before Elinor.

'Where did you go when you left Weald Hall?'

'You knew of my visit there?'

He gave a harsh laugh. 'My dear Madame de Sange, when Mistress Boreland took you off to stay with her, everyone in Town knew it was as a prospective bride for her son!'

The blood warmed her cheeks, but Elinor retorted with spirit.

'Since my affairs are such common knowledge, sir, you have no need of my explanation!'

'Oh, pray don't play off your airs on me!' he returned impatiently. 'I know – from sources that I believe to be reliable! – that you went to Weald Hall in early December and that you made a somewhat hasty exit on Christmas Day!'

'Your sources are most assuredly reliable, sir!'

He pulled his chair closer to her own and sat down.

'Yes, but they do not tell me why you were obliged to run away.'

'It is very simple, my lord. Boreland knew I had the ruby and he wanted me to give it up to him.' She paused, frowning. 'I do not think he himself recognized me, but he had visited Lord Thurleigh and upon his return he came directly to my room and challenged me. I did not know at that point why Thurleigh should be so anxious to have the ruby returned to him. He is after all so rich that he could purchase a dozen such jewels! It was not until much later that we discovered why this one was so important.' She looked up to find Lord Davenham's eyes fixed upon her, a deep frown upon his brow. 'You find my story too incredible, sir?'

'It seems odd to me that Lord Thurleigh should allow such an important jewel to go astray in the first place.'

'On the night I – met – Lord Thurleigh and his accomplices, one of them must have put the stone into my pocket, not realizing its importance.'

'But why did Thurleigh not come after you and recover his property? Would you have me believe that the innocent child you have described could outwit such a powerful man?'

Elinor's green eyes flashed. 'You would rather believe that he gave me the stone in a moment of infatuation?'

'I do not *want* to believe it, Madame, but it is by far the more credible story. There is no telling what a man might do for a beautiful woman.'

For a long moment their eyes remained locked, then with a sigh Elinor looked away. She did not know why it was so important to her that he should understand. 'We fled to France the very night Papa was killed. Mama had relatives there, who took us in.' She put up her chin, saying with brittle cheerfulness, 'So you see, my lord, how I thus evaded the powerful marquis!'

'But now that Thurleigh knows you are in England, he is most anxious to find you, even lowering himself so far as to come to me for information.' He observed her startled look and shook his head. 'You need not worry, I did not give you

218

away. Indeed, at that time I knew no more than he did where to find you. He did, however, tell me that you had escaped from Weald Hall. Is it true Boreland set his dogs to hunt you down?'

'Yes, it is true.' She forced herself to speak steadily. 'I had reached the cover of the woods before I heard the hounds in pursuit. I chanced upon a lane, which I guessed would lead me to the London road. Happily for me a – a traveller was abroad, and hearing the commotion he came to investigate and took me upon his horse.' She paused to smile briefly. 'He was only just in time, too, for as he took me up the dogs were snapping at my heels!'

'You had not arranged to meet this man?'

She looked surprised. 'No indeed, sir! Until that evening I did not even know that I would be leaving Weald Hall.'

'And he carried you safe away.'

Elinor hesitated. 'Yes. He carried me to safety.'

'And what is his name, this gallant knight who came so opportunely to your rescue?' Davenham could not resist the question, nor prevent the sneering tone of his voice.

The lady looked away, but not before he had observed the glitter of tears in her eyes.

'Ralph Belham. But you need not concern yourself with him, my lord. He is no longer alive.'

The viscount fought against his desire to comfort her.

'You appear to have a rare talent, ma'am. Any gentleman who falls within your sphere comes to an untimely end!'

'Perhaps I am cursed,' she murmured, covering her face with her hands.

In an instant he was beside her, his arms drawing her close so that she was obliged to rest her head upon his shoulder.

'No, no, forgive me, Elinor. I should not have spoken so!' His cheek rested against the chestnut curls. 'You are involved, yes, but not to blame for these deaths! I cannot look into your lovely face and believe you are anything but the victim of a cruel fate. Oh, my dearest love, pray dry your eyes.'

She pulled away and stared at him in horror.

'Good God, sir – what is this?'

He gave a shaky laugh. 'God knows I have fought against

219

it, but from the first time I saw you I was attracted to you as to no one before! I fear you have bewitched me.'

With a sob she turned away, angrily wiping her eyes.

'Have you not insulted me enough?' she cried. 'You have from the start despised me, accused me of being in league with the likes of James Boreland and Lord Thurleigh, questioned my honour and suspected me of witchcraft! And now, when I have told you my story, laid open every scar and bitter memory that you might better understand me, you repay my efforts by making May-game of me!'

'No, Elinor, I swear that is not so—'

'And I have never given you leave to use my name!' she flashed, spots of rage flying upon her cheeks.

'I beg your pardon, Madame—'

'How dare you!' she continued, paying him no heed. 'How dare you think that I will suffer your taunts and insults! If it were not for the fact that I have promised to help Lord Hartworth I would leave here this instant! Oh how I hate you! You cannot know how much I despise you, my lord!'

Davenham stood rooted to the spot while her tirade raged over him. He remained silent, his face pale, and only by the quivering of a muscle at the side of his mouth did he betray his emotion. When the lady paused for breath, he said in a tight voice, 'I beg your pardon for my outburst, Madame. It was mistimed, I admit, but I was not aware that my attentions would be so abhorrent to you. It shall not happen again.'

'You may be assured I am most relieved to know that!' she threw at him, still in the grip of her own anger. 'I have suffered much in the past, my lord, but nothing – *nothing* could be less welcome to me than a declaration from you! Do you understand me?'

'Perfectly, Madame.'

For some incomprehensible reason Elinor found his calm acceptance of her invective even more infuriating. Dashing away a tear, she threw one last taunt at him.

'And I will furnish you with even more evidence of my – my *murderous* talent! Ralph Belham died at the hands of the very man who was pursuing me! By some mischance he met James Boreland upon the road one night last winter and in an exchange of shots he killed Boreland but himself took a bullet in the stomach. R-Ralph was able to g-get back to the inn, but he – he died before we c-could fetch a surgeon.' She drew a shuddering breath and added bitterly, 'Do you think I can exonerate myself from all blame in that tragedy, too? I tell you, sir, that I hold myself most decidedly culpable for the death of Ralph Belham, but it only increases my determination that the men whose names are inscribed on that blood stone should all be brought to justice, and I will not ask forgiveness of *my* sins until they have paid for *theirs!*' She stopped, her breast heaving with emotion as she fought to regain her composure, then, with a muttered 'Excuse me' she ran to the door.

'Madame!' the viscount's voice halted her as she was about to leave the room. 'Please – Elinor, you must believe that I am honoured by the disclosures you have made to me. If I can be of assistance to you in any way, at any time, pray do not hesitate to tell me.'

Elinor did not look back, but he saw her nod her head before hurrying away.

CHAPTER TWENTY-ONE

My Lord Thurleigh wins the trick

When the Earl of Hartworth had completed a late and leisurely breakfast, he enquired after his son and was informed that the viscount had ridden out. Glancing out of the window at the grey sky and steady rain, his lordship opined that no one would wish to remain out of doors longer than necessary on such a day and he left instructions that the viscount should be sent to him as soon as he came in. In the event it was nearly two hours before Lord Davenham returned, and a while longer before he appeared before his father, the inclement weather making it necessary for him to change his sodden clothing. He found Lord Hartworth in the library, seated at the large desk with his account books spread out in front of him.

'You wished to see me, sir?'

The earl looked up from his books and his shrewd eyes did not fail to notice the pale face and grim demeanour.

'Yes indeed, Jonathan. You talked with Madame de Sange this morning, as I suggested?'

'I did, sir,' came the short reply.

A gleam of understanding appeared in the older man's eyes.

Lord Davenham gave his attention to smoothing the snowy lace ruffles that covered his wrists.

'I am thinking of going back to Town, sir. I had formed the intention of leaving in the morning, if you have no further need of my services.'

'This is rather sudden: may one enquire the reason you

wish to leave us so abruptly?'

The viscount turned away. He said with difficulty, 'I think – indeed I am sure – it would be more comfortable for Madame de Sange if I were not here. We – cannot agree on a number of points, and I have no wish to cause the lady further pain by inflicting my presence upon her for any longer than is necessary.'

'I take it the lady rejected your suit.'

'She has left me in no doubt of her feelings towards me!' came the bitter reply, which caused his father to smile, but he said merely that they must wait to hear what Lady Hartworth had to say to her son's plan.

When the matter was mentioned to that lady, she cried out vehemently against the idea of her son leaving them so soon. The reason for so sudden a departure – that there were a great many matters in Town requiring the viscount's attention – she dismissed as nonsense, and accused her son of becoming bored with his family and preferring the gay life he was used to in London They were gathered in the drawing-room, as was the custom before dinner, and when Elinor came in Lady Hartworth immediately drew her into the discussion.

'Elinor, my dear, how glad I am that you were able to join us for dinner! Is your migraine completely cleared? So tedious for you to be obliged to keep to your room all day!' She beckoned to her guest to come and sit beside her. 'Do help me persuade Jonathan to give us a few more days of his company. He has been with us such a short time and already he is declaring that he must return to Town.'

Elinor blushed faintly and could not bring herself to look up at the viscount as she replied.

'I am sure, ma'am, that only the most urgent business could persuade Lord Davenham to leave you.'

'But Hartworth has informed me that we shall ourselves be returning to London in a few days! Surely Jonathan's business can wait a little while, that he may escort us.'

Elinor's eyes flew to the earl.

'Is it true, my lord? You go to London?'

He nodded. 'I hope to be back in Hartworth House by Friday. I want to hand over the ruby to those loyal to the King.

I think it best that you come with us, Madame. You will be safer under my protection than alone in your own house.'

'You see!' cried the countess. 'Davenham has but to delay his journey for another three days! And besides,' she added, 'I have this minute remembered we are to dine out tomorrow night. Squire Goodrow and his sister called this afternoon and pressed me so earnestly to accept that I could not find the heart to say them nay. Of course, I made no mention of you, my dear,' she continued, turning to Elinor, 'for we agreed from the start, did we not, that you were to remain here in strict seclusion?'

'I wish you had found some way to put off this engagement, Mama.'

'I know, Jonathan, I do not like it myself, to be going out and leaving dear Elinor by herself, but Miss Goodrow was so persistent, and we have excused ourselves from dining with them so many times in the past that I found myself quite at a loss.'

'It is never a good idea to offend one's neighbours, Davenham,' put in the earl. 'You will attend tomorrow night, sir, with as good a grace as you can muster. The Goodrows do not keep late hours, and you may make an early start for Town the following morning, if you think it necessary.'

The viscount looked far from pleased, but he merely inclined his head.

'As you wish, sir.'

Lord Hartworth smiled benignly at his son and the evening proceeded in what Elinor could only describe as a most uncomfortable fashion. Dinner seemed interminable, and when at last the ladies withdrew, she was able to tell her hostess truthfully that she had the headache and to retreat to the seclusion of her bedchamber.

The bright sunshine to which she awoke did nothing to lift Elinor's spirits, and it was with some trepidation that she entered the breakfast-room the next morning. She was relieved to find only the countess there, a casual enquiry eliciting the information that the gentlemen had taken advantage of the fine weather to ride over the earl's extensive estates. Elinor was thus able to avoid the viscount until the evening, when the family gathered in the drawing-room before travelling to the Goodrows for dinner. She delayed as long as she dared in changing her gown and tarried so long that the earl's carriage was at the door before she came down-stairs, entering the drawing-room just as the family were preparing to leave.

'Ah, my dear,' remarked Lady Hartworth, her cloak already about her shoulders, 'how unfortunate that you must remain here alone. However, it cannot be helped and I have told Fletton to serve your dinner in here by the fire. So much more comfortable for you than to sit in that draughty dining-room by yourself!'

'Thank you, ma'am.' Elinor bent to receive my lady's salute upon her cheek, and smiled farewell to the earl who was hold-ing open the door for his wife. She then turned to face the viscount; for an instant she was transported back to their first meeting in Paris, for then, as now, she had been impressed by the simple style of his attire, which so complemented his lean, handsome face. On that occasion he had been dressed in black, but now he wore a plain velvet jacket and breeches of the darkest blue, the severity of his raiment relieved only by the froth of snowy lace at his neck and cuffs. As was his pref-erence, his dark hair was unpowdered, and confined by a thin velvet ribbon. Elinor noted his gleaming riding-boots and the heavy greatcoat thrown over a nearby chair, and could not resist an enquiring glance. A faint smile lightened his features.

'I never travel by carriage if I can ride.'

'And you will be leaving in the morning?'

'Yes. I intend to make an early start.'

'Then let me wish you a good journey, sir, for I doubt I shall see you again before you leave.'

'Thank you.' He took her hand, wondering that her fingers should tremble as he raised them to his lips. For a moment they looked at each other, both wishing to speak, neither knowing how to begin. A discreet cough from Lord Hartworth broke the spell.

'It is time we were away, Davenham.'

With a final bow the viscount snatched up his greatcoat and strode out of the room. When the door had closed upon her Elinor stood for a few moments, listening to the receding footsteps, then she ran to the window, peering out into the fading light. Unfortunately, the drawing-room was at the back of the house and gave her no sight of the drive. She ran to the glazed door that led out on to the terrace, and after a few moments spent struggling with the catch she managed to open it. She stepped out. The terrace ran the length of the house, but a high wall at each end prevented her from seeing the earl's carriage as it moved off, although the sounds carried clearly to her on the still air. Disappointed, Elinor went back inside. The air was chill, but before settling herself by the cheerful fire that blazed high in the hearth, she went off to the library in search of a book with which to while away the evening.

Elinor jumped. The delicate chimes of the drawing-room clock were telling her it was nine o'clock. She must have dozed off in her chair after Fletton had removed the dinner tray. Her book lay open on the floor beside her and as she bent to retrieve it she wondered what had roused her; most likely the thud of her book falling to the ground, she reasoned. The fire had burned low, and Elinor was about to send for more wood, then decided against it. Perhaps she should go to bed, there was after all no reason for her to wait up. She shivered, feeling suddenly cold and a little nervous. The house was silent save for the ticking of the clock, and Elinor gave herself a mental shake. She was being childish: had she never been alone in a house before – and could you call it being alone when there was an army of servants below stairs! Elinor glanced about the room. Only the candles in the wall-brackets by the fire had been lighted, giving that area a cosy glow, but leaving the rest of the large room in semi-darkness. Her eyes moved to the windows. Every one was closed, and she had herself fastened the terrace door. She got up. Perhaps if the heavy drapes were pulled across the windows she would feel more secure and dispel this feeling that someone was watching her. She unfastened the ties that held the drapes on the first window, allowing the heavy velvet to shut out the night. Yes, that was undoubtedly an improvement! She moved on to the second window, then to the terrace door, but as her fingers closed on the ties, a figure stepped out from the shadowed embrasure and caught her in a vice-like grip. She gave one startled cry before a large hand was clapped over her mouth. Elinor's eyes widened in alarm as a second figure came out of the shadows, and she found herself looking into the cruel face of Guy Morellon, Marquis of Thurleigh.

'Good evening to you, Madame. We have not been formally introduced, of course, but I have no doubt you remember me. If you promise to behave, my groom will take his hand from your mouth.' He saw her nod, and at his sign the servant removed his hand, still pinning her arms so that she could not move.

'How did you get in here? How did you find me?'

'It was too simple. I followed Davenham when he left Town, and a little surveillance soon proved that my instinct was correct. Since then I have had the house watched, and when I learned that the estimable earl and his family were gone out, I decided it was time we – ah – renewed our acquaintance. So obliging of you, Madame, not to bolt this door when you came in earlier. It was such an easy matter to force the catch.'

'But I am not alone – the servants—'

He laughed softly. 'Oh come now, Madame. You know the servants are in their own quarters and in all probability enjoying some of their master's wine. There is very little chance that they would hear you, even if you were unwise enough to make the devil of a noise – which I would not advise you to try,' he added. 'Jason, my groom, would most certainly prevent you, and I should perhaps warn you that he is very experienced in subduing spirited fillies – is that not so, Jason?'

The man bared his teeth in a cruel grin. 'As you say, my lord.'

'Then at least let me sit down,' said Elinor, her brain racing. 'Surely there can be no harm in that?'

'As you wish.'

The marquis pointed to one of the chairs beside the fire,

taking one opposite for himself. As she sat down, Elinor noted that he had put himself between her and the door, while the groom stood at a little distance, watching them both. The marquis sat back, crossing one booted foot over the other and regarding her with chilling amusement.

'Well, Madame de Sange – or would you prefer me to call you Elinor? I remember that night we met very well, you see.'

'You may call me what you will. It makes no difference to me!'

'Then it shall be Elinor,' he purred. 'Where is the ruby, my dear? I take it you still have it!'

'It is safe. You will never find it.'

'But I have no intention of searching for it. You will tell me where it is.'

'Never.'

'My dear child, do you really think you can hold out against me?'

Elinor threw back her head, squarely meeting his gaze.

'Answer me one thing, sir. That night at the Black Goose – since you have told me how well you remember it – was it you who killed my father?'

'I seem to recall there was some impudent fellow who dared to challenge me. His impertinence was justly rewarded.'

At his careless words Elinor's cheeks grew as white as her petticoat. Her voice was barely above a whisper when she spoke again.

'Then I will never help you! Do you not believe me? Pray tell me, what else can you do to me now? Thanks to you I have no family to be threatened, and I care nothing for myself. My only wish now is to see you punished for the traitor you are!'

The marquis was no longer smiling. He got up and came to stand before her. Elinor kept very still, hoping he could not hear the fearful pounding of her heart.

'Perhaps you will be more co-operative when you realize I am in earnest.' He turned to his groom. 'Hold her!'

The servant moved behind Elinor's chair, pinning her down. Thurleigh raised his hand and hit her hard across the face. Her head snapped back, her senses reeling.

'Tell me where to find the ruby!'

Elinor tasted the blood in her mouth. She shook her head, tensing herself for another blow, but it never came. A door banged somewhere in the house, a rumble of voices and footsteps could be heard coming towards the drawing-room. Signalling to the groom to return to the window embrasure, Thurleigh strode across the room to stand behind the door, drawing his sword as he went. Still dazed from the blow she had received, Elinor looked up as the door opened and Lord Davenham stepped into the room. At the sight of her he stopped, his hand moving instinctively to his own blade.

'Elinor! What the—!' His words were cut short as the marquis stepped up behind him and delivered a stunning blow with the hilt of his sword, which sent the viscount crashing to the floor.

'Jonathan!' With a cry Elinor flew from her chair and fell to her knees beside the unconscious form. The groom stepped forward to pull her away, but his master waved him aside, his cold eyes gleaming.

'This is all very touching, my dear,' he drawled, watching her closely, 'but content yourself, he will recover. Unless you give me occasion to take further action.'

She turned towards him, her body poised as if to shield the viscount.

'What do you mean?'

'Jason, take the lady to one side while I deal with the viscount.'

The groom roughly dragged her away, and through Elinor's mind flashed the vision of Ralph Belham, his laughing face glowing with life and energy as he had told her, *Care for no one, child, 'tis the only way to survive*. But Ralph had broken his own rule. He had become too fond of her and now he was dead, along with her father and her mother – how many others would perish before this matter was ended?

'Well, my dear? It is up to you.' Thurleigh flourished his sword, placing the tip at the viscount's throat.

She gave a strangled cry. 'No! No more, I beg you! I will give you the ruby.'

The marquis waited.

'If I tell you – do you swear you will not touch him again?'

'But of course, my dear. Just give me the jewel and the viscount shall be spared.' He saw her hesitate and added, 'You have my word, ma'am.'

'It – it is in the library desk, in one of the drawers. But it is locked and Lord Hartworth has the only key.'

Lord Thurleigh nodded, and returned the sword to its sheath.

'Where is the library?'

'Directly across the hall.'

'Very well.' He pulled two of the tassled curtain-ropes from their hooks and tossed them to his groom. 'Tie her to a chair while I am gone.'

Passively Elinor allowed herself to be bound to one of the chairs, making no protest as the bonds pressed into her arms. The groom had just finished making her secure and was admiring his handiwork when the marquis returned.

'I have it.' His lips parted in a smile that was as terrible as it was triumphant. He glanced down at the viscount's motionless form. 'You are a very fortunate young man, Davenham. This young lady has undoubtedly saved your life tonight.'

'Do you think you are above the law?' cried Elinor. 'When I tell them you broke in here—'

'And do you think you would be believed? You have no proof. Who would believe the word of a nobody?'

'Lord Davenham and the earl will know the truth!'

'Mere speculation,' replied the marquis, making for the terrace. 'And unfortunately for you, it comes too late, my dear. Soon I will be in a position of such power that not even the King himself will be able to stop me!' Then, laughing, he stepped out into the darkness and was gone.

CHAPTER TWENTY-TWO

A return to Town

Slowly regaining consciousness, the vicount became aware of the sickening pain that throbbed in his head, and a distant voice calling his name. He opened his eyes, but the room was spinning round so much that he closed them again, groaning.

'Oh, Jonathan, thank God! I thought you would never wake.'

He risked opening his eyes again, this time moving his head towards the voice, which sounded vaguely familiar. His vision blurred and cleared and he stared at Elinor, blankly at first, then in horror as he realized she was bound to her chair.

'Oh my poor girl!' He struggled to his feet and staggered across the room, fighting down the nauseating dizziness as he fumbled with her bonds. 'Who did this?'

'It was Thurleigh!' Once untied, she rubbed her arms where the ropes had bitten into her skin. 'Jonathan, he has the ruby! We must go after him, he has been gone but half an hour!'

'We'll deal with that later,' he replied. 'First, we'll get you some brandy.'

'No!' cried Elinor, close to tears. 'Don't you see, he will destroy the brooch!' She jumped up, but her legs would not support her, and she would have fallen had not the viscount caught her. Holding her close, he guided her to a sofa and obliged her to sit beside him.

'I'm sorry, my lord, I am not usually so feeble!'

'I know – my Lady of Stone!' He smiled. 'And pray, must you

go back to calling me my lord? I prefer you to call me by my name.'

The lady flushed. 'It was merely the stress of the moment that caused me to do so, sir, I assure you!'

The viscount went to the sideboard and poured two glasses of brandy, giving one to Elinor.

'Drink all of it, there's a good girl. It will make you feel better, then you can tell me what happened.'

She eyed him frostily, but did not argue, merely taking the glass and sipping resolutely at its contents. Lord Davenham, she noted, drained his glass in one gulp. Elinor pushed her mind back to the events of the evening.

'The marquis forced his way in through the terrace door. He had his groom with him, and they overpowered me. I was closing the curtains when they came upon me and I could not call out for assistance.' She looked up at him anxiously but the viscount's smile reassured her. 'What of the ruby, my lord? Shall we see it again?'

'I doubt it. Thurleigh will not risk it falling into the wrong hands again. By the bye, how did he know where to find it? He could not search the house without the servants hearing him.'

Elinor finished her drink and sat turning the empty glass between her fingers, not daring to look up.

'I – I told him. I had to do so, for I could not bear— Davenham, I am so sorry!'

'Well, you must not blame yourself, child.' He sat down beside her again, removing the empty glass and possessing himself of her hands. 'I can see from the mark on your face that he did not treat you kindly. God knows what he would have done if you had not told him. It is better that you let him have the brooch than that he should hurt you further.'

'Oh, but . . .' She broke off as the sound of voices could be heard outside the door and in another moment Lord and Lady Hartworth came in. My lady's laughing conversation was cut short as she observed the scene, and she flew across the room to Elinor's side.

'My dear child, what has happened here! Get up, Davenham and let me sit beside the poor girl! Good gracious, your face, child!'

232

'It is but a scratch, ma'am. I am not hurt.'

'Perhaps, Davenham, you would be good enough to tell us what has occurred?' suggested the earl, stripping off his gloves.

'Unfortunately, sir, I can tell you very little of what happened,' said the viscount. 'I arrived here some time before ten, to be informed that Madame de Sange was still in the drawing-room. I dismissed the footman and came in here. I remember seeing Elinor slumped in her chair, but then someone hit me over the head and I lost consciousness. When I recovered, Elinor told me Thurleigh had been here and had forced her to tell him where the ruby was hidden.'

'He has taken the brooch, sir. It is all my fault, I have ruined all your plans.'

'Nonsense, child.' The countess patted Elinor's hands. 'We shall come about. I am only too thankful that you suffered no greater injury. And you, Jonathan,' she called across to her son, who was conversing quietly with the earl, 'have you recovered from the blow to your head? Perhaps I should summon Dr Grey to attend you . . .'

'Nay, Mama, save for a slight headache I am well enough now, and quite happy to set off after Thurleigh immediately, if you wish it, sir!'

The earl shook his head. 'No, Jonathan. I agree with you that there is little point in chasing around the country at night. I will tell Fletton to check the house is secure, but I think there is little chance Thurleigh will return. He will make it his business to destroy the brooch at the earliest possible moment. I think our best course would be to go to Town tomorrow and try what we can achieve from there.'

'I too am of that mind,' put in the viscount. He turned to Elinor. 'Madame, there is nothing more to be achieved tonight. Pray allow me to escort you to your room.'

'Yes, take her upstairs, Jonathan,' urged the countess. 'The poor child is looking quite worn down by all this!' She kissed Elinor lightly upon the cheek. 'Go along, my dear, and you need not be afraid to lean upon Jonathan, he is as strong as an ox!'

Elinor allowed herself to be guided from the room and, as

they crossed the deserted hall, she glanced up at her escort. The viscount's mouth was set in a harsh line, and his countenance so severe that her step faltered. Davenham looked down at her, and his face softened.

'Nay Madame,' he said, misreading her distress. 'I am anxious only to see you safely to your chamber. It is not my intention to inflict my company upon you longer than is necessary. Nor shall I attempt to press upon you those attentions that you have told me you find so abhorrent.'

'Did – did I say so?' she asked in a small voice.

'You did,' came the grim reply, 'and a great deal more.'

'Oh.'

They ascended the stairs in silence, Elinor grateful for the support of the viscount's arm, for her own limbs felt treacherously unsteady. When they had gained the landing, Elinor could not resist the temptation to ask, 'Why did you come back so early from the Goodrows, sir?'

'I wanted to talk to you before going to Town. It is not important.'

'Oh.' She stole another glance, discovered the viscount regarding her with some amusement and could not suppress a smile.

'Well, my lord,' she said, 'can we put our silly quarrels behind us and be friends, do you think?'

'I would like to try, Elinor.' They had stopped at her door, and the viscount removed her fingers from his arm. 'Goodnight, my dear.' He carried her hand to his lips and would have released it, had not her fingers suddenly clung to his.

'Jonathan! I have just remembered something Lord Thurleigh said before he left here – he told me it was too late to stop him, that he would soon be more powerful than the King himself!'

'He's planning mischief, we can be sure of that!' the viscount answered grimly. 'Mayhap we shall discover more in London. Don't look so anxious, child. We shall stop him, never fear! In the meantime, you should try to rest.' He squeezed her hand. 'Goodnight, Elinor. We will talk again in the morning.'

The earl's party arrived in London shortly before midnight two days later and thanks to my lord's foresight in sending a servant ahead to warn his household, they found rooms prepared and a light supper set out to welcome them. Despite the exhausting journey, it was a long time before Elinor slept. The viscount had promised to go personally to Knight's Bridge the following day to fetch Hannah to her, it being agreed that Elinor would be safer if she remained under the earl's protection, and the thought of seeing again one who had been as a mother to her filled Elinor with a mixture of delight and anxiety. So much had occurred, and she was not sure she could explain everything, even to Hannah. There was also a feeling of guilt for what her servant had suffered during the worrying months of her mistress's absence.

However, when Hannah Grisson arrived at Hartworth House and was shown into the small sitting-room where Elinor was awaiting her, all these nagging doubts were dispelled by the joy of the reunion. Lord Davenham, who had ushered Mistress Grisson into the room, observed their rapturous meeting before he quietly withdrew, leaving the ladies to their privacy.

'Oh Hannah, I can't find words to tell you how good it is to have you here!' cried Elinor between tears and laughter. 'It was wretched of me to leave you alone all this time, but indeed I could not help it!'

'Nay, Miss Nell.' Hannah patted her shoulder, her own voice gruff with emotion. 'I know you would have kept me better informed, had it been possible. It was enough for me to know you were safe.'

'So much has happened since I last saw you.' Elinor sank down upon the sofa, drawing Hannah down beside her. 'I hardly know where to begin.'

'Lord Davenham has told me much of your story, my dear ma'am.' The careworn face creased into a smile. 'Such a considerate gentleman, and when he told me that his father had been such a close friend of your own dear papa, I knew you were in good hands.'

'Did he also tell you about the brooch? It was vital evidence against Lord Thurleigh and I – I allowed him to regain possession of it!'

'Well, the viscount is a most resourceful gentleman and I daresay he will think of something,' replied Hannah complacently, displaying, in Elinor's opinion, a touching faith in Lord Davenham's abilities, considering their short acquaintance.

'Tell me,' said Madame, shaking off such ungenerous thoughts, 'in what order are things at Knight's Bridge? I understand Lord Thurleigh frightened away my staff.'

Hannah's eyes snapped angrily.

'Aye. He came to call, and turned the house out of doors looking for the brooch. When he couldn't find it he flew into a violent rage.'

'And the list, the one I obtained from Poyntz?'

'My Lord Davenham found it inside the family Bible, just as you told him it would be, and he has it safe now.'

'Thank heaven for that! But – poor Hannah! I am so sorry you had to suffer for my sake! Did the marquis hurt you?'

'Nothing more painful than such ravings and threats one would expect from a madman. I took little heed of it, but he terrorized the servants and they all ran away, save Cook and myself, and one poor dab of a maid who has nowhere else to go. Lord Davenham sent his own servants to help secure the house, and he has promised that they will continue there for the present.' She saw her mistress's frown and added defensively, 'I thought you would not object, Miss Nell, for I hardly liked to leave the house with only Cook and little Clara in charge.'

'No, of course not. You did right to accept his help.'

'And I have brought with me your clothes,' added Hannah, anxious to relieve the moment. 'The trunks have been taken up to your room ready for unpacking.'

'Then let us go upstairs immediately!' cried Elinor, jumping up. 'I have been living in country fashions and cast-offs for so long I am longing to step into one of my own gowns again!'

Later, attired in a gown of russet-coloured silk embroidered with green acanthus leaves, Madame de Sange made her way to the earl's book-room. There she found the viscount engaged in writing a letter. He rose as she entered and came to meet her.

'I was told you were still here,' she said, holding out her hands to him. 'I wanted to thank you for bringing Hannah to me. You have made a hit there, my lord! She thinks you a most competent gentleman!'

His eyes reflected her smile.

'If one wishes to win a lady's favour, it is always wise to be on good terms with her servant. Mistress Grisson has been with you a long time, I think?'

'Yes, for as long as I can remember. She was Mama's maid, I think, before she became my nurse. And she is extremely attached to me. That is why it was so good of you to fetch her yourself. A mere note summoning her to join me would have put her in a rare taking, but you were able to allay her worst fears. Thank you.' Realizing that he was still holding her hands, Elinor blushed and gently drew them away, continuing in a rallying tone, 'And you must also know, sir, that I am most grateful to have my own clothes again! I have been away so long I had forgotten the half of my wardrobe!'

'I am pleased to have brought you so much pleasure, ma'am.'

Elinor paused, running her fingers along the edge of the desk as she asked carelessly, 'Will you be staying to dinner this evening, sir?'

'Unfortunately not. I must return to my own lodgings in Warwick Street very shortly. Just as soon as I have completed the note I am writing for my father.' He indicated the letter lying on the desk, the paper half-covered with a neat, dark script. 'Of course. There must be any amount of business requiring your attention.' She smiled. 'I must not delay you any longer from your task.' She turned to go, but looked back when the viscount called her name.

'I may be able to call in for a few moments after dinner, ma'am, if you think you would not be too tired to receive me?'

She made him a small curtsy.

'I shall look forward to it, sir.'

'I pray you Mistress, keep still or I shall never finish your hair!' Hannah's stern voice called Elinor to order and she obediently assumed a posture of statue-like immobility, only her eyes dancing as she watched her old nurse's reflection in the mirror.

'Oh, do hurry, Hannah! It wants but a few minutes to dinner and I have yet to decide whether the pearls or the emeralds would be best with this gown.'

'Such a fuss over a quiet dinner with the earl and his lady! Well, the way your eyes are shining, Miss Nell, you have no need of jewels tonight!'

Elinor laughed. 'Pray you be serious, Hannah! Which is it to be?'

Before Mistress Grisson could give her opinion, there came a light scratching at the door, and Lady Hartworth hurried in.

'Oh Elinor, my dear, such a to-do! My lord has this minute come in and now all our plans must be changed!'

'What is amiss – the viscount?' cried Elinor, growing pale.

'No no, my love, 'tis nothing to do with Jonathan! Hartworth has learned that there is a reception at St James's this very evening in honour of some ambassador or other, and he has decided we should go! You look astonished, my dear, and indeed I cannot blame you! To be obliged to put on court dress at such short notice—' She broke off, as a sudden horrifying doubt assailed her. 'Heavens, Elinor, do you *have* a court dress?'

Mistress Grisson drew herself up and answered somewhat indignantly in her mistress's defence. 'But of course! Madame, do you not remember, we had the embroidered satin made up shortly before we left Paris. It will take but a minute to fetch it out.'

'Then do so immediately!' cried the countess. 'Oh – and you must powder your hair, Elinor! I have told Cook to put dinner back half an hour, which I hope will be long enough for me to achieve a creditable appearance! I must go now; I will see you at dinner – but hurry!'

Upon these words, she bustled out of the room, leaving

Elinor staring after her, feeling very much as if she was caught up in a whirlwind. Upon Mistress Grisson, however, the news that Elinor was to attend court acted like a spur, and she alternately coaxed and bullied her mistress into her clothes until, some forty minutes later, she was able to send Madame on her way, safe in the knowledge that no one would be able to fault her appearance. Elinor's chestnut locks had been heavily powdered and a touch of colour added in the form of a fine emerald aigrette that nestled amongst the curls. Emerald drops hung from her ears and a matching necklace was clasped about her neck, the brilliant colour enhancing the tiny green leaves embroidered upon her gown of gold-brocaded Italian silk. Gold lace ruffles trimmed the sleeves, a delicately painted fan hung from her wrist and matching shoes peeped out under the wide-hooped skirts, creating a picture of elegance that caused Lady Hartworth to utter a little cry of admiration when she caught sight of Elinor descending the stairs.

'Magnificent!' she cried, crossing the hall in her own lavishly embroidered silk robe. 'What a pity Jonathan will not be there to see you!'

'He is not coming with us to St James's? He said he might call here after dinner.' Elinor tried to sound unconcerned but she had an uneasy feeling that Lady Hartworth was not fooled.

'Well, if he does, the servants will tell him where we have gone –unless you would like to dash off a little note for him?'

Blushing, Elinor disclaimed any wish to contact the viscount and resolutely turned her thoughts to the evening ahead.

The spring night was chill, yet the crowded reception rooms of the palace were warm and airless, and Elinor made great use of her fan as she walked beside Lady Hartworth.

'Goodness, what a crush!' murmured the countess from behind her own painted fan. 'I can never understand why so many people wish to attend these affairs. Look, there's Lord Thurleigh and his wife.' She saw Lord Hartworth beckoning them and tapped Elinor's arm, saying in quite a different tone, 'Come my dear. Hartworth wants you to go with him – I think he is going to present you to the marquis.'

Looking across the room at Lord Thurleigh, Elinor shivered. Even in such a public place she was afraid of the man.

'Elinor?'

The concern in Lady Hartworth's voice gave her courage, and putting up her chin, Madame de Sange moved away from the countess and stepped up resolutely beside the earl, aware that Lord Thurleigh was observing their approach with an inscrutable stare.

'Ah, my Lord Thurleigh – my lady!' Lord Hartworth bowed low to the marchioness. 'May I present to you my young friend, Elinor de Sange?'

The marquis gave the smallest of bows, his eyes ever watchful.

'Your servant, Madame. You have but recently returned to London, I believe. Do you stay in Town?'

Elinor dropped a curtsy, but did not give him her fingers to kiss.

'I am for the moment residing with my Lord and Lady Hartworth. I consider myself fortunate to have found such friends here.'

'Fortunate indeed,' murmured the marquis, glancing across at the earl, who had engaged Lady Thurleigh in conversation. 'Tell me, Madame, after such a long sojourn in France, do you now plan to make your home in your native country?'

'I have yet to decide, my lord. There are certain – injustices – that need to be resolved.'

'Indeed? In my opinion the only injustice is that such a beautiful woman as yourself should still be a widow.' When she did not reply, he continued quietly, 'Set your heart on Davenham, have you not, my dear? Perhaps I could help you there, describe to him the delights that await him . . .'

A look of revulsion crossed Elinor's face.

'You sicken me!' she muttered, turning away.

Although she had not heard what was said, Lady Thurleigh had been observing Elinor closely while she talked to the marquis, responding mechanically to Lord Hartworth's conversation. Now with a word she excused herself and stepped forward, smiling brightly and holding out her hand to Elinor.

'What a pleasure it is to see you here, Madame de Sange! We have met upon occasion, but we have had no opportunity to converse. Pray Madame, allow me a little of your time now – come and sit down with me for a few moments.'

Startled, Elinor looked across at the earl for guidance. Lord Hartworth nodded slightly and she allowed herself to be borne away by the marchioness.

'Such a delightful young woman,' murmured the earl, watching the two ladies walk away together. 'And with such an interesting history.'

'Really?' replied Lord Thurleigh politely. 'I would not know.'

'No, of course. Even you, my lord, are not omniscient. Did you know, for example, that Madame met your old friend Julian Poyntz upon his last fateful trip to Paris, and that he was kind enough to furnish her with a list of names that he considered she might find – ah –useful?'

'Really?' repeated the marquis, but this time the watchful look had returned to his grey eyes. The earl appeared not to notice and continued his almost casual discourse.

'Yes. Madame has given the list to me for safe-keeping, and I have taken precautions to look after it. You may not credit it, my dear sir, but while I was at Hart Chase we were visited by house-breakers! Can you imagine?'

'Oh? Did you lose anything of value?'

'Nothing of any great importance.'

'I think, my lord, that you should consider yourself fortunate that no one suffered any hurt,' drawled Lord Thurleigh. 'I understand these ruffians can be very violent.'

The earl appeared to consider the matter.

'No,' he said at last, 'I think in this case it is the villains who should consider themselves fortunate, for although I have every confidence that I shall eventually bring them to justice by working within the law, if harm had been done to any persons living under my protection, I fear I should have been compelled to take matters into my own hands to avenge them.'

'You are so sure of catching these – villains?' asked Thurleigh, his lip curling.

'Oh yes,' murmured my lord. 'I am even now arranging the matter.'

With a smile and tiny bow, the earl turned and sauntered away, leaving the marquis scowling over their conversation.

CHAPTER TWENTY-THREE

The final hand

'Considering everything, a most successful evening.' Lord Hartworth allowed himself a slight smile as he leaned back against the luxuriously padded interior of the coach that carried the party away from St James's. 'I think our dear friend Guy Morellon understands that he must move soon, or not at all.'

'He did not look at all pleased after you had spoken to him,' remarked the countess, 'and I quite feared that some plot was being hatched when Lady Thurleigh walked off with Elinor. My dear, whatever did she wish to say to you?'

'Nothing to the point,' returned Elinor, puzzled. 'She asked me a little of my childhood, and if I had been happy, but all the time she seemed very nervous, and kept glancing towards her husband, as if she expected him to come over and drag her away. I confess I was a little surprised that he did not do so, after he had finished speaking with you, my lord, but instead he disappeared into the crowd, looking murderous.'

'Yes, I observed that,' remarked the earl. 'He immediately sought out Lord Thomas. I wonder. . . ?' He paused, then turned his attention back to Elinor. 'And Lady Thurleigh said nothing suspicious? She did not try to arrange a meeting, or ask you to call upon her?'

'No, for I was very much on my guard, as you can imagine, but she did not seem to wish me harm. Quite the reverse, in fact. She was quite concerned that I should be properly attended at all times. I found it very strange, for Lady

Thurleigh has been described to me as a very different creature.'

'Perhaps the marquis put her up to it. I can imagine that he
would be relieved to see his wife spending so much time talking with another woman – it is more usual for her to be
arranging an assignation with a gentleman!' observed the
countess, drily.

'You do not care much for the lady, my sweet?' murmured
the earl.

'Emphatically I do not!' came his wife's swift retort. 'The
woman has the soul of a strumpet. I should not wish a son of
mine to have such a wife, although in Guy Morellon's case it
is no better than he deserves!'

She broke off as the carriage drew to a halt outside the
earl's town house and the ladies had scarcely reached the hall
and shaken out their full skirts before they were informed
that Lord Davenham awaited them in the morning-room.
Without waiting to take off her wrap Lady Hartworth led the
way, greeting her son with a motherly kiss and demanding to
know why he had not joined them at the reception.

'There was no time, Mama. I arrived here only minutes
before you. And you are aware, dear ma'am, those receptions
are not my style. How was it? Crowded, as usual?'

'It was a sad crush,' she sighed. 'Too many people for
comfort. I wonder why we make so much effort to dress for
these court functions? It is far too crowded to display a gown
to advantage.'

'Well, there is ample space here, Mama, and I will say, you
look splendid – both of you,' he added, smiling at Elinor.

'What did you learn tonight, Jonathan?' asked the earl,
following the ladies into the room and closing the door.

'My man discovered that Thurleigh's people are in constant
readiness to leave Town at a moment's notice. As you know,
that is nothing out of the ordinary for the marquis, but this
time his good lady must be ready to leave with him, and that
has set the household by the ears.'

'I can well imagine it!' smiled the earl. 'We must watch him
carefully. I don't want him to slip through our fingers. By the
by, what do you know of Lord Evelyn Thomas?'

The viscount shrugged.

'Very little, save that he is now a Lord of the Bedchamber and Thurleigh has struck up an acquaintance with him. They have a common taste in gambling hells.'

'A strange alliance,' mused the earl, 'especially as Thomas was Cumberland's protégé. I think we should look more carefully at that young man.'

'But what of Thurleigh?' cried the countess impatiently. 'Surely you should lay your suspicions before the King's ministers, my lord. You alone cannot expect to thwart his wicked plans!'

'The marquis is a powerful man, my dear. I need proof of his treachery before I dare go to the King.'

'And the ruby would have provided it,' muttered Elinor, 'had I not let it go!'

Lord Davenham came across the room to take her hands.

'You must not blame yourself for that, Elinor. In fact, I have a plan, and if it works, the marquis *can* be arrested for treason.'

She looked up at him hopefully. 'Poyntz's list?'

He shook his head. 'That merely confirms that five men met together all those years ago, but they could have been meeting for any reason – to agree a plan of support for the King, for example. No, what we need is a written statement from the only other man mentioned on that list who is still alive. Bishop Furminger.'

'Will he confess, do you think?' murmured Lord Hartworth. 'The fellow lives in fear of Guy Morellon.'

'Oh, I think I know a way to make him tell us what he knows.' Davenham smiled, turning his gaze towards Elinor. 'But I shall need your help, Madame de Sange.'

The viscount called at Hartworth House at an unfashionably early hour the following morning, and he was pleasantly surprised to find Elinor ready and waiting for him. She could not have had more than a few hours' sleep, yet he thought she looked more beautiful than ever in a simply cut bronze walking-dress with a serviceable cloak thrown over her arm. It was a bright, sunny morning and they made good time to the village of Islington, arriving at Bishop Furminger's leased residence just as that gentleman finished his substantial breakfast. A servant carried the news of their arrival to the little parlour, then silently gathered up the breakfast dishes on to a tray as his master studied the viscount's card.

'Davenham. I don't think I know the gentleman. . . .'

'But you will see me, all the same.'

The bishop looked up in surprise to see that Lord Davenham had followed the footman into the room, at his side a tall lady wrapped from head to toe in a black domino. He dismissed his servant and smiled benignly upon the visitors. Doubtless a pair of star-crossed lovers wishing to be married at once – a common story!

'Well now, what can I do for you? You must excuse me, ma'am, if I do not get up.' He waved at his bandaged foot. 'A touch of gout, you know! Pray be seated, both of you, and tell me how I can help you.'

'I think we prefer to stand.' The viscount's response was cool. 'We will not stay long. Our business concerns the Marquis of Thurleigh.'

The reverend gentleman's smile froze. He said cautiously, 'I know very little of Lord Thurleigh. In fact I have not seen him for quite some time.'

'But you know he is a supporter of the gentleman over the water.'

'I – I have no idea what you mean, sir! I think it would be best if you were to leave . . .' The bishop's hand reached out for the bell-pull, but dropped again as the lady spoke for the first time.

'Can it have slipped your mind, sir, that you were one of a small group of traitors who were waiting to join Charles Stuart in 'forty-five? If he had not turned back at Derby, you would have marched with him to London.' She had pushed back her hood before speaking, and the Bishop stared in horror at Elinor de Sange. The years had changed her from a pretty child to a beautiful woman, but there could be no mistaking the rich chestnut hair or the green eyes that now glittered as they stared at him. 'I see you remember me, Bishop Furminger.'

He licked his dry lips.

'My child, I was haunted by your face for months after that night – I could not forget! But I was powerless to help you!' he cried in anguished tones. 'Thurleigh would have destroyed me!'

'Now you shall help us destroy him,' said Davenham. 'You will denounce him as a traitor.'

Thurleigh will kill me if I do that!'

'And *I* shall kill you if you do not!'

Furminger shrank back in his chair as Elinor drew an evil-looking knife from the folds of her cloak. He managed a shaky laugh.

'You mean to frighten me, Madame, but it will not work. You would not harm me!'

'I shouldn't be too sure of that, Furminger,' put in the viscount. 'Consider for a moment: Poyntz is dead, so too are Rowsell and Boreland.'

'And you, too, would be dead by now,' added Elinor, 'if Lord Davenham had not suggested you would give evidence against the marquis. I am willing to let *you* live, in exchange for his destruction.'

Furminger's naturally ruddy countenance grew pale and he looked imploringly at the viscount.

'The woman's mad! Davenham, I pray you take the knife from her, she is not safe!'

'Give me a written statement concerning Thurleigh's involvement with the Stuart cause and I will ensure Madame de Sange does not harm you.'

The bishop twisted in his chair, thinking quickly.

'I cannot accuse Lord Thurleigh without incriminating myself.'

Lord Davenham smoothed over the ruffles that covered his wrists, replying calmly, 'If you speak out against the King's enemies, I have no doubt the Crown will be merciful.'

There was silence; to Elinor's stretched nerves it seemed to go on for ever.

'Very well. I will tell you what I know.'

'Good.' Davenham crossed the room and tugged at the bell-pull. 'Call for some paper and ink. You can write it down immediately.'

'No! How can I be sure that once you have my statement you will not let this – this madwoman murder me?'

'You have my word on it,' replied the viscount. 'Once I have your written statement I will return to Town, taking Madame de Sange with me.'

'And leave me here to Lord Thurleigh's mercy, once he discovers what I have done?' he cried, aghast.

The viscount regarded the gentleman of the cloth with undisguised contempt.

'Very well, I will take you to Town with me now, and deliver you into the hands of Henry Pelham. He is a sick man, but still the King's first minister. You may tell him of Thurleigh's treachery. Will you trust your safety to him?'

The servant was at the door. After a brief hesitation, the bishop sent him away with orders to pack an overnight bag.

'And pray you, Madame,' he said testily, when the servant had departed, 'put away that fearsome blade, or I shall not travel in the same coach with you!'

It was well after noon when the viscount's carriage made its way back into London and the late spring sunshine had given way to grey clouds that spread across the sky from the west, promising rain before nightfall. They had reached High Holborn, and the bishop was once again complaining that the jolting of the carriage caused unbearable pain to his gouty foot, when they were hailed by a gentleman on horseback heading out of town. Davenham let down the window and looked out, whereupon the rider turned his horse to come alongside the carriage.

'Hello, Davenham! Thought I recognized your rig!' He glanced past the viscount into the carriage and raised his hat in a cheerful salute. 'Madame de Sange, ain't it? Servant, ma'am.'

'What is it Derry? Have you a message for me?'

Lord Derry shook his head, saying with his usual insouciance, 'No, nothing like that, Davenham. Just thought you might like to know the mob are on the move. They're rioting in St Giles again. Lucky I ran into you or you'd have driven right into it. Best turn off if you want to avoid trouble.'

' 'Fore Gad, my lord, let us turn back at once!' cried the

bishop, his voice rising.

'No need for that sir,' replied Lord Derry cheerfully. 'Just make a slight detour. You'll be safe enough.'

Davenham nodded and gave instructions to his coachman. With a friendly wave, Lord Derry turned his horse and rode off, while the viscount put up the window, his face grim.

'I say we should turn back!' cried the bishop. 'Unless you wish us all to be murdered.'

'Don't be such a fool, man!' retorted Davenham. 'We'll turn off towards Lincoln's Inn Fields and avoid St Giles.' He smiled at Elinor, sitting pale and quiet in her corner. 'Don't worry.'

Once off the main highway the carriage made its way slowly along the twisting streets, lurching and swaying over the uneven cobbles. Elinor gazed anxiously out of the window, expecting at any moment to see a ragged crowd appear and attack their carriage, but the roads were deserted and they saw no one until they reached St Martin's Lane, where they found houses and shops alike closed and shuttered, and looking north, a cloud of black smoke darkened the sky. Davenham ordered the coach to stop, and leaned out of the window to speak to a young lad who was running down the road. The boy paused, breathing hard.

'Aye, my lord, they seem set to come this way. They've fired a tavern on the corner of Long Acre, and the Lord only knows what else beside! The King's dead and the Frenchies are even now on their way! By your leave, I must get home!'

The boy ran on, and Davenham gave the word to his coachman before resuming his seat.

'Doubtless you both heard what he said.'

'I did sir!' Furminger's round face was suffused with fear and wonder. 'It puts matters in a completely different light! With the King dead I'll not speak against Thurleigh until I know how things stand!'

'Don't be ridiculous, man! Do you believe everything you hear in the streets?'

Elinor turned anxious eyes towards him. 'You think it's not true?'

'In all honesty I don't know, but I'm taking you both to

Hartworth House until the riot subsides. You will be safer there.'

The carriage moved on westwards and, as they rattled past one of the many narrow streets, the viscount's eyes were drawn to a heavily laden travelling carriage waiting at one corner. For half a minute after they had rumbled past he sat frowning heavily, then with a smothered exclamation he jumped up and shouted new orders to the coachman.

'Good heavens, sir, what now?' cried Furminger, his voice a mixture of alarm and annoyance, but he was ignored. The coach gathered speed and they bounced and jolted over the rutted lane, before swinging around a corner and coming to a stand before the gates of Leicester House. Almost before the coach had stopped, the viscount had leapt out, shouting over his shoulder as he went for the others to wait there for him. After the briefest hesitation, the bishop hauled himself out of his seat and descended from the carriage as quickly as his bulk and bad foot would allow, muttering that nothing would persuade him to remain alone with a murderess.

It took Elinor but a second to decide to follow him, pausing only to take from its holster the horse-pistol that the viscount kept in his carriage. By the time she reached the flagway, Davenham was coming away from the house. She ran up to him.

'What is it, sir, what do you suspect?'

'I'm not sure. Perhaps an attempt to kidnap the Princess and her children. I have just ascertained that the princes are here with their mother today. I'll wager 'tis no mere coincidence!'

'And the carriage we passed. You think – Thurleigh?'

'I'm sure of it!' he muttered grimly.

'Well, you have put the staff on their guard,' remarked Furminger, hobbling up to them. 'Let us continue to Hartworth House.'

The viscount shook his head, thinking rapidly.

'Take Elinor back to the carriage. I'll join you presently.' With that he set off back along the narrow street through which they had come, and soon found what he was looking for: a small plain door set in the wall, doubtless one of the service doors of Leicester House. He tried the handle and the door opened easily, startling the two footmen who were hurrying along the inner passage.

'My Lord!' cried one. 'After your warning we were just coming to check—'

The viscount cut him short. 'Never mind the explanations. Lock the door behind me and make sure it stays locked.' He stepped back on to the street and heard the sound of heavy bolts being pushed into position on the inside of the door. Glancing down the street he allowed himself a grim smile as he saw that the black bulk of the travelling carriage had pulled a little closer. A solitary figure in a grey frock-coat alighted and was approaching with an ungainly stride. The man checked when he saw the viscount, then his hand reached inside his coat to pull out a pistol.

'So, Davenham, you are here before me!' Lord Thurleigh's cold eyes flickered past Davenham, and a sneering smile curled his lips. 'And Madame de Sange. How charming to see you again!'

The viscount glanced around, a frown in his eyes.

Elinor shook her head at him. 'I could not leave you.'

'You had best give me that pistol, my dear,' drawled the marquis. 'I assure you I can fire this one before you even have time to lift your own.'

She looked at the viscount, who nodded, and she handed the carriage pistol to the marquis. He tucked the weapon into his pocket. The sounds of the mob could be heard quite clearly now, and the smell of burning filled the air.

'I would advise you to take the lady home, Davenham, and quickly. The mob are coming this way.'

'Is that your work too, Thurleigh? No wonder your groom developed such a liking for low company!'

The marquis bowed. 'But of course. My man has been working on them for weeks. It takes very little to rouse the mob, Davenham. They are no more than savages, after all. A few guineas, a little gin. . . .'

'So that was your plan. To have the King assassinated and take the Princess and her children away from here. But what next? Is your allegiance to the Prince of Wales, or to the Stuart?'

251

'My allegiance, naturally, is to the winning side. Cumberland's man carried out the deed and the country will think the duke plotted the King's death, and the disappearance of the heir to the throne. If the people decide to remove Cumberland and offer the crown to the Stuart, I shall make sure there are no Hanoverian brats alive to make trouble. If not . . . well, I think I can rely upon the young prince's gratitude for keeping him safe during this period of unrest.'

'But your plan won't work, Thurleigh,' the viscount interrupted him. 'I have warned the servants. You will not see the princess or her children today!'

Lord Thurleigh's eyes narrowed suspiciously. He waved Elinor and the viscount away from the small service door, then, keeping his eyes and the pistol trained upon them, he reached out one hand to try the door. It did not yield. None of them noticed a second cloaked figure descend from the travelling carriage. The marquis raised the pistol.

'So, Davenham, you think you have foiled me? I warned you I will brook no interference in my plans.'

Elinor stepped forward, placing herself between Thurleigh and the viscount.

'It is my fault Davenham is here. *I* vowed your destruction.'

The marquis laughed, regarding her coldly. 'You think you can save him again, my dear? I gave you his life once in exchange for the ruby, but this time it won't work. I am quite happy to put an end to you both—'

'No!' Margaret Thurleigh's voice rang out and she hurried up to her husband, her dark cloak flying out behind her, the hood slipping back from her unpowdered curls. 'No, my lord, you must not!'

'Put away your weapon, Thurleigh,' Davenham advised him. 'Can you not see the game is finished?'

'A game is never finished until the accounts are settled!' retorted the marquis.

Lady Thurleigh grasped his arm, saying urgently, 'No, sir, you cannot kill the woman!'

Her husband shook her off roughly and cocked the pistol. 'Can I not, my dear? I think I shall prove you wrong!'

He took aim. Davenham pushed Elinor behind him and the

marquis laughed harshly. 'You think to save her? You fool, I shall kill you first, then—'

'*But she is your daughter!*'

The words checked him. He lowered his arm. All eyes turned to Lady Thurleigh as she stood nervously twisting her hands together, her green eyes staring. 'You thought I had given birth to a still-born son, did you not, dear husband? But there were two babies in my belly – *two!* One was the boy-child, dead at birth, but the other was a girl, a big, lusty girl, Thurleigh! Do you remember? I was visiting my sister in Oxford and big with child. I detested the condition, so fat and ugly, but you cared little for my discomfort, is that not so, Husband? You were too busy with your gaming and wenching to take an interest in me! I was never first with you.'

'I took you to wife, did I not?' he threw at her, only to hear her scornful laugh.

'Because I refused to let you bed me until you had made me so!'

'But the child,' he reminded her sharply, 'tell me!'

'They came before their time. That was another nightmare, my lord! I vowed after that I would never go through such pain again. Two babies!' she laughed. 'I knew then how to pay you back for my suffering. My maid was acting as midwife, you see, and the babes were born long before the doctor arrived. I told her to take the girl away and drown her. No one need ever know, but she wouldn't do it. I would have smothered it myself, but she pleaded with me, said she'd smuggle the baby out of the house and find a wet-nurse.' Lady Thurleigh looked across at Elinor. 'I learned afterward that she had found someone, a learned gentleman and his wife, grieving over the death of their own babe, just a few hours old. More than that I did not want to hear. By the time the doctor arrived, we had removed all traces of the twin birth, and presented him with your stillborn son, my lord.'

Thurleigh stood like a statue, only his eyes seemed alive, blazing in the livid face.

'It cannot be true,' he said at last. 'It is a tale you have fabricated, though God knows to what end.'

'Oh 'tis true enough.' She pointed at Elinor. 'Only look at

her, my lord. Is not the likeness sufficient to tell you that she is my daughter? And as for her father – you know well enough that you kept me safe from all other men until you were sure I was carrying your child. This lady can confirm that she was born at the same time that I was brought to bed one November night, four-and-twenty winters past.'

'But why? Why, Margaret? How could you give away your own – *my only child?*'

My lady threw up her head, her face alight with hatred.

'It was the one weapon I had to curse you with, Guy Morellon. My vengeance! I knew how badly you wanted a child!'

For a full minute husband and wife stared at one another, then the disbelief left Thurleigh's face to be replaced with a look of pure fury. He raised his pistol, took deliberate aim and fired. The bullet found its target. Without a sound, the marchioness staggered back and collapsed, lifeless, to the ground.

The shot brought Thurleigh's servants running from the carriage, but they stopped at a distance from the little group, uncertain what to do. Elinor knelt beside Lady Thurleigh, searching for signs of life. Horrified, she stared up at the marquis.

'You have killed her. Your own wife!'

'She was a whore. I curse myself that I could not resist her – or you! You should thank God, my dear, that I didn't rape you with the others that night at the inn. Oh, I very much wanted to, only I knew my clap-ridden body couldn't manage it! *You* must pay for this, Elinor de Sange.' He drew the second pistol from his pocket. 'You've damned me to hell, between you! Join your mother in Hades, witch!'

The viscount lunged at him and Elinor could only watch in horror as they grappled for the pistol wedged between them. A shot rang out and the two men ceased their struggle. The pistol fell to the ground with a clatter and the marquis pushed his opponent away before he himself staggered drunkenly against the wall. He leaned there, fighting for breath while a dark stain gradually spread over his waistcoat. Davenham turned to Elinor, holding his hand out to her as she knelt beside Margaret Thurleigh's body.

'Will you never do as you are told?' he scolded her, but gently, his voice unsteady. 'I wish to God you had gone back to the carriage, and not witnessed this.'

'I know. I am sorry – you are not hurt?' Her anxious eyes searched his face, then, reassured, she leaned against him, resting her head upon his shoulder.

'And at Hart Chase – Elinor, is it true you gave Thurleigh the ruby to save my life?'

'Yes.' She spoke without lifting her head. 'I wanted no more killing. I wanted my own wounds to heal.'

Davenham held her close, but a slight movement caught his attention and he looked up in time to see Lord Thurleigh sliding one hand into his pocket. With a smothered oath the viscount swung himself between Elinor and the marquis.

Thurleigh gave a feeble laugh.

'Have no fear, Davenham. I've no weapon hidden about me!' He withdrew his clenched fist and held it out to Elinor. 'Pray, madam, come closer.'

Hesitantly, with Davenham at her side, Elinor approached the marquis. His breathing was laboured and his voice when he spoke was barely above a whisper.

'This was part of your mother's dowry.' He dropped a velvet pouch into her hand. She tipped out the contents of the pouch and looked down at the jewel she was now holding. It was the ruby, reset now as a pendant with a thin gold frame and threaded on a velvet ribbon.

'Now it belongs to you – Daughter!'

Elinor jumped back as if he had hit her, and he laughed at the revulsion in her face.

'Aye, that's a burden for you to carry through life, is it not? You will never be free of me now!' Thurleigh gave a soft laugh, ending in a gasp of pain. 'The final irony, my dear, is it not?' He coughed, and with a last desperate effort came away from the wall, his hands reaching out for Elinor, who shrank away from him, but life had gone from the marquis. His eyes looked at her unseeingly for a brief moment before he crashed to the floor.

Davenham put a supporting arm about Elinor's shoulders,

very much aware now of the approaching mob, for he could plainly hear their yells and screams, the breaking of glass as they found some window unshuttered. A pall of smoke hung just above the rooftops, casting an eerie gloom over the streets.

'Come. We must leave here before we are caught up in the riot.'

'But we can't leave them!' cried Elinor, her face pale in the half-light.

The viscount looked around and beckoned to Lord Thurleigh's servants, still hovering anxiously a few yards away.

'Your master and mistress are dead. Take their bodies home. You have the carriage.'

'Wait!' Elinor knelt once again beside the body of Lady Thurleigh. Carefully she placed the ruby pendant about the dead woman's neck. 'There are too many memories with this stone. It would be best if it were buried with this unhappy woman.'

She rose and walked with the viscount back to his coach, leaving Thurleigh's men to their unpleasant task. As they walked away, some instinct caused Elinor to glance up at the windows of Leicester House. She caught a fleeting glimpse of a woman's face at a first-floor window. The next instant it was gone.

CHAPTER TWENTY-FOUR

My Lord Davenham concludes the game

The viscount guided Elinor back to the carriage to find his servants anxiously awaiting his return and only too willing to set off for Hartworth House. The bishop was huddled fearfully in one corner and, as the door was shut upon them, he cried out in a shrill, querulous voice, 'Damme sir, but you took your time! I had given up all hope of seeing you again. Indeed, I would have driven on had your coachman been at all agreeable, but the dratted fellow refused to move until you was returned.'

'Calm yourself, Furminger.' The viscount's voice was cold. 'We were gone less than ten minutes.'

Sitting quietly in her own corner, Elinor was surprised to hear his words: had only minutes passed since she followed the viscount into the side street? Events had moved so rapidly that she could not yet comprehend it all. They travelled quickly through the empty streets, only the bishop's anxious remarks breaking the silence within the coach. His presence prevented any conversation between Davenham and Elinor, and she could not be sorry. For the moment her thoughts were in too much turmoil to be put into words. Furminger continued to grumble and peer anxiously out of the window, but the streets were deserted as news of the rioting spread and the only signs of life were the occasional ragged figures hurrying to join the mob, hoping to gain something from the looting that would inevitably occur. Davenham and Elinor maintained their silence, each lost in thought, until they reached the Haymarket, when a cry from the bishop caught their attention.

'Ah, that's more like it!'

Elinor glanced across to see what had brought about this sudden change in tone, and observed Bishop Furminger sitting bolt upright, staring out of the carriage window. Sounds of marching feet could clearly be heard approaching and moments later a body of uniformed men filed past the carriage.

'Now the army has been called out we shall soon have order restored.' Davenham smiled at Elinor. 'And in a very few moments from now you will be safe within my father's house.'

'But it is no thanks to you, sir!' cried the bishop. 'Tarrying so long with the mob almost upon us. I tell you, I had begun to fear for our lives.'

The viscount gave a short laugh. 'There's only one life that interests you, Furminger, and that's your own!'

The carriage drew up outside Hartworth House and Davenham escorted Elinor inside, pausing only to order the waiting footmen to attend the bishop. They found both Lord and Lady Hartworth awaiting them and their appearance was greeted with great relief.

'Thank heaven you are safe!' cried the countess, embracing Elinor and drawing her towards a sofa. 'My dear child, you look worn out! Come and sit by the fire – let me take your cloak, child, then you can tell us everything. When we heard the mob were rampaging though the streets I was terrified lest you should be attacked.'

Lord Davenham turned to the earl, saying urgently, 'Before anything else, sir, tell me – what news from the palace? We heard on the streets . . .'

'The King is safe. I went to St James's as soon as you had left the house this morning. As one of the Lords of the Bedchamber, Lord Thomas would naturally be attending him, so I dropped a word in several quarters and when Thomas realized he was under suspicion he soon broke down and confessed all he knew. It seems he allowed himself to become deeply in debt – mostly to Lord Thurleigh. He undertook to kill the King because Thurleigh promised to look after his family. The alternative was debtors' prison, and his wife and children thrown penniless upon the streets.'

'Poor devil!' muttered Davenham.

'As you say, my son.'

Lady Hartworth was bending over Elinor, coaxing her to drink a glass of wine, but at her husband's words she looked up.

'Whatever may happen to Lord Thomas, sir, can we not do something for his family?'

'I shall see they are not destitute, my love. You have my word on that. But what of your business, Davenham? Did you see the bishop?'

'We did. He agreed to speak against Thurleigh, but so great was his fear of the marquis that I was obliged to bring him here for safe-keeping, although what has occurred since then . . .' He paused. 'Thurleigh is dead, sir.'

'Good heavens!' Lady Hartworth sank down beside Elinor on the sofa, her hands pressed to her cheeks. The earl received the news with slightly less astonishment, merely nodding and asking if the bishop might now retract his evidence.

'Oh, I don't think he can do that, my lord. He has said too much. Of course, he may try to lessen his role in the affair, but we still have the list that Julian Poyntz wrote out for Elinor. I think he must still confess.'

'Good. Where is the bishop now?'

'I've given orders that he should be put in a guest-room and made comfortable there. I suggest you keep him there, sir. I've had as much of the fellow as I can stomach on the journey here!'

'You said the marquis is dead, Jonathan!' My lady looked puzzled. 'How did you learn of this?'

'I killed him, Mama.'

The countess gave a faint shriek.

'Go on, my son,' the earl urged him.

Davenham's eyes went to Elinor, who was looking dazed and pale. With a visible effort she rose from the sofa and went up to him.

'You must tell them. Everything.'

'Are you sure, Elinor? There is no need—'

'Yes, there is. It must all be told.' She pressed his hands and summoned up a small, tight smile before stepping back, then, with a murmured apology she picked up her cloak and left the room.

Elinor made her way to the comfortable apartment that had been assigned to her. There she found her maid waiting to help her to change her dress. She dismissed the girl with an order to send Hannah upstairs, and when she was alone she carefully laid the cloak over the back of a chair before sitting herself before her mirror. She scarcely recognized the face that stared out at her, the features so pale and drawn: rather she saw the face of Margaret Thurleigh, and in her head rang the words that lady had screamed at her husband: *She is your daughter – your daughter—*

'Mistress Nell, you sent for me?' Hannah's anxious voice broke in upon her. 'When I heard that the mob were on the streets I could not rest until I knew you were safe.' The old woman broke off as Elinor turned from the mirror, in her eyes a look of such anguish that Hannah was obliged to smother a gasp of dismay. Covering her anxiety, she chided Elinor, as she would have done a child. 'Oh Miss Nell, now look at your muddied petticoats! We will have you out of them and into bed in a trice, never you fear, and I shall fetch you a nice hot brick for your feet, for it's a good rest you need. . . .'

Elinor put up a hand.

'Later, perhaps, but first we must talk.' She rose and began to pace the room, trying to collect her thoughts. 'Hannah, how long were you with my mother?'

'Why, that's a strange question, ma'am! To be sure, I can remember as plain as anything. I became her personal maid just before her marriage to your sainted father.'

'Then you were with her when I was born?'

'But of course, Miss Nell. Haven't I told you time and again that I used to rock you to sleep when you were a babe?'

Elinor came to stand directly before her, taking her hands and looking into the older woman's face with such an intense stare that Hannah shifted uncomfortably.

'But were you *present* when I was born, Hannah?'

'Miss Nell, I—'

'Am I truly the child of Ambrose and Helena Burchard?'

'Really, Madame, there's a question to ask me!' cried Hannah, turning away.

'There is no one else to tell me, and I must know the truth!'

There was a long silence that seemed to Elinor to press mockingly upon her. When at last the answer came she felt strangely at peace.

'You were a foundling, Miss Nell. Brought to our door one night by a serving maid who had heard that the mistress had recently been brought to bed but had lost her own child within hours of its birth.'

'What month was it?'

'Why, November, Miss Nell. It was so very cold and the girl begged us to take you, saying that if we did not she would be obliged to put an end to you. The old master said it was a miracle, a gift from God he called you, and he himself carried you up the stairs to my lady's room. She took to you at once, Miss Nell, for you were a dear little scrap.' She looked appealingly at Elinor. 'Pray, ma'am, don't look like that. I swear they could not have loved you more, had you been of their own flesh!'

'I know it, Hannah. I think I should like to be alone for a while. Will you send down my excuses? I shall not require dinner.'

'But Madame, we have not yet changed your dress.' Hannah moved towards her, alarmed to see her green eyes bright with unshed tears.

Elinor waved her away. 'No. Please, just go.'

Alone once more, Elinor sank down upon the nearest chair. She scarcely noticed her cloak thrown over the chair-back, her mind trying to grasp all she had heard that day. Hannah's story confirmed what Lady Thurleigh had said, but Elinor had never really doubted it. The likeness between them was too strong. What was it Lady Hartworth had said? *The woman has the soul of a strumpet!* She felt the tears welling up inside her. Such a woman, then, was her true mother. She could bear that – she thought that she could even bear to be the bastard child of one of the lady's many lovers. It would be preferable to being Thurleigh's daughter.

A black despair settled upon her. She had been cursed from the start, bringing nothing but death and unhappiness to those around her. Elinor leaned back against the cloak and became aware of a solid object beneath its folds. She remembered then that she still had the knife with which she had threatened the bishop. Davenham had given it to her that very morning on their way to Islington. Sweet heaven, it seemed a lifetime ago! She recalled that he had drawn her attention to the intricate craftsmanship of the leather and silver scabbard, and the delicate engraving of the family coat of arms upon the blade itself. He had translated the motto for her – *Honour is all*. Proud words for a proud family.

Elinor was aware of an almost physical pain twisting within her: if she had truly been the daughter of Ambrose Burchard, then perhaps she might have been accepted by Lord and Lady Hartworth, despite her history, but a foundling had no place here. A bitter little laugh escaped her lips. What was she thinking of? She was no foundling – worse than that! Dear God, would that she had never been born! *Honour is all*. The words came back to haunt her. Dashing a hand across her eyes, she reached into the pocket of her cloak and drew out the dagger.

In the morning-room, the viscount gave a full account of his meeting with the marquis. Lady Hartworth's cheeks had grown quite white during the tale, and her eyes were wide with astonishment when her son disclosed Lady Thurleigh's intervention. When he had finished, Davenham waited for a reaction from his audience. Lady Hartworth looked towards the earl.

'Can such a story possibly be true?'

'It would appear that Thurleigh did not doubt it.'

'The poor child. Then she must be his heir!'

'Only if she wishes to claim kinship!' put in Davenham swiftly. Aware of his father's scrutiny, he added, 'Elinor and I are the only ones alive who heard Margaret Thurleigh's confession, and if Elinor does not wish for the connection, I shall not force it upon her.' He paused. 'I intend to marry her, you know.'

'I had guessed as much.'

The countess stared at her husband. 'You do not object?'

'On the contrary,' he replied. 'The child was reared as the daughter of one of my oldest friends. I see no reason to think of her as anything other than that.'

Two strides brought the viscount across the room to stand before his father. Taking the earl's hand he bowed low over it, his lips just brushing the thin fingers in filial respect.

'Thank you, sir.' His voice was unsteady, but there was no mistaking the glow of happiness in his blue eyes.

'Well, 'pon my word!' exclaimed the countess, taking out her handkerchief and dabbing at her eyes. 'I fear this is all too much for me. Such a deal of events and surprises in one day.'

'Do you mislike the match, Mama?'

My lady waved one white hand.

'No, no, I have grown very fond of the child, but to find that she is the daughter of. . . .' Her voice trailed off in a shudder of revulsion. The viscount moved over to the sofa and sat down beside his mother. Taking her hands in his own he looked at her, a slight frown darkening his eyes.

'Mama, you cannot blame Elinor for an accident of birth. She was raised in a very different world from that of Guy Morellon, Marquis of Thurleigh. Also, I learned today that she saved my life. The night the marquis broke into Hart Chase, it seems she traded the ruby for my life. I doubt Elinor would ever have spoken of it, had not Thurleigh mentioned the matter.' He hesitated before continuing slowly, 'Elinor de Sange has become the most important person in my life, Mama, and if it causes a rift between us then I am sorry for it, but I mean to marry her, if she will have me.'

'Oh my dear boy!' Lady Hartworth clung to him, smiling tremulously as she tried to blink away the tears. 'Of course you must marry her, if that is what you want. But I pray you, allow me a little time to grow accustomed. It has all happened so suddenly.'

'Of course, Mama! Elinor also will need time to recover from the events of the day. God knows what she must be thinking.' He rose. 'I must go to her. Pray excuse me, Mama – sir!'

As he reached the door, the sound of raised voices floated

down from the half-landing, where Hannah Grisson was engaged in a heated altercation with the butler. Catching sight of Lord Davenham, she pushed past the servant and hung over the banister.

'Oh, sir, pray come up at once! I fear my lady is dead!'

The viscount flew across the hall and took the stairs two at a time.

'She has locked her door, my lord!' cried Hannah, as he came up to her. 'I knocked and called out to her, but she did not answer, and when I looked through the keyhole I swear I saw a dagger upon the floor!'

Davenham ran up the second flight of stairs, his face grim as he approached Elinor's door. After briefly trying the handle, he set his shoulder to the door and in a matter of seconds there was a splintering of wood and the door flew open to reveal Elinor lying on the floor, the unsheathed knife beside her and a small bloodstain upon her bodice.

'Oh, my poor babe!' exclaimed Hannah.

She started forward but the viscount was there before her, dropping on one knee beside Elinor. He saw the faint throb of life at her neck.

'Fetch the doctor, quickly!' He lifted Elinor gently and carried her across to the bed. 'The blade glanced off the boning of her corset.' He gave a shaky laugh. 'I never thought to be grateful to this fashion for tight-lacing! By the time the blade had cut through the padding and reached the rib-cage, the force was not sufficient to do more than scratch the skin. I think she has merely fainted, but we must remove her gown to be sure.'

Hannah almost hustled the viscount out of the way.

'This is a woman's work now, my lord,', she told him briskly. 'I am much obliged for your help, but you need have no fear in leaving Miss Nell to me.' Observing his look she said in a softer tone, 'Off you go, sir, and don't worry. I have nursed my mistress through many a crisis. She will be safe now.'

For more than a week Elinor kept to her bed, she slept a great deal, and would take but a fraction of the nourishing dishes with which Hannah tried to tempt her. She developed a fever and grew delirious, reliving the recent events that had rocked her life. Upon one occasion she awoke from a particularly vivid dream to find a gentleman sitting beside the bed. It was dark, and there were no lights near the bed to disturb her rest. She lay still for a moment, trying to make out the shadowy figure beside her. Sleep still clouded her mind and she lifted her hand a little from the covers.

'Ralph?'

'No, Elinor. Go back to sleep.' Davenham's voice came to her from a great distance. She wanted to smile, to tell him she was glad he was beside her, but the effort was too great and she drifted away again into slumber.

The fever passed, but it left Elinor weak and listless On the doctor's advice, Elinor was lifted from her bed each morning and made comfortable upon a day-bed which had been drawn over to the window, so that she could look out upon the small pleasure garden that had been built to the earl's design. As spring passed into summer the garden bloomed with colour, providing a delightful prospect for the invalid, although she scarcely seemed to notice it. Every day the viscount came to sit with her for an hour, reading from books that might amuse her, or bringing her news of her acquaintance in Town. He was careful to avoid any mention of Lord Thurleigh or any other matter he thought might upset her, yet all his attempts at entertainment evoked no response. Elinor would listen to him in silence, a closed look upon her face that seemed to shut out the world. Davenham was in despair. It seemed no amount of coaxing would bring the fire back to those green eyes that now gazed at him so indifferently.

Lord Hartworth was aware of his son's growing anxiety, noting the grim set of his mouth after each visit, and at length he decided it was time to try a different approach. On a particularly sunny morning, Lord Hartworth visited the sick-room. Hannah had just finished making Elinor comfortable upon the day bed when the earl entered.

'May I come in? If you will permit me, Madame, there are a few matters I should like to discuss with you.' He gestured to Hannah to leave the room, then he drew a chair towards the day-bed and sat down. 'My son fears to upset you, but I know you are a young woman of considerable spirit, Elinor Burchard, and you deserve to know the truth.' Receiving no response, the earl turned his gaze to the window. 'I cannot remember looking at the garden from this point before. I designed it, you know. It is looking beautiful this morning, do you not think so? Although I do think the roses on the west wall should have been cut back a little harder. They look decidedly untidy.'

'I like their wildness.'

Not by so much as the flicker of an eyelid did he acknowledge that anything unusual had occurred, although he was well aware that Elinor had spoken to no one since the fever had abated. He merely nodded, his eyes still fixed upon the window.

'Perhaps you are right. I came to tell you that Bishop Furminger has now made his confession to the proper authorities. You will be pleased to know that he will now be judged as he deserves. Also, His Majesty is very grateful to you for your part in bringing the traitors to justice.'

He paused, turning slightly to observe her as he spoke again. 'You should also know that the bodies of Lord and Lady Thurleigh have disappeared.'

Elinor's eyes widened slightly.

'I sent to Lord Thurleigh's town house the day after his death, as soon as the streets were safe again, but it seems Thurleigh's servants never returned there.'

'Then, the ruby has gone, too.'

'Yes.'

Elinor gazed blankly out of the window.

'It was in truth a blood stone. I pray it will not curse another family as it has done mine.' Her eyes fixed themselves upon the earl. 'Is there no hope of learning the truth?'

'I fear not. A search of the area brought to light the burned-out shell of a large carriage, but there were no means of identifying it. I think we must face the possibility that the marquis and his wife may never be found. Which brings me to the point of my visit.'

A tinge of colour crept into Elinor's pale cheek, but she

continued to meet his gaze.

'My lord – you know of Lady Thurleigh's disclosure?'

'Jonathan told me.'

She looked down at her hands, clasped together in her lap.

'You should also know, sir, that the story is borne out by what I have learned from Hannah. There seems no reason to doubt that I am ... I am the daughter of the Marquis of Thurleigh.' Her voice was scarcely above a whisper and a fleeting glance at the earl's face told her nothing of his thoughts. 'I am sorry – I fear I have inconvenienced you long enough, sir. Regretfully I do not yet have the strength, but if you would be good enough to make the arrangements for me, I shall of course remove from your house at the earliest possible—'

'If that is your wish, Madame; I can only wonder that you have not spoken of it sooner.'

The earl's tone was perfectly reasonable, but still Elinor winced.

'In truth, my lord, I have been refusing to consider the matter. I offer you my apologies, for I know you will want me gone from here.'

'You know nothing of the sort, young lady!'

She drew out her handkerchief. 'I am sorry, my lord.'

'And I wish you would rid yourself of this tiresome habit of apologizing for everything! I have no idea why you should think it necessary to do so. Doubtless you mean to tell me you are sorry for saving my son's life?'

She afforded his words a watery chuckle. 'Indeed, sir, I could never do *that*!'

'Then let us get back to the matter in hand. From what Davenham has told me, the servants were too far away to hear Lady Thurleigh's story, so the only people who know of your parentage are in this house.'

'Is that not enough?'

'Answer me one thing, child.' He ignored her interruption. 'Do you wish to acknowledge the connection?'

She stared at him. 'Of course I do not!'

'Don't forget, Elinor, that the marquis was a very rich man. I believe the title must pass to a male heir, but the best part of his property would go to any legitimate child of his marriage.'

Elinor shook her head.

'I have more than enough for my needs. I should be desperate indeed before I could be induced to touch one groat of his fortune!'

'That is as I expected,' said the earl, rising. 'Well, let them fight it out amongst themselves, all those distant relatives who will now turn up, claiming their part of the Thurleigh inheritance. As for you, child, if you are content to be known as the daughter of Ambrose Burchard, I see no reason why that should not be the case. Indeed, I think it is the greatest compliment you could pay my old friend.'

'Th-thank you, my lord.'

'And perhaps I could persuade you to take a little stroll around the gardens later. I think you will find that upon closer inspection you will agree with me about the roses.'

With a smile and a bow, he turned and walked out of the room. Elinor, dazed by the effort the interview had cost her, rested her head against the cushions to consider all that had been said. After a few moments her eyelids drooped and when Hannah came into the room a little while later she found her mistress in a deep slumber.

Following the earl's visit Elinor made rapid progress. As summer reached its height the earl and his household removed to Hart Chase, where the countess hoped Elinor would benefit from the country air. The house at Knight's Bridge was given up and Elinor was persuaded to make an indefinite stay with Lord and Lady Hartworth. No longer obliged to hide away, she could now take part in the picnics, rides and parties that were arranged between the neighbouring families and with these mild entertainments she passed away the summer months. Lord Davenham had not accompanied them, and if Elinor was missing his company, she gave no sign, nor would she admit even to herself how many hours were spent in useless fantasies. She conducted herself with calm assurance and such an air of serenity that Lady Hartworth was convinced they had mistaken the matter.

However, the earl would not be drawn; he merely smiled knowingly and went about his business.

At the beginning of September, Lord Davenham sent a message to say he would be joining his parents for a brief visit. Elinor heard the news calmly, thinking that after such a long separation she was well able to cope with meeting the viscount again. Yet when he entered the library at Hart Chase two days later, she could not prevent the colour rising to her cheeks. The earl and his lady had gone out to visit friends and Elinor was alone, engaged in making a fair copy of a household inventory when Lord Davenham walked in. Taken by surprise, and furious with herself for blushing, her embarrassment was complete when her pen spluttered, blotting the neat lines of figures she had just completed. The viscount's harsh look relaxed as he watched her.

'I find that very encouraging,' he remarked, stripping off his riding gloves. 'I am not sure whether you are *pleased* to see me, but at least you are not indifferent to my arrival!'

She laughed and came around the big mahogany desk, holding out her hand to him.

'How could I be indifferent, when you have made me spoil my whole morning's work? How do you do, my lord?'

'That's much better!' he told her, holding on to her hand and smiling down at her in a way that made her heart pound uncomfortably. 'I was afraid you would greet me as coldly as you bade me goodbye.'

Elinor felt the heat in her face. She disengaged her hand and turned away from him.

'Was I cold?'

'As an iceberg,' he assured her cheerfully.

'Well, you could hardly call your own manner friendly!' she retorted, nettled. 'And then to remain in Town, with never a word to us for so long!' She broke off, conscious that she had allowed her feelings to get the better of her.

'Have you missed me, Nell?'

'Of – of course not!' She tried to recover her ground. 'We are so busy here, I have no time to think of anything. . . .'

'So busy in fact that you are reduced to copying out lists of

269

household linens,' he interrupted her, picking up the inventory; then he tossed it aside as his eye alighted upon another scrap of paper. 'Too busy to miss me?'

His eyes gleamed as he held up the scrap, upon which were drawn and embellished the initials JD in a very elaborate script. With a gasp Elinor put her hands to her cheeks.

'I – I must have been day-dreaming!' she cried, a look of dismay upon her countenance. 'Pray, give it to me.'

She reached out, but with a laugh, Davenham snatched back his hand, holding up the paper.

'Come here and take it.'

'Wretch!' Elinor stepped forward, stretching up to take the note from his hand. She became aware of how close she was standing to Lord Davenham and could not resist the impulse to look at him. In that brief second he bent his head and kissed her. The touch of his lips triggered the longing she had kept locked away for so many months. She returned his kiss fiercely, revelling in the contact as he wrapped her in his arms and pressed her to him.

'Oh Nell, I have wanted to do this for so long!' he muttered.

Elinor said nothing, but gave a little moan of pleasure. Her arms tightened about his neck as if to hold him there forever.

Later, when Davenham was sitting in an armchair with Elinor curled up on his lap, he said, 'Oh Nell, I've missed you! I cannot tell you how many times I have wanted to ride down here and ask you to marry me, but I told myself you need time to recover. Not for the world would I rush you.'

She buried her face in his shoulder.

'Oh, pray do not talk of marriage! You must see how impossible that is. I don't deny that, at one time, I had hoped . . . but now everything is changed.'

He held her away from him, frowning into her face.

'What is it, Elinor? Would an offer from me be so repugnant to you?'

Her eyes filled with tears.

'Not to *me*, my lord,' she managed to say, her voice breaking, 'but to you – and your family. . . .'

'Here, take this,' he said, giving her his handkerchief. 'When you have dried your tears, perhaps you will tell me what makes you think my family would object to our marriage?'

Having dutifully wiped her eyes, Elinor took a deep breath and began to speak, her fingers folding the viscount's fine lawn handkerchief into tiny pleats as she sought her words.

'You all see me as – as an obligation. Despite what your father says, I am the daughter of his bitterest enemy, scarcely the wife he would choose for you! And your mama made it quite plain to me that she regarded Lady Thurleigh as little more than a – than a—'

The viscount put an end to her explanation by the simple if ruthless expedient of kissing her, after which he told her lovingly not to be such a goose.

'You cannot be held responsible for the misdeeds of your ancestors – why, if you cared to read my own family history I daresay you would find any number of rogues amongst them. In fact, if I remember correctly, the first earl was no saint, married his first wife for her fortune, then poisoned her off so that he could marry some cousin of the king, which is how he came by the earldom. Then, of course there was the fourth earl, Robert, who had his own mother clapped up for treason—'

'Oh, pray be quiet!' cried Elinor, between tears and laughter. 'How can I make you understand that this case is quite different?'

'You won't,' he said, looking at her with such a glow in his blue eyes that her heart began to pound in the most erratic manner. 'I can assure you, Madame, that I have my parents' full approval for the offer I am about to make you. Not that it is necessary, for I have been my own master for years, you know, but I suspect that you would not even consider my proposal without my family's blessing, am I right?'

'You are, my lord.'

'Very well, then! In our eyes, my love, you remain the much-loved daughter of my father's dear friend, and nothing would give us greater pleasure than a union between the two families. Well, Madame de Sange?'

She rose and moved away from him, still kneading the handkerchief between her fingers.

'You are aware, Lord Davenham, that I have had a – a very *varied* life?'

'I am. And I hope we shall enjoy a very varied marriage! I will do my best to make you happy, Elinor.'

She smiled at that. 'But could I make *you* happy, Jonathan? You would not be the first man in my life, you realize that?'

'Of course, but does my past worry *you*? No, of course not. It is time to forget the past, Elinor, unless, perhaps, you are still in love with this fellow – Ralph Belham?' Anxiety added a rough edge to his voice. 'You spoke his name, you know, during your illness. I thought then, perhaps—'

She shook her head, a faint smile curving her lips. 'He told me he was not for me; at the time I could not believe it, but now I see that he was right. I owe him a great deal.'

The cloud lifted from the viscount's brow.

'Then what is there to prevent our marriage?'

'If only I could be sure you would not regret it!'

He lifted her hands to his lips, kissing each of her fingers in turn.

'No one can be sure of the future, Elinor, but I will try my best to make you happy. I love you very much, my dear. Will you consent to be my wife?'

She nodded, smiling mistily through her tears.

'Yes,' she whispered. 'Oh yes, Davenham, I will!'